IMMORTAL TREASURES

Paranormal fantasy

SJ. Turner

A Cozy Reads Publication
Release – August 2022

IMMORTAL TREASURES
By SJ. Turner

ISBN: 978-1-7777646-8-5

Cover Designed by Ambient Studios

TABLE OF CONTENTS

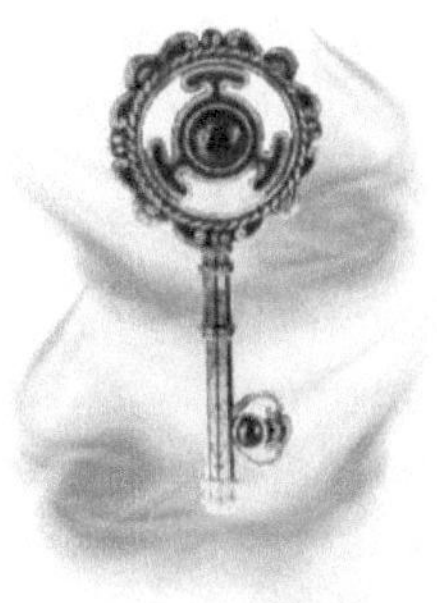

CHAPTER 1 ~ THE DISCOVERY

As Clara digs into the box of eighteenth-century treasures from the old Stepney Castle, she notices the spine of a rather basic tome lights up. She peers across the room at her two daughters, busying themselves with an array of artifacts. "Helen, Patricia, I think you two should look at this."

Exchanging glances with her sister, Helen sets down the small golden carousel she's been examining and moves in next to her mother. "What are we looking at?"

"Whoa! Am I seeing that correctly?" Patricia steps forward, her eyes shifting between her mother and Helen. "Did that book just glow?"

"Mmhmm. The aura of magic here" —*she passes her hand above the box*— "it's something I haven't felt in ages. Definitely old magic."

"What would a vampire family be doing with a magical book?" Helen asks, her brows drawn tightly together.

Patricia's face contorts in disgust. "The filthy demons probably sucked the witch dry and stole her grimoire."

"Oh, stop." Unamused at her daughter's response to such a priceless item, Clara reaches in to retrieve the leather-bound treasure. She wipes the dust from the cover, her voice dropping to a mere whisper as she reads the name aloud. "Laurent."

Opening the old tome, she slides her fingers through its leaves. "From the quality of paper, I'd say this is from around the seventeenth century." Carefully turning several thick parchment pages, she finally grasps the remaining bulk of the book and flicks through with a sigh.

"What is it?" Helen stares down at the turning pages as her face contorts. "What's wrong?"

Patricia jams her hand on her hip. "Yeah, I hate when you leave us hanging. Just tell us already. Did you find something vulgar?" She slaps her fingertips off her forehead. "Pfft. What am I saying? Of course, you did. There would have to be something appalling, like blood spells, to interest a vampire. Right?"

Clara's shoulders sag as she closes the cover. "No, I didn't notice any blood spells. Here." She hands the journal over. "Have a look for yourself. Tell me what *you* find."

Confusion clouds her face as she flips the pages. Finally slamming it shut, she twists her lips and holds the book out toward her mother. "This is friggin' empty!"

"Mmhmm." Clara runs her thumb across her bottom lip, staring at the journal in her outstretched hand. "I noted that too."

"But we all seen the glow," Helen protests. "And one can't deny the magic searing through the cover."

Clara flips her hand toward the old tome. "Have a look for yourself. Maybe *you* can see something in there."

Scanning the pages, Helen finally stops, her nose nearly touching the paper as she squints. "Hm, just when I think I've spotted a word, the darn thing disappears. Like here—" She shoves the book under Clara's nose and jams her finger to the page. "See here? Does that say forest?"

Patricia bends to get a better look, her fingertip landing on the page next to her sister's. "I can't identify anything that resembles *forest*, but I certainly recognize *crazy*." She smiles at her mother.

"What do you think, Mom?" Lifting her finger, she points at Helen. "Can you see *crazy*?"

"I'll show you crazy, you little tart!" Helen grabs Patricia's hand, giving her a shove.

"Oh, no. You didn't!" Patricia's face reddens, a fireball swirling to life in her hand. "I'll show you a tart, you old bladder bag!" She releases the ball of flames toward her sister.

Spreading her fingers, Helen gives her hand a flick. "Bomba de auga!" she shrieks, sending a water bubble to douse the fireball and leaving Patricia sopping wet.

"Oh, for the love of the Goddess!" Clara shouts, stepping between her two daughters. "Knock it off! I can't believe that after half a century, I'm still refereeing you two," she sighs. "Now, pull yourselves together. We need to discuss this Timekeeper Journal."

They freeze, peering at their mother with wide eyes, their question ringing in unison. "A Timekeeper Journal?"

Taking her seat, Clara turns the book over in her hands. "Yes, I believe so. I've never known anyone personally to have held one before, though I have heard stories." She runs her finger over the name on the cover, watching the letters glisten as she traces each one. "See that? That tells me it's found the correct bloodline. Though neither myself nor either of you can read it."

"I don't understand," Patricia utters, staring down at the book as though it were a foreign object.

"Well," Clara continues, "these journals are created by the keeper of time and sealed to two specific bloodlines. First, the named" —*she gestures to the name on the cover*— "and second, the interpreter."

Helen draws her bottom lip between her teeth and tilts her head, narrowing her gaze on her mother. "And by the keeper of time, you mean—"

Clara gives a slight nod. "The Goddess, Hecate. The triple goddess, keeper of the keys, some will even argue she is the keeper of time in the magical realm. Call her as you wish, but as you know, none is stronger when it comes to magic. She controls our elements and could appear to us in the form of the maiden, mother or quite possibly the crone, and we would never know. We've seen subtle hints of her work before. So, as much as this may seem like a rare find, it shouldn't be a big shock to us. In fact, I've heard mutterings of great Ancina being a direct descendant. But, like everything else, that is just another story passed down through the family."

"Pfft. No way," Patricia spits. "Are you trying to say *that*," she points down at the book in Clara's hand, "was created by the Goddess?"

"I believe that's entirely possible, or at least someone just as powerful." Holding the journal out, Clara peers up at her daughter. "If you don't believe me. Try to burn it."

Helen throws her hand over her mouth with a gasp. "You can't be serious!"

Clara shrugs. "Why wouldn't I be? If it is a Timekeeper Journal, as I suspect, then it can't be tampered with or destroyed."

"And if it's not a Timekeeper Journal?" Helen asks.

"Well, we all agree those pages appear blank. So if I'm wrong, then there's nothing to lose. On the other hand, if I'm correct, the journal will be undamaged, and we'll know for certain." Clara drops the book at Patricia's feet. "Go ahead. Give it your hottest flame."

Thunder cracks as Patricia raises her hands, and bright blue arcs dance along her fingers. She takes one last look at her mother. "I hope you're sure about this." Clara tips her head, flipping her hand out toward the book. "All right. Remember, this was your idea." She drops her hands, sending brilliant blue bolts toward the journal, but they're simply absorbed.

Helen's mouth drops open. "How on earth is *that* possible?"

"I must have missed it." The air thickens as Patricia takes a breath and raises her hands again. "Let me give it another go."

Clara turns her hand out. "If you must."

Again, Patricia strikes the old book with her hottest charge. The cover lifts slightly as though it were taking a breath, but it remains undamaged. Shaking her arms out, she stares at her mother. "I've never encountered anything able to withstand that kind of heat. That should be dust by now."

"Mmhmm." Clara reaches down to pick up the book. "You can't destroy something willed and protected by the Goddess."

Drawing her brows together, Helen stares at the perfectly unscathed journal in Clara's hand. "So what do we do with it? None of us can read it."

Clara takes a deep breath. "Well," she says, leaning back in her chair. "I can think of one other person that hasn't tried."

"No way." Patricia folds her arms across her chest while shifting her weight to one leg. "You can't be thinking of Olivia!" Clara shrugs. "That's ridiculous! She despises magic. You won't catch her within ten feet of that dang thing."

"Then I suppose we won't tell her. Will we."

"You can't do that to her," Patricia scoffs.

"We can, and we will. Every witch, including Olivia, is obligated to complete the tasks —whatever that may be— set out within a Timekeeper Journal. So we have no choice but to make that happen," Clara says, stuffing the journal back into the box she initially pulled it from. "Besides, with Summer Solstice coming, I have been adding a little Mugwort to her tea each morning, hoping to open her sixth sense. It's time she starts acknowledging who she is. Maybe it will help her open up to this as well."

Helen snickers. "I've been adding a little mugwort to her bedtime tea."

Pacing in front of them, Patricia throws her hands in the air. "I can't believe you two! How can you do that to her? She's only recently stopped having those damn nightmares again."

"Oh, she'll be fine. We'll just tuck this box aside and let them find each other. From what I know, these journals not only seek out their interpreter, but it draws them in—calls to them. She likely won't be able to resist it."

"I want it noted that I'm against this." Watching Helen retape the lid, Patricia points down at the box. "Feeding Olivia to that vampire diary is insane."

Helen bursts into laughter. "You make it sound as though the pages have teeth."

"Fair enough. Your protest has been noted. Now, shove the box back with the rest of them," Clara directs. "She has already promised to come in tomorrow to help us unpack. So, whether you're against it or not, you best not breathe a word to her." She glances down at her wrist. "It's late. I think we should call it a night."

CHAPTER 2 ~ THE DREAM

A savoury scent fills Olivia's nostrils as an old woman grabs a bundle of tightly wrapped white sage and wipes the sweat from her brow. Lighting one end in the fire, she begins to move around the circle with the smouldering herbs, cleansing the boundary with the smoke. Though her voice remains low, the words carry enough energy to force the flames higher with each spoken syllable.

When she meets her starting point, she kneels in front of the pit and places the smoking wrap at her side. Her hand wraps around a jagged piece of clear quartz she found by the shore—a scarce find in England indeed.

With a deep breath, she drags the ragged edge across the soft pad of her palm, tensing as golden beads of fluid rise to the surface. Letting a slight pool gather, she tips it into the salt bowl and closes her fist to stop the flow. Her thin, feeble fingers work the mixture together while steadily sprinkling bits around the stone enclosure. Then, with a whispered rush of words through the flames, the old woman spreads the last grains of salt along the fire's edge.

She sinks to her knees, drawing a black obsidian from her pocket—something she collected from the burned-out witch's camp long ago. A once sharp-edged crystal now clearly smoothed by use and time. Cradling the stone in the palm of her hand, she methodically passes her thumb across the surface while silently staring into the flames.

Dawn creeps closer, and the fear of nothing appearing begins to seep into her soul. Still, she remains steadfast, and moments before night gives way to the day, the obsidian heats in her hand. Images launch from the flames. A story she feared it would tell. The town is coming for her. There is no hope for a trial—they plan to drag her straight to the cross.

Images continue to flicker, a blazing film before her eyes. And although she flinches as they ignite the pyre, the final vision is what makes her gasp. Her fingertips press against her lips as she stares into the diminishing flames. "How could this be?"

She falls back on her haunches, her voice a mere whisper as she gazes up at the night sky. "Oh, my dearest, forever fated are our lives to be entwined."

At last, the restless sun stretches its beams across the meadow, and the old woman appears to proceed about her day as she would any other. She draws a pot of water from the well, places it over the fire, and makes her morning tea.

After her last sip, she swirls the remnants three times to the left, then three times to the right before turning the cup upside down on the table. After the tea leaves settle, she lifts the cup into her hands, twisting it slightly to examine the results. She draws her bottom lip between her teeth and gazes out the window of her tiny cabin. "Very well," she says, taking a deep breath as she stands and stares down at her cat. "I suppose tonight it is."

Draping a fresh bed linen over the table, she chooses only the items she intends to save. One by one, she lays them on the cloth— a few tinctures, her satchel of crystals, and of course, her grimoire. Pulling the corners together, she ties them into a neat package with another piece of fabric and smiles down at her feline companion.

"Well, Paene. Let's take this out to the big yew. Hopefully, my daughter knows enough to find it there."

After securing the bound parcel in the old tree out back, she makes another cup of tea and grabs a handful of smoked meat. "Come, my friend. Let's eat while we wait." She settles into her rocking chair on the front porch and holds a piece of cured meat out to Paene. "Only on a cold day in hell shall that foul-smelling priest catch me off guard."

Not long after the sun begins to set, distant voices carry on the evening breeze. Some laugh, some even curse as their footfalls move closer. "Go on now. Stay out of sight, and I'll call for you later," she whispers, running her hand down Paene's back. She pulls herself to her feet as the torch lights finally brighten the path. "Father Gordon. Might I ask what brings you so far out this late in the evening?"

The priest scowls. "You do, Witch." He waves his torch in the air, his voice rising as he directs his men. "Seize her!"

His men hastily stomp forward, tugging her arms behind her back, but she doesn't attempt to struggle. Instead, she stares into the eyes of the priest as he clutches his crucifix, holding it out in front of him. Spit flies from his mouth as he hollers, "You can lay no curse upon me, witch! Our Lord protects me." Then, cowardly tossing a jute sack at her feet, he waves his hand as he turns. "Put it over her head. She can't cast spells if she can't see."

The ignorance of the priest is almost amusing. She could effortlessly have these men crawling on all fours crying like babies if she so chose, but she knows that's not what fate has in mind.

"O—liv—via!" The high-pitched tone of Clara's voice echoes throughout the old four-bedroom house as she yodels out her granddaughter's name.

Mr. Green, Olivia's cat, squeals as she springs up in her bed and begins taking inventory of the surrounding room – *cream-coloured walls, burgundy drapes, the picture of my parents.* She examines her young hands and releases an exhaustive breath. "What a weird dream."

She checks the clock beside her bed—6am. Rolling her eyes, she flops back and pulls the covers over her head. With any luck, her grandmother will walk right past her room. But, of course not. Any hope of that happening is instantly removed when the door flings open, and Clara steps through with a snort. "Oh, I don't think so, darling. You promised to help at the antique store today. There are only a few more days until it opens."

Tugging her puffy down duvet tighter to her chest, Olivia groans. "Come on, Gran. It's Saturday. Can't I have one more hour? You woke me in the middle of the craziest dream. It felt so real."

"No, I'm afraid there are no more hours. We can talk about your dream once you get downstairs. There are still a ton of items to go through, and the store opens in less than a week. We're running out of time, and you promised to help today." She watches her snuggle in a little deeper and shakes her head. "Getting comfortable is not getting up." With that, Clara sends the duvet tucked in at her side, sailing across the room with a mere flick of her hand.

She promptly rolls over, her mouth agape as Clara raises her finger. "Nah-uh, don't say a word. A promise is a promise. Now, time to get up."

As Clara heads for the door, the defiant *"yeah yeah,"* causes her to spin on her heel. Her salt and pepper hair swishes over her shoulder as she walks back with her hand raised. "Don't even think about going back to sleep Olivia Parker. The next time I come up here, not only will I flick you right out of that bed, but I'll give you a severe bout of acne."

"You wouldn't!"

"Wouldn't I?" A smirk forms on her lips as she raises her brow. "You could test me if you'd like, but I suggest you get up and get dressed. Breakfast is on the table. In case it slipped your mind, the sign for the storefront is being installed this morning. Now stop being difficult, and let's go. We have a busy day ahead of us."

"Ugh!" She groans, swinging her legs over the side of the bed, her gaze landing on her crumpled bed cover across the room. "Fine! But don't think for one minute I believe you would actually toss me out of bed or tarnish me with acne."

"Mmhmm. You believe what you like," Clara replies, shutting the door behind her.

Clara Redfearn is not a wicked woman, but she's certainly not one to be tried. She may not look a day over fifty, but at ninety-two years old, she's perfected her skills. Not minding your manners when you speak to one of the oldest witches in London could have you croaking like a frog if you're not careful. Of course, that's not something Olivia has ever seen her do, but she's sure she could.

Though her primary connection is with Mother Earth, Clara acquired and refined some very crafty skills over the years. One of her many talents involves capturing the souls of those passing or stuck in limbo and transferring them to their final photographs or a likeness. As a result, the house holds a few lively photos and statues. Mind you, she mainly dabbles in potions for things that make life a little happier—plentiful gardens, brighter flowers, sweeter fruit and manicured lawns.

Around town, many know her as the medicine woman choosing to visit for her tonics, unaware she's a witch, of course. Instead, most believe her to be a herbalist with tinctures treating anything from acne to ageing. They claim *Redfearn medicines* work better than any doctor could prescribe.

Olivia recalls overhearing a story of Clara's true power being put to the test. A few members at Eternal Flame Coven—a name given years ago by Clara's great grandmother Annabel—beckoned her to visit a young man in town. Not that the words black magic would have been spoken aloud, but the whisper of such a thing rang through the coven.

After seeing several doctors, including London's best, Dr. Preston, none could find anything medically wrong with him. Yet, the young man became progressively worse. Finally, after losing almost twenty-nine pounds by the second week, doctors admitted him to the London general hospital.

As the story goes, a few weeks earlier, a fight occurred at the local pub between the young man and a couple from out of town. No one knew the couple, but they claimed the woman uttered a few words, stomped her foot and spat at his feet. The following day the young man fell violently ill.

Clara agreed to visit him at the hospital and claimed the room stunk of rot when she arrived. He had struggled to breathe as perspiration saturated his bed, periodically vomited and screamed of pain that could neither be defined nor explained by doctors. No physician would have been able to cure what ailed him. Just as her coven members' feared, the young man lay stricken with a death curse.

Taking her two daughters, Helen and Patricia, Clara waited until late in the evening to enter his hospital room. Working as quick as possible, they secured him to his bed, then sprinkled fresh earth gathered from the stream behind their house at his feet. Clara then laid a talisman she created out of clear quartz and black tourmaline over his heart.

Next, strategically draping sacred herbs around his body, they chanted a release while circling him with smouldering sprigs of cleansing white sage. Finally, the young man laid still, the stench of rot began to clear the room, and his breathing returned to normal. Helen swears she saw a dark shadow spring from his body, though neither Clara nor Patricia ever confirmed such a thing.

The following morning, the doctors scratched their heads in disbelief as they watched him happily stroll from the hospital. The town of Stepney would have loved to catch a glimpse of the magic performed to create a miracle that day. On the other hand, Olivia has been doing everything in her power to avoid it.

Considering her lineage, that may sound crazy, but magic teeters on a fine line of love and hate for her. Sure her mother's bloodline overflows with good, but her father? Pure evil. He invited the dark side in, leading them to a terrible death. The question is. Which blood is dominant in *her* veins?

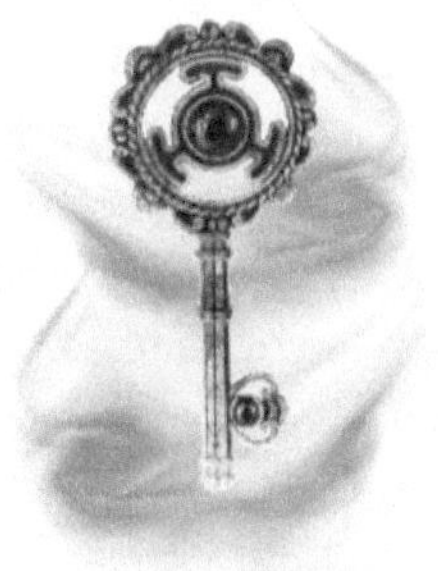

CHAPTER 3 ~ LET'S BE SAND-WITCHES

Twisting a napkin in her hand, Patricia acknowledges Clara as she enters the kitchen. "Morning, Mom."

"Yes, what a beautiful morning it is." She stares down at the tangle of tissue in her daughter's hand and raises her brow. "At least for some. What's on your mind? You may as well spit it out before you shred that poor thing to pieces."

"I was just about to ask her the same thing, Clara dear," the woman in the portrait, sitting on the shelf among Clara's spices, huffs. "She's been at that poor napkin for the last ten minutes."

Tossing the napkin down, Patrica slaps her hands together, ridding her fingers of paper particles and takes a deep breath. "It's nothing. Just lost in thought, I suppose." She feigns a smile, looking up at the portrait of Aunt Millie before meeting her mother's gaze. "Though I was thinking. What if Olivia and I went to the beach today? You know, a solid day to recharge and sort my scattered thoughts may do me some good and—"

The woman in the portrait laughs as Clara rolls her eyes. "Oh, come on now. We both know that's nothing more than an excuse to keep Olivia out of the store."

"Fair enough. It is an excuse. But I don't believe we should be pushing her toward that thing."

"I don't think you understand. This is a timekeeper journal, not just some silly artifact." Leaning against the counter with her teacup in hand, Clara stares at her daughter. "And look, Olivia is twenty-one. If you ask me, she's been coddled for too long. Besides, you must admit that book is here for a reason, and she's the only one who hasn't set eyes on it yet. Not to mention, there are a ton of practical pieces in there. These artifacts could interest her, even help ignite her call for magic." Clara glances over at Helen as she enters the kitchen. "Morning, honey, she smiles, her attention quickly shifting back to Patricia. "We've all witnessed some activity surrounding her these last few months. We need to let this happen. Perhaps this was sent for that exact reason—to entice her back into our world."

Helen pulls a pan from the cupboard and peers over her shoulder. "Let me guess. Olivia?"

Patricia holds her teacup to her lips and closes her eyes. "Who else."

Olivia lifts the window, allowing the sweet smell of lilacs to seep in from the small bush below. A relaxing scent she's always looked forward to in the early summer months. She takes a deep breath, inhaling the fresh morning air, and drags on her jeans while her ears perk to the dishes clanking downstairs and her Aunt Patricia's lively laughter. A comfortable reminder that most heartaches and loss eventually heal with time.

'Meow'

She peers down at the shiny black fur of her most trusted friend, Mr. Green, and recalls the dark evening they met. He appeared out of nowhere the night her parents died, offering reassurance as he curled himself around her in the back of the ambulance. His fur, black as coal, shone like diamonds as he purred his way into her heart, staring at her with his pale green eyes. When he finally snuggled in beside her, laying his head on her lap, their inseparable friendship began.

Now, nearly fifteen years later, the black furball swirls around her leg, gazing up at her with those eyes that closely resemble her own. "Well, good morning to you too, Mr. Green." She scoops him into her arms and kisses his forehead. "I'm sorry if I startled you this morning. I think that dream startled me a little too." She scratches the top of his head before gently setting him back on his feet, then turns toward the bathroom. "I suppose we should get ready before Gran comes back up, huh?"

'Meow,' he cries a little louder as he trots along behind her and hops up on the vanity. He sits twisting his head as he watches her brush her teeth in the mirror, then sticks his paw into her small basket of hair ties. Pulling it out with a band dangling from his nail, he juts it toward her. She glances down at his offering and laughs, replacing her toothbrush before taking the hairband. "Sure, why not? I like red too."

Drawing her auburn hair back into a ponytail, she strides from her room with her furry companion quick at her heels.

As she reaches the stairs, a familiar chipper voice greets her from the end of the hall. "Good morning, young lady." She peers up at the plaster bust of a man in a top hat as he smiles and tips his head.

"Good morning, Uncle Chester," she waves, continuing downstairs toward the kitchen. When she reaches the bottom step, she stops to take in the bright, cheery atmosphere of the room. Her nostrils flare to the citrusy brew simmering on the stove and the spicy scent from the hammock of dried herbs hanging above.

She finds herself studying the multitude of glass jars filled with different waters lining the window sill—*full moon, seawater, high tide, low tide, lake water*. The assortment is astonishing. Her eyes follow the vine of heart-shaped green leaves along the edge of the ceiling to the beautiful but deadly moonflowers that hang in every corner. They've been there her entire life, yet somehow everything seems different this morning.

A mug juts out in front of her as she steps into the room. "Morning, sleepyhead! Care for a cup of tea?"

"Mmm, thank you."

At fifty-seven, Olivia's Aunt Patricia is the quirky one. With her short blond hair brightly streaked red and off-side comments, she could easily pass for a young thirty-five.

Okay, so there may be some benefits to being a witch.

Ever since her preteens, Patricia has been able to absorb energy naturally from the sun and electrical storms. Plus, she can draw flame from any fire and redirect it with pinpoint accuracy—a skill she inherited from her fire element father, Willard Redfearn. But unfortunately, he didn't make for the most stable warlock. He perished when he set his car ablaze one drunken evening, leaving Clara to raise their daughters on her own. Not that his presence could have ever been considered a significant contribution anyway.

Patricia's hand passes across her upper body, tiny blue sparks dancing along her fingers as her white shirt changes to yellow. When Olivia peers down at the bold lettering across her chest, she nearly spits her tea. 'Let's do lunch on the beach! We would make FAB sand-witches!'

Clearing her throat, Helen rolls her eyes. "All right, enough goofing off! Let's finish our breakfast, so we can get to the store. We still have a ton of stuff to go through and—"

"Oh, pull your broomstick out of your keister. The store sign is going up today—it's the big name reveal. We know," Patricia affirms, cutting her sister off as she takes her seat at the table, chomping down on a piece of toast.

"All right, that's enough. Some days, I swear you two are still youngsters." Cradling her teacup in the palm of her hands, Clara exhales exhaustively. "If you two truly must act as sand-witches today—go." Her gaze flicks to Helen. "I suppose Helen and I could work some magic to unpack most of the boxes ourselves, and I guess you two can see the sign anytime."

"Pfft." Olivia dramatically scrunches up her face as she shakes her head. "No way, Gran. You've kept the name a secret for far too long. Besides, a promise is a promise. Remember?" She grabs her fork and glances at Patricia. "We wouldn't miss the reveal for anything. Would we, Aunt Trish?"

Dropping the remnants of her toast, Patricia dusts the crumbs off her hands with a halfhearted smile. "Of course not."

"Mmhmm," Clara smirks as she sets her cup down on the table and meets Olivia's gaze. "So, you mentioned something about a dream this morning."

"Yeah, I've dreamt about this old woman twice this week, but it always cuts at the same spot." Continuing, Olivia glances down at her grandmother's fingertips as they tap the table. "I'm watching her." She pauses and shakes her head. "Or, well, I think I am. I mean, I feel like a bystander—merely watching her. Yet, I'm burdened with her emotions, exhaustion, and even her pain as she drags the stone across her hand. And I know things only she would know, like where she got the stone from. A vision of an old burned-out witches' camp flashed through my mind when she pulled it out. There are moments I swear I am her." Swallowing, she takes a breath. "Anyway, she's attempting some kind of fire scry when she foresees a nasty old priest and his men coming for her. But for some reason, she refuses to leave her home. Instead, she sits on her porch, feeding her cat and patiently waits for them."

Clara's fingers stop as she draws in a deep breath. "Hmm. Apparently, there's a recent trend with an old witch appearing to us in our dreams." She sits silently for a moment, then shakes her finger toward Olivia. "Maybe she's trying to tell you to stop bottling up your magic – to accept who you are."

Olivia rolls her eyes. "I'm pretty sure that's not it, Gran. Seems like more of a warning, if anything. I mean, think about it. The priest and his men were dragging her off to hang on a cross when you woke me."

"Oh, don't be so dramatic. Warnings are usually quite clear. You must be missing something." Smiling, Clara stands. "Try not to let it bother you." She pats Olivia on the shoulder as she passes behind her. "Now, I require a few moments in the garden this morning. I woke with a strong desire for some rich earth between my toes. Does anyone else care to recharge before we leave?"

"Not me," Helen grins, tucking a couple of stray hairs into the pile on top of her head. "I bathed in the stream this morning."

Patricia waves on her way to the front door. "Nah, I'm good."

Stuffing a few bites of scrambled eggs into her mouth, Olivia grabs a piece of toast and follows her to the front porch. Though it's nothing more than waving her hand as she utters a few words, she would rather not be in the kitchen while Helen works her cleaning spell.

Helen, the oldest of the three siblings, has devised several helpful household spells over the years to ensure their days can be freed up quickly.

Since her preteens, she's been able to use water to her advantage in almost any way imaginable. With nothing more than a few carefully chosen herbs, a pot of boiling water and some strong desires, she can whip up an enchanted meal for almost any occasion. Not only does she have the ability to cook up some astonishing potions and protection spells, but Helen is considered the perfect host. She always has a pot of water simmering on the stove, and though you rarely see her move, your favourite beverage never empties.

CHAPTER 4 ~ THE SIGN REVEAL

Patricia tries to stifle a laugh as Olivia steps out on the front porch.

"What's so funny?"

"Honestly, it's rather amusing to watch you deek out as soon as you suspect magic is about to hit the air." She strides toward her with a grin. "You do know that sooner or later, magic will simply call on you. Right?" Flipping her hand out, she produces a bright blue ball of flames in her palm. As it slowly swirls, she gazes at her niece. "This is part of our life, Liv. It's who we are." She playfully bounces the fireball back and forth between her hands. Olivia's shoulders tense, and she takes a step back. Pursing her lips, Patricia rolls her fingers into a fist, dousing the ball of flames and perches herself on the railing. "Aw, don't look so timid. The summer solstice is tomorrow—a day filled with magic. Besides, your powers could be enormously helpful if you'd only give them a chance."

Olivia rolls her eyes, continuing toward the steps. "I don't want to work spells for fun or to have the best lawn in the neighbourhood or change the colour of my hair on a whim." She throws her arms out, turning back toward Patricia. "You know, in the real world, people actually go out for fun, fertilize the grass and buy hair dye." She pokes herself in the chest. "That's how I want to live." Tucking a loose tendril of hair behind her ear, she takes a breath. "Anyway, I wanted to see a movie with Jimmy tomorrow night." Her shoulders slump as she flops down next to her aunt on the railing. "That is if he ever returns my calls."

Patricia exhales as she picks a daisy from the patio planter and tucks it behind Olivia's ear. "You have to join us for the summer solstice. We're celebrating here this year, so I see little opportunity for you to escape." Walking down the steps, she pauses to glance over her shoulder. "And you know, Gran didn't even invite anyone to celebrate with us this year. Instead, she's kept it to a simple family celebration, hoping to lessen your anxiety." Tipping her head, she feigns a pout. "Come on, Liv. You can see a movie with Jimmy any night."

"But I don't want to be part of the summer solstice celebration," Olivia groans. "The entire day is filled with magic. Just the thought of it makes my heart race." She places her hand on her chest. "I swear. Feel it."

The front door slams behind her, and Clara's deep green eyes narrow. Tensing, she steadies for the inevitable lecture, though surprisingly, her grandmother pinches her cheek and offers her a smile on her way by. "Alrighty then, let's try to finish this up quickly. All those beautiful flowers we picked yesterday are still downstairs in the fridge. We need to make those into wreaths when we get home. I would prefer to hang them tonight, so they can greet the morning sun," she smiles. "Oh, I absolutely love summer solstice. Don't you, Olivia?"

"If you mean do I love the longer summer days, then yeah." She slides into the backseat with Mr. Green and flashes a forced smile. "Who doesn't?"

Sitting beside her, Patricia's white shirt changes to yellow as the words *'All right, I'm about to take some heat for you.'* appear across her chest. Shaking her head, Olivia lowers it into her hands.

"Hey, Mom. I'm not so sure Olivia wants to take part in the summer solstice celebration tomorrow, and personally—"

Clara slams on the brakes, cutting Patricia off and glares at her through the review mirror. "Personally, I think Olivia can use her own mouth if that's how she really feels." Her focus shifts. "Well, Liv? Is that how you feel? Do you honestly believe regenerating our energy and celebrating the gift of our inner light is unimportant?" Clara turns in her seat to face her. "Child, I've been patient with your fear of magic, but fifteen years is plenty long enough. There is no damn way I can allow you to ignore who you are completely. Whether you're willing to admit it or not, this is who we are."

Olivia's eyes spring to meet her stare. "Gran, I'm not trying to be disrespectful, but I'm terrified to think of what harm I might cause. I heard the stories of how my father's blood ran hot with evil, how he allowed his demonic call to overpower him and Mom that night. Remember how I set you on fire as a child?" She throws her hand out, pointing to Clara's arm. "What if I had seriously hurt you? Maybe these are warning signs. What if my inherited bloodline is laced with evil, like my father or grandpa?"

Clara's shoulders drop forward as she searches her granddaughter's face. "Oh, Olivia. Not all warlocks are evil, nor are their malevolent ways bred into their blood like their gifts. Some men are intense by nature, so when you add the gift of magic, they have a tendency to believe they are the almighty. That kind of arrogance breeds evil, and inevitably, that's what leads to their demise. It's not something passed down through DNA, child."

Pursing her lips, she tips her head. "As for you, I can assure you any wickedness your father could have introduced to you your mother dispelled long ago. Remember the chant you told me about—the one you said your mother kept repeating the night of the fire?" Her eyes soften as Olivia's face drops, recalling the evening that's been haunting her since she was seven. "Well, that's gone. And to be clear," she adds, glancing at Mr. Green curled up in Olivia's lap before turning to put the van in gear. "Animals cower, and nature withers when darkness touches it. Not the other way around. As I said, maybe there is a message trying to come through with these dreams. They could very well mean your magic is trying to push through the barrier you built around it. You can't hold it back forever." She waves her hand, dismissing the conversation. "Now, enough of this nonsense. Let's go pull this store together. Shall we?"

Olivia opens her mouth but quickly changes her mind, choosing to stroke Mr. Green's back instead. She can't seem to find a valid argument. Animals love her, and only a few days ago, the dead ivy on her desk came back to life with a simple touch of her finger. Mind you, she never mentioned the plant, but apparently, that hasn't gone unnoticed. As for the dreams of this old woman, as much as she hates to admit it, they leave her feeling more accepting – more alive.

When they arrive at the store on Ben Johnson Road, the boom truck is already out front installing the sign. Lifting Mr. Green into her arms, Olivia peers up, disappointed to see nothing but a large drop sheet. Nudging her, Helen points up to the cover. "You know, I'm willing to bet if you gave your magic half a chance, you would be able to flick that sheet right off there."

"Yes, well, you could do the same now, couldn't you."

Helen looks back up at the tarp and nods. "You're right. But how would that teach *you* anything?"

Strolling up beside them, Patricia throws her arm around Olivia's shoulder. "I hate to admit this, Liv, but she does have a point. You should work with your powers so you can control them rather than having them blast out of you like wildfire when you least expect it. You have to admit. It can't hurt to try. Right?" She lifts her hand, pointing two fingers toward the tarp. "All you have to do is will it to move as you swipe it away." She waves her fingers to the side with a smile.

"No way." Kissing the top of Mr. Green's head, she pulls him in a little tighter to her chest. "We can wait like everyone else."

"Aw, come on. What's the worst that could happen? Either it blows off, or it doesn't. It's not as if you're willing it to catch fire, Liv."

"No thanks. I'd rather not."

Sighing, Patricia glances up at the sign and waves her forward. "Meh, never mind. I think he's about to pull the sheet off anyway."

'Olivia.'

The hair on the back of her neck pricks her flesh as she turns to see a tall, dark-haired man standing on the corner. His muttonchop sideburns and nineteenth-century clothing catch her eye. Albeit, given the theatre's proximity down the street, this costumed man's presence is not entirely out of the question. However, someone has just gently tasted her name, leaving it hanging in the air at seven-thirty on a Saturday morning, and it seems he's the only one around.

As the nineteenth-century clothed man shifts his weight to search the length of the street, Olivia turns and taps Patricia's arm. "Aunt Trish."

But her gaze never wavers from the tarp as she pats the top of her niece's hand. "I know, I know. This really is kind of exciting. Isn't it? What do you think she called it?" Olivia's shoulders slump, realizing her aunt's attention is solely focused on the reveal. She glances back to the corner, but the man is gone. Just then, the unexpected thud of the heavy drop sheet sends her heart into her chest, and she grips her aunt's arm harder than expected with a gasp. Finally, Patricia spins to face her. "Hey, you okay, kiddo?"

"Yeah, a little jumpy, I guess."

There's not much sense in mentioning someone who is no longer there. Besides, she's felt a little strange all morning. In fact, her mind has been all over the place for a few weeks now. As for the man? He was likely nothing more than a figment of her overactive imagination.

Shaking off the eerieness, she turns her attention back to the sign. It's a beautiful piece of art. Custom carved out of light-coloured wood, it's been made to look scarred by time. The raised lettering is dark in contrast to the lighter background, and it bears the name Immortal Treasures.

Her focus shifts to her grandmother. She's standing with her fingertips pressed against her lips as she stares up at her long-awaited reveal. "I love the name, Gran, but couldn't you simply wave your hand and create the identical sign, if not better? I mean, you could use magic for something like this. Right?"

"Yes, I suppose. Though I do love it when my ideas come to life by someone else's hands."

"She has a point, mom," Helen declares on her way past. "And the payment would be minimal considering it's made of wood."

"What does she mean by payment? There wouldn't be a cost if you whipped it up yourself."

"Ah, but our gifts aren't entirely free, child. However, trees grow from the earth—my natural element. So, I can repay Mother Earth by planting a new seedling."

"Okay, then what would the payment be for the menial things like Aunt Trish changing t-shirt slogans or Aunt Helen's cleaning spells?"

Clara studies her granddaughter's face, then pats her hand with a smile. "Well, that's why we have the common altar. We give thanks for the little day-to-day things with small offerings. I'm sure you've noticed Patricia burns incense and keeps a fire burning on the hearth, and Helen adds a seashell or stone to the fountain daily."

Nodding, Olivia squints over at her grandmother. "And you, what do you do?"

Clara's smile grows. "Well, for one, I built the common altar. I personally made those bricks out of clay from our yard with my own hands. And I retain my garden, leaving offerings of herbs I've grown on the mantle. Of course, you can't forget the offerings we make on a larger scale during Imbolc, spring equinox or solstice. Such celebrations aren't merely fun get-togethers. They all have a purpose, Olivia." Cocking her brow, she glimpses up at the sign and points. "Is that your way of saying you don't like my sign?"

Bursting into laughter, Olivia shakes her head. "Goodness, no. I love the sign, Gran. Just curious. That's all."

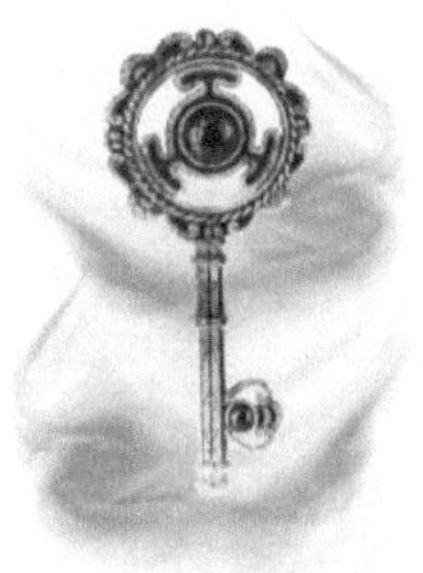

CHAPTER 5 ~ VAMPIRE TREASURES

"I have to agree. The sign looks great, mom, and the name—" Patricia shakes her finger with a grin. "Very clever. It certainly fits, considering the shipment of boxes we have to unpack today."

Smiling over her shoulder, Helen clicks the door open. "I'd say! I wonder what other wonderful little goodies we'll find. Personally, I'm quite excited to dig back in."

Olivia's brows pull together as she peers over at her grandmother. "What are they talking about? What makes these boxes so special?"

"Oh, they're not that big of a deal," Clara beams as she drapes her arm over her grandaughter's shoulder, guiding her toward the store. "They're nothing more than some eighteenth-century remnants that I was able to purchase at the auction from the old Stepney Castle. So far, it's only been some mismatched odds and ends, but you never know what we could find. Besides, the shipment has been fun to sort through if nothing else."

Stopping, Olivia spins out from under Clara's arm. "Wait! The Stepney Castle? You mean the old *vampire* castle?"

"Mmhmm."

"Are you sure we should have possession of this stuff? I mean, what if they really are vampires?" Her face tightens as she eyes the wall of boxes and steps inside, lowering her voice as if the undesirables might hear her. "After all, they are demonic descendants. Right?"

Patricia laughs, yanking on her white cotton gloves. "Well, they are bloodsuckers. That alone tells me they're not of a divine nature." She tips her head, looking at Olivia from under her brow. "Let's hope you have some magic in those lofty little fingers of yours. We may need your help if they decide to turn up to reclaim their stuff."

"For the love of the Goddess, will you two knock it off," Helen snickers, lifting a box to her table. "Don't forget witches are on the good ol' demonic descendant's list as well. Anyway, Liv, I wouldn't worry too much. I would say if their castle has been vacant for at least a century, and mom scored all this at the auction—" She gestures to the multitude of boxes lining the back wall and the items covering her table. "I think we can safely assume they have moved on or possibly even met their demise somehow. Besides, I haven't sensed any vampires around these parts in decades."

Helen pulls an old book out of the box and turns it over in her hands. "Oh, my goodness. Why in the world would someone consider sending this to auction? Shouldn't this be in a museum?" She holds up the barely worn hardcover bound in sheepskin and reads the title. "Just look at this! I mean, are you kidding me? Cassandra Fam'd Romance 1652," she grins, flipping the book to show Clara the front cover. "How steamy do you think this is?"

"Oh, for pity's sake. I can assure you that book is nothing like the smut you read. If I'm not mistaken, the story revolves around a bogus plot to murder King Charles II." Clara points to the corner shelf. "Why don't you slide it into one of those clear bags over there? I don't doubt it's fairly valuable. I have some artifact boxes in the basement we can use once we sort through everything."

Patricia slides a box in front of Olivia. "I swear this box is calling out your name. Poor lonely thing, sitting all by itself over there in the corner. Maybe the evil vampire king of Stepney has something special in there for you." She winks, a playful smirk dancing on her lips as she turns to grab a box for herself.

Olivia's hand flies to her hip, her head swaying side to side as the corner of her mouth pulls into a scornful sneer. "Haha. Honestly, now that I think about it. I would rather play with this vampire stuff than magic. What is the worst thing a vampire can do? Drink some blood and live forever?" She grabs the lid, slides her hand through the slit in the top of the box and yanks back one side with a squeal. "Ow! Damn it!" Pulling back her hand, she notices tiny red beads rising to the surface and shoves her finger into her mouth.

"What happened, Liv? Vampire bite you?" Patricia jokes.

Scrunching her face, Olivia pulls her finger from her mouth and holds up the digit for examination. "No – no vampire. Just a box lid. Dang thing managed to draw blood, though," she whines, jamming it back into her mouth.

"Ew!" Patricia cringes. "That's gross! Not even an hour among vampire junk, and you are already sucking your own blood? You're seriously disappointing me, Liv."

Shifting her weight, Olivia tips her head to glare at her aunt. "Real funny, Aunt Trish. I didn't want to drip on anything valuable."

"I agree. No bleeding on the priceless items." Clara points to the doorway behind the stack of boxes. "There are bandages in the bathroom. See that you use one."

"Nah, I'm okay, Gran. Nothing more than a tiny scratch. It's not even bleeding anymore." She holds up her finger, then waves her gloves in the air. "Anyway, you don't need to worry. I know enough to wear my gloves." She pushes the cotton over each finger, slaps her hands together then pulls open the other side of the cardboard lid, releasing a cloud of dust. Choking into the back of her hand, she blinks the grit from her eyes. "All right, now *that's* disgusting. I'm pretty sure I just inhaled a good chunk of the eighteenth century."

Clara peers up from the table of trinkets she's been meticulously itemizing. "Now-now, you should consider yourself fortunate. Do you have any idea how many people would pay dearly to get a whiff of this eighteenth-century dust?"

"Yeah? Well, they can have it," Olivia bites, her tone sassier than intended, but the dust is quickly forgotten as her sight sets on a deep blue satin bag. She reaches in to retrieve it, admiring its pristine condition. Gently pulling the gold cord, she opens it up and tips out the contents. A gilded set of child-sized utensils clatter to the table — each piece with an intricate embellishment carved on the top. Carefully running her cotton-gloved finger over the initials C.L. along the stem, Olivia peers up at Clara. "Hey Gran, if the Laurent family are indeed vampires, why would they have children's utensils?"

Clara leans back in her chair, pushing a strand of hair behind her ear as she squints across at her granddaughter. "Well, Julien and Clarentina Laurent aren't just any old vampires." Before finishing her sentence, she pulls herself to her feet and heads for Olivia's table. Sitting next to her, Clara takes up the small spoon to admire it. "We are talking about two originals. Their exact creation date is still unclear, but we have records showing them emerging from the darkness during the early seventeenth century." She shrugs, turning toward Olivia. "As for them being able to have children, well, I don't know the exact science behind it, but they could, and they did. Clarentina gave birth to two boys."

She sets the utensils down and walks back over to continue tagging items. "You know, great-gran Ancina left a tale behind of personally meeting Mr. Laurent." Olivia's head springs up, and her eyes widen as she listens intently. "Oh yes," Clara confirms with a nod. "She claimed he saved her from being set ablaze by the town. But, of course, that's merely a tale that has been passed down through the family. Although I believe it, there's no proof it's true."

"Wait." Olivia's brows knit tightly together as she contemplates her grandmother's words. "A vampire helping a witch?"

"Mmhmm. Gran Victoria swears her grandmother Annabel told her all about it, and you don't get any closer to the source than that."

"But I thought vampires and witches are enemies?"

"Indeed we are! Vampires are the *true* spawn of Satan. They would love nothing more than to tap into our magic, and by that, I mean drain it straight from our veins," Patricia exclaims, dramatically slapping her forearm.

A snicker comes from the opposite side of the room, and Olivia cocks her head toward Helen. She may not have a comment, but she clearly finds Patricia's remark amusing. Shaking her head, Olivia turns her attention back to Clara. "That tale makes no sense, Gran. It must be exactly that – a fable. Why would a vampire save an enemy if not to drain her of her magic?"

Slowly shaking her head, Clara shrugs. "No one truly knows. When I asked my grandmother the same question, she claimed that fate laid down its cards that evening. That eventually, time would reveal the connection." She takes a deep breath, staring off with a brass timepiece in hand. "As for old Hattox, she didn't get to tell the whole story to anyone. From what I can gather between old family journals and stories I've been told, she met her fate on old Gallows Hill shortly after. But, unfortunately, the story seems to end there with no record of where her body is."

"Maybe this is it." Helen gestures to the multitude of boxes with a smile. "Perhaps this is the connection fate had in mind. Maybe we're meant to become rich from these Laurent treasures."

Laughing, Clara holds up the beautifully carved brass trinket box and twirls it around in front of her. "I'm not convinced any of these little beauties can make us famously rich, but I am sure some may be worth a pretty penny." The childlike smile that spreads across her face draws a chuckle from Helen. "Personally, I am quite content to keep finding these wonderful little timepieces." She places the box down in front of her and grabs a tag. "They all have such lovely detailing, don't you think, Olivia?"

"Yes, Gran." She glances up to acknowledge the item, absently pulling open the lid on her third box. "They're all stunning pieces." Fanning away the plume of dust, she reaches in. A nervous sensation twists her stomach as her fingers graze the smooth leather cover of a book. It's an eerie feeling, though easily ignored, until she grabs the spine. Then, a bit stronger than static, an unexpected jolt sets her back in her chair with a squeal.

Clara's head shoots up, peering at her over the table of stock. "You okay, Liv?"

"Hmm? Oh. Yeah. I just got a shock. All this dust must be causing static electricity." Avoiding their stares, she ducks down and reaches back into the box.

A tingle moves up her arm as she grasps the binding of an old leather-wrapped book. Pulling it out, she turns it over in her hands and reads the name stamped on the cover — Laurent. Though it looks relatively plain, the prickling sensation says something entirely different. She wants to put it down, but something about this basic old tome arouses every fibre of her being.

As she runs her fingertip over the embossed lettering, every hair on her body rises, twisting her stomach into a nervous knot. She gently opens the cover as Mr. Green tangles himself around her ankle with his usual offering of reassurance. Peering down, she scratches the top of his head. Finally, her eyes return to the book—to the first perfectly uniform inscription, Julien Laurent—SOV.

The face of the man on the corner flashes before her. He's so close that she can see the flecks of gold through the blue in his eyes. Olivia's heart thumps, and she tugs her hand back with a gasp, bounding to her feet as the old book falls to the floor.

Across the English Channel, Cassian Laurent is leaning across his desk, gazing out across the rolling hills that lead to the small village of Commana, France, when his world stops. He straightens, spinning toward Gabriel. He must've phased out during his sired brother's rant. Not that Cassian needed to hear it, it's the same rant they've all taken turns with for what seems like forever.

"It's been more than a century! How can he have eluded us—"

Gabriel's frustrated words cut off abruptly, and Cassian can only assume they've seen the same thing. A young girl sits holding a leather-bound journal—she couldn't be any older than twenty. A golden glow emanates from under her finger as she leisurely runs it over the text.

"Christ! A reader," Cassian blurts, meeting Gabriel's stare.

Together they turn toward the thundering footsteps approaching the den. Cassian's younger brother, Elias, bursts through the door with his jaw slack. "Did you see that?"

Running his hand over his chin, Cassian nods sluggishly. "Indeed I did."

Gabriel jumps to his feet. "It's finally her, isn't it? The master of the timekeeper! She'll know where to find Roger and the key!" He jabs his hands into his hair with a toothy smile. "Cripes! We can finally bring Julien back!"

"I'm not sure," Cassian shrugs, his gaze distant as he tries to recall the girl's image. "She's so much younger than I had imagined, and she's – well, quite frankly, she looked timid. Not at all what I was expecting."

"Oh, for Christ's sake, Cash!" Elias shouts, throwing his hands in the air as he steps into the room. "Of course, she's the one! I don't care if she's nineteen or ninety. Shit, I don't care if she's scared out of her wits. We need her! After all these years, that girl is the only one that's been able to read that cursed book." In a flash, he's standing in Cassian's face. "I don't care what you say. We're going to go get her!"

Cassian shakes his head, raising his finger in the air. "Oh, no, no, no. If we saw the same thing, you must've recognized how scared she was. This will need to be handled with a subtle approach—something neither of you is capable of. The last thing we want to do is scare her off by having three vampires show up at her door. Besides, someone needs to stay here with mom. I'll go."

Gabriel's brows tighten as he glances between his brothers. "Come on, Cash. It's not like Clarentina would be alone. Soloman's here. We can't do anything for her at the moment anyway. She's still refusing to eat. Hell, one of the maids even offered her wrist to her, and she still wouldn't budge."

Closing in on Gabriel, Cassian's eyes darken. "Then you'll tell her we've found the witch who can help us bring our father back. You'll be the one to convince her that she needs to feed in order to gain her strength for his return—that he'll need her." Pointing in Gabriel's face, his jaw tenses. "You seem to have forgotten who fought for your life when you were dancing with death. She never gave up on you. Without her persistence, father would never have changed you.

In fact, beetles would be pushing dirt about your bones at this very moment. You're best never to forget that."

"Whoa. Easy, Cash." Elias places a calming hand on his older brother's back. "He wasn't being disrespectful. It's his sire bond to father."

Gabriel's shoulders slump as he lowers his gaze, and visible regret dullens his smile. "Cash, I'm sorry. Elias is right. I got caught up with the anticipation of finally having a way to bring Julien back." He shakes his head and flops down on the sofa with a heavy sigh. "Forgive me. It wasn't my intent to sound callous."

"Look, I understand, little brother." Cassian feigns a slight smile. "It has been an incredibly long time. We're all anxious." Walking over to the window, he stares out over the small village. "It's been a few years since we've been back in London. As I recall, the Windsor Clan was quite unruly when we were there last."

"You can say that again." Elias walks in behind the bar and pulls out a bottle of bourbon. Setting three glasses out, he begins to pour. "The smell of their halfbreed sire was all over the raucous bunch, yet he was still nowhere to be found." He hands each of his brothers a drink and smiles. "Somehow, I believe this is about to bring him out of hiding."

"I do believe you may be correct." Cassian takes a sip of his drink, glances at his pocket watch and tips his head to Elias. "Anyway, I suppose I should get ready. Hopefully, this won't take any longer than a few days." He shoots a look between both brothers. "I'm sure you two can command yourselves accordingly while I'm away."

"Don't be ridiculous. You know we will," Elias grumbles, his lips tight as he glares at his brother. "You just concern yourself with getting her and the journal back here. We can't make promises to mother if you can't deliver. So don't pander to the young sorceress, or I'll have to pay a visit to our little witch friend myself. Oh, and" —*he raises his brow, waving his hand along the length of Cassian's body*— "you might want to wear something a little more twenty-first centuryish."

Cassian looks down at his favourite breeches and smirks. "Right. I suppose a change might be in order."

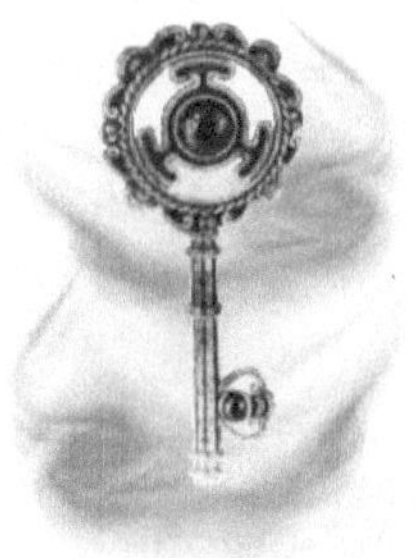

CHAPTER 6 ~ THE JOURNAL

Back at the antique store, a wide-eyed Olivia stands staring down at the leather-bound mystery. "You sure you're all right, Liv," Clara asks, straightening in her chair as she wipes her forearm across her brow. Her eyes land on the journal at Olivia's feet. "You do seem a little skittish."

Releasing her arm, Olivia forces a smile. There is no way she's about to let them think she's gone mad over some silly vampire stuff. "Yeah, of course. I'm fine." Picking up the book, she places it on the chair. "Just super thirsty all of a sudden."

Helen peers up from her crouched position on the floor. "Too much dust, honey?"

"Yeah, that must be it." Olivia finishes off her water and tosses the bottle into the trash. "I don't believe I've been subjected to this much dust since we cleared out Aunt Millie's belongings."

"You sure you're okay? Cause you look like you've seen a ghost." Patricia walks toward her, wiggling her fingers as her smile grows. "Ohhh, or maybe that box you cut yourself on has been laced with vampire venom. Let me see your teeth."

Olivia rolls her eyes. "You're really not being funny, Aunt Trish."

"Aw, come on, Liv." Patricia slings an arm across her shoulders and tugs her against her side. "You know I'm only teasing. All this vampire stuff gives me the heebie-jeebies too." She steps back, holding her by the shoulders at arm's length and scans her face. "Why don't I take you home? I'm a little drained myself."

Clara checks her watch before peering up at the two of them. "I think we've accomplished a fair bit here today. Why don't we all call it a night? I'd like to make a few flower wreaths for tomorrow's summer solstice anyway. It will give the dust some time to settle, and we can pick up where we left off on Monday." She pinches Olivia's cheek, winking as she passes. "I woke you early. You could likely use a good night's rest. You'll be fine by tomorrow."

"Yeah, I'm sure you're right." Olivia holds the old book up, ignoring the tingle that travels along her arm. "Hey, Gran. Mind if I take this home to read?"

Clara studies it for a moment and shrugs. "I don't see why not. It appears to be an old journal. Did you check to see what's inside?"

"Mmhmm, I took a quick peek, but you're right. It does resemble some kind of formal family diary. What do you suppose SOV stands for?"

"SOV is an abbreviation used for sovereign. As I said, Julien Laurent wasn't simply any old vampire. He was first to be created and was deemed the king." Her smile broadens. "I'm curious if there's any mention of Mr. Laurent's encounter with great-gran Ancina in that diary."

Helen points to a crate next to where she's been sitting most of the day. "I found a few other old books over here. Mom said we were going to keep them for our library at home. So you may as well take the entire load of them."

"You don't have to twist my arm," Olivia grins, placing the leather-bound treasure on top as she takes up the crate. "I can't wait to see what they wrote about back then—how they lived. The script is absolutely beautiful."

"Bloodsuckers? Likely how their victims tasted," Patricia cringes. "What else would they have to write about? I highly doubt they were farmers."

Olivia twists her lips, tipping her head toward her aunt. "Perhaps this journal will prove they weren't vampires at all. I mean, did you ever think that could have been just a story to stir up the town." She shakes her head incredulously. "Pfft. Have none of you read To Kill a Mockingbird? Remember the whole misconception of Boo Radley?"

Helen erupts into laughter as she stands from her crouched position and places her hand on her lower back. "Liv, please. As we sit among these belongings, there is no way you can tell me that you don't sense the vampire presence in this room. That would be pure denial, honey."

Waving Helen off, Patricia rests her arm across her niece's shoulder. "Meh, pay her no mind. I suppose I'm a little curious myself of what those blood-sucking demons may have written about."

"Right." Rolling her eyes, Olivia kisses her teeth. "Come on, Mr. Green. Time for us to go." Shifting the crate of books to her hip, she struts toward the door.

"No, really. I am curious about what you'll find in there."

"Well then, if I read anything juicy, I promise to share. You know, so we can start a fang club." Smiling over her shoulder, she pushes open the door.

"Ahhh! Good one, Livy!" Patricia grins, snapping her fingers as she points at her. "You make me proud."

Chuckling, Helen opens the hatch on her way around the van. "I'm glad your humour is back, kiddo. I'll admit, that dang dust was getting to me too at the end."

The lighthearted moment soon passes as Olivia slides the crate into the back, and a soft breeze tussles her hair. An eerie shiver runs down her spine, and she spins to check behind her. Catching a glimpse of nothing more than a shadow disappearing down the alley, she takes a step toward the darkness.

"Hey, you coming?" Patricia calls out as the van door slides open.

Glancing back, Olivia peers down the empty alley one last time before shutting the hatch. "Yeah. Yeah, I'm coming."

Laughter fills the van as the conversation centres around the summer solstice celebration on the drive home. Still, Olivia can't keep her thoughts from drifting back to the leather-bound timepiece sitting in the crate behind her. A part of her wants to forget about the wretched old thing, but the urge to reach back and grab it is indescribable.

When they pull into the driveway, Clara puts the van into park and leans over the steering wheel. "Well, I think we've had a fairly productive day." She swings around, peering between the two seats at Olivia. "How are you feeling, Liv? Any better?"

Her focus still centred on the journal, Olivia's head pops up to meet her grandmother's stare. "Hmm?"

"I said, how are you feeling?"

"Oh, I'm okay, Gran. I'm sure it was just the dust." Sliding the door open, she steps out of the van, her gaze landing on a shadow by the old oak tree. Squinting to have a better look, she leans forward, but whatever it was, has disappeared into the darkness. She takes a deep breath and mutters to herself as she opens the hatch. 'For crying out loud, Olivia. Stop letting your imagination run wild. Do you want everyone to think you've gone mad?' Just then, a warm hand comes to rest on her shoulder, and she nearly jumps out of her skin.

"Whoa, what's up, buttercup?"

She gasps, her hand flying to her chest as she spins to face Helen. "Oh, Christ, Aunt Helen."

"My goodness, honey. I didn't mean to spook you, but who other than one of us could it possibly be?" Helen bends around her, peering out into the darkness. "What is it that you see out there anyway?"

Olivia shakes her head. "Uh, nothing, I guess." Tucking her hair behind her ear, she forces a smile. "I suspect it's all this vampire talk. You know how overactive my imagination can get—simple shadows can make me jumpy."

"Well," she looks around, then flares her arms out with a smile, "if it makes you feel better, the only thing I see out here is us, crazy old witches," she snickers. Leaning into the back of the van, she reaches for the bag and stops to point at the crate. "You need a hand carrying that in, honey?"

Olivia shakes her head. "No, thanks. I got it," she smiles, pulling the crate toward her.

The two sisters watch as she trails into the house behind their mother. "I think it's safe to say she read something in that book," Helen sighs.

Patricia nods as the door closes behind them. "Yep, she sure did." She threads her arm through her sister's. "I have to admit. I worry a bit about that. I hate the idea that she's being called on by that damn vampire diary. Let's hope mom has a plan to keep her safe. Anyway—" She grabs the spool of wire in Helen's hand and tosses it back in the van with a grin. "If Olivia isn't helping make the wreaths this year, a little magic will get that job done in no time."

Dropping the crate of books beside the stairs, Olivia reaches up to scratch Mr. Green's head. "All right, Gran, what can I do to help?"

"Nothing. Your aunts and I can take care of the flowers. You get some rest so you can enjoy yourself tomorrow."

Olivia's eyes shift from her aunts standing in the kitchen doorway to Clara. "Gran, honestly. I'm—" she starts but is abruptly stopped by her grandmother's raised hand.

"No. I won't hear it. You've been off all day, and I want you to enjoy yourself tomorrow. I know you were looking forward to going out with Jimmy. So you can invite him here." She waves her hand dismissively. "Now, take your books up to bed and get some rest. You can let us know if you find anything interesting in there over breakfast."

"Okay, fine, but remember I offered." She kisses Clara goodnight and grabs the crate. "Come on, Mr. Green. I guess we'll see you guys in the morning."

"Goodnight, Liv. Don't let the vampires bite," Patricia calls out as she turns toward the kitchen.

"Still not funny, Aunt Trish," she hollers back.

Clara leans across the kitchen table, her voice a near whisper. "None of us were able to read that book, yet from Olivia's reaction and question about SOV, I'd have to say she read something. Considering a timekeeper journal reveals itself only to the intended party, we must assume she is the journal's interpreter."

Helen rests her chin in her hand, staring across at her mother. "How crazy is that? The one that fears magic is the one to get called upon."

Leaning back in her chair, Patricia raises her hand. "Okay, wait a minute here. Has anyone given any thought to the fact that the journal belonged to vampires? Or that Olivia has no idea what kind of power she even possesses, or better yet, how to use it." She folds her arms, looking between her mother and Helen. "I think a shielding spell is in order."

"Look, I know you're concerned, but shielding her is not the answer. We've all sensed Olivia's power." Clara taps her fingers on the back of the chair as she paces. "How she's been able to suppress it this long is a mystery."

"Suppressing it or not, she hasn't learned how to use it. For crying out loud! She hasn't even attempted the simplest of spells since she was seven!" Patricia runs her hands through her hair and flops her arms down on the table. "How do you suppose she will protect herself when a vampire decides to appear, huh? Cause we all know that they will start surfacing once she begins reading that damned thing. That is the way those journals work, isn't it?"

"No one is one hundred percent certain how they work. We're running off guesses and hearsay. Regardless, she's been around magic her entire life. This is not as foreign to her as you might think. Once Olivia starts reading that diary, she won't be able to deny her abilities. I'm certain of it." Clara places her hands on the back of the chair and gazes up the stairs. "I'm not only convinced that she will call upon her magic when necessary but that she'll also be able to use it. Control might be an issue," she tips her head to the side, "but I believe she'll be a quick study once faced with no other options."

"Are you crazy?!" Patricia stands, throwing her hands out. "Every vampire tied to that journal will be seeking her out! You said yourself that whatever is in there must be something of great significance. Something that vampires will require a witch's assistance with." Pursing her lips, she cocks her head toward the steps. "They'll want Olivia. They have no idea she hasn't been actively practicing."

"Yes, that's true. I do suspect we'll likely be visited by vampires very soon. Still, the journal has chosen her, and she does seem drawn to it. There's no way that we can stand between them. One thing I know for sure is that timekeeper journals hold much power of their own. I'm sure it will not let her rest until she resolves the matter it has set out for her. That is its entire purpose. We can't tamper with fate by shielding her from what comes calling."

"Besides, if the vampires need her help, they won't want to harm her," Helen adds matter-of-factly.

"Really?! And what about the bloodsuckers that will want to stop her," Patricia asks. "You can't be foolish enough to believe there aren't some ready to interfere. Maybe I need to articulate the major issue here since you two don't get it?" She slams her hands down on the table. "Olivia – doesn't – know how – to use her – powers! Haven't you noticed that magic frightens her, for god sake?"

"Yes, you've made your point abundantly clear, and we are aware of the situation. It's something Mom and I spoke about earlier. But, to make our point just as clear, it's time that Olivia embraces the world of magic she was born into. She's no longer a child, and though we know that we can't force her" —*taking a deep breath, Helen sways her head from side to side*— "we may be able to bend her will a little."

"Pfft." Patricia throws her hands up, slumping down in her chair. "Well then, so much for not tampering with fate, huh."

Clara pats Patricia's shoulder with a reassuring hand. "Oh, come now. It's merely a little shove to help her open up. We only want her to accept who she is and embrace it. I wouldn't consider reducing her fear tampering." Shrugging her head toward the stairs, Clara pushes in her chair. "Why don't we go see if she's reading the journal? I'd like to get a better feel of her reaction to it."

Olivia sets the crate beside the bed and places the leather-bound book stamped Laurent on her nightstand. She shimmies between the soft cotton sheets, propping her back against the headboard and pulls the covers up around her hips. Once she's comfortable, she reaches for the journal and drags it to her lap. Her hand smoothes over the worn leather, allowing the quiver of exciting fear to arouse her senses.

In the dim light of her room, the golden glow that trails under her finger is much more prominent as she leisurely traces each embossed letter. She draws her bottom lip between her teeth and gently opens the cover to reveal its contents. Her heart rate increases as her hand hovers over the first inscription, Julien Laurent—SOV.

The appearance of the same man's face causes her to pause. *Clearly, this is not my imagination.* It's so vivid that she could swear he's standing right in front of her. His oval-shaped face is framed with jet-black hair, and his deep blue eyes seem to be looking directly into hers. The cover slams closed as her hand flies to her chest, and she stares down at Mr. Green. "Christ! Maybe I am going crazy, but I swear it's Julien Laurent that I've been seeing."

Clara slowly steps back from Olivia's cracked door and turns to her daughters. "Well, it does seem as though she has read something. I couldn't distinguish what she was chattering to herself about, but whatever it was seemed to have startled her. That fear of hers is going to be an obstacle we'll need to clear."

"As soon as she's asleep, I'll whisper into her ear. Hopefully, I can dispel most of her fears and restore her need to pursue her calling," Helen shrugs. "It worked to dismiss her nightmares when she was a child. I'm not sure I can ignite her passion for magic again without disturbing that block, but it's worth a try."

Folding her hand into the crevice of her elbow, Clara curls a finger around her top lip. "Yes, I agree. It can't hurt to try." She tips her head. "I'll continue to add a little mugwort to her tea each morning for the next week. It does seem to have made her more receptive. Unless it really is just the journal that's drawing her in."

"Goddess help us," Patricia grumbles, throwing her hands in the air as she stomps down the hall. "You two have lost your minds."

Unaware of the audience outside her door, Olivia grabs her phone, sending Jimmy a message. 'Hey! I haven't heard from you in a couple of days. Is everything okay?'

Tossing the phone on her bedside table, she pulls the string on her lamp, allowing her mind to play in the shadows moving across her wall—something she loved doing as a child. The full moon's glow passes through the rustling leaves outside her window, creating an array of dancing figures. Similar to that of a shadow puppet show, the drama unfolding is left entirely to her imagination. The wind shifts the tree limbs, creating new images so quickly that her mind can barely keep up. *A cat sitting on a branch, a bird in flight, creepy hands, a man sitting on the window ledge.*

Fear shoves her stomach into her throat as she bounds forward. "Solas air!" she yells, turning the light on as her head flips from the wall to the window. Her hand falls to her chest. "Christ!" she gasps, staring at the open window. "I could have sworn someone was sitting on that ledge."

She darts for the window, pulls her burgundy drapes shut and takes another look around. Finally deciding that no one else is in her room, she slowly makes her way back to her bed while checking over her shoulder. Sliding under the sheet, she lies back on her soft feather pillow and pulls the string on her bedside lamp. As she closes her eyes, she sighs with relief. 'That's it! No book, no shadows, no more imaginary men! Just sleep, Olivia.'

But sleep won't come that easily. Her eyes pop open, "Did I just use magic to turn the light on?" She stares at Mr. Green as he rolls up against her leg and purrs. Covering her head with her pillow, she groans, "Ugh! What the heck is happening to me?" Squeezing her eyes shut, she prays for sleep.

CHAPTER 7 ~ SUMMER SOLSTICE

"Wakey, wakey, Sunshine! The summer solstice has arrived!" Olivia hears Patricia's playful tone as she taps on her door in passing.

"Ugh, you've got to be kidding me," she moans, turning away from the blinding rays beaming through her bedroom window. "I could have sworn I shut those damn curtains last night."

Her first instinct is to cover her head and go back to sleep, but she knows that's pointless. Her grandmother will come up next if she does. Flipping her blankets back in a huff, she begins to roll out of bed when something digs into her side. Her arm tingles and her heart begins to race as she runs her hand across the oddly familiar worn leather. "What the hell?"

Nearly knocking her cat to the floor, Olivia pulls the journal from her side and leaps from her bed, dropping it on the crate next to her nightstand. Scanning her room, she jabs her hands into her hair and takes a deep breath. "I'm not sure what's happening, Mr. Green, but I think I might be losing it." Her pale eyes stare down into his as though he may have an answer. "I did put that damn book on top of that crate last night. Didn't I?" His purr gets louder as he steps up under her hand and flops onto his side. "Pfft. I talk to you way too often. What would you know, anyway?"

Scratching his belly, she grabs her clothes and takes a sip of the tea left on her nightstand. She's not sure why but suddenly, she's not so concerned about the wandering journal or even a day surrounded by magic. In fact, she's kind of looking forward to the firewalk and making her flower boat. As she opens her bedroom door, the sound of her aunts and grandmother singing filters up the stairs. It's a witches' song she's heard every year since she was a child, sung to the beat of 'The Lion Sleeps Tonight.' Though she has always tried to deny it, it's a pretty catchy tune.

Unable to help herself, she begins singing along as she marches down the stairs to the kitchen.

Around the fire, the sacred fire, the witches dance tonight

The Witches-Way, the Witches-Way…

Under the moonlight, the radiant moonlight, our powers will flow tonight

So stoke the fire, the mighty fire, and we'll jump the flames tonight…

Dancing her way into the kitchen, Olivia grabs the teapot, swaying her hips to the lively beat. Spotting her unusually cheerful niece, Patricia retrieves a mug from the hook under the cupboard. She keeps time with the sway of Olivia's hips as she slides the cup across the counter. "I see you got my wake-up call. Are you ready for the summer solstice festivities today?"

"Yeah, I guess," Olivia shrugs. "I mean, I've given it some thought, and I know how much it means to Gran. Besides, I suppose you might be right," she grins, turning to face her. "I can't avoid magic forever."

"Whoa!" Patricia steps back, scanning her from head to toe. "What have you done with my niece? Not that I'm complaining. I'm actually quite thrilled." She holds her arms out, shimmying as her bright pink t-shirt displays the phrase, 'Thank you, Goddess! You've healed her!'

Olivia rolls her eyes, attempting to contain her smile as she throws her hands up. "Yes! Thank you, Goddess. You've healed me!" she jokes. "The celebration can finally begin!" Her giggle drawing Helen and her Grandmother's attention.

"Ohhh," Helen shrieks, rushing to hug her. "I knew you'd come around, Liv!"

"I can't tell you how thrilled I am that you've decided to join us." Clara grabs one of the flower crowns from the table and sets it on Olivia's head. Adjusting it slightly, she steps back to have a look. "You look like the perfect solstice princess." Kissing her on the cheek, she glances up at the clock. "I suppose I had better get dressed then. The day is a wasting!" she beams.

"Oh—" She turns back with her finger raised. "I know how much you love McNally's strawberries, and truthfully" *—She smiles mischievously—* "I fully anticipated you to join us. So I ordered two baskets. Helen's going to make us her famous strawberry shortcake. Anyway" *—she shakes her head, returning to her original thought—* "when I spoke with him, he had mentioned his wife is having difficulty with her hips again. So I prepared a batch of great Ancina's elixir." She points to the small brown bottle on the counter. "It's right over there. I was hoping you might make that exchange for me this afternoon."

Olivia's smile grows. "Of course, Gran." She hasn't heard her grandmother ramble like this since she announced her plans to open an antique store.

A smile lights up Clara's face as she grabs the edge of her nightdress and heads for the stairs. "Take the van, and don't be too long! I'm so glad you're feeling better. It may just be us today, Olivia, but we're going to have a magical day," she calls out over her shoulder as she continues up the stairs. "Oh, we'll have a maypole and flower wreaths in every corner! It's going to be wonderful!"

Patricia tosses her the keys to the van. "You just made your grandmother a very happy lady." She takes a sip of her tea and leans against the counter, peering at Olivia over her cup. "Did you read anything juicy in that old book last night? Care to share the details with your auntie?" she winks.

"Nope. Though, between you and me, there's something strange about that book. On the one hand, I really want to read it, but on the other, it weirds me out. Anyway, no. I didn't. I decided to shadow gaze instead."

"Hmm, weirds you out, huh? In what way?"

Olivia shrugs. "I don't know. Probably because it's the oldest thing I've ever held."

"Maybe. Or it could be the fact that it belonged to bloodsuckers," Patricia says, baring her teeth as she forms her hands into claws.

"Nah. The fact that it belonged to vampires doesn't bother me anymore. It did at first, but once Aunt Helen reminded me that witches are included on that demonic descendant's list," Olivia says, making air quotes with her fingers. "I have decided that list means nothing. I might not like magic, but my family is full of the sweetest witches I know," she smiles.

Patricia's face hardens. "We are *nothing* like bloodsuckers, Liv."

"Aunt Trish, you can't be serious? Have you looked in the mirror lately? You barely look older than me, and you're almost sixty." Olivia throws her arm out towards the staircase. "And what about Gran? She looks pretty darn good for somebody that's almost a hundred. That's not because we're human."

"What can I say, Liv? The goddess has been kind," Patricia smiles. "Look, it's the summer solstice. It's not a day to be talking about bloodsuckers. As for your shadow scrying, it's one of the oldest forms of witchcraft. Did you know that?" Olivia rolls her eyes as Patricia takes a sip of her tea and nods. "I'm not even kidding. It's a real thing. What did you see?"

Olivia fiddles with the keys while looking at her from the corner of her eye. "Um, I think a cat, some creepy hands, a bird—" She stops toying with the keys and stares up at Patricia. "And a man sitting on my window ledge. I will admit that freaked me out a little." Olivia laughs, shaking her head. "But, of course, there was no man on the ledge. Just a shadow from the tree and my crazy imagination."

Patricia feigns a grin. "All right, so I suppose shadow scrying isn't the most reliable. Especially with an imagination like yours.

Anyway, go." She shoos her toward the door. "You have strawberries waiting for you, and I'm sure old lady McNally could use that tincture. Be careful and hurry back. You're the only fun one around here."

On her way to McNally's farm, Olivia tries calling Jimmy again. With no answer, she leaves him another message about the solstice celebration at the house. "...Even if you don't want to come tonight, please call me back. You haven't answered me in days. I'm starting to wonder if I should report a missing person."

Surprisingly, the drive to McNally's farm is quiet for a Saturday afternoon, allowing Olivia time to take in the tranquillity of the surrounding scenery. Though she's been coming out here since she was a child, the beauty of the area never fades. The tall trees that hang over the narrow dirt road sway gently in the summer breeze, permitting only a hint of the bright afternoon sun to peek through the branches. She draws in a deep breath turning into the driveway, her senses filling with the sweet smell of fruit and fresh-cut grass.

Mr. McNally greets her with a warm smile and two large baskets of fresh berries in hand. "Olivia dear, it's so nice to see you."

"It's always a pleasure coming out here, Mr. McNally." She holds out the bottle of great Ancina's elixir and opens the hatch on the van. "Gran asked me to give this to you. It's for Mrs. McNally's hip."

Tipping his head, he smiles. "That grandmother of yours, I don't know what we'd do without her medicines." He tucks the bottle into his shirt pocket and pats it with a grin. "It'll be good to have the missus back up and mobile again. Be sure to thank her for me, will you?"

"Of course," Olivia smiles, loading the berries into the van.

On her way home, she tries Jimmy again, but there's still no answer. Refusing to leave yet another message, she tosses her phone on the seat and taps her fingers on the steering wheel. "What are you up to, Jimmy Prescott?"

Back at the house, Olivia steps out to whimsical music carried through the air. "Hey, there you are," Patricia calls out, stepping through the front door. "Need a hand?"

Opening the back hatch, she shakes her head. "Nah, I'm fine, but please tell me they'll play some better music today. This makes me feel like I'm lost in Wonderland with Alice."

"Oh, come on now. These are the opening songs. They call out to our elements." Patricia tips her head toward the backyard. "This one is calling out to mother earth."

Olivia raises a brow, and they break into laughter. "Right, well, the music will get better with more wine," Patricia chuckles, pushing the door open with her elbow. "So, did Jimmy call you yet?"

"Nope. I guess he's busy."

"Who's busy," Helen asks on her way into the kitchen. Her face quickly brightens at the sight of the baskets on the counter, and her original question is long forgotten. "Oh, good! The berries are here."

Patricia grabs Olivia's arm, spinning her toward the back door. "Yes, and they're all yours."

As Olivia walks out into the backyard, Clara holds her arms out with a wide smile. "Happy awakening, Olivia!"

Her eyes narrow as she cautiously steps up next to her grandmother. "What do you mean, happy awakening?"

Clara places an arm over her shoulder and hands her a drink, fanning her arm out. "Well, we're celebrating the awakening of summer, of course. Look around," she exclaims, pointing out the flower wreaths that decorate each tree, the tables and even the rear of the house. "Have I taught you nothing? Need I remind you that it's the summer solstice, dear."

"Of course not, Gran. How could I have forgotten? I'm just not sure I've ever heard you refer to it as an awakening." Olivia's eyes trail across the expanse of the large yard. There's a table full of food, and next to it, an old wooden desk with a stack of coloured paper, flowers and tea lights." She points. "Where have I seen that old desk before?"

But before Clara can answer, Olivia spins toward the common altar, where the sweet scent of jasmine burning lures her in. She's always loved the smell of jasmine incense. Her mother always had it burning in their house when she was little. There, on the mantle, two cones and several sticks smoulder while a pot of water hangs over a flickering fire. Then just beyond the altar, near the back garden, she spots a tall maypole with multi-coloured ribbons draped from the top ring. "Holy, when did you put that up?"

Squinting up at the stately standing maypole decorated with bright green foliage and vibrant summer flowers, Clara grins. "Magic, my precious child, magic."

"But I thought it was only going to be us here today? That is what you said. Isn't it?"

"Oh, relax. Of course, it is. But that doesn't mean we shouldn't celebrate properly. Does it?" Winking, she points to the desk by the edge of the yard. "Don't forget to make yourself a flower boat and send it off with your fondest desires down the river."

"Are you kidding? It's the one thing I've been looking forward to all morning. Well, that and Aunt Helen's strawberry shortcake," she giggles. Usually, Olivia feels tense during such an occasion – enchantment seeping out from every angle. She's still not sure why, but she feels strangely comfortable today. Mr. Green rubs against her ankle, and she bends to pick him up. Stroking the length of his back, she smiles. "And don't worry, I'll be sure to grab a pebble while I'm down there for the firewalk too."

"Now that's my girl." Scratching Mr. Green's head, Clara's smile broadens. "Then I'm not going to hold you up. Go on and make your boat. Oh, and be careful with that old desk. It used to belong to great-gran Ancina."

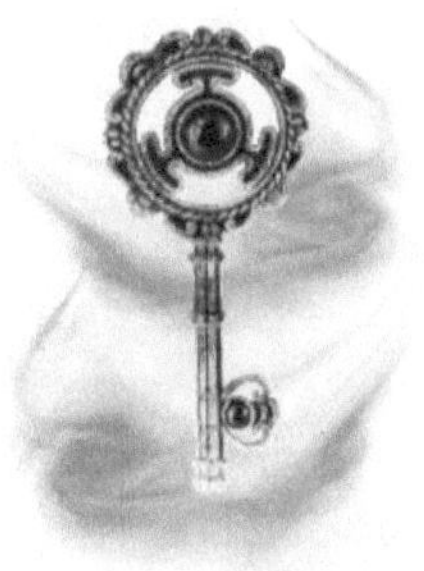

CHAPTER 8 ~ JIMMY

Olivia sets Mr. Green down and makes her way over to the desk stacked with coloured paper, flowers and candles. Taking a seat, she picks out a sheet of peach paper and a pen and stares across the garden. Before she realizes she's written anything, Patricia sits down next to her with her own paper in hand. "Hey, kiddo. How are you making out?"

"Meh, I'm still thinking."

"Really? It doesn't look that way to me," Patricia grins, tapping Olivia's paper with the tip of her pen. Together they stare down at the freshly penned desire on the peach sheet of paper in front of her. Olivia's mouth drops open as Patricia begins to read it aloud.

Goddess Hekate – keeper of the keys.
This is my greatest wish.
Hear my plea.
A true love is my desire.
His hair dark as the night,
and his skin fair as the day.

He'll need strength to keep me grounded
and unbridled passion to set my soul ablaze.
I can be patient, but can you send him before I'm gray?

Patricia laughs, tapping her pen between her front teeth. "So, I guess it's safe to assume Jimmy didn't call back. Huh?"

Olivia shakes her head, joining her laughter. "No, he didn't, but I didn't write that. I must have grabbed a piece of paper that someone else had already written on."

"Nice try, Liv." She points to the page with a smile. "That's your handwriting. Besides, I saw you scribbling something on my way over here. I'd have to say, whether you realize it or not, that is your fondest desire. I'd set it to sail if I were you."

"You watched me write this?" Patricia nods, and Olivia sets the pen down to reread it. "That's so strange. I don't recall writing anything at all."

"Well, it must be a subconscious thought then," she shrugs. "Why don't you fold it up, and let's set these babies to sail."

"Sure, why not? What have I got to lose, right?" Folding up her boat, Olivia adds a few flowers and grabs a candle. "Right behind you."

With a flick of her finger, Patricia lights their candles, and as they set their dreams to sail down the creek, Olivia gazes over at her. "So, what was your wish?"

"I can't tell you that. If I do, it may not come true." Winking, she sits down and pats the ground beside her. "Come sit. Let's enjoy mother nature while we recharge." She rubs her hands together, making tiny blue sparks dance along her fingers.

Olivia giggles. "I swear that was one of the most popular party tricks when I was younger." She kicks off her sandals, making herself comfortable next to her aunt. "I may not need to recharge, but I'll gladly enjoy the tranquillity with you." She leans back, presses her fingers into the moist earth, and lets the cool water run over her feet as she closes her eyes. When she finally sits forward, it feels as though the afternoon has leapt past them. One minute they're soaking up the energy of the surrounding elements. Next, the setting sun is casting shadows by the minute. "For the longest day of the year, it seems to have escaped us much quicker than I thought."

Patricia rolls her head across her shoulders, a refreshed glow brightening her cheeks. "That tends to happen when we recharge."

"Hmm." Olivia peers over at her furry sidekick rolling in the tall grass. "Well, whatever the case, we should probably head back up. Gran's going to be upset that we're not up there."

"Yes, she is," Helen declares as she crests the opening of the path behind them. "Elizabeth stopped by to meet you."

"Who's Elizabeth? I thought it was just going to be us here today."

"You mean she wanted to read her!" Patricia stands glaring at her sister as she brushes herself off. "That's exactly why I kept her down here. I had a feeling mom invited her. You two need to realize that Olivia's not a damn sideshow."

"No, she's not, but mom feels it would be good to see how much she's opened up."

Olivia rises to her feet, waving her hands through the air as Mr. Green hurries to curl around her ankle. "Okay. Don't talk around me as if I'm not even here." Her eyes narrow as they bounce between her two aunts. "Now, who exactly is Elizabeth," she demands, slamming her hands on her hips. "And why might she want to see how much I've opened up? And what the hell does that mean—opened up? Opened up to what exactly?"

"Elizabeth is the high priestess at the Eternal Flame Coven. She's gifted with the ability to read a witch's strengths—their abilities." Patricia glares at Helen. "She can tell what elements you've made a connection with and how much power you yield."

"I thought Gran was the high priestess, and why would that matter anyway? You all know I have no intention of using magic."

"Well—"

Patricia steps in front of Helen, cutting her off. "It doesn't matter, Liv. Not one bit. Things will happen on their own. When and if you're ready. As for the high priestess, well, mom stepped down some time ago. She only assists when asked."

"Oh. I guess I really haven't paid attention."

Helen rolls her eyes with a huff. "Right, well, she left anyway." She spins to walk back up the path. "The sun is beginning to set, and mom wants you to light the bonfire. It's time for you two to come up now so we can have dinner. Mom's itching to watch Olivia do the firewalk."

As they watch Helen storm up the path, Olivia's phone vibrates, and she reaches in to pull it from her pocket. Staring down at the screen, she shakes her head. "I guess better late than never." She flashes Jimmy's text to her aunt. *'Hey, Liv. Sorry, I should have gotten back to you sooner, but my dad was in town. I'm on my way over now. Can you meet me at the stream? You know how much I hate being around all that hocus pocus.'*

"Hocus pocus, huh?" Patricia rolls her eyes.

"He doesn't mean anything by it."

"Right. That kid is lucky I like him, or I'd zap his ass." She picks up a pebble and tucks it into Olivia's pocket. "Anyway, I'll go light the fire and bide you some time with the two old ladies but don't be too long, or Gran will send me back down to get you." Scanning the tree line, she winks. "Be mindful. I've heard there have been a lot of wild animal attacks lately."

"Don't worry, Aunt Trish. I'll be fine, and I won't be long. It doesn't sound like he's going to stay long anyway."

Nodding, Patricia purses her lips and turns, heading up the trail toward the house. As she reaches the top of the hill, she throws a ball of flames at the stack of wood in the pit to ignite the fire. Clara spins, her smile fading as she looks into the shadows behind her. "Where's Olivia?"

"She'll be up soon. Jimmy's meeting her down there."

Helen takes a deep breath and hands her a piece of strawberry shortcake. "I don't like that boy, and I'm very uncomfortable that she told him we use magic."

"Meh, you don't like anyone. I happen to think Jimmy's sweet, and besides, it's not like anyone would actually believe him if he said anything." She stuffs a forkful of cake into her mouth. "Oh my goodness," she moans, pressing her fork against her lips. Her eyes roll back in her head as she speaks around a mouthful of cake. "Damn, this really should be illegal."

Waiting for Jimmy, Olivia is sitting by the river's edge with Mr. Green, absorbing the beauty of her surroundings. The constant flow of the stream becomes the backdrop for the night melody of croaking frogs, buzzing tree beetles and chirping crickets. Leaning back, she inhales the fresh earthy scent of damp moss that surrounds her and stares at the night sky. Though it's not quite a full moon, it shines brighter than ever tonight.

The snapping of branches coming from behind, accompanied by Mr. Green's low growl, causes her to sit up and peer over her shoulder. As Jimmy's silhouette emerges from the bushes, she quickly gains her feet, strolling toward him with a big smile. "Hey! I'm glad you came. I've missed you." She throws her arms around him, but he barely hugs her back. "I was starting to worry when you hadn't returned my calls. I almost called in a missing person," she jokes.

But something about his demeanour is off. She's dated Jimmy throughout high school, and he has never responded to her like this. His smile has lost its glow, and his hug is cold and distant. Even his usual charm is falling flat. He coldly steps back, swiping his thumb across his nose with a stiff nod. "Yeah, sorry. I guess I should have called."

Then as he drops his arm, an old leather bracelet on his wrist catches her eye, and Olivia reaches out to touch the new accessory. It has a charming blue stone tightly wound into well-aged leather. "Is that a lapis," she asks as he quickly tugs his wrist from her hand. Her eyes jump to his. "Geez, I'm sorry. I didn't mean to – I mean, I've never seen it before. Is it new? It looks like an antique."

"Um, yeah. It's a family heirloom— a gift from my dad," he says, shaking his shirt sleeve down to cover the stone.

"It looks like something straight out of Gran's store." She glances at his hand, resting on the cuff of his sleeve. "Okay, Jimmy, what's up with you? You're acting strange."

"Nothing's up with me." He drops his arm, shifting his weight to one leg. "I forgot you've been helping your Gran at the store." Taking a step toward her, he chucks his chin. "So Stepney castle, huh?" She nods, her eyes still focused on his bracelet. "Have you found anything interesting? Like anything that confirms that they were real vampires?"

An image of the journal flashes in her mind sending her stomach into knots. She's not sure if it's a warning, but until she sees the Jimmy she's familiar with, there will be no telling him about that. "No, nothing but a bunch of old trinkets. Why the sudden interest? You've never cared about Gran's store before."

"Come on, Liv. What's with all the questions tonight?" He tugs her forward, resting her back against the silver birch at the bottom of the path. "Forgive me for showing a little interest in what you've been up to these past few days. As for your Gran's store, sure, I might be a little interested since I have gotten this." He holds out his wrist, shaking his leather bracelet. "But really, I'd be foolish not to ask about the stuff from the Stepney Castle?"

She reaches out to touch the bracelet as he jerks his hand back. "You're very protective of that piece. Maybe you should take it and go home," she says, dropping her hand as she turns to walk away.

"Olivia, wait!" He lunges forward, grabbing her arm. "I'm sorry. I told you, it's a family heirloom, and it's still new to me. So I guess I might be a little overprotective of it."

"That's no excuse. If it were that priceless, you wouldn't be wearing it, Jimmy. Besides, I'm around antiques all the time. I know enough to be careful. I only wanted a closer look."

Tossing his head to move the bangs from his eyes, he slips his arms around her waist and pulls her closer. "Look, I don't want to fight with you. I missed you. Can't we just have a nice evening?"

Her eyes meet his, and an eerie chill runs down her spine. She shakes her head. "No. You know what? As much as I wanted to spend this evening with you. I've changed my mind. I don't think tonight is a good idea after all. Something doesn't feel right."

"What? Come on, Olivia. I said I was sorry." He tries to tighten his hold, but she pulls away.

"No. I'm serious. You haven't returned my calls in three days. The only explanation you've offered is that your father was in town. Something that has never stopped you from calling me back before. Then there's this new heirloom" —*she steps back, pointing to his wrist*— "that I'm not even allowed to have a closer look at and a sudden new interest in my Gran's store. Every fibre of my being is telling me something isn't right."

Tugging her back, he forces a smile. "Olivia. You're being silly."

"And that! You've NEVER called me Olivia, yet it comes so freely for some reason tonight." As she attempts to pull free, she grasps his wrist and freezes as an image of a blond biting into his shoulder flashes through her mind. Her mouth drops open as she jumps back, snapping the bracelet off in her hand. "Vampires? That's where you've been!"

Creases form on his forehead, and for the first time since he has arrived, Jimmy looks nervous. He reaches for her, but she continues to step away. "What the hell are you talking about, Liv?"

She dangles his bracelet in the air, trying to control her shaking voice. "Vampires! As soon as I grabbed this, I saw them. Where did you get this thing, Jimmy? Unless your father has fangs, this is not a family heirloom."

"You don't know what you're talking about. You've been playing with that vampire stuff" —*he throws his hands in the air with a chuckle*— "now everyone is a vampire. I told you. It's this place and your crazy family. The magic here plays tricks on your mind." His voice softens as he takes another step toward her. "Why don't you give me back my bracelet? Then we can talk about this."

"There is nothing to talk about, Jimmy Prescott," she carefully steps back as branches snap in the distance behind him. "You stay away from me!"

His face hardens as he takes another step toward her. "Liv, you're being ridiculous."

"No, Jimmy, I don't think I am. I want you to go."

But her words seem to fall on deaf ears as he lunges forward. "Yeah? Well, I'm not going anywhere, Olivia. Not without you. Now give me back my bracelet!"

Her voice is laced with fury as her arms fly out. "No! Go to hell!" she screams, pushing him back with a strength she never knew she possessed.

Lightning flashes in Patricia's eyes. "Olivia," she says, dropping her plate at Helen's feet as she darts toward the path leaving a bright blue bolt trailing behind.

A loud hum permeates the air, and Olivia's eyes dart from her shaking hands back to Jimmy, watching as he slowly regains his feet. "What the hell was that, Liv?"

But she's just as shocked as he is as her hair stands on end and bolts of electricity shoot from her fingertips. The bright bolts of light seem to tear through an invisible wall in the forest, creating a black hole behind him. He glances over his shoulder as he skids backwards through the leaves, his face paling as he reaches out. "Liv, please. Grab my hand!" But she just stands shaking her head. "Liv! Help me!"

As tears stream down her face, Olivia looks down at her hands. "I - I don't know what's happening. I can't stop it." Frozen in place, Mr. Green circles her ankles as she watches an unseen force drag Jimmy, back through the dirt.

"Damn it, Liv, help me!"

But Jimmy's cry is left unanswered as he's quickly lifted off his feet and sucked back into the darkness. Electricity crackles in the air and every hair on Olivia's body stands at attention as small blue bolts flash along the edge, sealing the hole. Her eyes stay fixed on the area where he stood, but there's nothing left. Only a blip of smoke, the smell of sulphur and the skidmarks his feet left remain.

The smoke begins to clear, and a tall thin man appears from slightly beyond where the hole had been. As the pale male steps out from the lingering cloud, she sees a flash of Jimmy being bitten. "It's you! The one I saw biting Jimmy," she stammers, stepping back.

"Tsk-tsk. That wasn't a vision you were entitled to, young sorceress." His eyes narrow, fixing on the bracelet dangling from her clenched hand. "I see you have destroyed not one but two of my trinkets. I suppose I'll have to do this all on my own now." He steps toward her, stopping as she drops the bracelet and throws her hands out.

"Stay back," she yells, praying that whatever had stopped Jimmy will happen again.

He cautiously looks over his shoulder but quickly turns back with a sinister sneer, and his canines bared. "Aw, now isn't that a pity. It looks like the little witch has run out of steam."

There's little hope of escaping his clutches when a set of deep red eyes glare down at her, but that's not about to stop her from trying. She turns, but before taking her first step, she hears a roar and tussle moving away from her. Spinning back, she sees nothing but a blur of movement disappear between the trees. Her knees shaking, she raises her trembling hand to her lips and expels a breath.

"Olivia?!" Patricia calls down the path.

"Over here, Aunt Trish."

Just then, a cool hand gently grasps her arm, and she jumps back with a squeal. She covers her mouth, her heart thumping as she scans a tall, dark-haired man. He's standing only a few feet in front of her when he raises his hands. His voice is soft and silky as he speaks her name. "Easy, Olivia. I'm not here to hurt you. My name is Cash - Cassian Laurent. I heard you cry out and came to see if I could be of assistance." A crooked smile dawns on his face as he points toward where the portal had been. "I saw you had handled that feeder quite well, and I truly thought you had that pleb, but—" His words hang mid-sentence as he turns, dodging a bright blue ball of flames. His hands once again raise in defence as he peers into the darkness. "Easy now. I'm not here to—" he starts when an angry female voice cuts him off.

"Back the hell away from her, Bloodsucker!" Patricia finally appears from between the trees as another fireball wizzes past Cassian's head. "Take one step closer to my niece, and I'll turn you into a pile of ash." He steps back, watching as she runs to the safety of her aunt's side. Patricia grasps Olivia's chin, moving her head from side to side. "Are you all right? Did he bite you?" Her brows draw together as she peers out into the forest. "Where's Jimmy?"

Shaking her head, Olivia tries to decipher what she's asked. "Bite me? No. Everything happened so fast." She flails her arm out, pointing to Cassian. "I'm almost certain he saved me from that vampire." Tears well in her eyes as she looks back to where Jimmy had been standing. "I—I don't know where Jimmy went."

Patricia's face reddens as her palm ignites, her eyes narrowing on Cassian. "Tell me what you did with Jimmy."

"That's truly unnecessary," Cassian says, pointing at her flaming hand. "I came merely to assist young Olivia. As much as I would like to take credit for this Jimmy's departure, that had nothing to do with me. That credit goes to your niece."

Olivia stares over at him through teary eyes. "Is it you that's been following me?"

"No, I'm afraid not. I just arrived this evening. Though considering my brothers and I saw you the moment you cracked the journal, I think it's safe to assume I'm not the only one seeking you out."

"The journal from Gran's store?"

"The timekeeper journal. It was created for my father, Julien Laurent, centuries ago by an extraordinarily powerful witch. You're the only one who has been able to read it in over a century. My brothers and I know very little of it other than it will locate the witch who can help us."

Tears trickle down Olivia's face as she looks at her aunt. "But I can't help you."

"You must. You're the only one who—" Cassian starts when Patricia flicks her wrist, producing another ball of fire in her palm.

"Last chance, Bloodsucker! Shut the hell up!" She glances at Olivia. "I need you to focus, Liv. What happened to Jimmy?"

"I—I don't know." Her body trembles as she shakes her head and points to the bracelet at her feet. "I grabbed his bracelet and saw the red eyes of a vampire staring back at me. I shoved him, and – and the strength I had," she shakes her head. "He—he flew back." Confusion clouds her face as she looks down at her hands. "My hands. I couldn't stop them from shaking and—and my fingers. Blue bolts shot from my fingers. Then" *—She points to the tree line—* "a pocket opened up over there, and I couldn't move," she cries.

The comfort of her trusted companion swirls around her ankle, and she crouches to pick him up.

"She opened a portal," Cassian offers, quickly ducking as another fireball rushes toward his head.

Tucking Olivia behind her, Patricia glares at the attractive ancient one standing before them. "For the love of the Goddess, Vampire! Shut up! I didn't ask you."

"Vampire?" Olivia's eyes dart back to Cassian. *He looks nothing like the vampire I saw. That thing had defined fangs and red eyes—precisely as I'd expect them to look. Not perfectly combed hair and an expensive suit. Clearly, Aunt Trish is mistaken.*

Helen places a hand on her shoulder. "Yes, sweetie. A vampire. They don't all come with red eyes, and their fangs bared."

"Yes, I am a vampire," he confirms, "but I did not come here to harm you, Olivia. You have no idea the kind of power you possess. My brothers and I have been waiting more than a century for you, but as I had feared, we're not the only ones." He points back to where the portal had been. "I believe Jimmy may have been one of Roger Windsor's feeders. That bracelet at your feet, that's a concealing anchor. It tethers him to his owner while concealing his bite marks. I haven't seen one in centuries. My best guess is that he was sent for the journal, or possibly to lure you back, then he would have become one of Roger's fledglings." He takes a step closer. "I assure you he will not be the last. Others will come for you and the journal. We can help each other."

The image of someone biting into Jimmy's shoulder flashes before her, and she toes dirt on the bracelet. "Feeder? You don't mean—" Her head drops with the sag of her shoulders as she chokes back her final words.

Cassian's gaze lowers. "Yes. I'm sure you've heard of the excessive amount of wild animal kills these last few months. Do you really believe they're wild animals?" She stares at him, unsure of what to think. He places his hands behind his back, cautiously taking another step forward. "Together, we can stop this." She shakes her head. "As soon as your touch brought that print to life, my brothers and I saw you, Olivia. After what happened here tonight, I'm certain others did too."

Stepping up next to her granddaughter, Clara digs her barefoot into the earth and raises her hand. "I suggest you stop right there, or I'll be wearing your head as a charm."

Cassian stares down at her planted foot and bows his head. "As you wish, Ms. Redfearn." He looks up, his dark eyes anchoring on Olivia's as he slowly steps back. "Just know that when you're ready, and you need me" —*his gaze flits across the three ladies before landing back on Olivia*— "and make no mistake, you will need me to battle the Windsor clan. All you have to do is call for me." He places his hand on his chest. "Just yell, Cash. The moment you do, I'll return." Then, without another word, he disappears into the trees.

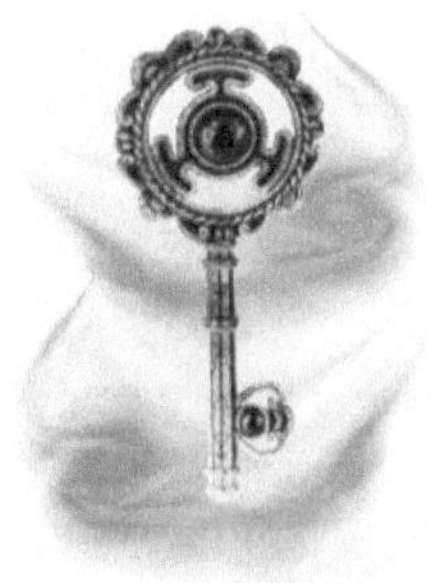

CHAPTER 9 ~ I CAN SEE THEM!

Clara's forehead furrows at the black cat purring in Olivia's arms. "I find it rather odd that Mr. Green didn't react to the vampire's presence. Don't you?"

Slamming her hand on her hip, Patricia huffs as her glare bounces between her mother and Helen. "You're concerned over how a damn cat responded? Do you have any idea how much worse this could have been?" She pulls Olivia against her side. "I bloody told you two this would happen!"

"What? What are you talking about?" Olivia steps back, glaring at her aunts and grandmother. "Told them what would happen? And what did Cash mean others would come for me? What the hell is going on?"

Closing her eyes, Clara pats Olivia's hand and takes a deep breath. "Hush now. Everything will be fine." The muscles in her face tighten as her dark green eyes spring to meet Patricia's. "As I recall, I told you that her magic would be there when she needed it, and clearly, it was." Now, let's go back up to the house where we can discuss this in the privacy of our home."

"Wait." Olivia turns back to where they had been standing. "What about Jimmy? How do we get him back?"

"Oh, you mean the sweet one?" Helen peers at Patricia out of the corner of her eye as she bends to pick up the bracelet. "Well, the simple answer is, we don't. My best guess would be that you sent him back to where he belongs." Knocking the dirt off, she peers down at the piece of ancient jewellery and runs her thumb over the stone. "Goddess, help us. No wonder your magical instincts kicked in." She shivers, squeezing her eyes shut as if trying to scrub away the vision. "You know this thing means that whoever that vampire was, he has a witch working with him, right?"

"Well, of course, he does. Seems we work together these days," Patricia scoffs.

Following Clara up the path, Olivia can hear the constant crackle of the roaring fire. "I'm sorry I ruined summer solstice for you, Gran."

"Nonsense. We may not enjoy a full evening, but you will still complete your firewalk. If ever there were a time to toss away the old and steady for the new, it's now."

Olivia peers up at her through tears of disbelief. "But, Gran. I can't."

"Nah-uh. I won't hear of it." Clara tips her head toward the firepit. "Now, take out your rock and walk, Olivia. It's only three times around." Raising her hand, she circles it toward the fire. "Let's go, and be sure to release as many unwanted memories, bad events and fears as you circle until only the good remain."

Helen places a flower crown on Olivia's head and kisses her cheek. "I'm sorry, Liv, but she's right. If ever there was a night you needed to do this. Tonight is that night." Turning to join her mother and sister, they watch as she struggles to pull herself together.

Trying to push back the events of the evening, she pulls the rock from her pocket. Staring down at it, she takes a deep breath and runs her thumb over the rough surface. *'You can do this, Olivia. It's only three small circles.'*

As she sluggishly begins to walk around the pit, she allows the ugliness to flood her mind. Jimmy, the fire that took her parents, fighting magic inside her that continuously tries to spill out, a journal that wants to control her, and now vampires.

"That's it, Liv. Now toss your stone and let go of all that dreadful darkness," Patricia calls out as she begins her final lap. "It's time to think of only the good in your life."

Releasing an exhaustive breath, she throws the pebble into the flames. *'Good?'* A tear trickles down her cheek, and she quickly swipes it away. Inhaling deeply, she raises her head to the sweet smell of lilacs from the nearby bushes and burning jasmine on the altar. Her shoulders draw back, and she focuses on filling her mind with things that have made her smile. *'Sitting with Mr. Green in Gran's garden, feeling warm rain on my face, enjoying the day at the beach with Aunt Trish.'* For the first time tonight, she feels a smile tug at her lips. She takes the last few steps. *'Family game night, Aunt Helen's ginger lemon tea, Mr. Green's snuggles.'* Realizing she's completed her walk, she stops and turns to face her family, her lips pulling into a smile. Clara wraps her arms around her. *'And the comfort of Gran's hugs.'*

Patricia flicks her hand toward the blazing fire. "Submergo," she says, dousing the flames.

"I believe some calming tea is in order." Helen glances over her shoulder as she heads for the backdoor. "Lemon ginger tea work for everyone?" Without waiting for a response, she disappears into the kitchen.

"Go on ahead. I'll be right in." Clara bends to pick up Mr. Green and hands him off to Olivia. "I left my sandals among my roses."

Entering the kitchen, Olivia places Mr. Green on his feet, and as her eyes fix on the table, her arm juts out. "Who brought that down here?"

Helen's gaze follows the length of her outstretched arm to the leatherbound diary, and she shakes her head. "It sure wasn't me."

Taking her seat, Patricia puts her hand up. "You know you can count me out."

"But I know for certain I put it on top of the crate of books in my room this morning."

"Well, mom did say it's magical, that it has a mind of its own." Helen drops a slice of lemon in the pot of boiling water on the stove and flicks her hand toward the table. "Gingiberi ti citrea," she says as four cups of lemon tea appear in the center of the table.

The room grows quiet as Clara enters and takes a seat. Pulling a mug in front of her, she chucks her chin toward the chair across the table. "Sit." Her gaze steadies on Olivia. "I know this seems like a lot to accept in one evening, but there's more we need to discuss before we all turn in."

"More?" Olivia's shoulders slump and Mr. Green hops onto her lap, purring as he nudges his head under her chin. "How about you start by telling me what's really going on with this journal and what did Cash mean when he said more would come for me? Maybe we should call him back. He's the only one that trusts me enough to tell me anything—the only one who recognizes me as an adult. Vampire or not, you should never have sent him away. Clearly, he is not like the other vampire. Cas—" She starts to yell out when Clara grabs her hand, halting her.

"Olivia, stop. I understand you're upset, but you need to calm down. We're not your enemy. Besides, at this point, we probably know more about the journal than he does, and that's not much." Clara's chest heaves with her breath as she purses her lips. "Look, once I realized none of us could read it, we had to try and calm your fear of magic and open your senses."

"Nah-uh." Raising her hand, Patricia shakes her head. "Do not include me in that statement. I was against meddling from the start."

"Oh hush," Clara scowls. She turns her attention back to Olivia, patting her hand reassuringly. "I'm sure you must have been feeling a bit different these past few days, and I believe I can explain why. You see, this isn't just any old book. We're dealing with a timekeeper journal. If it feels like someone has been following you around, that's because it likely has, or I suppose I should say whatever presence it's powered by has been. We believe you are the interpreter of the book."

"That doesn't explain what Cash meant. What did he mean by more will come for me? More what? More vampires?" Olivia's brows draw together as she throws her hands up. "And why would this book choose me? I have so many questions for him. Like, let's start with what SOV really means cause I'm not buying the whole sovereign explanation anymore. From what Cash said, it sounds more likely that it means save our vampire, and I can't do that. I'm not even a real witch! I can't do anything."

A mischievous grin plays on Helen's lips as she pats the table. "Oh honey, don't be so naïve. Of course, you can. You're the only one that can read that damn journal for one. We can't do that." Her brows lift as she folds her arms and leans across the table, her grin widening as she winks. "And, incidentally, let's not forget that less than an hour ago, you sent Jimmy crying all the way back to hell. That's not exactly something just anyone can do, Olivia."

"Sweet Goddess!" Clara dabs the perspiration from her chest and forehead. "Can someone open the window, please?" she asks, glaring at Helen.

"And Jimmy? Will this magical book bring him back?" A tear runs down Olivia's cheek as she searches the faces around the table for an answer.

"No, I don't believe so," her grandmother says softly. She reaches out to take her hand, but Olivia pulls it back. "Look, Olivia. There have been so few timekeeper journals that little is known of how exactly they will present themselves. We know the basics. They will choose by who and when they are read. They will seek out the intended party and will not let them rest until the matter set out is completed."

"But why me, and what about Jimmy," she shouts, her head dropping into her hands.

"We're not sure why it has chosen you, but you must embrace your abilities to be able to work with it. This journal has a purpose. The entries it contains are to make you understand why this journey is so important and help you achieve the goal set out." Clara takes a deep breath. "Forget about Jimmy, Olivia. There is nothing we can do for him. He fell prey to the wrong vampires."

Thunder rolls above as Patricia stands. "Oh, for pity's sake! Take the kid gloves off and stop dancing around the real answer. That's not what she bloody asked!" Pacing, she stops directly in front of Olivia, places her hands on the table, and stares directly into her eyes. "Look, Liv, the vampires that are mentioned in that journal? They will come. Either for your help or to try and stop you from completing your task. That's what Cash meant. Jimmy was a feeder of one of the vampires in that journal, and they likely compelled him to pursue you. They fed off him. And there are no twisting words there. He's gone, and he's not coming back."

"I'm giving her the information I have. I can't speak for what Cassian said." Scowling over at Patricia, Clara rubs Olivia's hand. "What we do know is timekeeper journals are magical. A rare creation by the keeper of both good and evil. Their purpose is to record critical events in a specific lineage that will, at some point, help solve an inevitable problem. No one physically writes them, Liv, and no one but the intended party can read them. Each entry will help explain your journey in some way." She takes the journal in her hand and flips the pages. "These pages? They're blank, all but the odd word. At least to us. But you, I saw your reaction last night when you put it down. I'm not sure what you saw in here, but you can clearly read it."

Mr. Green jumps up on the table, nudging Olivia's hand, leading her to absently run it down his back. "What do you mean they're blank?" She reaches for the journal and flips it open to the very first page. "Look! Right here," she exclaims, poking the page. "This list of names, it's not just that I can read them – I see their faces!" Running her finger down the list, she begins reading each name aloud.

"Julien Laurent" —*she pauses as the dark-haired man she saw the previous day reveals himself*— "He has dark hair and muttonchop sideburns. He looks as if he's from the nineteenth century. In fact, the first time I saw him was outside the store the other morning." Shaking off the strange feeling she's been fighting since the first moment she held the journal, Olivia runs her finger over the next name.

"Clarentina Laurent," she stammers as a woman with a perfect porcelain complexion appears before her. "She has long, wavy brown hair that cascades over her shoulder, and her eyes are a cornflower blue. Her lips are the colour of crimson, and if you want my honest opinion, she looks the spitting image of one of my china dolls."

"There's a whole list of them, Gran." Her voice rises with frustration. "Cassian Laurent, Elias Laurent. I can see them!"

A gasp fills the room as all eyes focus on a grey mist encompassing two bodies only steps away from Olivia. Cassian and another man appear, steadying themselves with their hands extended defensively as the mist dissipates around them.

Chapter 10 ~ Sure! Accommodate The Bloodsucker

Clara places her hand over the page. "Olivia, stop!" She gestures to the two men. "We can see them too."

"What the hell are you doing back here, vampire?" Patricia asks as she readies herself with a fireball in hand.

The two peer around the room, locking their stare on Olivia. "It seems we were summoned here."

She knows she should feel afraid, but oddly enough, their presence isn't frightening. Instead, outside of a bit of confusion, she feels calm for the first time this evening. She points to herself. "Are you claiming that *I* summoned you both here?"

"Yes." Cassian nods. "This is my brother, Elias."

"At your service." Elias bends slightly at the waist, freezing as his gaze drops to the journal. When he attempts to step forward,

Cassian grabs his arm. "What? I merely wanted to have a look." He scowls, yanking his arm free. "Might I at least suggest we prepare before the young sorceress carelessly calls out any more names on that page? If she continues, we could end up with a room full of unwanted vampires."

"Well, I'll be damned." Placing her hand over her mouth, Helen leans back in her chair, staring at the two brothers.

Standing to face them, Clara points at the journal. "If that's so, why didn't Julien or Clarentina appear when Olivia said their names?"

"They were smart enough to know I'd be waiting," Patricia sneers, twirling the ball of flames in her hand.

"Not exactly." Cassian glances over at her, his shoulders dropping with a sigh. "Our father has been dead since the nineteenth century, and his absence currently incapacitates our mother. As a result, she's been trying to end herself by starvation."

"Not an easy task for an original," Elias adds.

"But I saw their faces." Olivia peers up at them, closing the journal. "In fact, your father has appeared to me a few times in the past few days."

Clara turns, scanning Olivia's face. "You've seen him other than just now and outside the store?"

"Mmhmm. At first, I wasn't sure who he was. I was actually starting to think my mind was playing tricks on me, so I was afraid to say anything. At least until this came along." She gestures to the leather-bound treasure lying in front of her. "When I read his name in here, and he appeared in front of me, it was only then that I realized I had been seeing Julien Laurent."

"Well, that explains why you've been so jumpy." The fireball in Patricia's hand fades as she spins toward her. "Why didn't you say something, Liv?"

She shrugs. "I did try the other morning at the store, but when I finally got your attention, he was gone. Besides, I was worried you'd think I had gone mad."

"Hm, does this only happen when you're near the journal? Was it Julien that spooked you while you were grabbing the crate," Helen asks.

"Maybe. I'm not sure who that was. I've seen many fleeting shadows these last few days. But now that I think about it. It does seem to happen most when I'm close to the book."

Clara sits back down, nodding as if something has suddenly sunk in. "Now I have to wonder how many others are following this journal" —*she waves her hand toward Olivia*— "or rather following you. How many other names have you read in there?"

"Only the ones you heard tonight." She places the journal on the table and raises her hand. "I promise. The images kind of startled me."

A smile stretches across Elias's face. "Wait, if she can summon us, she must be able to summon Roger. His name has to be in that book." He slaps Cassian's arm. "This is going to be so much easier than we thought!"

Patricia puts her hands up, stepping closer to the two vampires still standing in the corner of the kitchen. "Oh no. Now you wait just a minute. I don't care who Roger is or why you need him. Olivia will not be calling on him or anyone else, for that matter. It's bad enough we have two bloodsuckers standing here."

"I have to agree." Clara gestures to the book in front of her granddaughter. "That journal has a purpose, and Olivia will follow it through, but she will not be calling vampires here at your whim. We cannot interrupt or interfere with the intended order set out in that journal. To do so could have an undesirable outcome. Not just for Olivia but your family as well."

"But Roger—" Cassian moves in front of his brother as he attempts to take another step forward.

"Hold it right there." A fireball appears in Patricia's palm as she cuts him off. "If Roger is required, the journal will let Olivia know! Now, I suggest you both get out of here."

"We will gladly leave, but we didn't come here of our own free will. The master of the journal summoned us here, and she will need to release us." Casually walking past Patricia, Cassian stands in front of Olivia, slightly bowing his head. "As long as you hold that book and the answers we require, we" —*he motions between himself and Elias*— "are at your service."

Olivia gazes up at him, her eyes wide. "Master?"

Groaning, Helen rolls her eyes. "You've got to be kidding me." Pouting, she slumps in her chair. "Why couldn't it have chosen me?"

"Oh, for crying out loud, Helen. Will you shut up," Patricia scowls.

Clara clears her throat. "All right. That should be easy enough." She turns her hand out toward her granddaughter. "Go ahead and release them. I think we can all use a good night's rest. We can have another look at that journal in the morning."

Olivia flips the journal over, her shoulders lifting into a shrug. "Well, it's not like this book came with instructions. What do I do? Do I simply say you're released?" Her gaze lifts to the brothers as they nod. "Oh, um. You're released," she says, her brows raising as Elias vanishes before her eyes. "Wow, I can't believe that worked." But her eyes quickly narrow on the tall vampire left standing by the counter. "I don't understand. Why are you still here?" He shrugs, and she waves her hand as if shooing him off. "I said, I release you." But Cassian doesn't budge. Her brows drop as she twists her lips. "I don't understand, Gran. I released him."

Clara takes a deep breath, her hand falling from her cheek to the table. "Yes, verbally, but apparently, you didn't mean it," she sighs. "It's curious, but you must feel the need for him to stay for some reason."

Olivia's cheeks redden as Cassian lowers his head with a smirk. Dropping into her chair, Patricia flops her elbow on the table, pinching the bridge of her nose as she shakes her head. "Ah, damn it, Liv. Not you too."

Helen taps her teacup, whispering, "Calor" to heat its contents, then smiles at Cassian with a shrug. "I think this could work in our favour. You know. Having a vampire on our side in case any of the *bad vamps* appear."

"There's no such thing as a *good vamp*, you twit," Patricia scowls.

"Well, Cash did—" Olivia starts when Clara clears her throat.

"That's quite enough." Taking a deep breath, Clara grips the edge of the table and peers over at Cassian. "All right. Well, since it appears that we'll have a houseguest for a while, I suppose I should go make up a room."

Springing forward in her seat, Olivia peers around as if she may have missed a hidden door. "But we don't have a guest room."

"Right. As I said, I will have to make one." A forced smile tugs at Clara's lips as she stands and rotates her hand in the air. "It's nothing a little magic can't take care of. You three go on to bed." She waves them off. "I'll see that Cassian gets settled in."

"Sure, why don't you just accommodate the bloodsucker," Patricia huffs, kicking her chair back as she stands.

Clara glares at her daughter. "Let's not forget that a much stronger and wiser force created that timekeeper journal. That means we must do whatever it takes to ensure Olivia fulfills her obligation to it."

"Fine! What shall we do next? Are we to line up and let the vampire drain our veins for breakfast because it's convenient for some magical book?" Slamming her chair against the table, she storms toward the stairs. "Let's go, Liv." Turning back, she narrows her eyes at Cassian and points her finger. "I'm sealing our doors tonight, so don't even think about coming near our rooms."

The corner of Cassian's mouth tugs upward as he tucks his hands into the front pockets of his trousers and rocks back on his heels. "I get the feeling your daughter doesn't like me, Ms Redfearn."

"Yes, well, this may feel unethical for all of us, but it is something we'll have to adjust to for now. Besides, she'll come around eventually." Turning toward the back of the house, Clara waves him forward. "Come with me, and I'll get you set up. Mind you." She pauses, glancing back over her shoulder. "After that display, you may want to consider sealing your own door to ensure she doesn't set you ablaze."

Halting next to a wall at the far end of the house, Clara looks up at an old black and white photo and taps on the frame. "Aunt Millie, I'm afraid I need to switch your bedtime location for a little while. We have a guest."

Cassian's brows raise, his eyes bouncing from Clara to the picture.

"Yes, I'm sane." Clara smiles over her shoulder. "Well, mostly."

The woman in the photo turns her head. "The panel is still out on that, Clara dear," she winks.

"Sorry to disturb you, Aunt Millie. It's good to hear that smart tongue of yours is still quick as a whip after all these years."

"Yeah yeah." The woman's head in the photograph turns from side to side, peering around the room. "Did you say we have a guest? Who might this guest be?" Stepping aside, Clara fans her hand toward Cassian, and the woman's eyes widen. "A vampire!" she shrieks. "Since when do we consider a vampire a guest? Have you lost your mind, Clara dear?"

Lifting the photo from the wall, Clara places it on the mantle. "Aunt Millie, this is Cassian Laurent. He's the son of an original, and his stay here is tied to a timekeeper journal. So I expect you to be nice."

"A timekeeper journal, you say? Ah, well, that may change things a little, I suppose." The woman in the portrait shifts her eyes to Cassian, letting a scowl settle on her face. "You can rest assured that we'll keep our eye on him all the same."

"I'm sure he won't be any trouble." Walking back to where the picture had been, Clara glances over her shoulder. She looks back at Cassian's bewildered expression and snickers. "You'll get used to the house, and it will get used to you. It's been in our family for centuries, and it definitely has a mind of its own." Pulling a white stone with dark gray stripes from her pocket, she curls her last three fingers around it and places her hands against the wall above her head. "Ostium." The tips of her fingers light up as she cuts out the outline of a door.

The house begins to shake, and Cassian takes a step back, his eyes growing as a doorframe appears around the cutout. "Cherolaba," she says, drawing a small circle near the edge. A shiny brass doorknob forms before their eyes, and Clara takes hold of it, swinging the new door open. As she steps inside the empty space, she lifts her hands, crossing them above her head. Then, slowly lowering them, she snaps her hands toward each corner. "Exorno." Pieces of furniture begin to appear throughout the room.

Cassian shakes his head as the once empty room becomes a fully furnished suite. It's equipped with everything a guest would require, including a desk, sitting area and private entrance to the backyard. Clara pokes the end of her finger with her ring and dabs a print above the inner doorframe. "Might I have your index finger, please?" He holds out his hand, watching her curiously as she pricks the end of his as well. "Press your print above the door leading outside. Yours will allow your family into your room, and mine will stop them from entering the rest of my house. At least until they're invited," she smiles. He dips his head, acknowledging her rules as she takes one last look around at the new addition. "Very good then. I assume this will be adequate."

"Yes, thank you, Ms. Redfearn. I do appreciate your generosity."

Tucking her stone back into her pocket, she turns toward him, her face void of expression. "Well, as you might have noticed, I would do almost anything for my only granddaughter." Clara's eyes narrow. "That includes anything to protect her."

He clasps his hands behind his back. "I would expect nothing less."

"She has an obligation to the timekeeper journal, and I will ensure she fulfills that obligation," Clara continues. "So as long as she feels she requires you, you're welcome here." Taking a deep breath, she forces a smile. "Now, how will you sustain yourself? I can't have you thinking of us as dinner."

A smile tugs at Cassian's lips. "Of course not. You don't have to worry about any such thing from a Laurent. I assure you we are quite civilized these days, Ms. Redfearn. With your permission, I'll have my house steward bring me some—" He stops, shifting his weight with a chortle. "I can have him take care of that."

"Right." Clara gives a curt nod. "Be sure that you contact him then."

"Let me make the house rules clear, Bloodsucker. There will be no feeding on anything with a heartbeat in this house," Patricia calls out as she storms down the stairs.

Cassian moves with the swiftness of a vampire, meeting her at the bottom step. His eyes slowly move from hers to the throbbing artery in her neck. "As delicious as that pulse of yours sounds, Patricia. It's considered rather uncivilized these days to nourish ourselves with talking prey. Luckily for you, that went out with the nineteenth century." Winking, he adjusts the cuffs of his suit jacket and slowly begins to walk away when he turns back with his finger raised. "Oh, and I'd appreciate it if you'd stop calling me bloodsucker. The term is rather repulsive. My family and friends call me Cash. However, you can call me Cassian or Mr. Laurent." Stepping into his room, he gives a slight bow. "Thank you again for your generous hospitality, Ms. Redfearn. I guess I'll see you ladies in the morning."

"Pfft." Patricia glares at her mother. "He has some nerve! He should know that he wouldn't be welcome inside these walls if it weren't for that damn magical vampire diary and *you* allowing it."

Helen walks into the living room as Patricia storms past her. "Whoa. I see someone isn't happy about our guest."

"Well, as long as Olivia and that journal require his presence — he will be here. So I suggest we all get used to it."

Pressing the loose strands of hair against her head, Helen shrugs. "I think he's rather dashing. Besides, he seems harmless."

"Oh, for pity's sake, Helen." Clara rolls her eyes, pushing her way past. "Let's not forget it's the vamp glam attracting you. Now, pull yourself together and go to bed. We can talk to Cassian tomorrow. I'd like to see just how much he knows about the journal."

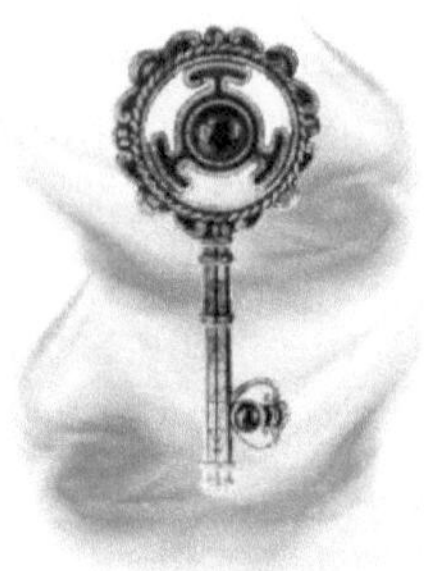

CHAPTER 11 ~ SHARING A MEMORY

Olivia rests against her headboard. The firewalk might have helped for the moment, but now that she's alone with her thoughts, the evening's events come rushing back. The sight of someone biting down on Jimmy's shoulder and him reaching out for her as he disappears is still fresh in her mind. Holding her hands out, she turns them over, eyeing them for some sort of change. *'I can't believe these hands created a portal. Surely Aunt Helen was joking when she said I sent Jimmy to hell.'*

"Knock, knock." Patricia's face appears between the crack of Olivia's door as she pushes it open and peeks in. "Can I come in?"

Dropping her hands, Olivia pretends to busy herself with adjusting her bedcover before peering up. "Yeah, of course."

Sitting on the edge of her bed, Patricia takes hold of her hands and smiles. "I remember examining mine too the first few times I was able to call on fire." She turns Olivia's hands over, running her thumb along each finger before releasing them. "You know, I recall these hands changing the colour of Gran's roses when you were little." Her smile broadens. "I was peeking around the garden's opening watching you play among the rosebushes – I think you were about seven then. Anyway, I heard you talking with a bird." Patricia sniggers. "I swear. You were having an actual conversation with this tiny sparrow when you asked what colour it liked. The next thing I know. You closed your hand and opened it finger by finger, changing all the rosebuds around the tiny bird blue.

"Aww, I remember that day," Helen says, peeking around Olivia's door with a grin. "We were so happy we had finally gotten rid of the nightmares that were plaguing you."

Clearing her throat, Patricia shoots her a dirty look. "Anyway, we must have watched you for a good twenty minutes changing the colour of the rosebuds."

Helen pulls a chair alongside Olivia's bed and nudges Patricia's leg with her foot. "I also recall us arguing about which elements she was making a connection with." She smiles at Olivia's chuckle.

"Really?"

"Oh yes," Patricia nods. "I had seen a bright blue glow around you periodically for some time, but Helen wouldn't believe me."

"Yeah, yeah. I didn't want to admit you could be developing a connection with mother earth and fire when I hadn't seen you connect with our water element yet. So I invited you to the stream to collect some sun-charged water. We knew one of them had to be your main connection, and of course, I was praying you would join me. Do you remember?"

Olivia grins. "Yeah, I think I do remember that day. I had forgotten to change back one of the blue roses. I tried to pull your attention from it by asking if I could pick a couple of pretty rocks for the fountain, but it was too late. You had already seen the blue bud," she says, pointing at Patricia with a smile.

"I wanted you to feel comfortable with your magic. That's why I had pointed it out – as if it were a new blossom. I was hoping you'd say you had done it. But, instead, you held that little secret tight to your chest and drug Helen off toward the stream."

"Hmm, I did enjoy that day, although I believe that's the evening I decided to shut magic down."

Patricia takes hold of Olivia and Helen's hands. "Can you share it with us, Liv? Show us how you recall that day. It's been a long time since we've shared a memory."

"I can try." Olivia grabs Helen's hand, the three of them forming a circle. Then, as Olivia closes her eyes, she projects the remainder of that day, pushing all her senses out through their bond.

Running ahead of Helen, Olivia stops to admire the enormous common altar. Her eyes draw upward to the ornate sun hugging the moon that's set into the large chimney— something reminiscent of the yin and yang. She can feel Helen watching as she runs her hand across the handmade bricks, taking in every dip and crevice as she makes her way across to the water basin. When water beads trickle on her fingers from the small waterfall, she giggles, flicking the droplets at her aunt.

Laughing, Helen nudges her away from the common altar. "All right, little missy, this isn't a place for playing." She waves her forward, continuing toward the stream. "Come with me so we can fill these jars, and you can get your rocks."

Helen's shoulders relax as she takes a deep breath and crouches to dip the jars into the stream. Her attention quickly diverts to Olivia's giggle. "Hey, that tickles."

Tightening the caps, she tucks the jars into her pocket and quietly makes her way toward her niece. Olivia is sitting on a rock with her hand in the water, where a medium-sized chub is swimming back and forth, rubbing itself against her hand. A few feet back, two more chubs are swimming in their direction. "Now, what have you got here," Helen asks, lowering herself to sit next to her on the rock.

"I was looking at the stones, and he swam up to me." Olivia looks over with a big smile. "I think he's petting himself."

"It does kind of look like that, doesn't it?" Helen rises to watch as the other fish make their way toward her hand. "And it looks as if he's called his family to come and say hi."

"Aw, I wish I could take them home."

"Now, Olivia, you know we don't take anything from nature unless it serves us a purpose. So, unless you intend to eat them, I think you should say goodbye to your fish friends for now. I need to get back and make dinner."

Olivia's face drops as she bounds to her feet. "I'm not having fish."

Laughing, Helen places her hand on her shoulder. "No, we're not having fish."

Later, sitting around the dinner table, Clara takes a bite of her chicken and watches Olivia push her vegetables around her plate. "Are you not hungry tonight, child?"

"Not really."

She gazes up at the blue rose in the centre of the table. "You know, I've never had blue roses in the garden before. It's quite lovely." She sets her fork down on her plate, dabbing her mouth with her napkin. "In fact, I don't believe anyone has ever changed the colour of my roses." Taking a sip of her tea, she pushes her plate off to the side and gestures for Olivia to do the same.

"Am I in trouble?"

"Goodness, no. I merely thought we might give some magic a try. And since you seem to like plants—"

Clara waves her hand in a small circular motion above the table. "Soli Potted," she says with a flick of her hand.

"Whoa!" Olivia sits back in her chair, her eyes wide as a small flower pot filled with soil appears in front of her. "How did you do that?"

Helen pats her on the shoulder with a chuckle. "One thing at a time, little one. Now hush. You need to focus on what Gran is teaching you."

Olivia's wide eyes bounce between Clara and the flower pot. "But you don't even have a wand! Harry always uses his wand."
Clara's face drops, and her daughters break into laughter as she peers up from the pot. "Harry, huh? And who might this Harry be?"

"Harry Potter, of course," Olivia says matter-of-factly.

Patricia clears her throat, trying to contain her laughter. "She's referring to the boy from the book we've been reading."

"Oh, of course, Harry Potter." The corner of Clara's mouth tugs slightly upward as she turns her focus back to Olivia. "Well then, your first lesson is that your hand is the only wand you need. This isn't a fairytale, darling." Olivia nods, and Clara points to the fruit bowl on the table. "Now, grab an apple and push one of the seeds into the dirt. You're going to use your energy to sprout a sapling."

"Really, Gran? You think I have magic in my hands?"

Clara smiles. "I sure do. I believe you hold a great deal of power in you. You simply need to learn how to access it." She chucks her chin at the bowl of apples. "Well, come on. Let's give it a try, shall we?"

Olivia cuts open an apple to dig out a seed, pushes it into the soil as directed, and smiles at Clara. "Okay, what now?"

"Good. Now, let the pot rest in the palm of your hand while you hold the other slightly above and repeat after me. Mother Goddess, I ask of thee. Show me the power that resides in me."

Reciting after Clara, Olivia stares down at the pot with pursed lips.

"Do you feel anything?"

Shaking her head, Olivia glances up. "No, not really."

"Hmm, try touching the soil with your finger." As she carefully places her finger against the soil, Clara smiles. "That's good. Do you sense the temperature of the soil rising?" She nods, acknowledging the warmth. "Wonderful. Now I want you to picture the growth of the seed. Imagine it splitting open, allowing the tiny sprout to make its way between the two halves. Do you get the sensation of it pushing through the dirt?" Clara sits back, studying her granddaughter's face as it tightens with concentration.

She looks up, still holding her finger to the soil. "I guess I can imagine it, but I don't feel anything."

Clara clasps her hands together, resting them against her chin and takes a deep breath. "Well, maybe you're still a bit too young." Standing, she pats Olivia's head. "Why don't you set it up on the window sill, and we'll try it again in a few days?"

She stares down at the flower pot with a long face. "Okay."

As Clara leaves the room, Patricia pushes a candle into the centre of the table. "Aw, don't look so disappointed, Liv. I have something else we can try."

"I truly think I need a wand, Aunt Trish.

Patricia chuckles. "You don't need a wand, honey. This is all about concentration. See that candle? Focus on the wick. Imagine it igniting. Feel the heat from the flame. Then extend your finger toward it like this and say one simple word" —*Patricia lifts her hand, her finger directed at the candle*— "Flamma!"

Olivia's face glows with the ignition of the wick. Her head spins toward her aunt. "That is so cool!"

"Submergo," Patricia says, dousing the flame. "Now, you try."

Olivia places her hands on the table. "Okay." She sets her sight on the wick, takes a deep breath and imagines the flame. Her thumb and forefinger rub together involuntarily as Clara enters the room.

"You know, I was thinking—" Clara says, drawing Olivia's attention toward her.

'Whoosh'

Flames burst from Clara's sleeve. Squealing, she pats at the sleeve as Patricia quickly extends her hand. "Submergo!" she shouts, dousing the fire.

The colour in Olivia's face washes away with her tears as she jumps to her feet, sending her chair flying out behind her. Patricia reaches out. "Liv, it's okay. It's just a sleeve," Clara says with a calming smile. "Besides, this is not the first time I've caught a misguided flame."

"Liv, honey, you had it," Patricia beams. "Let's try again."

Tearing out of her grip, Olivia storms off, hiccuping cries echoing against the walls as a trail of light streams behind. "No, I don't want to try!"

Olivia loosens her grip, and Patricia shakes her head. "Wait. There's more that you wouldn't have seen that day. Let me show you."

Clara sighs, watching Olivia disappear up the staircase. "I'm afraid this was too soon for her."

Left staring at the empty stairwell, Patricia squeezes her eyes shut and shakes her head. "Christ, did you see her glowtrail?"

"What's all the commotion—" Helen stops at the doorway, waving her hand in front of her face. "Oh my, what is that stench?" Her brow lifts with sudden realization when she spies Clara's burnt sleeve. "Ah, I see. A little mishap with the candle lesson, huh?"

"Yes, and you could say it has left her quite upset." Patricia slumps down in her chair. "However, she did leave one hell of a glowtrail with her hasty departure."

Picking up her teacup, Helen takes a sip. "Glowtrail, huh." She tips her head from side to side. "Okay, fine, she might have made a connection with fire, but she's still so young. If you think about it, we didn't figure out our true element until we were at least eleven or twelve."

Patricia throws her hands up. "Yeah, well, she's not us, and she did it! Her concentration may have been thrown off, but she did it!" She leans back in her chair, folds her arms across her chest and peers over at Clara. "I believe she may even be able to harness two main elements. She may not have had any luck with the apple seed tonight, but she had an audience. If only you could have seen her out in the garden today, mom."

"And the way she responded to the altar and interacted with the fish," Helen adds. "The fish have never swam up to me like that."

"Yes, well, I'm afraid this" —*Clara holds her sleeve out*— "may have just set her back."

Patricia lets go of Olivia's hand with a sigh, breaking the circle. "I blame myself for you shutting magic down, Liv. We thought we had hidden the memories of the night your parents died—of the fire. I should never have gotten you to try lighting the candle."

Her eyes meet Patricia's as the corner of her mouth tugs upward. "You could never fully hide them, and you certainly couldn't erase them. Besides, you were right. If I had of just kept my focus." Her gaze turns to Helen. "Those fish, though—" She laughs. "I had forgotten about that."

Helen's head falls back with laughter. "And the look on your face when you thought we might have them for dinner – priceless!"

Clara opens the door to Olivia's room and stands staring at the three of them with a warm smile. "It's nearly two in the morning. You three should be in bed. What could possibly be so funny?"

"We were just reminiscing," Patricia winks at Olivia. "But you're right." She walks over to the door and puts her arm around Clara. "It's time for bed. Sweet dreams, Liv."

Blowing her a kiss, Helen flicks her hand toward her nightstand. "Gingiberi ti citrea," she says, leaving a cup of lemon ginger tea behind.

Olivia lifts the teacup to her lips, inhaling the citrusy scent before tasting it. "Mmm, lemon ginger tea. My favourite. Thanks, Aunt Helen." Taking another sip of her tea, she sets her cup down on her nightstand and smiles. "Goodnight, Gran."

"Get some rest, child. I'll see you in the morning."

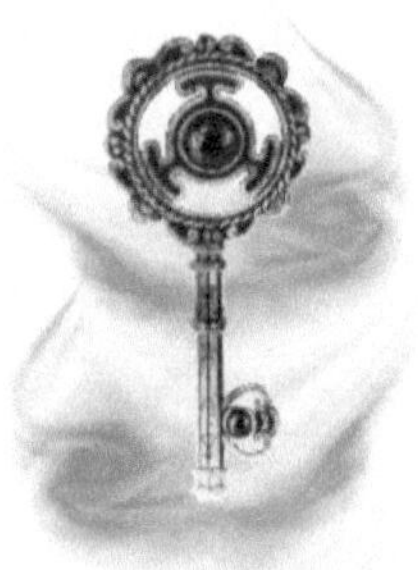

CHAPTER 12 ~ THE NIGHTMARE

Watching the door close, Olivia pulls her duvet tight to her chest and snuggles in. She takes a deep breath, releasing the craziness of the day as she feels the weight of her body seep into her pillowed mattress. A loud shriek from downstairs wakes her, and she leaps from her bed. Her tiny hand hesitates on the bedroom door before pushing it open to step over the thick line of salt. The air is heavy with smoke as she cups her hand over her mouth and pinches her nose to block the fumes when her sight lands on an old woman. Calling out to her, she frantically waves her forward. "It's going to be all right, Olivia. You must ignore the shadows and keep moving."

As she skittishly feels her way down the hall, the dark shadows dance through the plumes of smoke illuminated by the flicker of light below. Olivia's heart pounds against her chest, and she stops, wrapping her hands around the bannister to peer down into the light. No matter how often she has this same dream, nothing can prepare her for what she's about to see. A circle of flames surrounds her parents, and horror steals her voice. The fear on her mother's face as she kneels beside her father sends chills down her spine. Stuck between the floorboards, he claws at the wood, desperately trying to keep himself from slipping through. Olivia tries to scream, but no sound comes from her gaping mouth. Finally, when her mother spots her, she yells, "Olivia, run outside as fast as you can and get help!"

The old woman's hands wrap around her arms, and Olivia is standing at the front door before she even realizes they have moved. Flames lick at the walls and ceiling around her as she peers back at her parents. The old woman is now at her mother's side as she stretches her arms skyward. Together they repeat the same words over and over again – words Olivia can now recite by heart.

> 'Terra, Ignis, Aqua, Ventus,
> I summon thee
> Earth by divine earth,
> make the ground one with me.
> Fire ignite to illuminate the way,
> Water douse the evil,
> Air carry it far away.
> Mother Goddess, protect my daughter!
> Olivia – Olivia – Oliv—'

Olivia screams as the ceiling crashes, cutting off her mother's final words.

Her heart slams against her chest as her damp cheek meets coolness, and an intoxicating scent of masculine spice fills her nose. A firm hold envelopes her as someone calmly strokes the length of her hair, gently rocking her side to side. "Shh, Olivia," a deep voice rasps soothingly against her head. "I've got you. You're safe. It was only a dream."

"What happened?" She hears her grandmother ask, her voice fading as if she met understanding before completing her question.

Again the deep voice soothes her as it rumbles over her neck. "You're all right, Olivia. I want you to listen to the crickets."

She nods as a cool touch brushes across her forehead, and her body begins to slowly relax. As darkness drapes over her thoughts, she sees nothing but stars—hears only the quiet chirp of crickets and feels the refreshing chill of an evening breeze. Her head sinks back into her pillow as a light brush of lips meets her forehead. "Sleep well," the deep voice echoes in the distance.

"I can't believe you let him in her room last night," Patricia says, flopping down in the chair across from her mother. "He could have—"

"Calmed her fears and ensured she fell back into a restful sleep," Cassian says with confidence as he enters the kitchen. He grabs the chair next to Clara. "Mind if I join you?"

Patricia rolls her eyes as Clara extends her hand. "Please. I had intended to come and thank you. I'm grateful for the way you responded to Olivia's nightmare last night. She hasn't cried out in the night like that in a very long time."

Helen waves her hand over the table, delivering three teacups in the center. "I think the eventful day yesterday may have stirred up some memories." She looks over at Cassian. "Can I get you something?"

"No, thank you. My house steward came by this morning." Their shoulders tense with his words, and he raises his hand. "Not to worry. I've obeyed house rules. Nothing with a heartbeat."

Gagging into her fist, Patricia turns her head. "So disgusting."

Picking up her teacup, Clara cradles it in her hands. "I must ask. How did you get to Olivia's room so quickly last night? I'm directly next door, and you were already there by the time I got to her."

Patricia bounds to her feet, pointing an accusatory finger in his face. "I knew it! You're the bloody reason she screamed." Her glare shifts to Clara. "I told you he couldn't be trusted!"

Cassian calmly shakes his head. "I hate to disappoint you, but it was not me that caused her to cry out. Olivia barely began to scream as I was making my way to her room." All eyes dart in his direction, and he quickly raises his hands. "Wait. I know that sounded inappropriate, but I can explain. A nightmare was the cause of her crying out. My intent was merely to calm her and erase the bad dream. Nothing more."

Patricia's eyes narrow as she folds her arms. "And how could you have possibly known she was having a nightmare?"

"I could see it—feel her fear."

Taking a deep breath, Clara closes her hand, pressing the inside of her fist against her lips as she shakes her head. "You can see our thoughts," Helen asks, her cheeks turning rosy as she peers up at him.

"Yes. Well, not entirely. Only if I concentrate on them."

"Okay," Clara says, dropping her hand as she turns to glare at him. "Care to explain why you were concentrating on Olivia's thoughts last night?"

He folds his arms over his expanding chest and leans back in his chair. "Truthfully, I had hoped to see what she had read in that journal. I thought she might have read further into it than she cared to share. But instead, I saw her dream or rather her nightmare. I could feel her distress and felt the need to soothe her fears."

"I was expecting you to lie." A smile slowly works across Clara's face as she speaks. "I had forgotten you were born to two originals – I guess you're not able to."

Patricia leans back and stretches her legs, crossing them at the ankle as she looks him over skeptically. "Then tell us. What exactly did you see when you invaded Olivia's private moments?"

"Look, it wasn't just a dream. From what I saw, she was reliving a traumatic childhood event." He shrugs, releasing the breath he had just taken. "I made her forget the dream—showed her the night sky and gave her thoughts of serene sounds in its place." His voice hardens as his stare meets Patricia's. "I wouldn't harm her."

"Well, of course not." Helen sets her teacup down, forcing a smile. "You need her."

Standing, Cassian places his hands on the table, making eye contact with each of the three ladies one by one. "Yes, my family may need her, but that's not why I chose to help her last night. I'm confident her nightmares will not change the commitment she has already made to the journal." He straightens, placing his hands in the front pockets of his trousers. "Olivia has one of the purest hearts of anyone I've had the pleasure of knowing in centuries. Continually reliving a nightmare of that magnitude could destroy it. Now, if you'll excuse me, I think I could use some air."

Narrowing her eyes, Patricia stares over at her mother. "What do you mean he can't lie?"

"No, I don't believe he can." Clara takes a sip of her tea, meeting Patricia's bewildered stare. "My grandmother Victoria told me many years ago that originals were created with the inability to lie. Like anyone, they can dodge answers by repeating the question as idiocy to avoid the truth, but they cannot blatantly tell a lie. Julien and Clarentina were both originals. They must have passed that onto their children."

The sun's rays brighten the room as Olivia cracks open her eyes. She can hear the chatter downstairs but can't quite make out the conversation. Turning to look at her alarm clock, she's amazed at how refreshed she feels at 8 am. Usually, her butt would be dragging, and she'd be praying for a few more hours.

A friendly 'Meow' comes from the bottom of the bed as she swings her feet over the side. "Good morning, Mr. Green." She reaches over, rubbing his head as she walks to the window. An aromatic scent of lilacs tickles her senses as she peers down across the yard. Inhaling deeply, her sight sets on Cassian leaning against the oak near the back corner. He looks completely out of his element with a foxtail dangling from his mouth like a farmer.

Snickering, she pulls on a pair of shorts and a tank top, nudges the journal aside and grabs one of the old books from the crate. When she opens the front cover, she notices an inscription. *'To my dearest friend, Julien. Daniel DeFoe.'* Flipping it over, she reads the title aloud. "Roxana: The Fortunate Mistress by Daniel DeFoe. Hmm, I wonder if Cash ever met Daniel? This seems like a fair enough reason to speak with him. Don't you think," she asks her furry friend, tucking it under her arm as she heads for the door.

As she walks downstairs, her stomach grumbles at the smell of bacon. "Morning." She inhales exaggeratedly through her nose, taking a seat at the table. "Mmm, I could smell bacon before I even hit the stairs."

"You look well-rested," Helen chirps, placing a plate of bacon and eggs in front of her.

"Thank you." Setting the old book on the table next to her, Olivia picks up her fork. "Yeah. It must have been your tea. I haven't slept that well in a long time."

Clara forces a smile as she pats her hand. "I'm happy to hear that. Maybe once you've had some breakfast, you could try reading a little further into the journal instead of one of those old novels," she says, pointing to the book at Olivia's side. "The sooner we can figure out what it's all about, the sooner things can get back to normal around here."

Patricia leans forward. Resting her elbows on the table, she drops her head to her hands. "For the love of the Goddess. If you insist on having her read that damn thing, can we at least agree on not reading any names aloud?"

"She must read whatever is in front of her. Though I see no reason to visit a list of names."

"Sure, but can we wait till a little later, Gran? I thought I'd sit by the tree out back and read something that won't bring visitors for a bit," Olivia smiles. Standing, she grabs her book and two slices of bacon from her plate. Dropping a piece in front of Mr. Green, she turns toward the backdoor.

Her gaze locked on Olivia, Patricia spins in her chair. "Hey, wait. Where are you going?"

"Like I said, I'm going to go read." She holds the old book up. "Plus, I wanted to talk to Cash. This book was addressed to Julien and signed by the author, Daniel Defoe. He died in like the eighteenth century. I'm curious if Cash knew him. You know, like a family friend or something."

Patricia swings around, staring at the door as it closes. "Okay. What the hell just happened? I mean, Really? Suddenly she's BFFs with this bloodsucker?"

Clara purses her lips and nods. "Mmhmm. I am finding it a bit curious myself. The only explanation I have is the journal. And, maybe you haven't noticed Mr. Green's demeanour, but he doesn't seem the least bit concerned about Cassian's presence." She gestures to the cat, lazily licking the grease off his paw as he watches Olivia out the back window. "So, I'm confident we shouldn't be either. After all, his judge of character has always been impeccable."

"Um, is it just me, or did anyone else notice that Olivia didn't mention or even seem to realize she had a nightmare that shook the house last night?" Helen tosses a sprig of pine into the pot of boiling water on the stove and squeezes in half a lemon. The water begins to bubble, and a thick mist rises to the ceiling. "Mundet," she mutters, pushing the steam through the room with her hands. Within seconds, the kitchen fills with a light smell of citrusy pine, leaving a gleaming shine behind. She wipes her hands off on her apron, hanging it next to the stove and shrugs. "Cause that's not the type of nightmare that goes unmentioned. I find that particularly odd," she says, taking her seat at the table.

Clara nods, taking a sip of her tea. "Mmhmm, I noticed, but it wasn't something I was about to bring up."

"I think he used his bloody hypnotic bullshit on her for more than a dream exchange. That's what I think," Patricia says, storming over to the back window.

CHAPTER 13 ~ JUST DON'T RUN

Olivia's pace slows as she nears Cassian, still leaning against the tree at the back of the yard. He shifts his weight, and she stops, a gasp leaving her lips as her heart begins to race. "You don't have to fear me, Olivia."

She pulls her bottom lip between her teeth, trying to reel in her anxiety as she steps closer. "I'm not afraid," she lies. "I just wasn't sure if I should disturb you."

Turning, the corner of Cassian's mouth tightens into a slight smile. At that moment, Olivia can tell her attempt to conceal her panic isn't working. "You're not disturbing me," he says as he advances with slow short strides. "I was merely in need of some air."

She tilts her head, her lips twisting as she focuses on his heedful movements. "If you're the predator, why does it look as though you're the one who is carefully calculating each step as you approach me?"

Cassian smirks, bowing his head slightly before meeting her gaze. "Not only are you tremendously inquisitive, but you're very observant."

"I'm sorry." Heat immediately rushes to her cheeks. "Sometimes I ask the silliest—"

He raises his hand. "Olivia, it's fine." He takes a step closer. "I believe, given our circumstances, we should have this discussion. Though I must ask one thing of you."

Her head bobs as she shrugs. "Sure."

A slight breeze tussles her hair, and he closes his eyes as his nostrils flare. "You must not run from me."

Her chest expands, and a hint of his spicy cologne hits her senses like fresh baked goods. She clears her throat, moistening her lips as she brushes the stray strand from her face. "I have no reason to run. You don't intend to hurt me. Do you?"

"No." He takes another step toward her, leaving an arms-length between them and tucks his hands into the front pockets of his trousers. "I can assure you I have no intention of hurting you."

"Okay," she says, squinting with a tinge of uncertainty.

"I'm a vampire, Olivia."

"I know that, Cash."

"Yes, but you should know that your words mean nothing when it comes to how you feel. I can hear your heart beating, smell your fear and sense the rise of your body temperature all before you get within 100 yards of me."

Her heartbeat picks up, and she watches him shift, his brow lifting as he tips his head. "I am usually a master of control when sensing the human body's emotional reflexes. And make no mistake, I haven't thought about sinking my teeth into a living being that hasn't offered themselves to me for over two centuries. My family is one of the only clans that survive on donors' blood. However, I have never been as drawn to the scent of anyone's blood as I am to yours."

A wave of fear forces a quick intake of breath, and she can feel the warmth working through her limbs. She takes a step back, and Cassian raises his hand. "Wait, please. Forgive me. I don't mean to frighten you. What I mean is the heat of your fear" —*he cautiously extends his hand toward her*— "it lends a heady scent to your blood that is almost unbearable to deny. I don't want to risk triggering your flight response on top of that. I'm afraid I may not be strong enough to fight the urge to come after you." Pacing in front of her, he runs his hand through his hair. "Damn, this was meant to caution you, not frighten you further."

Shaking her head, Olivia meets his gaze. "I'm not afraid of you, Cash. If you wanted to" —*she stumbles, searching for the right words*— "kill me. You had the perfect opportunity the other night by the stream. Instead, you protected me from the other vampire."

"Olivia, I require you. I have no choice but to ensure your safety." Swallowing, his gaze moves from her pulsating artery to the book in her hand. "Your heart is racing."

She watches as he turns to pick another foxtail and twirl it between his fingers. "Wow, Gran wasn't kidding about you not being able to lie, huh?"

Turning back to face her, Cassian slowly shakes his head. "It's not about being able to lie, Olivia. I don't want to lie to you."

Heat floods her cheeks. How could she have fallen for his vamp glam her aunt was talking about? How stupid could she really be? All promises forgotten, she drops the book in her hand and darts for the backdoor. Hearing that he only protected her because he requires her cut like a knife. How could she have let herself believe he helped her for any other reason? Why would he? He's a vampire—cold, void of life and emotion.

Stopping, she places her hand on the common altar and peers over her shoulder, expecting to meet the hungry eyes of a vampire. But he's gone. She spins, checking the expanse of the yard, but there's no sign of him. With a breath of relief, she continues toward the house.

When she enters the kitchen, Helen's cheery voice greets her before the door has a chance to close. "Hey, buttercup. I thought you were reading." She spins with a basket of empty jars in hand, her smile fading as their eyes meet. "What's wrong?"

"Nothing. I'm just a little tired." Olivia rubs her stomach as she turns for the stairs. "Monthly cramps. Nothing a nap won't fix."

"Hmm, all right, but let me know if you need anything for them." She holds up her basket with a smile. "I'm going to gather some water for my collection. Gran's at the store, and Patricia is here somewhere."

"I'm good, but thank you." She starts up the stairs, her eyes bouncing off the mumbling walls as an uneasy sensation travels up her spine. Intensifying as she nears the top step, she stops, timidly glancing over her shoulder at the empty staircase. "Oh, for crying out loud. Calm down, Olivia," she grumbles, opening the door to her room. "What were you thinking anyway? Of course, it's all about the journal."

Her bedroom door slams behind her, and the novel she hoped would spark conversation sits mere inches from her face. "You forgot your book by the tree," a deep voice rasps. She stumbles back, fumbling behind her for the handle as she meets Cassian's stare. His nostrils flare as her heart rate increases, and the corner of his lip rises, revealing the slightest glimpse of his fangs. "Miss Parker, you are a terrifyingly reckless young lady." He drops the book to his side and steps forward, resting his opposite hand above her head.

"I—I'm sorry. I needed," she stammers.

"You were embarrassed."

"No," she bites back.

"Yes. You assumed I meant that I require you merely for the journal."

Her chest heaves, a tiny squeak escaping as he backs her against the door. When he lowers his head to hers, she closes her eyes. "I believe I may have mentioned that I have never been as drawn to the scent of anyone's blood as I am to yours," he slowly articulates next to her ear. Inhaling deeply, he runs the cool tip of his nose along the length of her neck. Olivia swallows. "Maybe you misunderstood me when I said I require you. Perhaps I should have said you stir something in my otherwise void existence. Something I haven't felt in a *very* long time," he says, his voice deep and sultry as his lips brush against her flesh. "I must tell you. I have imagined what you'd taste like, Olivia. And I am absolutely certain your warm sweet blood would indulge my palate."

"You—you thought about tasting me? Like you want to?"

"More than you could ever understand." She squeezes her eyes shut as his tongue glides along her collarbone. "But I would never allow myself such a pleasure out of fear that I'd never be able to stop," he sighs.

Tap tap tap

"Liv? You in there?" Patricia calls through the door.

Her eyes spring open. The cool of his touch and his spicy scent still penetrate her senses, but Cassian is gone. The book he held is now sitting on the side table. She takes a deep breath, expelling it through loose lips, and pulls the door open.

"Hey, kiddo! I thought you were reading." Patricia looks her up and down, her stare leaving a glaring question mark as she passes by her outstretched arm. "What's up? You look winded."

The corners of her mouth turn down as she shakes her head. "No, I'm fine." Her gaze follows her aunt to the window, and she throws her arms up, feigning a smile. "Cash looked as though he needed some time to himself. So I came back in," she lies.

Pushing the heavy burgundy drape aside with the back of her fingers, Patricia peers down into the backyard. "I had thought I saw you speaking with that parasite" *—she tips her head toward the window—* "did he say something to upset you?"

"No." She walks to the window and peers down at the vampire under the tree. His shoulder resting comfortably against the trunk and his legs crossed at the ankles, he appears to be casually reading a book. One would never imagine he was mere inches from her jugular a moment ago. "I mean, yeah, you did, but he did nothing to upset me. He was telling me about his family." She looks at her aunt. "Did you know they are one of the only clans to survive off donors' blood?"

"Oh, well, isn't that less beastly of him. Are you proposing we should give the bloodsucker a medal?" She rolls her eyes. "Look, I'm not getting into what donor means with you now, Liv, but think about this for a moment. He could compel someone to do his bidding and bam! Donor!"

Turning, Patricia wipes her hand over her face as if to wash the filth of her statement away and scrunches her nose. "No matter how you say it, still gross. Anyway, that creature is not why I came up. What do you say we try some magic before Gran gets back? The sooner you get through this vampire quest, the sooner we can have our house back." She bats her eyelashes and playfully nudges her shoulder, slathering on a big grin. "C'mon. What do you say?"

Olivia shrugs, twisting her lips. "I don't know. I never had any luck in the past."

"That was the past. We'll start slow. Besides, you know you have to start somewhere."

She looks out the window at Cassian, then turns back with a bright smile. "Okay, fine, but only if Cash helps."

"What?" Patricia slams her hands on her hips. "No! He's a bloodsucker, Liv. How the hell is he supposed to help?"

"I don't know," she shrugs, walking back toward her. "I mean, he is one of them, right? So it might be helpful if he could show us what we're up against."

Folding her arms, Patricia purses her lips, her shoulders lifting with an exaggerated breath. "Fine. Go get your new BFF and meet Helen and me in the kitchen. But if I accidentally kill him, it's not my fault."

"No! You're not allowed to hurt him," Olivia hollers, watching her stomp out of her room.

"Now, what fun will that be?" she grins, winking over her shoulder as she approaches the stairs.

Sighing, Olivia moves back to the window and peers out at Cassian, still perched against the tree with a book in hand. *'How is it that I can read your family journal, but you're so closed off to me?'*

Just then, his eyes lift from his book to meet hers with a smile. Her heart thumps. Releasing the heavy curtain, she steps back from the window.

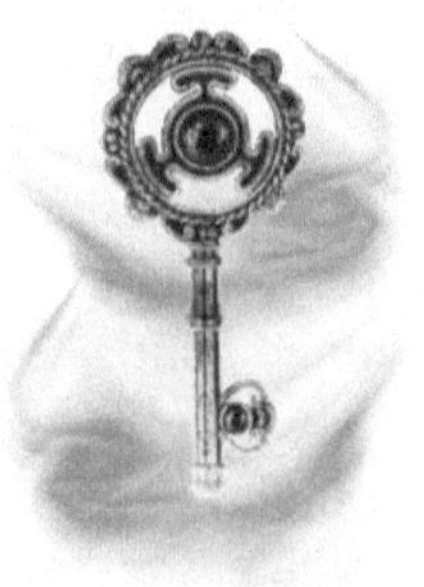

CHAPTER 14 ~ THAT KIND OF POWER

UGH! Stop being a damn coward, Olivia!

Padding down the stairs with a purpose, she storms toward the door. Her pace slowing as the screen slams behind her. He methodically turns the page, his hand resting across the book as he stares forward. "You are truly much braver than anyone gives you credit for, Olivia Parker."

"Hm? Oh. Or exceptionally stupid," she lowers her head, stepping in front of him. Toeing a stone with her shoe, she looks up. "Cash, I'm sorry I ran off."

He closes the book and drops his hand to his side. "I should have considered my words a little more. I didn't mean to—"

She cuts him off. "Please. I don't think we should discuss it. I believe I understand. All I truly wanted to say was that I'm sorry I was unable to release you when I summoned you and your brother. I hope you know it's not intentional. I have no idea why the journal chose me. I mean, it's ridiculous, really. I don't do the magic thing." Cassian straightens, watching intently as her arms flop at her side in frustration. A smile tugs at his lips, but he remains quiet. "I was thinking, and maybe it's because I had given thought to what you said. You know, how we could help each other. I never thought I would say this, but I think I could use a vampire on my side right now." Cautiously, she extends her hand. "So what do you say? Friends?"

His smile broadens, allowing the slightest glimpse of his fangs to appear as he reaches out to take her hand. As coolness closes around warmth, her heartbeat picks up once again. He inhales deeply, glancing down at their joined hands. "Yes, of course. Friends. But, to be clear, Olivia. I have always been on your side."

Her eyes drop to their hands. The cool sensation of his touch is almost equal to the tingle she receives when she handles the journal. She swallows, running her thumb over his index finger, recalling how close he was only minutes ago. Her eyes meet his emerging smile, and she inhales, straightening her shoulders. "Though, I should tell you. I'm afraid that I don't possess the powers you may need. In fact, magic makes me extremely uncomfortable."

"I recognized your fear the first time you read the journal. Though you seemed awfully determined to prove something the night you summoned my brother and me here." He turns her hand over in his, running his finger over her palm. "It might not be obvious to you because you've lived with it your entire life, but I can hear the magic singing in your veins, Olivia. I assure you. You are by no means powerless."

"You can hear my magic?"

"Most definitely," he nods. "It sings the most beautiful song—ignites my flesh. I haven't felt that kind of pull from anyone in at least a century." His lips tug into a smile. "In fact, I'd say that it's the same feeling my father described the night he saved the wit—" Cassian stops mid-sentence with an apologetic glance. "Forgive me. It's the same feeling my father described the night he saved the old woman from burning on the cross. The same woman who created the journal."

Patricia's face is pressed against the window frame, watching their exchange when Clara walks in. "What are we gawking at," she asks, taking a teacup from Helen's hands.

"Damn it!" Patricia exclaims, staring at their joined hands. "It's just as I had feared."

"What?" Clara asks.

"Goddess, help us! She just made a deal with that bloody parasite" *—she points out the window—* "the damn blood-sucking devil you let stay in our home."

Helen chuckles as Clara takes her seat at the table. "Stop being so dramatic, and come sit down," Clara groans, swirling her teacup before flipping it over on the saucer. "You mean, she shook his hand. Try not to overreact. Olivia is a bright girl. There's only cause for concern if she were to offer him her blood." Patricia gasps as her mother picks up her cup, turning it slowly to examine the leaves. "I'm sure that's something we don't need to be concerned about." When she's done, she turns it back over, places it on the saucer and pushes it into the center of the table.

"What?" Patricia slides in next to her, reaching for the teacup. "What did you see?"

Helen slaps her hand away as the cup and saucer disappear. "It's not your concern. If mom wants us to know, she'll tell us." She flicks her finger at the space where Clara's teacup and saucer had been. "Ministerio tea." A fresh cup of tea appears, leaving Patricia to flop back in her seat with a scowl.

Olivia pulls her hand back from Cassian's and turns. "I hate to disappoint you, Cash, but if that's the kind of magic you require, I'm afraid I can't help you. I know I don't possess any such power." Without another word, she walks back to the house.

Making no attempt to stop her, he picks up the old book he had been reading and watches her disappear inside.

"I thought you were asking the fang-a-saurus to join us." Patricia spins to face her niece.

"Yeah, I was going to, but he's reading and looks content. It didn't feel right dragging him from his book." She stares at the counter, her face tightening as she points. "Who brought that down here?"

"Brought what down here, dear," Clara asks as all heads turn in the direction of Olivia's accusatory finger. Her eyes land on the journal with a sigh. "Ah, well, I just got home, but I did tell you that it will persist until you fulfill your duty."

Olivia glares at her grandmother, poking her thumb into her chest. "My duty? And who makes these decisions exactly?"

A raspy cough from behind causes her to still as the woman in the picture clears her throat. "Why, the creator of the book, of course. It should be considered a great privilege, Olivia. Not a curse. In fact, to ignore the call of a timekeeper journal will most definitely bring darkness upon your entire family."

I can't read that wretched thing without Cash. Olivia's shoulders slump as she gazes around the room at her aunts and grandmother. "Fine. I'll read it, but—"

The back door swings open, and she spins to see Cassian with the old book in his extended hand. "I forgot to mention that I borrowed one of the books from your collection."

She straightens, gracing him with a smile. "Oh, no worries at all. They were once yours anyway, right?" Bowing his head slightly, he starts to walk off when she stops him. "Um. Cash? I was about to read the journal. Would you like to join us?"

"Yes. It would be an honour." He glances across the faces of the three other ladies staring back at him before meeting Olivia's gaze. "That is as long as your family doesn't mind, of course."

Olivia responds before anyone can speak. "Oh, they don't mind. After all, this is *your* family's journal. Besides, I'd feel safer knowing you're here. You know, just in case any vamps show up."

"In that case, it would be my pleasure."

Patricia flops back in her chair, rolling her eyes skyward, her shirt bearing 'FANGTASTIC' across her chest. "Not that we can't scorch a vamp or two on our own if needed."

"Oh, ignore her." Helen pats the seat next to her. "Come sit next to me. You might not have noticed, but my sister has been a little tense. Here I'll get you a drink." Leaving him no time to reply, Helen flips her hand over. "Rubrum," she says, looking over at him with a sultry grin. "If my sources are correct, your preferences would be red wine."

He takes the offered seat next to her with a gracious bow. "Thank you."

Patricia folds her arms, her brows heavy as she squints at Olivia. "But I thought we were going to work on your magic today, Liv?"

"And we will, but the journal is already down here. I mean, there's no reason why we can't practice tomorrow. Right, Gran?" Watching Clara nod, Olivia picks up the journal next to her trusted companion on the counter and runs her hand over his back. "Well, Mr. Green, are you ready to find out what's hidden inside this crazy old thing?"

As if he's as interested as everyone else, he jumps down and trots over to the table, sending a 'meow' back over his shoulder. "Okay, okay, I'm coming," Olivia chuckles, taking her seat at the end of the table between Cassian and Clara. She sets the journal down, lays her hands over the cover, and takes a deep breath. "I assume I should skip the list of names to avoid any unwanted guests and start reading from the first entry, huh?"

Patricia rests her elbows on the table, batting her lashes with a sarcastic grin. "Actually, I'd be perfectly fine if you didn't read any of it until we practice your skills."

Clara jams her elbow into Patricia's side. "Yes, dear. I think that would be best. Skip the list for now. I'm not sure we're ready to meet any more vampires until we know more about them." Her gaze shifts to Cassian. "No offence."

He raises his hand with a slight smirk. "None taken."

"Although, if they're from the Laurent clan and look anything like Cash, one or two more couldn't hurt." Helen nudges his shoulder with a wink when Clara clears her throat. "Oh, I only meant for backup."

"Seriously, Helen, knock it off," Patricia gripes, pointing an ignited finger at her.

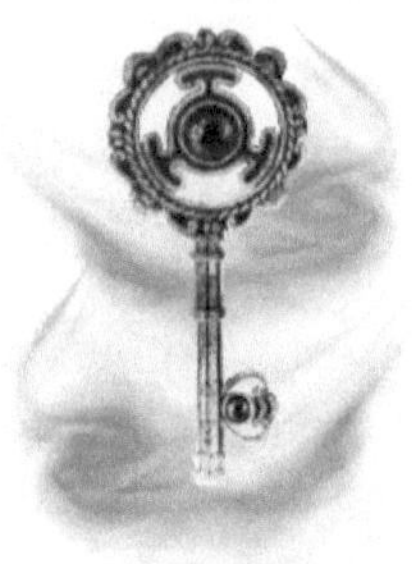

CHAPTER 15 ~ ENGLAND - JULY 12TH, 1612

Olivia opens the journal and runs her finger along the enticing inscription at the top. Ignoring the tingle that shoots up her arm, she reads it aloud, "England - July 12th, 1612 – Julien Laurent - SOV." Her heart begins to race as the smell of damp wood overwhelms her senses. Her hand stops, and she looks around. "Do you smell that?" Heads turn to look at one another with a shrug.

"Smell what?" Clara asks.

"The dampness of a forest." Everyone shakes their heads. "Odd." Lowering her gaze, she continues. "Two vampires, Julien Laurent and—" Her voice trails off, leaving everyone staring in anticipation.

Patricia leans in, slapping her palm off the table. "Liv? Liv where'd you go?"

As Olivia's eyes dart from side to side, her finger continues to trace each line. Helen reaches out, but Clara grabs her hand. "No!

Don't touch her. I believe she's actually inside the entry." She spins toward Cassian. "You said you could see into her dream last night—feel her emotions? Can you do that now?"

"Yes, I've felt connected to her since she first read the journal. She does feel a little anxious at the moment. As for the mind link, that was a bit different. She was calling out for help in her dream. I'm not sure if it will work in this situation."

"You have to try, please. We need to know where she is—what she sees. We need to be sure she's not in danger." Clara clasps her hands and peers down at Olivia's finger as it continues to fly over the page. "We don't want to disturb her as long as she's safe. Hopefully, we can bring her out by removing the journal if we need to."

"Hopefully?" Patricia's voice raises, flames prancing in her eyes as she slams her hands on the table and glares at her mother. "Why would you bloody send her in there if you weren't sure?"

"I had no way of knowing that she would mentally disappear inside the journal." Clara peers over at Cassian, her eyes pleading. "Please, make sure she's okay. I'm depending on you to let us know if we need to bring her out."

Cassian's lips tighten as he gives her a stiff nod. "I'll do my best, Ms. Redfearn." Closing his eyes, he opens his senses and reaches out to Olivia's mind.

Standing in the middle of a dense forest, Olivia can feel the chill of the night air settle on her skin. She reaches out to wipe the dew off a leaf, gasping as her hand swipes through the branch. Stumbling forward, she rubs her thumb and forefinger together, looking down at her moistened digits. "How is it that I can feel the moisture but not the leaves?" Her eyes flit from one tree to another as she takes in the sights and sounds.

"Yes. This is quite curious, isn't it," Cassian says, grasping the branch next to her, but she doesn't acknowledge his presence. He reaches out to touch her shoulder, but his hand travels straight through. "Yes, curious indeed."

The sound of thundering hoofs captures their attention, and they spin to see two deer darting directly toward them. Behind the deer, two men are gaining on them quicker than humanly possible. Olivia ducks behind the tall birch, watching as the deer pass.

"Father. Mr. Windsor," Cassian mutters as the rapid footsteps suddenly halt.

Olivia's heart begins to race as a branch snaps nearby, and she peeks out from behind the tree to see Julien standing only a few feet away. Somehow, he looks younger with his long black hair and beard to match. At least different from when she saw his image the evening before. He's wearing a vest-type coat, his sleeves are puffy with ruffled cuffs, and he has long leather boots that meet his breeches—something straight out of the Jacobean era.

She peers over at the three large stones on her right, noticing that their placement is reminiscent of a castle. "Lancashire Forest?" she asks as if someone can hear her.

As Julien turns toward Olivia, his gaze focuses beyond her, and Cassian steps forward with his hand on his chest. "Father? You can see me?"

But he quickly drops his hand, spinning with Olivia as she follows Julien's stare to the glow coming from between the trees behind them. He starts in their direction when a man with dirty blond hair and a reddish beard grabs his sleeve. "Hey! Where the hell do you think you're going?"

Olivia follows Julien's gaze, walking toward the light. As she approaches the tree line along the outskirts of old Lancashire, she can hear a distant chant. "Burn the witches! Burn them all!"

"Olivia," Cassian calls out, trying to grasp her arm once again. When he fails to connect with her, he withdraws, opening his eyes to the three ladies around the kitchen table.

Questions fly at him from all directions. "Did you see her? Is she all right? Where is she?"

The questions come so quickly that Cassian is unsure who has asked what. Finally, he raises his hands and nods. "I saw her. She's fine. She's in Lancashire Forest, but I was unable to communicate with her."

"What do you mean you couldn't communicate with her," Patricia asks. "I thought you had some kind of mind link, and if you couldn't communicate with her, how do you know she's all right?"

Drawing the corner of his bottom lip between his teeth, Cassian shakes his head. "I'm not exactly sure why. I could see and hear her, but she had no idea I was there. It's almost as if we were on two different planes. I touched the very same tree that her hand passed through. I'm afraid I can't explain that." He scans the faces around the table, his lips tightening into a pensive smile. "I am, however, quite certain that she is safe. From what I can tell, she is nothing more than an observer."

Raising her hands, Patricia closes her eyes. "Thank you, Goddess!"

Clara stares at her, taking a deep breath before turning her attention back to Cassian. "I do believe you may be right. I have heard of such a scenario before. Could you tell if you would have been alive during that time?"

Patricia scoffs. "He's never really been alive. He has no heartbeat, for pity's sake."

"My heart beats. The blood it pumps might be a different temperature than yours, but it still circulates," Cassian spits back. "I should remind you that I am the son of two originals, not a pleb or a created, as you call them."

Clara shoots her daughter a dirty look, then chucks her chin at Cassian. "Forgive Patricia's ignorance. That was not something we were aware of. Maybe you can educate us at a more convenient time if you're so inclined. But, for now, we're extremely grateful that you could at least tell us Olivia is okay." She pats his hand. "Could you tell what time or date she's in? Would you have been alive then?"

"Yes." He glares at Patricia. "In fact, I saw my father and Mr. Windsor. They were still friends and looked just as I recall when I was a young boy."

"Still friends?" Clara lifts her hand. "Never mind. I believe that might explain why you and Olivia are experiencing the world around you differently. You would have been able to touch that tree because you once belonged in that space and time. But, to Olivia, those trees are nothing more than a vision of a time long gone."

Helen waves her hand, producing a glass of red wine in front of Cassian and turns to her mother with a bewildered look. "But why wouldn't he be able to communicate with her? He's been able to before."

Clara runs her fingertips over her lips, then rests her chin on her curled fingers. "If I have to guess, I'd say it's because only Olivia is to be inside the journal entries." She takes a deep breath and leans back in her chair. "We can't forget that timekeeper journals are created with a power of their own. Olivia is the one that has been chosen to interpret the book, and I'm afraid we can't cheat it. So we'll simply have to wait for her to reemerge." Her eyes soften as they shift back to Cassian. "Though I see no reason why you couldn't at least observe along with her. If you wouldn't mind, that is."

Cassian's lips tighten as he gives a firm nod. "Of course." He closes his eyes, once again reaching out to Olivia's mind. Thankfully, she's where he had left her—Lancashire forest.

Julien halts for a brief moment, his focus remaining on the glow emanating through the branches. "Harold, you cannot tell me you don't feel that." He pulls free from Harold's grasp. "There's no way you can't sense the immense energy radiating through the air?"

Harold presses his lips together and looks around. "No, I feel nothing out of the ordinary, and I'd like to keep it that way. What the hell is with you, Julien? You haven't been yourself all day." His brows draw together as he searches Julien's face. "Look, I said nothing when you ripped the heads off your latest creations—deeming them all out of control. Sure, taking out your own clan was a little out of character, but that's what I appreciate most about you. You've always been merciless. But now this?" He shakes his head, throwing his hand out toward town. "Of course, I hear the chanting. But you're acting as if this is something new. They've been hanging and burning witches for weeks now. It never bothered you before. In fact, just a few weeks ago, we were cheering this very crowd on. So what changed all of a sudden?" He grabs Julien's arm and gives him a tug. "I'm not sure what has gotten into you, but you need to stop this foolishness, and let's go. We have a deer hunt to get back to and our own families to think about."

Olivia stares at Harold, her face heating with each heartless word. It takes every ounce of her energy to focus on Julien as he continues to gaze off in the direction of the voices. When he's finally heard enough, he tugs his arm free of Harold's grasp and glares back at him. "Foolishness is letting our plebs gorge themselves. Prepare for change, my friend, because many more are coming."

"One old hag has you this bent out of shape that you are willing to change life as we know it?"

Julien shakes his head. "No. The law has already been written and sealed with my blood. There will be no more reckless pleb creation. No more gorging. That's why I set up this deer hunt tonight. I needed to tell you. I rounded up the last of my rogue plebs this morning. They had the choice to conform, or I had to remove the life I gave them, and you, my friend, must do the same."

"That's ridiculous!" Harold stares at him in disbelief. "You destroyed your own clan?"

"To preserve humanity? Yes. Without question." His head swings back toward the chanting. "This discussion can wait until tomorrow," Julien says, waving him off as he steps closer to the tree line. "Tonight, precedence has shifted to a powerful witch. There is no way you can't feel her strength." Glancing at Harold, he touches his cheek. "My flesh feels alive for the first time in centuries." His hand continues down his chest. "If I didn't know any better, I'd swear my blood is pumping warm. Her energy is so intense."

Harold breaks into laughter. "Okay, Laurent. Stop being so dramatic. This apostle act is not fooling me one bit. I feel absolutely nothing." He raises his finger in the air, pompously cocking his head to the side. "Oh. No. Wait. I do feel something." He spins back to face him with wide eyes and an exaggerated grin. "I feel us burning right alongside that damn witch if we don't get out of here. Now stop this nonsense. We need to go."

Scowling at Harold, Olivia wants to scream but knows it'll be useless. They don't seem to acknowledge her presence at all. Though all is not lost when Julien turns to plead his case. "Look, the townspeople neither desire witches nor vampires. For all we know, we could be next on their weekly roundup—beheaded and tossed into the town's burning centrepiece. With all the untamed plebs you've been creating, they're bound to draw attention sooner than later. Maybe this is a sign. Who is to say it wouldn't work in our favour to help out an equally unfavourable foe?" Drawing in an unrequired breath, he slaps Harold's hand off his arm and directs him toward the bushes. "Go ahead and cower, but this is something I must do."

Leaving Harold slack jaw, Julien takes off toward the glow of the fire breaking through the trees. He halts at the tree line, taking cover within the foliage. Slowly, Olivia creeps up behind him and stares out between the leaves. Her hand flies over her mouth as she gasps. The sight before them is something she's only read about. Never did she think she would witness such a thing firsthand.

Erected in the city centre is a large wooden cross. Two women hang by their necks from each end of the crossbar, and clearly, they've already perished, but the third is still alive. She's tied to the primary beam, her hands and feet bound together behind the main post. Olivia can't see her face with the sack over her head, but she can see her moving—she's definitely alive.

Julien takes another step closer. "It's so strange. I know I hold no friendships with any witches. But this one? She feels so—" He rubs his arm. "So familiar to me."

Harold laughs, laying his hand on his shoulder. "You have no friends among the *breathing*, Laurent. Now, come on. Snap out of it. We already have to find another herd thanks to you letting our deer get away."

Olivia's fear spikes as men toss dead brush at the woman's feet. She can hear the torch-bearing crowd's chant echoing through the forest—the mob's roar becoming increasingly unbearable. "Burn the witches! Burn them all!"

Julien attempts to leap, but Harold grabs his jacket and yanks him back, his voice a loud whisper. "You crazy son-of-a-bitch! Will you forget about the witch! You're going to get us torched, for crying out loud!"

"No. The other two are already dead, but they're going to burn that poor woman alive."

"She's not a bloody woman!" Harold yells, rubbing his forehead. He stares at Julien, throwing his arms out in disbelief. "Will you think about this for a minute? If this witch is so powerful, why isn't she saving herself? Huh?"

"I'm not sure." Julien tilts his head toward the city center. "But just listen for a moment. Her heart is unusually calm for someone in her position. I'm telling you, there is something special about this witch. I must save her."

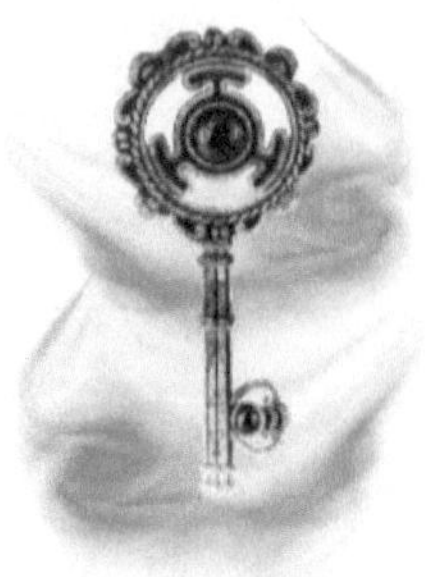

CHAPTER 16 ~ JULY 12TH, 1612
CONTINUES

Olivia's chest expands with hope, but then Harold throws his hands up, laughing contemptuously. "You've lost your bloody mind! She's ancient and certainly not worth your identity. No, let me rephrase that." His hand passes back and forth between them. "She's not worth **our** identity. For you to save her, it will take speed. Speed no human could possibly have. Those townspeople will be chanting off with the vamps head next." He throws his hand out toward the crowd gathered below and huffs. "Let them light the magic candle, and let's go find another deer."

A torch is tossed, igniting the pyre, and the sudden whoosh of flames causes Olivia's stomach to plummet. She turns back, but Julien's already gone. He's darting toward the city center, heading directly for the old woman on the cross.

Harold shakes his head, letting out a loud groan of annoyance as he takes off in the opposite direction, hollering back over his shoulder, "You're a damn fool, Laurent!"

Ignoring him, Julien leaps over the onset of fire, utterly oblivious that the once chanting crowd has grown deathly silent. *'Come on, Julien!'* Olivia urges as onlookers watch him extend his claws, slicing through the ropes that bind the old woman to the cross. He heaves her over his shoulder, then darts back into the forest, leaving a deafening silence, wide eyes and gaping jaws behind.

He's moving so fast that Olivia sees only a blurred shape as he passes. She's attempting to catch up when she's tugged off her feet by some kind of invisible tether. Within moments, Julien is striding alongside Harold as she loftily floats above.

"I've never known you to be so foolish, Laurent," he scowls, continuing to run. "You wasted a perfectly fine deer hunt and now managed to risk our very existence on a damned old witch!"

Olivia swats at him, huffing as her hand swipes through his head. *'Ugh! You selfish twat!'*

"Yeah, well, I've never known you to cower in a bloody bush nor take off running with your tail tucked like you did tonight," Julien scoffs, striding toward his castle on Laurent's Hill.

"I wasn't cowering! Never has any half-dead old witch been our concern! Consider for a minute how they constantly manage to get burned at the stake when they have these formidable powers. I'd say that's reason enough not to waste our time and abilities trying to save them. Either intelligence is not one of their strengths, or they've chosen to be there. Now, thanks to you, you stupid bastard, the townspeople will be looking for **us**!"

As they approach the castle, Julien slows his pace. "I'm sure no one was focused on my face." He stops in front of the gates and faces Harold. "Besides, you have nothing to be concerned about. **You** never left the safety of the woods."

Olivia squints against the darkness as Julien pushes open the heavy iron gates leading into the property. Her eyes immediately focus on the enormous round towers dominating the sky as the full moon illuminates the massive stone castle standing within. She follows the two vampires along the long gravel path, taking note of the family crest on each stone pillar as they pass.

When they reach the big iron doors, Julien sets the frail old woman on her feet and removes the sack from her head. With her smock torn and her face blackened from the smoke, she gazes up at him with an admiring smile. "Thank you. I am indebted to you." She turns toward Harold and scowls. "Contrary to what your friend here thinks. I promise you will not regret it."

Harold starts to speak when she steps forward, raising her crooked finger to his face. "Oh, hush, young man. I'll have you know that my powers are formidable enough to tell you how your greedy, hateful existence will come to an end." Her pale green eyes glisten, lighting with specks of gold as they stare into his. "You, Mr. Windsor, will die a horrendous death at the hands of a dear friend—a death that will be well deserved. You see, you can't hide what you've been doing forever."

Olivia is just as shocked by her words as Harold. Even Cassian takes a step back, unsure if this old witch might be able to see him and dish some undesirable fate his way, but that doesn't seem to be the case. As the shock of the old woman's words dissipates, Olivia can't help but smirk at Harold's unhinged jaw. After all, he was going to let her burn out there on that cross. He lunges as Julien steps between them to protect the old woman. "Whoa, hold on. I didn't save her so you could harm her."

"What do you mean, *hold on?* Didn't you just hear the old hag? She bloody hexed me!" He stretches his arm around Julien, shaking his finger. "You take that back, you scraggly old witch!"

She slowly shakes her head, calmly peering around Julien to meet his wild eyes. "I'm afraid I cannot, Mr. Windsor. That is your fate. It's not mine to change."

Olivia's not sure if the old woman has actually cursed him, has truthfully told him his fate or if she is just trying to scare him. Regardless, she has definitely struck a nerve. Thinking about that for a moment, she shifts her weight, folds her arms and stares at Harold. *'And quite frankly, your unease is rightfully earned if I do say so myself.'*

Slapping Harold on the shoulder, the corner of Julien's mouth tightens. "Come on now. Maybe you haven't noticed, but I am your only friend, and I have no desire to kill you" *—he shrugs, allowing his smile to fully surface—* "at least not yet."

"I'm glad you find this amusing," Harold scoffs, throwing his hand out toward the elderly witch. "You enjoy your evening with your new witch friend here. I'm leaving. I might see you tomorrow if the old hag's curse hasn't taken hold by then."

As the door closes behind Harold, Julien turns back to the old woman and gestures to a nearby chair. "Feel free to make yourself comfortable. You're safe here." He pulls a bottle of wine from the cabinet and holds it up. "Could I offer you a drink?"

Her eyes dart around the room, taking in the rich tapestries and paintings that adorn the stone walls. Then, scanning the high-arched ceiling, she nods. "Yes, thank you. I could use a drink to wash the taste of smoke from my tongue." She nervously wipes her frail hands down her filthy smock, turning her gaze to meet his. "Not that I'm not immensely grateful, but your friend had a valid point. Why would a vampire risk himself to save a withered old witch like me?"

Olivia's reoccurring dream and the story of her great-gran Ancina being saved by Julien Laurent flood her mind. She takes a good look at the old woman. Not that she has ever seen an actual portrait of her, but she does resemble the old woman from her dreams. The high cheekbones, the pert nose, and—Olivia squints to have a better look. *'And those eyes!'*

Julien tips his head slightly in her direction as he pours the wine. "Honestly, I'm not sure. I simply knew I couldn't turn away. There was a strange energy in the air—very strange indeed." He pauses, peering into the distance. "It was an exhilaration I've never felt before. Something familiar pulled me in your direction. It's difficult to explain, but I'd say it's similar to what I would experience if my primeval were in danger." His eyes scan the old woman curiously as he sets the bottle down. "I know that some may believe me to be heartless, and I have indeed done some unspeakable things—things I'm not proud of. However, I'd like to think I'm on a path to correcting my wrongs." His lips tighten as he drops his gaze. "I guess what I'm trying to say is that I may not have any witch friends, but that doesn't mean I'm opposed to your practices. In fact, now that I think of it, I'm not quite sure why our kinds don't get along."

She curls her fingers into a fist, resting her thumb against her lips and peers up at him. Her eyes search his face for a brief moment, then with a slow nod, she drops her hand and forces a smile. "I certainly don't believe you to be heartless, Mr. Laurent. After all, you did save me tonight. But surely you can't be so naïve as to not understand why our kinds don't get along. It has nothing to do with vampires being opposed to our practices. I'd say it's more that our blood is a delicacy. It can actually be addictive to your kind. Vampires gain twice the strength from feeding on a witch as they would from a human. Not to mention, you would gain some of your host's magical abilities for a very short spell. However, like any addiction, too much or too often could drive you mad."

Julien raises a brow, holding out a glass of wine. "Well, that is definitely knowledge I did not have." She graciously accepts the glass, holding it in both hands and dips her head. "I suppose it's lucky for both of us that I've already eaten then," he says, winking as he steps back.

A smile works across her lips. "Yes. I have been quite fortunate this evening, in more ways than one."

He returns her smile, taking a seat in the chair across from her. "I feel like I'm at a bit of a loss. It seems you already know who I am." He lifts his glass to his lips and pauses, his eyes searching her messy hair and soot-covered face. "Might I at least ask who I'll be sharing this glass of wine with this evening?"

The old woman peers down, swirling the contents of her glass. "Oh yes. I am quite aware of who you are, Mr. Laurent." She tips her head, finally meeting his gaze. "You're the first of the three original vampires created by the Divines fallen in the 14th century." Her eyes close as she nods. "And yes, I know you're not the evil one as some may believe." His brow lifts as he watches her take a drink, her pale green eyes meeting his as she continues. "Mmhmm. The creation of the three originals. I most definitely have heard the story. One powerful and noteworthy, one angelically beautiful, and the last devious to the bone."

"And I am aware which of the three you are, Mr. Laurent." Julien runs his finger around the rim of his chalice as he sits quietly, listening to her every word. "One bad apple truly can ruin the basket. I'm sure that's not a new phrase to you."

He lifts his gaze to hers. "I do believe I may have heard the phrase a time or two," he nods.

"The farmers often said it in the market when I was a girl. But, of course, that was a lifetime ago," she forces a smile. "Anyway, I understand all too well. The term witch is used quite loosely among the townies too. Most would have you believe anyone who doesn't attend church is a witch these days. But as I'm sure you know, that's simply not true. In my day, a witch meant someone who dealt with evil deeds. They would prefer to make you sick or even kill you." She pats her chest. "Me? I prefer to consider myself helpful—more of a cunning woman by nature."

"A cunning woman? Like a healer?"

"Mmhmm." She takes another sip of her wine and places her glass on the table between them. "Yes, indeed. Some do, in fact, call me a healer." Julien watches in amazement as she swirls her hand above her head, effortlessly tucking her messy hair neatly into place without ever touching a finger to it. "Well, at least that's what they call me to my face," she says with a toothy grin.

Olivia giggles as she follows her around the room, noticing she walks with a slight limp. She runs her hand along the mantle, her gaze fixing on the large family painting above the fireplace. "You have a lovely wife and children."

Julien stands, slipping his hand into the front pocket of his trousers, his head tipping slightly to the side as he clears his throat. "Thank you. Yes. Yes, I do. They're—"

"They're safe at your castle in France with Mr. Windsor's wife and child," she says, finishing his sentence. But when he shifts his weight, she places her hand over her mouth and glances back over her shoulder. "Oh, I'm sorry. Please, forgive me. Sometimes my sights slip right past my lips without a second thought."

Concern flashes across Julien's face for the first time this evening, and she turns to reassure him. "Please, Mr. Laurent, you have no need for concern. I was merely stating that you have a lovely family.

And, well, let's not forget you did just save my life tonight. Besides, I also have a child. Well, she's grown now with a child of her own, but they do always remain children to us, don't they?" Chuckling, she waves her hand in the air. "Ah, pay no mind to my ramblings. I'm an old woman, you know." Julien's shoulders relax, and her focus turns to two skeleton keys hanging from a chain near the mantle. Carefully lifting them from their hook, she holds them out to him. "These keys. They seem to yield no purpose. May I use them?"

Julien shrugs. "I don't see why not. They're just keys I had found on the grounds. I'm not even sure why I had kept them. You're certainly welcome to them if you feel they might be of use to you."

"Oh, the need for them is not for my personal gain," she says, making her way over to the sofa. She then smiles, gesturing toward the chair across from her. "Please, come join me."

Olivia walks over to stand behind Julien as she lays the keys on the table, and together, they watch as the old woman reaches into the pocket of her smock, pulling out two black stones. She carefully sets them into the hole at the top of each key and closes her eyes. Then, while uttering a few obscure words, she passes her hands above them.

The unlit torches hanging on the surrounding walls ignite. Julien's head shoots up to peer around, yet the old woman's focus remains on the keys. As symbols begin to appear along the key's shafts, Olivia speaks them aloud as each one emerges. "Earth – water – fire – air – spirit."

Helen is standing at the kitchen counter, stripping the buds from stems of lavender, when she hears Olivia's voice sing out behind her. She turns, watching Clara and Patricia sit forward. "Did she just name the elements?"

"Shh." Placing her finger to her lips, Clara nods. "She did, but by the look of it, she's still deep inside the journal."

Patricia tips her head toward Cassian. "Yep." She slumps back down in her chair. "And he still seems lost in her mind."

"Then I guess we'll have to wait," Clara says, turning her focus back to her book.

CHAPTER 17 ~ SOLOMAN

The old woman stills above the keys, a slight glow emanating beneath. When she finally pulls her hand away, the top has been transformed into Hecate's wheel with the tiny stone sealed in the center. Olivia's eyes grow wide as she places her hand over her mouth. She's never witnessed this type of magic, at least not firsthand.

Remaining silent, Julien watches as she pokes the end of her finger with one of her rings. She then squeezes the tip, letting the golden fluid drip on each stone. *'Gold blood, just like in my dream,' Olivia mutters.*

Her sight fixes somewhere in the distance, and she begins to mumble, passing her hands over the keys. As one hand hovers, the other reaches out toward his chest. With her fingertips pressed together, she twists her hand and inhales. The candles flicker, and Julien pushes back against his chair as a vibrant blue string threads from his chest into one of the keys. Lifting slightly, it falls back to the table as she drops her hands.

Finally, she leans back and expels a great breath. Her thin fingers reach down and grab the chain, holding the keys in the air. "When worn, the key not only will increase your strength, but most plebs, regardless of their sire, shall acknowledge you as their sovereign, abiding by your laws. Of course, there are bound to be rogues, but the majority shall be set on following your rule. However, this key's hidden beauty and main purpose is to resurrect a soul." She holds up one of the keys. "This one can serve any human, witch, or vampire, as I've garnished it with a sliver of my own essence." She lifts the second key and twirls it, letting the light of the moon reflect off the stone. "But, this one has been fused with yours. Therefore, it can only resurrect an original like yourself." She smiles, her head bobbing as if to answer his thoughts. "Oh yes, Mr. Laurent, the originals retained their souls."

Her smile broadens as she continues. "These keys will bring back the soul when used against any part of the deceased body. That means these" —*she lets the keys drop on the chain, swaying them in front of her*— "can undo a vampire's worst nightmare. They will recall the body at its time of departure and fully recreate it. Of course, there will be a few requirements, but nothing unattainable for your family."

He points at the keys. "Are you saying—"

"I'm saying that vampires, like any witch, human, or creature, require a prominent figurehead to rule their world, and as I see it, there is none more worthy than you, Mr. Laurent." He attempts to speak when she raises her hand. "I am aware of the things you have done while adjusting to your new life, but I'm also aware of how well you've adapted." She smiles. "The vampire population requires your strength and knowledge, and this key will ensure you have the ability to reign over your kind for an eternity." Pursing her lips, she tips her head to the side. "Mind you, there is one small catch."

"Catch?"

"Mmhmm. The key-bearing sovereign must only speak the truth." Smiling, she peers up to meet his gaze. "You can withhold information for the greater good, but a blatant lie you will be unable to tell. You can try, but the words simply will not form."

A small smirk tugs at the corner of Julien's mouth. "I can live with that." He runs his hand down his chest. "You mentioned the key is fused." His sight narrows on the golden charm. "The blue string?"

"Yes." She nods. "It's fused with the tiniest sliver of your soul. But, not to worry, Mr. Laurent, that's nothing you might miss, nor does it change you in any way." She closes her eyes, sitting silently for a moment. "I sense other vampires here in the castle. It might only be me, but I find it odd that they haven't come to greet the fresh blood. I'm sure they must be able to hear the ichor singing through my veins," she smiles.

Olivia's eyes narrow as she studies the old woman. *'Ichor? As in the royal blood of the God's?'*

"Ichor?" Folding his arms across his chest, Julien throws his hand out. "That explains the golden colour of your blood and why I was so drawn to you. I felt the energy." He rubs his arm. "Like nothing I've ever encountered before." Staring at her, he shakes his head. "Then you're a direct descendant of the Goddess?"

The old woman nods.

"Remarkable. I am truly honoured to be in your presence. Though please, I can assure you there's no need to fear the vampires on Laurent Hill. They only drink what our donors offer freely. Believe it or not, some humans rather enjoy a vampire's bite." Lowering his head, he picks up his drink. "I may not have always been an ideal sire, but as you noted, I have changed. I have now seen all my creations through their transition and helped them control their hunger." He holds his glass up. "I can assure you, you are safe here."

"I have no doubt of that." Smiling, she grabs the chain, dangling the keys in the air. "I am forever grateful for your kindness and hospitality. If there is anyone who can appreciate the recent change in your character, Mr. Laurent, it truly is me. For that reason and many others, I believe you have a soul worth preserving. We wouldn't want to ever see the likes of someone such as Mr. Windsor have a chance as sovereign. That could be catastrophic, especially to my kind." Her gaze moves to the large picture window. "I'd like to show you how these work since we are so fortunate to have the grace of the full moon on our side this evening."

"You really don't owe me anything. Simply knowing your name would give me great pleasure." Julien leans back, studying her face. "I can't help but feel a familiarity about you." He extends his hand in her direction, his lips tight with thought. "I'm unable to put my finger on it at the moment though I think maybe it's your eyes."

Shaking her head, she forces a smile and looks away. "My name is unimportant, Mr. Laurent, but I can promise you will know it before I leave. For now, why don't you call me what everyone else does— Old Hattox."

Olivia's jaw drops. *'It can't be.'*

"Old Hattox?" Julien's brows raise into his hair.

"Yes," she responds casually, placing her hand on the table. "Now, what do you say I show you some real magic?"

Dipping his head, Julien peers at her through his lashes. "With those keys? Aren't they to be used on a corpse?"

"Yes," she says matter of factly.

"But—"

Old Hattox rolls her eyes toward the ceiling as she falls back in her chair with laughter. "Not on you, Mr. Laurent. I want you to witness how they work. You certainly can't do that if you're dead. Now, can you? However, your primeval is perfect for such a purpose. I do sense his presence, don't I?"

He leans back with wide eyes. "Yes, but you can't be serious? You want to kill Soloman?!"

"Yes. Or, well, now that I think of it, maybe it would be best if *you* did. It would be much quicker that way, but, of course, whatever makes you most comfortable." Julien attempts to speak when she raises her hand, dangling the keys in front of her. "I assure you, there is nothing to be concerned about. He'll be back to his old self within a few minutes and none the wiser. But being your first creation, he has the strongest blood tie to you outside one of your sons."

Clearly, Julien is just as stunned as Olivia. He sits motionless with his hand fisted against his lips. Olivia shakes her head, her eyes bouncing wildly between them as she pleads pointlessly with the ancient vampire. *'Please don't, Julien. What if she can't bring him back?'*

Pale green eyes meet his with a note of sincerity that Julien finds hard to ignore. "I need you to understand the significance of this gift I'm giving you. These keys play a vital part in your future, Mr. Laurent. You have my word that I will bring him back. If for some reason I fail, and I won't, you have my permission to drain me."

His brows draw together, creating heavy creases in his forehead. "Let's be clear. I have no intention of draining you." Running his hand over his beard, he paces behind his chair before finally turning to face her. "Surely, there must be another way. Clarentina would never forgive me if something happened to Soloman. He's not only my first creation but a loyal member of our family."

"Mr. Laurent, not that the intention is there, but the fact remains as swiftly as you saved my life tonight—you're capable of taking it. I have even offered it to you if I fail. That should be enough to assure you of my abilities. Please. You must trust me."

Julien stares at her, his head slowly shaking from side to side. "Damn it. I have no idea why I'm agreeing to this." He removes his sword above the mantle and positions himself next to the doorway. Closing his eyes, he expands his chest, calling for his first and most trusted creation. "Soloman! Could you come to the den for a moment, please?"

As requested, Soloman steps through the door, and Julien draws back his sword. Olivia squeezes her eyes shut with the swift swoosh of his blade, and she cringes at the accompanying thud of Soloman's head tumbling to the floor. Her eyes spring open as his body teeters, and the old woman raises her crooked finger, sending his corpse back against Julien's chest.

He drops his sword, letting it clatter to the floor as he wraps his arms around Soloman's headless body. "Jesus Soloman, forgive me. This feels so wrong, my friend." His gaze meets the old woman's. "That damn key better work."

Olivia hangs her head. *'Oh, Julien. This is wrong on so many levels.'*

"Don't fret, Mr. Laurent. He won't recall this moment." She swings her arm out toward the table. "Bring his body over here by the window, and he'll be back to his old self before you know it."

Dragging Soloman's body over to the window, Julien lays him on the table. He cringes as she picks up his head and lays it against his severed neck. "The entire body is always nice to have when available, but it's not necessary for these keys to work." She hands him the chain. "Could you remove one for me, please?"

Removing the key, Julien holds them out to her. She grabs his hand, holding up her pointed ring. "May I? I require just a few drops."

Opening his hand, she pricks the end of his finger, letting a few drops of his dark blood drip into her palm. Then using it like paint, she draws the five elements on Soloman's flesh and tips the rest on the stone of one of the keys. Turning the key until the moon's glow reflects off the bloodied gem, she lays it over the severed pieces. "There. Now, just stay silent."

Closing her eyes, she slowly moves her hands over Soloman's body. Her voice rises and lowers with each change of direction. The key's stone begins to shine, becoming brighter as the metal takes on a golden glow. Olivia and Julien watch in awe as his body appears to ripple like wind over the water. His knees suddenly bend and fall back to the table with a thud—his abdomen expanding and deflating like a balloon. Still, the old woman continues chanting, unaffected by the grotesque display beneath her hands.

As a loud hum fills the air, every hair on Olivia's body stands on end. She steps back, watching a smokey fog drop over Soloman, lingering just above his chest. The fog lasts only moments before it dissipates, and the hum subsides. Julien tips his head, examining his friend. He opens his mouth, but before he can speak, a magnificent glow sprouts from the key—a blinding flash, nearly as bright as the sun. As it disperses, golden spikes move along the gash, flawlessly welding Soloman's flesh together. When the arcs fade, his wound is sealed, and the charred key clatters to the floor.

Olivia stares over at old Hattox in disbelief. She possesses a kind of magical power that Olivia has never seen before—the type of magic that has only ever existed to her in fairytales.

The old woman opens her eyes and looks down at the newly mended Soloman with a smile. She drops her arms, her eyes slowly drift shut with the slump of her shoulders, and she begins to fall. Narrowly catching her, Julien gently sets her down in the chair and jumps as the table jolts next to them. Now sitting, the big vampire looks dazed as he clears his throat and grips the wooden edges. "Sir? I fear to ask, but why might I be on the table?"

With a nervous laugh, Julien spins to meet the onyx stare of his house steward—his primeval vamp—his friend. He eagerly reaches his hand out with a gracious smile. "Ah, Soloman! It's great to have you back."

Swinging his legs over the side of the table, Soloman squeezes his eyes shut. "Back?" He squints, focusing on his sire. "I'm not sure I understand, Sir. Where exactly might I have gone?"

Slowly lifting her head, the old woman pats Soloman's hand. "You didn't go anywhere, young man. You merely fainted." With her other hand open, she twirls each finger into her palm one by one, clearing any blood from his body and the room with each dropping digit.

"Fainted?" The shock rings in Soloman's tone as he hops off the table. "But I'm a vampire," he says, rubbing the back of his neck. "I've never heard of such a thing. Could I have drank bad blood? Maybe we have some old stock."

"Oh, come now, Soloman. I'm sure our supply is just fine."

"Well, something must be wrong. The last thing I recall is you requesting my service." He scans the room. "But strangely enough" — *he shakes his head, motioning toward the entry of the den*— "I can't recall anything beyond entering that doorway." He stares down at the table. "Though I must say, the most disturbing image keeps flashing through my mind since I found myself sprawled out on this here table." His eyes narrow on Julien. "One of you lopping off my head."

Julien takes a step back, his eyes darting to the old woman before releasing a nervous laugh. "Have you gone mad, my friend? Me? Lopping off your head?" Julien pats him on the back, raising a brow as he nods. "One thing is for sure. That image certainly is a disturbing one."

Sitting forward, the old woman takes a sip of her wine. "I'm sorry, Soloman. I believe I should take full responsibility for this mishap. I've been working on a spell and wanted to show Mr. Laurent, but, unfortunately, these things tend to get away from me now and then. I do apologize if it played tricks with your mind." With her ring's point, she cuts the soft pad on the side of her hand and holds out her palm. "Here, have a sip of my blood. It will help clear any chaos it may have caused."

He stares at the golden syrup, licking his lips before shaking his head, then waves her off. "No, thank you, Madame. I could never indulge in such a generous offer. Besides, I'm sure there's nothing to worry about." His hands run along his neck as he peers between the old woman and Julien. "Thankfully, my head is still intact."

She places her hand directly under his nose. "No, truly, I insist."

Soloman's gaze slides to Julien for approval. "Go ahead, Soloman. This is indeed a very kind offering from such a powerful woman."

He bends to lick the small pool of ichor from Ancina's palm, and they watch a golden glow flash through his onyx eyes. "Thank you, Madame." Soloman bows slightly, his sight landing on the blackened key on the floor in front of him. Picking it up, he holds it out, twirling it between his thumb and forefinger.

"Ah! There it is," Ancina chimes as she leans forward with her hand out. "Thank you, young man. I do believe that belongs to me."

His eyes float between Julien and the old witch curiously before dropping it into her palm with a tense smile. "My pleasure, Madame." He bends slightly, his gaze meeting Julien's. "Well then, I suppose I shall retire to my chambers, Sir. That is if you no longer require me."

"Of course." Watching him walk from the room in perfect condition, Julien shakes his head. "That is the most incredible thing I have ever witnessed!" He runs his hand over his beard, still staring at the empty doorway. "I would never have believed such a thing possible before this evening."

CHAPTER 18 ~ OLD HATTOX

Old Hattox takes another sip of her wine, wiping her chin with the back of her hand. "I'm not convinced that *anything* is completely impossible, Mr. Laurent. I may have thought so at one time, and I'm almost certain the townspeople thought you saving me tonight was an impossibility." She smiles. "You know, I had an aunt that swore she could wander in and out of her body to travel through time." A cackle resonates from her throat as she throws her head back. "Of course, we all thought she was a bit crazy, but she was a powerful old woman, just the same." She runs her crooked finger around the top of her wine glass and tilts her head toward him with a grin. "When I think about it now, maybe she could. I guess it's all perception. I have visions of what I believe is the future, but I would never claim to have travelled there." Sitting silently for a minute, she runs her knuckles along her chin. "Anyway, even having such a gift would not have prevented me from being on that cross tonight."

Julien tips his head, peering at her through narrowed eyes. "Really, why do you say that? I know if I could see into the future and was about to be dealt with such a misfortune, I would figure out a way to avoid it."

"Nope. As much as we'd like to think we can tamper with our destinies, we cannot. Only fate gets to decide. Besides, I knew you would save me, for our paths have been intertwined for centuries."

"How so?"

"Come, let me show you." She reaches her hands out, wiggling her fingers. "You wouldn't believe me by my words alone."

He slowly leans forward, eyeing her hands as she reaches to rest them on either side of his head. "That's it. Now, just close your eyes," her voice is low and sweet as the images begin to appear.

Julien and Olivia gasp in unison. The visions Old Hattox is projecting may only be meant for Julien, but Olivia can see them too.

A beautiful young woman appears—a well-tanned Julien at her side. She's selling baked goods from a rickety wooden cart at the waterfront, with a cat curled around her ankle. Julien pulls away and leans back in his chair, heavy creases settling between his eyes as he studies the old woman questionably. "Can you not see," she asks, with a tilt of her head.

Curling his hand over his beard, he nods. "Yes. Yes, I can see. She was my first love. A beautiful young girl, but that was centuries ago." His hand drops and his eyes follow it to his lap. He sits silently for a minute, then lifts his head with a forced smile. "I was human then."

The old woman taps his knee. "Come, Mr. Laurent, please." Circling her hand, she motions for him to lean forward. "I'm not done. If you allow me to continue, this will all make sense in a few moments."

His eyes close as he leans back in, and her hands once again press against his head, allowing the images to commence. The same sweet girl runs crying through the muddy streets of London, cat licking at her heels as she covers her nose from the stench of rotting flesh.

Julien looks up. "I recall that year well – 1348. The year of my birth as a vampire."

The tiniest of a smile dances on her lips. "Shhh. Please, pay attention, Mr. Laurent."

A young priest stands before the young girl telling her that Julien had succumbed to the blue sickness. She sloshes through the mud and the rain, searching the face of each body left in the dank streets. Drenched, she stares at the fresh mounds of dirt surrounding her—the mass graves of those never to be named. Sobbing uncontrollably, she kneels next to the enormous yew tree they used to share lunch under.

Julien lifts his head, his chin quivering as he meets her eyes — the same pale green eyes he had stared into centuries ago. He reaches for her trembling fingers, brushing his thumbs over the top of her hands. "Annie Whittle?"

She nods, a slight smile tightening the wrinkles around her lips. "Yes."

He sits back, examining her face. "But how?" Letting her hands slide from his, he stands and walks over to the large window. "How is that possible? I haven't seen you," he glances back, turning his hand out toward her, "or, well, Ancina in nearly three centuries."

'Great- Gran Ancina!' Olivia places her hand over her mouth. *'Gran never mentioned they knew each other before he saved her.'*

She struggles to smile. "If you let me, I can show you. I wouldn't know how to tell you."

He kneels in front of her and takes her hands, placing them against his head. "Yes. Show me. Please."

Twenty-year-old Ancina stands beside a fire pit. Her trusted cat Paene is at her side as she tosses herbs into a large pot of boiling water. She's speaking in a tongue Olivia knows she shouldn't understand, but each word seeps in as if she's heard it her entire life. As Ancina reaches into the steam, misty fingers begin to crawl over her body until they envelop her entirely. Bolts of energy shoot from the fog in all directions, and when the air finally clears, nothing but the boiling pot and Paene remain.

Julien sits back, his brows tight with confusion. "I had no idea you were a—" He stops, tipping his head to the side. "I mean, it all makes sense now that I have felt your energy, heard your magic sing and witnessed the" *—he pauses, pointing toward her hands—* "the golden nectar. But I had no idea you descended from a Goddess."

"It wasn't something I could openly share. Much like today, I would have been hunted down. Sacrificed for the good of all mankind. We, too, are an abomination, you know," she chuckles, the corner of her mouth tightening. "Regardless, when I found out I lost you to the sickness—" her eyes fall to her hands in her lap. "Well, vampires didn't exist back then, or at least not that I knew of, and I lost everyone I cared about except Paene." She draws a deep breath. "All the power in the world means nothing when you're alone, but I had no physical way to end my days. Then I recalled the words of my grandmother. She told me almost daily that I was one of the 'hidden ones'— that Paene was my divitias immortales or my immortal treasure. I searched her old grimoire and found a spell marked with my name." Closing her eyes, Ancina shrugs. "I had nothing to lose, so I waited till the full moon and tried it."

"So this" —*Julien gestures to her ageing form*— "this look is some kind of masking spell?"

Her head bobs from side to side. "I suppose one could call it that." Holding her arthritic hand out, she turns it over for examination. "I only appear in human form to those close to me. Those I have chosen to hold within my heart over the centuries. I live among mankind as I choose now. Though my life, as Ancina Whittle, at least as anyone would have known me, that has most definitely well passed."

Julien presses his fist to his lips and shakes his head. "I'm not sure I follow. How are you here now?"

"I am here now because of you. The details are not important, Julien." Her eyes soften as they meet his. "I'd like to ask a question, and I hope you don't think me disrespectful for it."

"Of course not." He shakes his head. "Anything."

"The creation of the three originals has always been such a well-kept secret."

His eyes shift as he slowly wipes his thumb over his bottom lip. "It's not something I've ever shared. Nor do I believe any of the others have." Retrieving her glass, he walks over to pour them more wine. He glances up, though his gaze never entirely meets hers as he speaks. "Harold and I docked a few days earlier than we anticipated. During the two weeks it took us to sail from France, we accumulated several dead crew members and passengers. They began dying the day we left Marseilles. By the time we arrived in London, Harold had begun vomiting blood. I couldn't get warm, and the headache was nearly enough to blind me. I knew we were in trouble." He places her glass of wine on the table in front of her and settles into his chair.

"The shore was lined with clergymen awaiting our arrival. Presumably to give everyone the last rites." Julien leans back in his chair and stares into his glass. "Three of us were taken to an old decaying cabin next to the port. Harold, myself and a young passenger from Marseilles, Clarentina."

"Your wife," she says, taking up her glass of wine.

"Yes," Julien smiles. He takes a generous drink from his glass and sets it on the table between them before continuing. "A young priest lit a candle and told me to lie down on a bed of straw while two others helped Harold and Clarentina into the cabin. He offered me a drink of water, pushed a bucket next to me, said a prayer, and they left us to die." Julien shakes his head. "I will never forget the stench in that cabin. I'm positive many had perished in there before us." He swallows, wiping his hand over his mouth.

"Sometime during the night, I woke to a fully cloaked dark figure by my side. At first, I thought it to be one of the priests, but his lips never moved as he spoke. It was as if his voice echoed in my head. He said he could feel my struggle and that it wouldn't be long before I would succumb to my illness, but he could cure me." Stroking the stem of his wine glass, Julien looks up, the corner of his mouth tightening. "He did warn there would be a price—a small price is what he said." Forcing a smile, he lowers his head. "I never questioned the price. The offer came when I was at my weakest with a promise that I would forever be strong and safe from any future illness. All you have to do is say yes, he said." Peering up at Ancina, his eyes hold hers. "I was delusional and gave it little thought, if any. I just wanted to survive—to feel better. Then, before I knew it, I heard myself saying *yes*."

Julien places his glass down and stands. "Seeing him slice his boney wrist and offer it to me, I should have refused to drink from it. But I didn't. Instead, I found the coolness of his dark blood soothing." Running his hand over his beard, he turns to face her, finally meeting her gaze. "As he disappeared, his voice rang through my head with words I will never forget. *'Beginning tonight, you will live by the moon or burn by the sun. When hunger pains you, only the blood of a human will sate you. I've given you many gifts that you have an eternity to discover, my child. Be wise with your immortality.'* I tried to speak, but it was nothing more than a grating noise. As my eyes closed, my only thought was that I had just surrendered to the devil. That I was forever damned."

Olivia clasps her hands to her lips as Ancina swipes a tear from her cheek. "You're a good man, Julien. Not even the fallen could turn you completely evil."

He drops his gaze. "Don't be so sure. When I woke the following morning, I thought it was all a dream. Then Harold shifted, and it was as if all my senses heightened at once. I had to cover my ears. The distant clatter of dishes, the smell of the spice cart and fish near the port, feet shuffling across the stone pathway, and the steady heartbeats of every patron that passed. The sounds and smells were so intense. But none more appealing than the unsuspecting bypassers."

Julien paces the length of the room, his stare lost in the memory. "The door swung open, and the doctor's heartbeat hammered in my head like a drum. He smelled of sweat, dank linen and sweet copper, and though that may not sound appealing to you, that morning, it's all I wanted. I recall swallowing hard, trying to push back my vile thoughts, but when he leaned over to listen to my chest. I could see the blood coursing through the artery in his neck. My stomach ached. A pain that I could never describe. The need to taste his blood." He shakes his head at the memory. "Then, in a movement quicker than I thought ever possible, I tore into his vein. Draining him of his life."

"You can't blame yourself for your survival instinct, Julien. That doesn't make you evil." Her gaze drops to her hands, picking at the hem on her smock. "Am I correct to assume Clarentina and Harold were created the same night?"

"Yes." Julien takes her hand. "I hope you understand why I couldn't come back for you. I didn't know how to explain what happened to me, and I couldn't trust myself around humans." He bows his head. "It took a long time to understand my hunger and to control it," he wipes his hand down his face, "well, that is a whole other story."

"In no way did I believe you left me without word or reason." She offers him a smile. "I knew better. So when the priest told me you died of the blue sickness." She peers up at him, her eyes glistening as she shakes her head. "Well, with the plague ravaging our village, I never doubted him."

His brows draw together. "How did we ever find each other after all these years?"

"I suppose we must thank fate." Closing her eyes, she shrugs. "I first saw you during a fire scry only a couple of nights ago. I couldn't believe my eyes. As I said, I made peace with the idea you were dead, but then there you were."

Stepping back, Julien sits in the chair across from her and folds his hands in his lap. "Ancina, as you know, I'm married with children now."

She leans forward and grabs her wine glass with a chuckle. "Yes, Julien, and as you can see, I came as an old woman. One merely hoping to make peace with her past. I certainly don't want you to think my intentions were to disrupt your family." She takes a sip of her wine and sets her glass on the table. "Though I do believe that our destinies were meant to be entwined for a greater purpose. Why else would fate finally place you in my path tonight? You could have been anywhere in the world."

"True, though I'm thankful I was able to be there."

"Not more than me." Laughing, she shakes her head. "Though, can you imagine my surprise when I felt the cool touch of a vampire carrying me to safety?"

His head tips back with laughter. "Yes, I can imagine how shocking that must have been for you."

As their laughter subsides, she reaches across the table, holding her hand out to him. "You must miss the daylight. I recall how much you loved the sun. Can I see your hand?"

Julien places his hand in hers, and she pricks his fingertip with her ring, smearing the dark red blood around the tip. She closes her eyes, her voice somewhat of a hum as she begins to speak in the same old tongue she had projected earlier. He shivers, and she opens her eyes.

"Cold?"

His shoulders draw upward. "No. It's the oddest tingle. I felt it when I saw you through the trees from the Lancashire forest."

"Ah, yes. That would be our souls calling to each other." She licks the blood from the tip of his finger. "There. Now your bloodline will never have to fear the sun's rays again." A warm smile works across her lips. "Not to worry. Sharing your blood with your wife will allow her the same benefits."

Shifting in his seat, he peers up from under his brows. "You can read my mind?"

Ancina rolls her eyes. "Please. Did you honestly believe only vampires could hear another's thoughts?" She slowly rises to her feet and hobbles over to the window. Her voice is calm as she peers out at the full moon. "Oh, there is one last thing I want to be clear about. Your friend Mr. Windsor. I did not hex him."

His brows draw together as his smile fades. "Are you saying that was a real vision?"

She draws her shoulder up into a shrug. "Fate works in mysterious ways, Julien."

"But—"

Ancina holds her hand up. "I will tell you this much. Your friend Mr. Windsor has not only been going against your rule not to keep feeders against their will, but he has been slowly draining a witch. I believe his hope is to gain enough power to claim your throne by beheading the sovereign."

"But I have sons. He would have to kill us all," Julien says, shaking his head.

Closing her eyes, Ancina nods. "Yes." She takes a breath and reaches for her wine. "But I mustn't say anymore. I have already said much more than I should have." She finishes her wine, sets down her empty glass and hands him the remaining key. "I feel like I have accomplished what fate had intended tonight. I believe we've both made peace with our pasts. Please take care of the gifts I've given you. Somehow, I'm sure the Laurent and Whittle paths will cross again. Let's hope our bloodlines can work together." She blows him a kiss. "I have never stopped loving you, Julien Laurent." Finally, she waves her hand toward the table, leaving two scrolls and a leather-bound journal behind.

Olivia looks down at the gifts left by Ancina as her final words echo through her head. 'I'm sure the Laurent and Whittle paths will cross again. Let's hope our bloodlines can work together.' A smile nestles comfortably on her lips as she looks around the room. *'Oh, you've made sure our paths would cross again. Haven't you, great Ancina?'*

As Julien stares off in the direction where she had been standing, a slight smile tugs at the corner of his mouth. "I'm not sure if you can hear me, Ancina, but it was wonderful to see you again." He picks up the first scroll and unties the red ribbon.

Hurrying to his side, Olivia peers at the ancient scripture. It contains instructions along with the incantation required to perform the resurrection. Unfortunately, before she has a chance to read it through, Julien rolls it back up and excitedly grabs the second scroll. Sliding the ribbon off, he eagerly unrolls it.

My Dearest Julien,

I have granted you the resurrection key as a token of gratitude for the kindness shown tonight and to protect the kind soul I have always known you to be. There are a few minor details you must remember. It can only be used once, and it will only be successful as long as you don't allow yourself to resort back to the dark individual Mr. Windsor seemed so fond of. If at any time the key loses its golden glow, your soul has forever turned, and it will no longer be viable.

Along with the key, I have granted you a Timekeeper journal. This indestructible diary will record specific events in your life, starting with tonight's events.

Do not write in the journal, for the timekeeper can see all and will automatically record whatever may be necessary to convince its master to work their magic. Don't be alarmed if you cannot see the entries after tonight. When the time comes, I assure you all will be revealed to the intended eyes.

Be sure to keep these scrolls hidden well and separate from the journal. The master of the Timekeeper will be able to locate them when required.

Forever yours,
Ancina.

Running his hand across the top of the journal, Julien slowly opens the cover to the initial entry.

England – July 12th, 1612 – Julien Laurent—SOV.

He reads the first couple of paragraphs, confirming the evening events of him and Harold on their deer hunt. Then closing the cover, he holds up the chain with the remaining key. The light of the moon shines on the naturally black stone, casting a million golden stars across the walls as it twists in his hand. And when he finally slips the chain over his head, and the metal comes to rest against his chest, his shoulders rise. An unmistakable aura of strength surrounds him— the key supplying a type of power that cannot be denied.

He gathers the scrolls and the journal and heads for his bed chamber. Placing the two scrolls into the wall safe behind the large painting of his two sons, he resets the picture and slides the journal up on the bookshelf. "Thank you, Ancina."

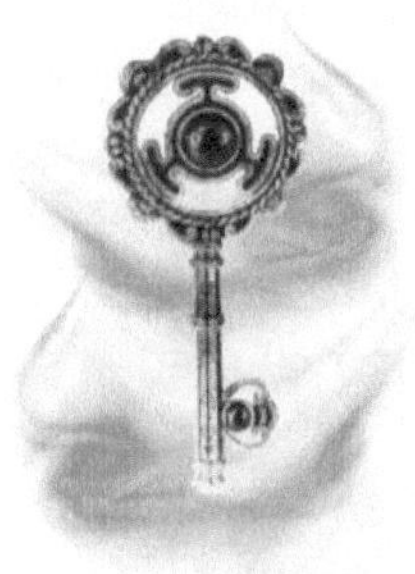

CHAPTER 19 ~ APOLOGY

The room goes dark, and Cassian opens his eyes. As he leans back in his chair, Helen springs forward. "What is it? What does she see?"

Blinking, he runs the back of his fingers across his jaw, his eyes scanning the ladies around the table. "Some century-old details have come to light, but unfortunately, nothing that will help just yet." Rubbing his hands along his thighs, he presses his back against his chair and peers over at Olivia. "She's been in there an awfully long time. Maybe we should pull her out of there for today."

"Finally, we agree on something." Patricia slaps her hands off the table. "That's the smartest thing you've said since you got here, bloo—" She stops herself, gracing him with a smirk. "Vampire."

As Clara shakes her head, Olivia's arm shoots into the air, the journal falling to the floor with a thud. "The safe," she yells.

Jumping, Patricia runs to her side, wrapping her arms around her. "Thank goodness you're back, Liv. You had us all worried."

"Gingiberi ti citrea," Helen says with a slight wave of her hand. A steaming cup of lemon ginger tea appears in front of her. "You must be thirsty, honey. Have a sip and tell us all about your adventure."

Clara peers over at Cassian. "The safe?"

Before he can answer, Olivia sits forward with wide eyes. "Yes! The scrolls are in the safe! Julien put them there." Her distant stare moves to his. "Behind a painting of you and your brother." She glances down at the old leather book at her feet. "He didn't hide the journal, just slid it into the bookshelf," she shrugs. "But I guess if no one can read it, it wouldn't have mattered."

His lips tighten into a smile as he nods. "I'm afraid the safe in Stepney has already been cleared. Though you're right. The journal was where he had left it. Completely untouched for centuries. I actually had no idea of any scrolls until just now. We had heard the story of the journal, even found it when we packed up the remnants of the castle, but our focus has been searching for the key. Roger had taken it, and we believe he still has it, but he's somehow been able to remain hidden."

Olivia picks up the journal and flips open the cover. "I can see if his name is on the list. There were only a couple left that I hadn't read."

A hand falls on the book before she can open her mouth. "Wait." Patricia leans over, covering the page. "You are not reading them out loud. The last thing we need is you summoning any more vampires here.

"I know." She pushes her hand aside to look over the list, but there's no Roger. "I actually only see two other names. In fact, I don't even see Ancina's name on here." Closing the cover, she sits back and takes a sip of her tea. "Maybe the list only names within your bloodline?" She squints up at Cassian. "Soloman, I remember Ancina saying Julien created him."

"Yes, before I was born. He's been our house steward for centuries."

"Who is Gabriel? I haven't seen him yet."

"My sired brother. He was turned by my father when he was eighteen." Shaking his head, he runs his hand over his mouth. "It's a long story" —*he points to the journal*— "one that may even come up in there, but he was our childhood friend." A shocked intake of breath comes from the opposite side of the table, and Cassian peers over at Patricia's wide eyes. "It's not as you may think. He was ill, had no one and was hours from death. My father wouldn't have turned him if he hadn't wanted it."

Helen's eyes droop as her smile fades. "Oh, the poor thing."

Cassian smiles over at her. "Yes, well, thanks to my father, he's fine now."

Resting her cheek in her palm, Helen taps her pinky against her nose. "Wouldn't they both be your sired brothers then?"

He leans back in his chair, studying her face for a moment. "Yes. I suppose you're right. Though I've never thought of Soloman as such. I've always known him as our trusted house steward."

Patricia slaps her hand off the table, raising her voice above the chatter. "All right, enough with the vamp family history. Don't you think we should find out what Olivia saw in this damn thing?"

Helen shrugs nonchalantly. "Cash already said it was nothing that would help."

Olivia turns to glare at her, and silence falls over the room. "How would Cash even know?" Her stare quickly shifts in his direction. "You were inside my head? So I'm not your interpreter. I'm like your personal movie projector."

"Now, Olivia, calm down. I asked him to check on you," Clara says, reaching for her hand, but she pulls away.

Pushing herself from the table, she glares at her grandmother. "Then why not just ask him what's in there? What do you need me for?" She throws her arms in the air. "Oh, right. He can only see it through me."

"Liv, wait," Patricia stands, but Olivia shoves past her continuing up the stairs. "Ugh!" she groans. "Well, now, that's just great. Obviously, she thinks I was part of this little plan too."

"She's fine. She just needs to get some rest." Clara turns to Cassian. "Maybe you could enlighten us. What was it that she saw?"

His eyes shift from the staircase, meeting her gaze as he leans forward to rest his chin on his clasped hands. "No disrespect, Ms. Redfearn, but it's not my place to tell you what unfolded while she was inside. She's the interpreter—the master of the journal, if you will.

Therefore, just as I shouldn't divulge anything that might interfere with the process, I believe it should be only her that shares its contents." Standing, he taps the table with the tips of his fingers. "I will say this. In the small portion I witnessed today, I learned things about my family that even I didn't know. I'm sure you will learn just as much once Olivia is ready to tell you what she has seen. Now, if you'll excuse me, I have an apology to make."

Cassian stands, his shoulders slumping as he makes his way up the stairs. "What do you think he means by that," Helen asks, turning her attention to her mother.

"I believe he may actually feel guilty for being in her head uninvited," Patricia says, resting her cheek on her hand.

"That's not what I meant," Helen snarls, rolling her eyes. "I meant about us learning much about our family that we didn't know."

"I'm not sure." Clara pulls her teacup toward her and stares into the steaming liquid. "I suppose we'll have to ask Olivia."

"Well, this is just great!" Patricia leans back, throwing her arms into the air. "You wanna remind me again why he had to be inside her head while she was reading? Now she doesn't trust her own damn family!"

Clara is about to take a drink of her tea when she sets her cup down and glares over at her daughter. "Because we have no real idea how this journal truly works. Did you know she could summon vampires by reading their names?" Without allowing for an answer, she raises her hand. "Exactly. None of us did. At least with Cash watching, if something happened to her in there, he could alert us or perhaps help pull her out. He was our safety net—Olivia's safety net." Tipping her head, she clasps her cup with both hands and slowly lifts it to her lips. "Or at least that was the thought."

Slowly making his way upstairs, the eyes in the pictures that line the walls follow Cassian's every move. And as he finally steps onto the top landing, a low chatter of voices fills the hallway. "I should inform you that I have pristine hearing. So stop mumbling. If you have something to say to me, go on and say it already."

"If they wanted you to hear, they would speak up."

He turns toward the deep voice at the far end of the hall. However, the only thing in that vicinity is a plaster bust of a man in a top hat perched on a wooden pedestal. Changing direction, he walks toward the figure. Standing in front of it, he carefully inspects each wrinkle, then reaches out and runs his finger along the rim of the hat. "What the hell is wrong with you, boy? Can't you read?" Cassian jerks his hand back as the statue tips its head toward the sign on the wall. "The sign clearly says DO NOT TOUCH!"

"Right." He tucks his hands into the front pockets of his trousers, taking a step back toward Olivia's room. "My apologies."

"You young vamps. Always taking liberties you're not entitled to," the bust huffs.

Glancing over his shoulder, Cassian smirks as he taps on Olivia's bedroom door. She's sitting on her bed with her knees tucked against her chest when she hears the tap. Ignoring it, she wipes the tears from her cheek and leans back against the headboard. Another 'tap tap tap' echoes across her room, then a muffled, "Olivia, can we talk? Please. I feel I need to apologize."

"Seems you're making a habit of that," the deep voice mumbles behind him.

He leans his cheek to the frame and presses his mouth against the crack of the door. "Please, Olivia."

Olivia wipes her eyes with the heel of her hands, takes a deep breath, and allows a slight smile to pull at her lips. "Come in before uncle Chester starts at you." Her puffy eyes meet his as he steps into the room.

"Right. I believe I just met your uncle Chester." He glances back toward the door.

"He can be grouchy, but he's harmless." Smiling, Olivia sweeps the stray tears from under her eyes. "There's no need to apologize, Cash. Gran already told me it was her idea for you to climb inside my head."

Pulling a tissue from the box next to her bed, Cassian hands it to her. "Yes, that may be true, though you should know that it wasn't done maliciously." He gestures to the chair next to her nightstand. "Mind if I sit?" Olivia shifts over, adjusting slightly to see him. "Your grandmother wanted me to ensure you were safe. Nothing more."

"That's not it, Cash. She wanted to be sure I wasn't leaving anything out. I think she's upset because here I am," she points to herself, "the one who doesn't like magic, yet I'm the only one who can read that stupid thing. I mean, you have to admit the entire concept is ridiculous!"

Shaking his head, he raises his finger. "No, Olivia. She was truly concerned that they might need to pull you out of the journal. It's a magical book. One that very few have had the chance to experience. No one really knows what it can do just yet." He shifts forward, sliding the chair toward her bed. "You know, I've never thought much of magic before. In fact, I've always thought of witches to be lesser beings. But now, being surrounded by your family and this house," he throws his hands out, looking around, "entire rooms created before my very eyes, talking pictures, talking statues. I'm still trying to wrap my head around it all. At any rate, my job was solely to alert them if you were in any danger so they could pull you from your trance."

"My trance?" she asks, her brows drawn tightly together.

"Yes. You were lost to the happenings within the journal. The thought was to remove the book from your hands if something went wrong. You know, break the connection."

"But I can't help you if I don't read it."

Lowering his head, Cassian clasps his hands. "I understand and appreciate that more than anyone, but like your family, I would not risk your safety." Standing, he walks toward the door. "Oh, and Olivia, I didn't tell your family anything. I believe it's up to you to share that with them."

Patricia is standing outside Olivia's door with her mouth open as she presses her back against the wall. "What are you doing?" Helen asks, reaching the top step. "Are you eavesdropping?"

Stepping away, Patricia places her finger to her lips and shakes her head. "Shh." She grabs her arm, pulling her toward the opposite end of the hall. "Of course not. I just wanted to make sure he wasn't trying to have her for dinner."

"Oh, stop." Helen tugs her arm free. "He's not going to risk losing the only one that can help him and his family."

"What is it that they need help with anyway? Why hasn't he just said?"

Pursing her lips, Helen shifts her weight. "His brother mentioned someone by the name of Roger."

Olivia's door opens, and Cassian steps into the hallway, his gaze landing on the two sisters at the end of the hall as he gently shuts the door. "Yes, finding Roger is one thing we need her help with." He walks toward them. "He holds the key to the puzzle." Shaking his head, he looks down at the floor. "But I wouldn't go against your mother. She's been kind to me, and I believe she's right. That book may have more than one purpose. Olivia will need to follow the journey it has mapped out for her. I've been waiting for over a century for my resolve. A little longer won't kill me."

"We'll see about that." Patricia takes a step closer to him, her finger pressing against his chest. "What are you hiding, Bloodsucker? What did you see?"

Their eyes meet as Cassian raises his hand and slowly pushes her finger from his chest. "I have nothing to hide. Now, if you'll excuse me, I think I'll return to my room." He begins to walk away and pauses, gripping the top of the bannister as he glances back. "Oh, and Patricia, in the future, you might want to think twice before poking a hungry bear."

She lifts her hand, swiftly producing a ball of flames and tosses it past his head, catching the fine hairs of his sideburns. "Patricia!" Helen squeals, reaching for her sister's arm.

A low growl resonates from his chest, and he pats the embers next to his ear as he slowly turns to face her. Then in a blink of an eye, Cassian is standing chest to chest with her. Yet Patricia remains unmoved. She stares into his eyes and snarls. "I'm not afraid of you, Bloodsucker. And I don't miss. So consider that your warning."

Olivia opens her door and peeks out into the hallway. "Hey, what's going on out here?" That's when flames from the silk flowers on the shelf catch her eye, and she covers her mouth, pointing at Patricia. "You threw a fireball in the house?"

Quickly throwing her hand out toward the flowers with a whispered *'submergo,'* Patricia steps away from Cassian. She slaps her hands together with a shrug. "I was simply showing your toothy friend here how swiftly I can respond to a threat."

"Hmm, yes, I'm sure," Clara utters, climbing the stairs with the journal in hand. Her stare fixes on Patricia as she motions behind her. "Don't you have an errand to run? I'm sure Elizabeth is pacing by now. She's been waiting for you to deliver that fire quartz for over an hour."

"I was just leaving," Patricia declares with a grin as she brushes past her mother, her voice fading as she disappears down the stairs. "Try to get some rest, Liv. I'll be back in a bit."

Meeting her daughter's gaze, Clara chucks her chin toward Helen's bedroom door. "Oh, um, right. I suppose I could use some more freshwater in my collection anyway. If anyone needs me, I'll be down at the stream."

"Cassian," —*Clara glances at Olivia before meeting his gaze with a smile*— "could you excuse us, please?"

"Of course."

Offering a slight bow, Cassian disappears, leaving Clara shaking her head as she stares at the space where he had been standing only a second before. "I'm not sure I'll ever get used to the speed of a vampire."

She holds the journal up to Olivia and gestures to her room. "May I come in? I think I owe you an explanation."

Pushing her door open, she musters a smile. "You can come in, but Cash already explained it to me, Gran. I understand why you had him read my mind or enter my head, whatever it is he does," she says, throwing her arms out. "But to ease your mind, it's like they don't see or hear me. I'm just there observing."

"I can't tell you how much of a relief that is. After witnessing you summon Cash and his brother here, we weren't sure what else could happen." She sets the journal down on Olivia's nightstand and brushes a strand of hair from her face. "I know I seem overprotective and pushy at times, but you're all I have left of your mother, Olivia. I live daily with the guilt that I failed to protect her."

"Gran—"

Clara raises her hand. "No, it's true. I could have insisted she remain with the coven, but instead, I asked her to leave because I couldn't condone her practices. I should have insisted she and Bryan live here, but instead, I suggested they get their own place because their ways frightened me. I would never have lost her to that damn fire if I had done either of those two things. I could have stopped it." She wipes a tear from her cheek and peers over at the picture of Diana and Bryan. "So, I'm sorry if you feel I betrayed you by asking Cassian to enter your mind, but I needed to know you were safe. You phased out on us."

Nodding, Olivia smiles. "Yeah, Cash told me. I guess I just felt like you didn't trust me to tell you everything."

"And you think I would trust a vampire more?"

Olivia shrugs. "You seem to trust him. You did move Aunt Millie and build on a guest room for him," she chuckles.

"I still have my reserves, but overall, I feel he's a genuinely kind being. Besides, Aunt Millie and the house will keep their eye on him." She pats Olivia's hand. "Now, how are you feeling? Care to share what you saw, or would you like to get some rest first?"

"I feel fine. Almost as if I slept while I was in there. I'm not tired at all."

"Fantastic!" Clara slaps her hand off her knee and stands with a wide smile. "I'll make us some tea. Mine may not be as good as Helen's, but I'm sure it will suffice. I'm dying to hear everything." Before Olivia has a chance to respond, her grandmother disappears out her bedroom door.

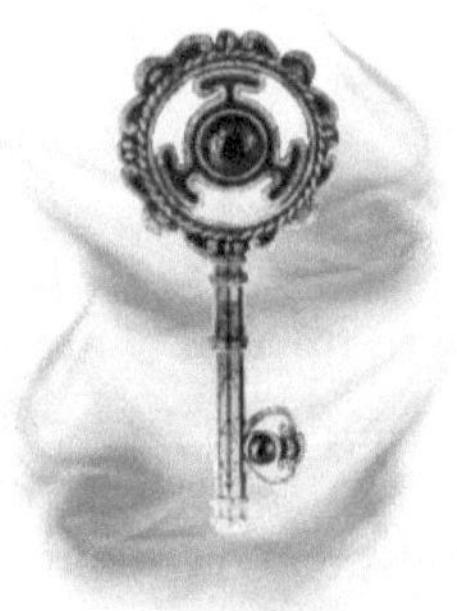

CHAPTER 20 ~ VISIT FROM HOME

Cassian pulls a bottle of special stock from the bar fridge Clara so kindly included in his suite during its creation, then runs hot water over a crystal goblet. He uncorks the decanter and slowly pours the deep red liquid into the heated glass. He chooses a random book from the bookcase, another thoughtful addition to his accommodation, and takes a seat by his bedroom window. Resting his feet on the ottoman, he peers out at the large oak where he and Olivia had stood earlier His mind drifts to the warmth of her hand in his — the sudden increase in intensity of her heartbeat. Taking a sip from his glass, he closes his eyes, savouring the sweetness on his palate, and imagines the nectar to be hers.

"Jesus, Cash. What's gotten into you?" Elias's voice cuts through his thoughts as he appears in the doorway to his brother's room.

Nearly spilling blood on his crisp white shirt, he bounds forward, the deep red liquid lapping at the rim of his glass as he sets it on the table. "Elias. I wasn't expecting you, brother."

"Clearly," Elias chuckles, strolling about his brother's room. "You know, you really should mind those dirty little thoughts of yours. I wouldn't be surprised if these witches can read them."

Closing his eyes, Cassian pinches the bridge of his nose. "Why have you come? Is it mother? Is she responding?"

Shaking his head Elias rests his arm on the mantle of the fireplace. "No. I'm afraid she's still unresponsive. Though I thought I should check in with you since we saw little miss lovely reading the journal again, and we had a couple of Roger's plebs visit the castle shortly after."

Cassian turns, narrowing his gaze on his brother. "I wondered how long it would be before they showed up there. How many?"

"Only two. Looking for the girl and the journal, of course." Elias shrugs. "Nothing we couldn't handle, but I thought you should be aware. It's only a matter of time before they locate her. Especially with you here daydreaming of sipping on her blood." Cassian shoots him a dirty look that is quickly returned. "Don't look at me like that. Go ahead and tell me you weren't." He throws his thumb over his shoulder toward the inside door. "Why do I get the feeling that you're falling for this witch, Cash?"

"Keep your voice down and watch your tone," he snaps. "It just so happens that Olivia is a very nice young lady. We've simply agreed to be friends."

"Friends?" he asks, his tone rising with his brows.

"Yes, Elias. Friends. Everyone can use a friend. And quite frankly, we need each other."

"For crying out loud, Cash. You seem to have forgotten she couldn't release you." Elias throws his hands in the air. "And now, I find you daydreaming of her—of *tasting* her."

"It was a simple misguided thought."

"Misguided. Yes. Well, that's a given." Elias snorts. "Maybe she has bewitched you. Did you ever think of that?" Cassian sets his book on the table next to his glass, watching Elias shake his head. "You know what? Never mind. You're the older brother here—the big bad sovereign. At least till father gets back. Right? I'm sure you know what you're doing. Besides, that's not why I came. Did she at least find Roger and the key in that damn book yet?"

"No. I'm afraid not." Cassian stands, brushing his hand down the front of his shirt, checking for drops of blood. "In fact, the book starts much earlier than we originally thought." He tucks his hands in the front pockets of his trousers and slowly walks toward Elias. "It turns out father and the journal's creator were once sweethearts, if you can believe that." The corner of his mouth tightens as he tips his head. "While he was still human, of course."

"What?"

"Yes. I was just as shocked as you." Cassian turns back toward the window and leans against the frame, staring out into the backyard. "Ancina Whittle. She sold spices at London's port. Father was a sailor—a human sailor."

"What the hell are you talking about, Cash? That's absurd. Father was an original. I recall him telling us he was once a sailor, but there's no way he could have been human," Elias argues, walking over to sit by the window. "He would have told us. Wouldn't he?"

Never taking his eyes from the view outside, Cassian shrugs. "I guess it wasn't on the list of things we needed to know." He glances at Elias's puzzled expression and offers him a quick smile before turning his gaze to the old oak tree in the backyard. "The three of them, father, mother, and Mr. Windsor were all created the same night. They are the originals, but they were also once human. He did tell us he met mother while he was a sailor. That she was travelling from Marseilles to London. He merely chose to leave out the part of them being ailing fragile humans. But I had the privilege of witnessing these things firsthand through my mind link with Olivia while she was inside the journal."

"I can't believe this." Elias shakes his head, dropping it into his hands. "So our family history is a lie?"

"Of course not, little brother. We all know father could not lie as long as he wore that key, and we both know he never took it off."

"So you're saying it was mother who lied to us then?"

"No." Cassian turns to face him. "We made assumptions, taking for granted that they were the first to be *born* into this life –

like us. But that's simply not the case. Instead, they were the first to be created. I would never have given it a second thought if I hadn't seen it myself. Did you ever think to ask if our grandparents drank blood?"

Elias rests back in his chair, his chest expanding as if taking a breath. "No, I guess I never have." Then, jutting forward, he squints up at his brother. "Wait. What do you mean Olivia was inside the journal?"

"Just as I said," he nods. "She begins to read but then quickly gets absorbed into the scenery. I've been inside her mind, and it's quite an amazing thing to witness. At first, I could have sworn she was standing there with them." Cassian runs his hand across his chin with a chuckle. "In fact, I watched her try to swat Mr. Windsor. Unfortunately, she's not able to make a connection with anything while she's inside. She's merely an observer, but that didn't stop her from trying."

"Oh, I would have paid dearly to catch even a glimpse of that," Elias laughs. "I am pleased to hear she doesn't fancy the Windsor men." He turns his hand out with a shrug. "Maybe that's why the book waited so long. To ensure there was someone who would feel as strongly against the Windsors as we do."

Cassian takes a seat on the ottoman in front of him, his elbows on his knees while resting his chin on his clasped hands. "Perhaps, or possibly it was waiting for someone of equal strength to the creator. The creator of that journal is Olivia's great-grandmother a few generations back. The practice of magic hid deep in darkness for a couple of centuries whiles the witch hunters were at their strongest, don't forget. It's only this last century it has been openly recognized again, and even then, most don't flaunt it."

"Wait a minute. This Ancina Whittle is Olivia's ancestor?" Cassian nods. "And you don't find that a bit strange?" Elias asks as he gains his feet. Raising his finger in the air, he slowly paces in front of the window. "Cash, you just told me this girl's great ancestor was once our father's lover." Stopping, he turns to stare at him, his eyes wide. "Now, the very book she created and gave him is pulling you, her ex-lover's son, and her great-great-granddaughter together. Think about that for a moment."

"I think you're being ridiculous," he laughs, standing to place his hand on his brother's shoulder. "It only makes sense that the two of us work together on this. We have a vested interest." He pours a second glass of blood and hands it to Elias. "Olivia not only learns about her ancestor but is driven to accept her birthright while learning the practice. All while helping us get our father back—something we've spent over a century trying to achieve." He picks up his glass and holds it up with a single nod. "I'd say it's a well-thought-out mutual win."

Taking a drink, Elias forces a smile. "Sure, well, call it what you like. All I can tell you is what I witnessed when I arrived. He sets his glass down, narrowing his eyes as he points. "Just don't lose track of why you're here, Cash."

Cassian sighs as the rear door to his room slams shut. Emptying Elias's glass into his, he stares out the window. "You forgot to bow to your sovereign, brother."

CHAPTER 21 ~ HOW DID THIS GET DOWN HERE?

Patricia chucks her keys on the kitchen table, her eyes fixing on Olivia as she enters the kitchen. "I thought you were getting some rest."

"I'm not tired, and Gran wanted to hear about the last journal entry."

All heads turn toward the rear of the kitchen as the back door swings open, and Helen strolls through, her eyes lighting up at the sound of the journal. "Eee," she squeals. "We're going to hear about your adventure now?"

Clara takes her seat at the table, gesturing for them to sit. "Yes. Olivia has decided to share what she has seen. I was going to make tea, but since you're here now" —*she smiles at Helen*— "I think it would be best if you did the honours."

"It would be my pleasure." Helen takes her seat, waving her hand over the table. "Gingiberi ti citrea," she smiles at Olivia. "For this occasion - your favourite."

Rolling her eyes, Clara flips her hand toward Olivia and dips her head. "Whenever you're ready, Liv."

The three ladies sit on the edge of their seats, listening as Olivia tells them everything she witnessed while inside the journal. Her own excitement ramps as she recalls the time spent with Julien and Ancina. "I realized something else," she says, running her hand down Mr. Green's back. "The dream I kept having of great-gran Ancina was like the initial unwritten entry of the journal. As if that first bit picked up from where my dream left off."

"You know, I believe you may be right," Clara shrugs, pulling a cup of tea toward her. "I had almost forgotten about your dream."

"Maybe she was trying to alert you to Julien," Helen says.

Olivia shakes her head. "I'm not convinced that was it. I didn't see Julien in my dream. Only in the journal."

"Where was the big yew tree you had mentioned? The one great-gran Ancina hid that goodie bag in. Do you remember?" Patricia asks. "Maybe great-gran Annabel never did get the stuff she had left for her."

"Now, that could be possible." Clara rests her chin on her fist and looks at Olivia. "I don't suppose the property looked familiar to you?"

Twisting her lips, Olivia shakes her head. "Not really. I mean, the area kind of reminded me a bit of Mr. McNally's lane, but that would have been ages ago."

"True. Though it couldn't hurt to ask him if there are remnants of an old house nearby. I know that she lived in this area. In fact, now that I think about it, you said great-gran Ancina wrapped her grimoire in that package she placed in the big yew tree. Gran Annabel raised me after my mother died, as you know, and that was one of her only complaints. That her mother never left her grimoire for her."

Olivia's eyes widen. "Do you really think that was the message she was sending me, Gran?"

"It's all speculation, but your aunt Patricia could be on to something. I'll call Mr. McNally in the morning." She peers up at the clock. "But tonight, I'm going to rest my weary bones. Helen and I have to finish itemizing the stock at the store tomorrow." Smiling down at Olivia, she winks, waving her finger between her and Patricia. "I thought I'd let you two be sand-witches tomorrow."

"Yeah, it's getting rather late. I guess I should turn in myself," Helen says, standing with her hand on her lower back. "This poor old body isn't as young as it used to be either."

"Pfft, a couple of old crones," Patricia whispers.

Olivia attempts to stifle her laughter as Clara turns sharply, sending a gust of wind toward Patricia and blowing her over in her chair. "I may be old, but my hearing is as keen as the vampire's in the other room. You might not want to forget that."

Brushing herself off, Patricia gains her feet with a chuckle. "For an old crone, you're still pretty quick, mom." Clara lifts her finger, and Patricia puts her hands up in defence. "It was a compliment! My way of saying thanks for the day off."

"Mmhmm," Clara says, waving her off as she continues up the stairs. "Sweet dreams, Olivia. Don't let your crazy aunt keep you up too late."

"I won't, Gran," Olivia giggles. "I'm going to bed soon too."

"So." Patricia turns to face Olivia. "I saw you and the bloodsucker holding hands earlier. You know, before you came in to read the journal." She raises her brow with a tip of her head. "What's up with that?"

"Pfft." Olivia rolls her eyes. "You mean when we shook hands? There's a big difference, Aunt Trish." Her gaze veers away from her aunt's convicting stare as she shrugs. "We agreed to be friends."

"Friends?" Patricia's tone rises with her brows.

"Yes. Friends. I thought it best to have a vampire on my side if one does show up. You all said vampires could start coming out of the woodwork once I started reading the journal. I mean, you saw how I was able to summon Cash and his brother. Right?" She waves her hand toward Cassian's bedroom door. "I prefer to have someone I can trust that is on an equal playing field here if one shows up unannounced."

"Trust, huh?" Patricia sits back, folding her arms across her chest. "You can't seriously think you need his protection?" She purses her lips. "Or that he might be superior to us. Do you?"

Olivia shakes her head. "No. That's not it."

"I'll have you know that I can torch him to nothing but mere ashes if I choose."

Cassian's door opens, and he steps into the living room, closing his door behind him. His eyes settle on Olivia. "Am I interrupting?"

Patricia's head swings in his direction, her eyes narrowing as she stares him down. "Is that really a question, Bloodsucker? You're here, aren't you?"

Olivia shakes her head. "No, you're not interrupting." Smiling, she waves him out to join them. "Aunt Trish was just saying goodnight. Weren't you, Aunt Trish?"

A frown settles on Patricia's face as she exhausts a breath and pats the back of the couch. "Right. I guess it is time for me to join the old crones." She flicks Olivia's ponytail and points to the ceiling. "I'll be right above." Her brow shoots up as her stare anchors on Cassian. "In earshot. Just call if you need me."

He runs his finger along the side of his neck with a smirk. "I assure you she'll be good."

"Don't test me, Bloodsucker," Patricia scowls, directing an ignited finger toward him. "You've seen how quickly I can—"

"Okay." Olivia bounds to her feet between them with her arms out. "Should I call for Gran?"

A snicker above the mantle causes them to turn toward Aunt Millie's portrait. "Clearly, he's trying to get a reaction from you, dear." Her smile grows as her eyes dance between Cassian and Olivia. "You can go to bed, Patricia. I'll keep an eye on them."

"Pfft." Olivia jams her hands on her hips. "I'm an adult! Besides, we're friends. Why can't you all realize that?"

"Twenty-one is barely an adult and a mere youngster next to this walking heap of dust," Patricia says disgustedly. "And to be clear, witches and vampires do not hold friendships, Liv. This beast" —she narrows her eyes, pointing at Cassian— "is just a bloodsucker who requires our assistance."

"Ugh! Goodnight, Aunt Trish."

"Fine. I'll just make myself a sandwich, then I'm off to bed." Patricia squints, raising two fingers to her eyes, then points them back toward Cassian. "Don't let the bloodsucker bite." Olivia rolls her eyes. "No. Really. Don't let him bite."

Shaking her head, Olivia flops down on the sofa. "I'm sorry. She means well. We've obviously never had a vampire in our home before, and she's been known to be a bit over the top sometimes."

Waving her off, he sits in the armchair across from her. "No need to apologize. I understand your aunt's concern." He leans back into the chair, crossing his ankle over his knee. "Our kinds," he waves his hand between them, "vampires and witches, that is. We don't typically hold friendships. Quite frankly, if I were brutally honest, most vampires would do anything to drain the magic from your veins. She's not lying about that."

"Well, they'd be sadly disappointed. There is no magic flowing through these weak little veins of mine."

He cocks his head, scanning her face. "It amazes me that you really have no idea of the power you hold." His hands grasp the arms of the chair as he straightens. "It's almost as if you've built a protective wall around it, sealing it away from even your own conscious mind."

His words have little effect on her as she reaches for her cup of tea and nestles back into the sofa. "Truthfully, I was very young the last time I tried to use magic." Taking a sip of her tea, she cradles her cup in her hands and shakes her head, staring into the distance. "I think I was about seven, and trust me. It did not go well. I lost my concentration and set Gran on fire." Closing her eyes, she shakes off the memory and sets her cup down. "I have steered clear of it since then."

Shifting his gaze from hers, Cassian nods. He recalls seeing her nightmare. Setting her Grandmother ablaze could cause enough trauma to build that kind of wall after suffering such a loss. "I can see how that might affect a young girl. Especially after what you endured." His stare pierces hers. "But I'm afraid I have to ask you to break down that wall and work on those skills again. I'm sure you must be aware that we will require that power you're hiding at some point."

"See now, this is where you all are confused." Olivia's voice rises. "I have no power, and even if I did as a child, I tucked that away so long ago that any spark I may have had is well gone by now. Besides,

I don't feel magical, and I certainly could not possess the type of power great-gran Ancina did."

Patricia leans against the living room door frame and forces a tight smile. "Liv, you must know how much it kills me to say this, but he's right. We should be exploring your strengths and working with them. We can all feel the energy you've been suppressing. It's time." Raising her hands, she turns her head and takes a deep breath. "Okay, there it is. I've said my piece. Now I'm off to bed. Sweet dreams."

Watching Patricia make her way upstairs, a smile slowly moves across Cassian's lips as he peers at Olivia from under his brow. "I believe she may be starting to warm up to me."

Olivia covers her mouth as she breaks into laughter. "What in the world gives you that idea?"

"Well, she did just side with me, and I haven't had to dodge any fireballs the entire evening," he says, his smile showing the slightest hint of his fangs. "I'd have to say that's a positive sign."

She tips her head from side to side, her smile matching his. "You do have a point. That's not a bad sign." As she leans forward to grab her teacup, her smile fades. Her hand passes hesitantly over the journal instead. "How did this get down here?" She picks it up, the familiar tingle shooting up her arm as she draws it toward her. "I know this wasn't here a minute ago."

Cassian shrugs, staring at the book in her hand. "No, I'm sure I would have noticed it if it were."

When she pulls the book into her lap, the cover flops open, landing on the page where she had previously ended. Her gaze drifts to Cassian as she holds her hand above the page and wiggles her fingers. "Do you think it's a sign? I mean, Gran said these things are compelled by magic—that they have a mind of their own."

"I don't know, Olivia. This journal has always been somewhat of a mystery to my family and me." His eyes narrow as his gaze darts between her and the book. "And the way it seems to compel a person as uncomfortable with magic as you are is a little more than interesting."

Pursing her lips, she leans back and studies his face for a moment while contemplating his words. Finally, she nods. "You're right. I do feel the need to reach for it—to read it. Though the sensation that used to scare me when I touched it is now somewhat inviting. Besides, the quicker I get through this journal, the sooner you'll have your resolve, right?"

"Yes, that's true, but don't you think we should wait until your grandmother and aunts are here?"

The corner of her mouth turns down as she shrugs. "Why? They trusted you to look out for me last time. You can come with me. Right? I mean, you can watch over me in here—make sure I don't get stuck or something. It's not like we won't tell them what we see." Olivia lays her hand on the page and instantly feels herself sway. Then, before she knows it, she's back inside the journal.

"Olivia? Ah, Damn it!"

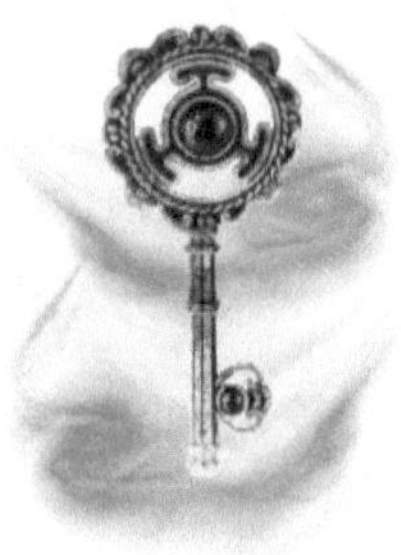

CHAPTER 22 ~ DAYWALKER

Cassian closes his eyes and reaches out to her mind when he finds her standing in his father's room.

A ray of light leaks across a wooden floor as Olivia glances around the massive room. She notes a large canopy bed with deep red velvet drapes just off to her right. It's a breathtaking piece of furniture—something her grandmother would feel privileged to see firsthand. The dark heavy wood is intricately carved along each post and across the canopy's edge.

Hearing a huff, Olivia turns to see Julien standing beside the window, his arms at his side and his eyes closed. His mixed emotions are not lost on her as another huff pushes from his lips. Finally, he reaches out and slowly draws the edge of the heavy drapes into the palm of his hand before suddenly pulling it open. As the sun's brightness streams into the room, he plasters himself against the wall, squeezing his eyes shut—his chest heaves. "Don't be such a damn coward, Laurent," he grumbles.

Olivia's shoulders stiffen as he timidly reaches forward to stick the tip of his finger into the sunbeam. But then, a slight smirk works across his face, and he pulls his back from the wall twisting the digit further into the sun's rays. His smile broadens, and he tugs his hand back to examine it before trying again.

She can't help but snicker at his reaction. Cupping her hands over her mouth, she waits with what is obviously shared anticipation as he excitedly rolls up his sleeve. Closing his eyes, he stabs his entire arm into the light. His eyes pop open as he flips his hand over in the sun, examining it. "Hah! Nothing!" he laughs, jumping directly into the midday sun. "Well, I'll be damned! Harold is never going to believe this."

Anxiously hauling his nightshirt over his head with one tug, Olivia quickly covers her eyes and turns her back. *'Whoa! Easy there, Julien.'* Raising her hand to shield her view, she strides for the door. *'I'll just wait out here.'*

Reaching for the handle, she can feel the chill of the metal but can't seem to grasp it. Her finger passes through the wood, and she pushes her hand forward, watching her arm disappear. *'Okay, here goes nothing.'* Taking a deep breath, she lifts her foot and steps through as if the door didn't exist. Once on the other side, she releases her breath and looks back at the solid wood slab, trying to collect her thoughts. *'Wow, that is not something I want to do often.'* She runs her hands down the length of her body, ensuring it's still intact. *'Such a horrible feeling. As if I separated cell by cell.'*

When the door bursts open, Olivia barely reclaims her thoughts before Julien darts downstairs. Grabbing his boots, he calls out to his house steward. "Soloman! I'm going to the Windsor's residence. I'll be back shortly."

The flash of someone entering the room startles her, and Olivia steps back, her hand flying over her mouth as her eyes focus on Soloman. He grabs a large hooded overcoat and rushes toward Julien as he watches him prepare to leave. "But, Sir! It's mid of day! Surely he'll be resting as you should be."

"No, thank you, Soloman. I won't be needing that. I'll be walking in the sunlight like everyone else today."

"Walking uncovered in daylight," Soloman gasps as he stands, holding the cloak open in his outstretched hands. "You can't be serious. It's the height of noon, Sir!" His words come out in a rush as he continues to thrust the heavy cloak toward him. "You must wear this. The sun. You'll burn on contact."

Julien hauls on his boots and peeks out the small window. "I'm fully aware of the time of day, Soloman. In fact, I believe a walk in the sun is just what I need. I've missed the warm rays, my good friend. Haven't you?"

"Sir, you're frightening me. I fear the witch may have cast an evil spell on you." He stands back, watching with wide eyes as Julien prepares to step out of the confines of his dark castle.

"Nonsense!" Pulling open the heavy door, Julien raises his forearm to shade his eyes and holds his hand out to Soloman. "Come, my friend. We've been cooped up in the dark for too long. Step out with me and feel the warmth."

Shaking his head, Soloman backs away, shielding himself behind the door. "Sir, I don't know how you're doing that, but I'm afraid I cannot. Please come back inside the castle before this spell wears off."

"It won't wear off." Turning to face him, Julien raises his arms, allowing the sun to drape across his body. "Come, Soloman. You must trust me. Just stick your hand into the light. You'll see. We've finally been freed from the curse of night."

"All vampires?"

"No, but my entire bloodline has. That includes you, my friend. Now, come out here," Julien says, waving him out excitedly.

Unconvinced, Soloman shakes his head. "Merely looking outdoors is nearly blinding, Sir. I haven't seen the sun in centuries."

Julien's laugh echoes through the halls as he grabs Soloman's hand. "Neither have I, my friend, but I assure you it feels wonderful." Soloman squeezes his eyes shut as Julien tugs him forward.

Olivia's heart melts at their elation as the sun's bright rays beam down on the two men. Massive smiles stretch across their faces as their laughter bounces across the open field.

Soloman stares at his hands, turning them over in the sun. "Incredible!" A smile stretches across his face. "How did this happen?" He peers over at Julien. "Your witch friend. So this was her spell?"

"One of them—yes." His smile broadens. "I must go see Mr. Windsor. Be sure to let everyone know that our hours around the castle have changed."

He rushes toward the coverage of the forest, dashing through the woods with Olivia tethered along for the run. Within moments, a large stone house appears through the heavy foliage of the vast chestnut trees. As they get closer, Olivia notices the sheer enormity of the place. She's not convinced it's a castle, but it's much more significant than any home of the current time.

The white brick is marred with dirt and moss, and the roof holds chipped slate shingles. Thick, rotting wood planks frame the handful of oddly placed windows covered with dark drapery, and the massive double doors are reinforced with metal bands and studs. Knocking once, Julien lets himself into Harold's residence and heads directly for the stairs. He bursts through a door at the end of the long hall. "Harold! Harold! You must see this!"

Harold shoots upright, his eyes springing open only to close again. "Julien?" Shielding his eyes with his hand, he squints. "How the hell did you get here? It's mid of day!"

"Yes! Yes, it is." Julien's hearty laughter fills the room. "I told you that old woman felt familiar. I knew her long ago—before we were created. That was Ancina Whittle."

"Aw, that's hogwash. Come on, there's no way you can believe that. Not even a witch can live that long."

Olivia raises a brow at his ignorance. "Oh, I beg to differ. Ancina showed me everything." He waves his hand through the air. "Nothing you can say will change my mind. I believe irrevocably. Anyway, the fact remains that she removed the curse of night from my entire bloodline. We can now walk in daylight just as when we were humans. Oh!" He lifts the chain holding the key from his shirt and dangles it in front of Harold. "And this! It's a magical key—a resurrection key. It will resurrect an original regardless of how they met their demise."

Harold's eyes narrow as he stares at the old key. "Is that so? Regardless of how they met their demise, huh? Even if they were beheaded or had their heart ripped from their chest?"

"Yes! I saw it!"

"Now, that's absurd," he laughs.

"Is it? I mean, look at me. Just look at the gift she has granted me. How can you not believe?" He walks over, yanking open one side of the heavy curtain allowing the sunlight to beam across his flesh.

Wailing, Harold throws the blanket back over his face. "For crying out loud, Julien! Shut the bloody curtain!"

"Sorry," Julien smiles, "but I had to show you I'm telling you the truth."

There's a tap on Cassian's shoulder, and he opens his eyes in response. "What is she doing in the journal," Clara asks, her jaw tight with scorn. "And why didn't you come get me?"

"Ms. Redfearn," he blinks, trying to adjust his eyes. "I promise it wasn't intentional. The journal had appeared on the table. She only placed her hand on the page, and she was lost to it. So I thought it best to keep an eye on her, nothing more."

Staring down at him, she exhales through her nose. "I have been told these journals can be quite persistent." She tips her head toward Olivia. "All right then, where exactly is she?"

"It has taken her to my father's first time as a daywalker. He's at Harold's, showing him his new ability," he smiles.

She turns toward the kitchen. "Very well, I suppose I'll get a tea and join you then."

With a nod, Cassian closes his eyes to rejoin Olivia's vision within the journal.

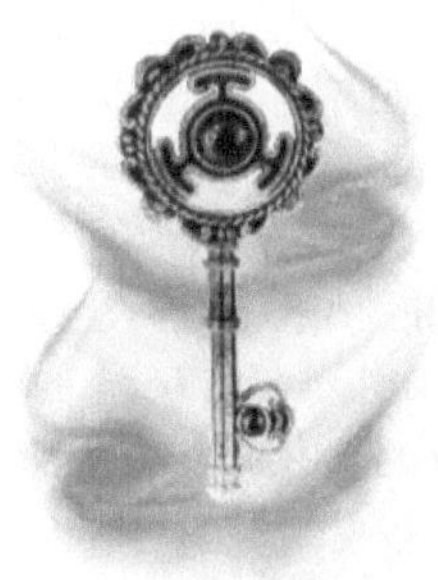

CHAPTER 23 ~ DAY MOON

Julien shuts the curtain, and the room goes dark. Olivia can't see a thing. Only the uplifting sound of children's laughter surrounds her as the room slowly brightens. Finally, she finds herself standing in a large sunny room, watching two young boys dancing by the window. They're having so much fun running back and forth through the sunbeams that, for a brief moment, Olivia can almost feel their joy.

That joy, however, quickly dissipates with the sound of a woman's raging voice breaking through the boys' laughter.

"Gladys! I told you the curtains must stay drawn during the day! My children are sensitive to sunlight!"

Barely able to make out the dark hair poking around the corner, Olivia walks over for a closer look. She recalls seeing this stunning woman with her porcelain complexion and dark wavy brown locks before – Clarentina. Her cornflower-blue eyes cautiously stare past Olivia, warily peeking around the corner to curiously watch the children dance through the sun. She looks horrified as she puts her arms out and calls to them, "Cassian, Elias, come to me now. How many times have I told you, you must stay out of the daylight? It's incredibly dangerous to our kind."

Olivia studies the delight on the faces of the two young brothers. Her heart skips at the thought of witnessing their first experience in the sun.

"Aw, ma!" The older boy with jet black hair pouts as he squints up at her. "But we're better now, just like Annie said. She said it wouldn't burn us anymore, and it doesn't. This doesn't hurt at all. It feels nice, like a warm bath." He raises his hand, twisting it in the sunbeam. "Look! See? No flames."

Clarentina pulls his arm down. "Cassian, please. You're frightening me." She studies him for a moment. "Did you say, Annie?" He nods, and she shakes her head. "We don't have any Annie here, son."

"Yes, we do! She's the really pretty one. She opened the curtains and promised that even father knew it to be okay."

Pursing her lips, Clarentina stares down at him as his younger brother wraps his arms around her waist with a squeal. "Cash is right, mama! And so was Annie. The day moon doesn't hurt. It feels so warm!" He tugs her skirt, trying to coax her toward the sunlight. "Come feel it!

'Annie?' Olivia looks around. *'They can't be talking about Ancina. Can they? They said young, and she was old when I saw her with Julien.'*

Another woman, one Olivia is unfamiliar with, comes scurrying down the stairs with a young blond-haired boy in her arms. "Clarentina, is everything okay? I heard you cry out."

Crouching, Clarentina wraps her arms around the two boys and kisses their cheeks. "Oh, Harriet. Forgive me for disturbing you and young Roger. The boys gave me a bit of a fright this morning." She straightens, looking down at her children. "I'm not sure how you two managed to come away unscathed, but I assure you I cannot play in the sun." She points toward the stairs. "Now, go on and pack up your things. We're going back to London. Tonight."

"Aw, come on, ma!" Cassian protests, grabbing his brother's arm and lifting it in the air. "Look, Elias and I are fine!"

"Yeah, mama. It didn't hurt us. I like the heat on my skin," Elias pouts.

"Yes, well, you're very fortunate. You could have been seriously hurt. Now go and get ready." Clarentina folds her arms, turning back to face Harold's wife. "I'm sorry, Harriet. I know it's only been a few days since we arrived in France, but I need to discuss this whole thing with Julien. If nothing else, maybe we can convince the men to come back with us." She looks around the room. "You haven't run into a housekeeper by the name of Annie, have you?"

"No." Harriet rubs Clarentina's arm. "And please, there's no need to apologize. I would want Harold at my side at a time like this too. Thank goodness they're all right." She kisses the child in her arms and turns for the stairs. "Roger and I will be ready to leave when you are."

'Roger? The same Roger that Elias and Cash are looking for?' Olivia looks around the room as, once again, everything goes dark. Her stomach flips, and she closes her eyes, waiting for it to settle. Then as she opens them, she is standing in the middle of Julien's den again. He and Harold are sitting at the same table Solomon had been mended on. Several empty wine bottles litter the table while they sit, sipping from their fancy chalices and laughing. *'These two share the oddest friendship,'* Olivia chuckles.

The sound of a heavy door slamming startles her, and Olivia spins to nearing footsteps as Clarentina's voice sings out. "Julien, darling. Are you home?" She rounds the corner holding Cassian and Elias's hands. There's a lightness in Olivia's chest as their mother releases them, and they run toward their father.

"Daddy, we played in the sun!" Elias spits out excitedly.

Throwing his arms in the air, Julien roars with laughter. "You did? That's wonderful!" He glances over at his wife as she shifts her weight to one leg and folds her arms. Her gaze pierces his as he pats the boys on the shoulder. "Why don't you boys go upstairs and play? You can tell me all about your adventure later. I think your mama and I need to talk."

The muscle in Clarentina's jaw tightens. "Mmhmm. Indeed we do, Julien Laurent."

Slapping his hands together, he watches his boys dart upstairs and turns to her with a wide grin. "I didn't expect you back so soon." His arms wrap around her waist, and he draws her against him, his eyes anxiously searching her face. "But, I am awful glad you're home. As you might have guessed, I have some remarkable news to share with you, my love."

"Mmhmm." She places her hand on his chest to push back. "I suspect you do." As her eyes trail to Harold at the opposite end of the table, she dips her head, forcing a smile. "Good evening, Harold. I'm afraid Harriet took Roger straight home."

Olivia's gaze flits to Harold at the end of the table. *'So Roger is Harold's infant son, but why do they need him so badly? And why couldn't Cash have just told me this?'*

He returns her feigned smile with a stiff nod. "Evening, Clarentina. I should be getting home to the Mrs. then." Emptying his glass, Harold pushes back from the table and chucks his chin at Julien. "I'll be seeing you. Don't forget some of us still hold moonlight hours."

When the room clears, Julien sits back down. His rosy cheeks nearly reach his eyes as he takes his wife's hand. "Clare, you're never going to believe what has happened. Just look!" Tapping his cheek, he pulls her down onto his lap. "Do you see this? I have a tan!"

She stands with her hand on her hip and stares down at him. "No, darling. That's a burn, and you mean to tell me you knew of this and didn't tell me? Do you have any idea how frightened I was when I found our children playing in the sun today? I was horrified!" Her scowl softens as she takes his face in her hands, her thumbs caressing his pink cheeks. "Tell me how such a thing is possible. And why would you send some Annie to deliver the message to our boys instead of speaking with me?"

"My love, forgive me if they scared you, but this happened late last night." His eyes narrow. "Annie? I did not send—" His brows shoot into his hairline. "Ah, yes. Annie. Well, I would have come to France today to tell you personally if you hadn't come back first."

"Well, spit it out already. How did this happen?"

"Simply put, the curse of night has been lifted, my love." He pulls her into his arms. "My entire bloodline can now walk freely in daylight. Isn't this a blessing?"

"Of course, it's a blessing, but how? How did this come to be?"

"I saved—" He pauses, and Olivia smiles, realizing his wife may not understand him risking himself for his first love—a witch. "I saved an old woman from burning, and in return, she lifted the curse of night."

"A witch!" Her hand rests on her lips. "You're telling me you saved a witch! Are you insane, Julien? Were you seen?"

"No, my love. No, of course not. It was dark, and it happened so quickly."

As the clarity of his words dawn, Clarentina tilts her head. "You said your bloodline, but I do not carry your blood. That means I remain vulnerable to the sun's rays."

The corner of Julien's mouth lifts. "No. You may not be of my bloodline. However, we do share blood," he grins, leaning in to kiss her cheek. A shy chuckle rises from Clarentina as she swats his chest. "It's enough to allow you to walk in daylight as well. I already thought to ask, my love." Stepping back, he reaches into the neckline of his shirt. "Oh..." Pulling out the chain, he holds up his newest treasure. "And this! It's a resurrection key."

Clarentina tips her head, her eyes narrowing as she examines the shiny skeleton key dangling from his fingers. "A resurrection key? What on earth would we require that for?"

"We may be immortal, but we're not completely indestructible." Julien lifts his finger, pausing any further questions and waves her toward the safe. He then pulls out the scroll that Ancina left behind and hands it to his wife. "Here, read this. It will explain it better than I can."

She carefully studies both scrolls before rolling them up and handing them back to him. "I can't read what I assume is the spell, but they do seem like interestingly valuable gifts." She turns the journal over in her hand, flipping through the first few pages. "If indeed they work, that is."

Julien grins. "Oh, they work, my love. That first entry was written all on its own."

"I see nothing written in this book, Julien. These pages are blank." She stares down, squinting at the page. "Actually, it does look as if there could be letter impressions there, but certainly nothing I can make out," she says, handing it back.

He takes the journal and examines the blank page. "I swear something was written in here. I had read the first entry myself. Though she did mention that after last night it would only be visible to the intended party." He sets it back into the safe with the scrolls and turns to face her. "But the key, I saw its power with my own eyes. Remember those old keys I found out back?" Clarentina shrugs. "Well, that doesn't matter, but she used one to prove they work and left me this one." He holds up the scroll. "This scroll with the instructions appeared on the table along with that journal as she disappeared. It's a timekeeper journal. It writes itself as major events happen."

Confusion clouds her face as she shakes her head. "Wait a minute. Did you just say she proved the key worked?"

Julien looks uneasy as he steps back. "Yes. But before you get upset, hear me out." He takes another step back. "I had to remove Soloman's head for just the briefest of time."

Clarentina's eyes widen. "You did WHAT?!"

"Yes, but he's fine." His confidence returns, and his eyes meet hers as he grasps the key again. "She mended him completely—" he holds the key higher. "Using one of these. Right before my eyes!"

"Soloman is part of our family! How could you do such a thing?"

Olivia wraps her arms around herself at the shrill ring of Clarentina's voice. For a woman that looks delicate, there's no doubt she's fierce when driven into protection mode.

Julien quickly draws her against his chest and kisses her forehead. "Oh, my love. He's perfectly fine. I swear. He has no idea anything happened."

Pulling free of his arms, she walks toward the staircase, shooting him a backwards glance. "Soloman? Soloman!"

Appearing at the top of the stairs, Soloman dips his head. "Yes, madame?"

Her hand falls to her chest as the tension in her shoulders release, and her voice calms. "Oh, forgive me, Soloman. I didn't mean to yell," she smiles. "It's great to see you. As you might have noticed, the boys and I have returned home early from France. Could you be a dear and check that they're in their rooms for me, please?"

"Of course, Madame." Returning her smile, he bows. "Welcome home."

Clarentina follows Julien over to the table, sitting across from him. Shaking her head, she stares at him blankly. "I can't believe you would even consider doing such a thing."

"Oh, come now, my love. It didn't happen as you may think." He reaches out to take her hand. "I watched her create the keys. It was like nothing I had ever witnessed before." Clarentina leans forward, resting her chin on her hand. "I swear, this woman's power was beyond magnificent. Besides, how else was I to know if it would work?"

"I still don't understand how you trusted a witch, Julien!"

"My love, please. She wasn't just any witch. She was a cunning woman—a healer."

Clarentina's eyes narrow. "I know what a cunning woman is."

"Yes, well, she needed someone from my bloodline, and Soloman being my primeval, was the best match."

She sits up, her back bar straight. "Surely you wouldn't have considered using one of our children?!"

"Of course not," Julien says, his eyes falling from her piercing gaze. "If you could have felt her energy, saw the creation of the keys, you would not be questioning my decision Clarentina. In my heart, I knew it would work, but I had to see it for myself." He pulls the key out of his shirt and holds it up. "The twin to this key and a mere drop of my blood mended Soloman before my very eyes. I swear to you. I witnessed a true magical miracle last night."

"Mmhmm." She closes her eyes, her chest expanding with a breath she truly doesn't require. "Or perhaps you made another deal with the devil, Julien Laurent."

CHAPTER 24 ~ DEVIL'S TAVERN

The room around Olivia darkens, and it feels as though she's being sucked through a vacuum. Her aunts have now joined Cassian and her grandmother in the living room. They've been observing the pages magically flip, and her finger continue to scan across them, line by invisible line, while anxiously waiting. When her eyes close and she finally jolts in her chair, Patricia taps Clara's hand. "Mom! I think she's coming out."

But then the page flips, and Olivia's finger continues to move along the invisible lines. Helen huffs, waving her hand in the air to produce another pot of steaming tea. "Well, It seems that was a false alarm. We may as well have some breakfast. Who's hungry?"

Olivia is standing in complete darkness as the sound of a crowd gradually gets louder. As she steps forward, a pungent stench of stale alcohol hangs in the air. Her eyes slowly begin to focus on an old stone building with a wooden sign in the window that reads Devil's Brew. Walking up to the entrance, she places her hand on the swinging door, stumbling as her body floats through. *'Ew!'* She shakes the chill from her body, glancing back at the undisturbed door. *'Okay. There is no way I will ever get used to that.'*

Spotting Julien and Harold at a nearby table, she heads in their direction. As she passes by two drunks at a neighbouring table, she hears them mention Old Hattox. Olivia moves closer, glancing up at Julien and Harold. From the look on their faces, they seem to be listening too. "I can't believe they finally got to Old Hattox." The drunk slams his cup down, sloshing ale on the table. "She was one of the best damn healers in London."

Swaying in his seat, his drunk friend looks up. "You saw her hanged?"

"Yup, did so. They hanged her up on Gallows Hill. Saw it with my own eyes." He wipes the back of his hand across his lips. "Some kid claimed she was one of the Pendle witches." He shakes his head. "Poor old hag."

His friend flops his head into his forearms and peers up through his brows. "Yep. Poor old hag."

A drunkard from the neighbouring table leans over. "Old Hattox? I heard her body was 5

missing when they went back to cut her down. They think someone stole it, but I say she tricked them. She was a powerful ol' hag, you know."

"Pfft. Hardly. I'll bet the wolves got her," another calls out from the back of the tavern.

Laughing, Harold slaps Julien's arm. "Did you hear that? What a waste of your time, saving that old witch."

"It wasn't a waste of time. You seem to have forgotten that she gave my family and me the type of freedom our kind only dream about." Julien lifts the chain around his neck, jingling the key. "Not to mention life security."

"Well, I hope you enjoyed your month of freedom 'cause she's dead. Her spells probably died with her, you fool."

Olivia grins. *'That's not the way it works, Harold. Spells need to be reversed.'*

Taking a drink of his ale, Julien looks at the key before tucking it back into his shirt. "That's ridiculous! You're the fool for being so narrow-minded. These gifts could have been yours as well. Instead, her magic is alive and well in my bloodline alone. How do you think my wife and children are now able to enjoy daylight hours?" Cocking his head, a smirk grows as Harold's grin slowly fades. "As for this key" — *he pats his chest*— "the spell has already been set, sealed with blood. Only two people know the real secret it holds, and now one of us is dead."

Leaning back in his chair, Harold studies him for a moment. "You never did tell me exactly how that key is of value."

"Yes, I did. I told you it can resurrect the dead—"

Rolling his eyes, Harold slaps his hands off the table and leans back in his chair. "That's it? You've been going on about *the great power* this key holds," he leans forward, pointing to the chain around his friend's neck, "and that's it?" Flopping back, he throws his hands up, laughing. "Damn, Julien. I can bring someone back from the dead too." He leans back in, folding his arms across the table with a cocky grin. "In fact, we both can, and we don't require no damn key to do it."

Julien glances around the room as he leans across the table. His eyes lock with Harold's as he lowers his voice and nods. "Sure, a human near death, but not a vampire who has lost his head or had his heart ripped from his chest."

Harold sits back, running a hand over his beard. "I remember you telling me the old hag showed you it worked. How did she do that exactly? Are you telling me she killed someone—a vampire? I mean, if that's what the key is capable of, there would be no other way to show you. Right?"

"Yes."

"What!" Harold's voice rises above the crowd. "Who?"

"Shh." Straightening, Julien holds his hand out in front of him and peers around the room. "Keep your voice down." He leans back in, cradling his mug in his hands. "Soloman, and as you have seen with your own eyes, he's completely fine."

"You're insane, Laurent!" He leans back against his chair, his brows knit tightly together. "What if it didn't work? You risked your primeval's existence on the word of a scraggly old witch?"

"I could feel the power surrounding us when she created them." Julien shrugs, sitting back in his chair. "I knew it would work. I witnessed the magic at work as markings engraved themselves along the shaft. Saw the stones glow as they embedded into the top of the keys. I'm telling you, they danced to life right before my eyes."

"Yeah, well, I remember being there that night too." Harold sits forward, his teeth clenched as he points his finger in Julien's face. "As I recall, you carelessly risked *my* identity. In fact, it's starting to look like our mighty sovereign has lost all respect for his own kind. And now, at a crucial time when vampires are being hunted as regularly as witches, you Laurent are walking freely in daylight. Who would ever suspect you now? If anyone is at risk of losing their head for suspicion of being a vampire" *—he sits back and jabs his thumb into his chest—* "it's me. As far as I'm concerned, I'm the one who should have that key. Not you."

A loud belly laugh fills the room as Julien slaps his hand off the table and leans in. His eyes narrow as the muscles in his jaw tighten. "You've gone mad," he growls. "As I recall, you cowered in the bushes. You would have let her burn. Besides, Ancina told me what you've been up to." His nostrils flare. "I have given you far too much grace, Windsor. You still haven't taken care of the plebs you carelessly sired and left to fend for themselves. We agreed they needed to be blood-tamed or eliminated by now. And another thing, don't think I'm unaware you've been holding human feeders against their will. Something I ruled against almost a decade ago. Not to mention the witch you hold captive among them."

Harold sits staring at him, the muscle in his jaw tensing as he leans back in his chair. "In fact," Julien continues, "Ancina informed me of your plan to use your pleb army and the witch's blood to gain enough strength to try and overpower my sons and me. That your big plan was to attempt to claim my throne. So as far as I'm concerned, you deserve nothing more than the fate she promised."

Standing abruptly, Harold slams the table against Julien's chest, sending their drinks across the floor. "Is that so? You've chosen the love of a scraggly old hag over one of your own?"

Julien leaps to his feet, his fists clenched at his sides as he snarls. "Yes, that's so. Your betrayal has not gone unnoticed, nor will it be left unanswered."

"May your witch rot in hell for meddling. Regardless of what you think you know, Laurent, you should take heed to what I'm about to say. It's only a matter of time before the throne and all the liberties that go with it become mine." He steps forward until they're standing toe to toe. "See this face? I want you to have a good look at it. 'Cause this" —*Harold circles his face with his hand*— "this will be the last thing you see when I remove your head to take what should've always been mine."

Watching Harold storm toward the door, Julien holds his arms out. "You know where to find me, Windsor. My boys and I will be waiting!"

As Cassian's eyes spring open, Clara bounds forward, sending Mr. Green to the floor. Her eyes dart between him and Olivia. "Is that it? Is she finally done?"

Olivia's hand drops to her side, and the journal slams shut, but she remains still. Four sets of eyes focus on her—waiting.

"Okay, what happened in there?" Patricia scowls at Cassian. "Why hasn't she opened her eyes?" He shrugs, and she turns her glare on her mother. "Why hasn't she snapped out of it yet? Pull her out!" she demands.

"Calm down. I'm not sure. She's been in there longer than usual. Just give her a few minutes."

Finally, Patricia reaches for the journal as Olivia bounds forward, knocking it to the floor. She jumps back with her hand on her chest and gives the old tome a kick. "Jesus, Liv! You scared me half to death."

The tension in Cassian's shoulders finally releases, and his eyes meet hers as he offers a slight smile. "Well then, I think I'll retire to my room and let you ladies discuss this last entry." He places his hand on Olivia's shoulder, giving it a gentle squeeze as he passes. "Just call should you require me."

Nodding, Olivia peers up at her aunt. "I'm sorry, Aunt Trish." She reaches up to give her a hug. "I felt like I was falling through a dream. You know how when you wake just as you're about to hit the ground?"

"Ew," Patricia laughs. "Say no more, kiddo. I hate those dreams."

"We're just glad you're back, dear." Clara shifts in her seat, watching Helen shoo Mr. Green from the top of the journal.

"Come on, move it. I want to see if we can read anything in here now." A nasty growl resonates from the naturally friendly cat as he swats at Helen's hand. She steps back. "Whoa. What's gotten into you, kitty cat?" Scowling at Mr. Green, she pulls her hand to her chest. "Gees, you'd think *you* owned the dang thing."

Carefully studying the cat, Clara rests her hand on Helen's arm. "I'm not sure why he's reacting the way he is, but best to leave him for now. Why don't you get Olivia some breakfast so she can tell us where she's been."

"Breakfast?" Olivia's eyes dart to the morning sun peeking through the drapes of the big bay window. "Last I remember, it was—"

"Bedtime? Yes." Patricia points to the journal. "You've been in there all night."

Olivia places her hand over her rumbling stomach and glances around at the anticipation-filled faces as everything she's just witnessed comes flooding back. Though she saw some great moments, she still can't say that anything stood out as helpful yet. She leans down, shooing Mr. Green from the journal and flips the pages. "I can't believe you guys waited up all night. You must be exhausted."

Patricia stuffs a cushion under her arm and grins. "Sleep is overrated. Besides, you can't honestly believe we would leave you in there by yourself. Do you?"

"I wasn't alone. Cash was with me."

"Exactly," Patricia scoffs, folding her arms across her chest.

Olivia's face drops as she flicks past Harold leaving the Devil's Brew. "I don't understand. I can tell there's more here, but I can't read it anymore."

Helen sets a plate of pancakes and a cup of tea down as her stomach responds with a grumble. "Here, it sounds like you could use some nourishment. Why don't you eat up? Then you can tell us about your adventure."

"Thanks, Aunt Helen. Though I don't believe I've found the answer yet and, well, to be honest" *—she peers around at the curious faces—* "I'm not sure the rest of the book was meant for me."

Lost in thought, Clara stares at her, slowly running her finger along the crease of her lips before dropping her hand to the table with an exhaustive breath. "Of course, it was meant for you, dear." She forces a smile. "Timekeeper journals only have one interpreter. I believe you may need to hone in on your skills before you're able to read any further."

"Skills?"

"Yes. Meaning you need to work on your bond with the elements—strengthen your abilities." Olivia's regret in asking is instantaneous. She should have known her grandmother would leave no room for question. "Now, there must be something that sticks out from your time in there. What happened?"

Cutting into her pancakes, she stops for a moment and peers up. "Well, I guess I'm still learning who everyone is. I did finally discover Roger is Harold's son, but he certainly hasn't done anything wrong. At least not yet. I mean, he's only a toddler, for goodness' sake." She shrugs. "Even Cash and his brother were so young. I witnessed them playing in the sun for the first time." Her smile brightens as she recalls watching them dance through the sunbeams. "It wasn't all bright and cheery, though. I did hear about great-gran Ancina's hanging on old Gallows Hill, and I was privy to a rather heated argument between Julien and Harold at a tavern - the Devil's Brew." She tips her head, looking off into the memory. "In fact, Harold threatened to remove Julien's head to retrieve the resurrection key great-gran Ancina created for him."

Helen draws her feet under her bottom, pulling her nightdress over her knees. "Then I'd have to assume this is where it starts getting interesting."

"And possibly why Cassian chose to turn in as soon as he ensured Olivia was out safely," Clara says, pulling herself to her feet. She pats Olivia's shoulder on her way past. "I'm pleased you've become more open to reading the journal. Though if you insist on jumping into it on your own, perhaps it's time to concentrate on your magical strengths. I truly believe connecting with the elements may be required for you to continue reading anyway."

She may have presented it as a suggestion, but it was clear there was no choice.

Clara's attention shifts to Helen without waiting for a response. "If you're coming with me to the store this morning, that's enough chitter-chatter. I'm leaving in a half-hour."

Patricia leans back next to Olivia with a mocking grin. "Well, that won't be me. Thankfully, you gave me the day off. So I think I may stick around the house today and keep Liv company."

"You mean make sure she keeps her distance from Cassian," Helen chimes as she heads for the stairs. "In case you haven't noticed, he's harmless when it comes to Olivia." She places her hand on the bannister and looks back over her shoulder. "You, on the other hand, should be careful. You could become his lunch."

Flipping her hand, Patricia produces a swirling ball of flames in her palm. "Pfft. I do wish him luck, sister dear."

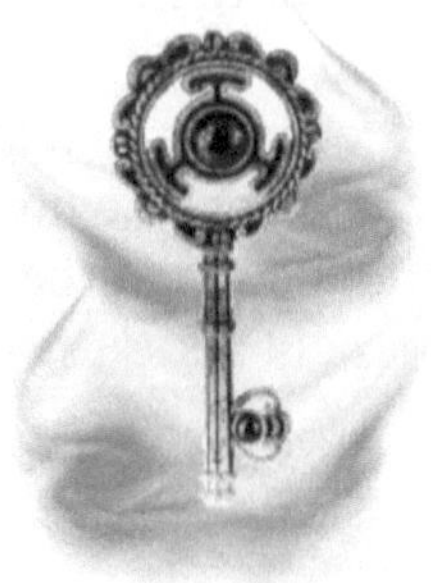

CHAPTER 25 ~ I LIVED THAT NIGHTMARE

Olivia lifts a fork full of pancakes to her lips and pauses. "I really wish you would try to get along with Cash. He's not like other vampires."

"Oh, Liv. Tell me he hasn't reeled you in with that damn glam of his. Look, let me enlighten you." Strolling over to the mantle, Patricia carefully picks up the bracelet Jimmy had worn the night of Summer Solstice. Holding it out in front of her face with her thumb and forefinger, she gives it a twirl. "Do you realize how Cassian knew about this—what it was?" Before Olivia can answer, she tosses it at her. "Let me tell you how. He recognized it because he has used them."

Olivia gasps, dropping the bracelet on the table as the red-eyed vampire biting into Jimmy's shoulder flashes before her. "No."

She shakes her head. "I don't believe that, Aunt Trish. Even if he did, he said he hadn't seen one in centuries. Besides, people change."

"See, that's the thing. He's not a person, Liv. You seem to keep forgetting he's a vampire—a hunter by nature. They look like harmless everyday people, but they can compel the innocent. Making them fall madly in love or having them do anything they ask. Then, as soon as their prey is comfortable—" She bares her teeth, slapping her hands together in front of Olivia's face. "They bite! They're not about to show you their true form right away. You'd never let them close."

"True form?"

She points to the bracelet. "Like the ones you saw when you touched that charm."

Olivia shakes her head. "Cash is nothing like them. He doesn't feed on people."

"Don't be foolish, Liv. The blood he's having shipped in here isn't synthetic. That's straight from the veins of living, breathing humans."

Standing, Olivia grabs her plate and starts toward the kitchen. "That's different. The blood is freely given. Not taken, and he's not sinking his teeth into anyone with a pulse."

"Don't be so sure about that," Patricia calls after her.

Cassian's bedroom door opens, and he stands, leaning against the doorframe. His eyes are fixed on the pulsing artery in Patricia's neck as she turns to face him. She shifts her weight, and he slowly lifts his gaze to meet hers. "You don't like me. That much is staggeringly clear, Miss Redfearn." Pushing himself off the frame, he straightens and takes a calculated step toward her. "Though beyond being a refined vampire and not at all what you were expecting, I haven't a clue why."

Disgust furnishes Patricia's face as she takes a step closer. "Refined?" Her shoulders rise with her feigned gagging. "Is that how you see drinking blood?" His irises enlarge, and she shakes her head, dropping her gaze from his. "Don't even try that on me, Bloodsucker! I am not susceptible to your hypnotic bullshit." She turns with her finger raised. "As for your eating habits, they're nothing short of animalistic, barbaric, inhumane, not to mention downright disgusting."

The springs in the old sofa protest under his weight as he takes a seat and runs his fingers across the worn flowers in the material. "Some would call chawing on a steak the same. Yet you nearly licked your plate after dinner last night, didn't you?"

Out by the rose garden, Olivia sits with her knees tucked against her chest while Mr. Green lies lazily at her side, soaking in the sun. She's been replaying the conversation with her aunt for the past forty-five minutes. Finally, she looks skyward as if the answers might fall into her lap and asks, "Cash, please tell me Aunt Trish is wrong. Tell me you're not holding those people captive to drain their blood."

"Screw you, Bloodsucker!" Patricia spins, tossing a fireball at the empty seat on the sofa where Cassian had been only a moment before.

"You have my word, Olivia. I am not holding anyone captive."

"Oh," Olivia gasps. Holding her hand to her chest, she stares up as Cassian appears between the opening in the hedges. "You startled me. I can't believe you heard me."

"My apologies. Yes, I heard you, and none too soon, I might add." She glances at him quizzically as he sits on the grass next to her, draping his arms over his knees. "Your aunt and I were having a rather heated discussion, and as usual, I don't believe she was happy with my response." He picks a blade of grass, twisting it between his fingers and smiles. "Let's just say I felt the heat as I was leaving."

"I see." Olivia covers her mouth in an attempt to stifle her laugh. "For the record, fireballs are more of a toy to her. You'll know when she gets really ticked. The skies will darken, and thunder roars. She won't be tossing fireballs any longer. Her fingers will ignite, and she'll simply strike." Drawing in her cheeks, she lifts her hand and points. "Pew," she spits, making the sound of a laser. "Hot blue beams. Hot enough to cut metal."

Cassian chuckles. "Well, let's hope I never upset her to that degree then." His face tenses into a frown as he shrugs. "I realize that our lifestyle, our necessity for blood. At least for most, it isn't the easiest to understand." He drops his head between his arms, staring at the ground. "Being born into this life, this isn't something I learned to live with. This is who I am. Though I understand that my father struggled for many centuries to adjust."

"Cash, I don't mean to change the topic, but—" She pauses as he tosses the blade of grass he's been twirling in his fingers and rises to his feet. "Um, I need you to know—"

He holds his hand out, glancing over his shoulder at the backdoor. "Can we continue this elsewhere? I'm not sure I should be this close to the house with things being as heated as they are. I think your aunt could use some time to cool down."

She stares at his outstretched offering for a moment and nods. "All right," she forces a smile and reaches for his hand. When her warm fingers meet the cool of his palm, her body tenses. He pulls her forward, and her cheek nearly collides with his chest. The strange intoxicating male spice that fills her nose is oddly so familiar. She quickly steps back as an image of her laying against his chest floods her thoughts. Her questioning eyes meet his, but before she can speak, he nods.

"Yes, Olivia. It was me that calmed the fears of your most recent nightmare. I felt your fear, the guilt that had consumed you over your parent's death, and I couldn't allow you to suffer from such a belief."

"I'm not sure I understand." Squinting, she peers up at him through her lashes. "How could you know about my— I mean, I haven't had a nightmare in quite some time now."

"The night you summoned us here." Cassian shifts uncomfortably. "Everyone was in bed when the sound of your heart racing filled my ears." His eyes drop from hers. "I could sense your fear." He licks his lips. "My mind connected to yours, and I saw your dream." Shaking his head, he takes a step closer. "I'm unsure if you screamed aloud or unconsciously, but I ran to your room when you cried out for help."

Olivia stands staring at him in silence. She's never shared the dream in its entirety with anyone, not even her aunts or grandmother. "You saw my dream? The death of my parents?"

He lowers his gaze. "Yes, but my focus wasn't the dream, Olivia. I came to you because of what I felt—what you felt. The terror, the guilt. I couldn't leave you with that."

Turning away, she starts toward the path leading to the stream, then stops. Keeping her head low, she turns back to face him.

"You may have been able to relieve me of its horror for one evening, but I will always relive that night." Her voice raises with her gaze. "You can't just erase something of that magnitude, Cash. No one seems to understand that. It's not as simple as forgetting a bad dream." She pokes herself in the chest. "I actually lived that nightmare!"

Before she can walk away, two strong arms envelop her shoulders, drawing her into the intoxicating scent of spice. She's never been one for the cold, but the coolness of his chest feels comfortable—safe. His head rests on hers. "Olivia, I realize that I may not be able to remove that horrific moment from your life completely. However, I will do my best to exchange those nightmares for beautiful dreams whenever possible."

Stepping back, she smiles up at him. "You're really making it difficult for me to hold up the whole *'vamp witch rivalry'* we're supposed to have."

"I see no need for us to be enemies." The slightest hint of a smile plays on his lips as he fans his hand toward the path. "Shall we?"

They're sitting along the river's edge, enjoying the tranquil sounds of rippling water and chirping birds, when she turns to see him running his hand down Mr. Green's back. "Cash—"

"Olivia, I believe I already know what you're going to ask. It's about the vamp glam," he holds up his fingers, making air quotes, "right? I have heard it mentioned a few times in the last few days."

Laying her head on her folded arms, she feigns a smile. That's not what she had planned on asking or rather telling him, but it is a point of discussion she had also intended to visit. "Well, you're right. That topic has come up plenty."

He tips his head, offering a slight smile. "Yes, I've heard, and I'd love to tell you differently, but I'm afraid it is true. We have a built-in charm to lure humans, but that's not something I can control. It's not an amulet or talisman that I can simply take off." He scratches behind Mr. Green's ear, smiling as the friendly feline pushes his head against his fingertips. "And it doesn't usually work on cats."

"I trust Mr. Green. He's always been an excellent judge of character." She shifts uncomfortably. "Though that's not really what I was going to say. I'm not sure why, but I'm unable to read any further into the journal. At least for now."

"I know."

She sits up straight, cranking her body toward him. "You knew?"

"Your thoughts aren't entirely private, Olivia."

A frown settles on her face as she squints over at him. "I guess that means I should be able to release you."

"You can try if you'd like, but if it's all right with you, I think I'd like to stay for now. I believe your grandmother may be right. That you may have to work on connecting with your magic" —*twisting his lips, his eyes dart to the side*— "or connecting with your elements. I'm not exactly sure which it is, but I think that could draw some unwanted attention which means you may need me here more than you know."

Olivia nods. "I'd appreciate that. I know how much this means to you and your family, and I promise I'll do what has to be done to continue."

"I know you will, and you have no idea what that means to me." He offers her a warm smile. "Now, enough of that. I know you have something else on your mind. What is it you've been wanting to ask?" Holding his hand up, he pulls his fingertips toward him as if to draw it out of her. "Come on, let's have it."

"Well, I have been thinking about how you easily stitched a new dream over my nightmare. It's a form of compulsion, right?"

"I suppose some might consider it compulsion, though my father always referred to it as dream weaving. It's not something the average vampire can do though my father also had the ability. My mother claimed it was something gained from the wit—" he pauses to correct himself. "My apologies. I meant Ancina."

"Witch doesn't bother me. It may have been a derogatory term in the eighteenth century, but not today," she shrugs. "I must remember to ask Gran about dream weaving. So maybe Aunt Helen was right about us being on the same demonic descendant list."

Peering over his shoulder at the path, Cassian chuckles. "Yes. I suppose."

"You use compulsion on someone while they're awake. Right?" He nods. "So you could compel someone to give up their blood willingly or even have one believe they've fallen in love with you if you chose."

Cassian's gaze meets hers briefly before dropping to her lips, then lazily moves back to her eyes. "Yes. We've established I have the ability to compel someone, Olivia, but I have not—"

His words cut off at the heavy footfalls coming from behind. They turn to face the path as a panting Patricia breaks through the trees. Her cheeks are a deep red, nearly matching the surrounding spider orchids that colour the treeline. "That's a bloody lie, you parasite!" Her eyes flit to Olivia. "He just tried his hypnotic shit on me before he pulled his disappearing act." She steps toward him as they gain their feet. "Tell her the truth," she demands as the sky darkens and thunder cracks overhead.

Olivia stands, her gaze bouncing between her aunt and Cassian as they exchange words.

"I have only spoken the truth." His eyes shoot back to Patricia's. "I will admit, for a brief moment, I was tempted to compel you because, quite frankly, I'm tired of dodging fireballs." He tips his head with a shrug. "I would much prefer if we could get along, especially since we are currently sharing a dwelling."

Patricia's head falls back with laughter, her smile slowly fading as her gaze meets his. "Fat fangy chance, Bloodsucker!" She swings her hand, releasing a fireball from her hip as if she's pitching a softball directly toward Cassian's chest. He ducks, but the flaming ball of death carves a path through the back of his suit jacket, setting it ablaze.

"Aunt Trish!" Olivia squeals as she rushes to pat out the flames.

"What?" Peering at her niece, Patricia purses her lips. "Come on, Liv. It was just a fireball. I could have zapped him."

"But you still hit him!"

Taking a deep breath, Patricia releases a heavy sigh. "Oh, all right. Submergo." Her eyes narrow on Cassian. "One of these times, there will be no putting you out. You should think about that, leech."

He shrugs off what's left of his jacket and begins to unbutton his charred shirt. "Fair enough, Patricia. I believe we've firmly established that you and I will not be friends. Though I wish you could understand that I am not here to make you uncomfortable. In fact, I may actually be of assistance when other vampires show up."

"Right," she sneers, turning her attention to Olivia. "We really should test your given abilities today. Whatever that book wants, I can almost guarantee you'll need to use whatever goddess-granted gift you have. So please put your big girl panties on, and let's get this over with. The sooner we can relieve ourselves of this," her eyes stroll the length of Cassian's body, "this mutant. The better."

He tips his head toward Olivia. "It pains me to say this, but your aunt is right. It's probably best to at least figure out where your strengths lie." Placing his hand on her shoulder, he smiles. "I'll be in my room if you need me."

Watching him disappear, she turns to her aunt with a pout firmly in place. "You didn't need to do that. Cash is here only because I couldn't release him."

Patricia tips her head, the corners of her mouth tightening into a sarcastic grin. "Yes. Well, maybe you should give that another go then. Hmm?"

"Aunt Trish."

CHAPTER 26 ~ UNINVITED GUESTS

Taking a deep breath, Patricia drops her folded arms with a huff. "Okay, fine. Let's see if all this sun has done anything for you." She points to the large stone at the edge of the river. "See that big rock? Stand back and watch this."

Extending her arm, she points to the jagged corner near the top of the boulder. A blue bolt zaps the edge, blowing pieces of stone into the stream. "There," she says, blowing on the end of her finger with a smile.

Olivia stares at the stone with wide eyes. "I can't do that!"

"Of course, you can, Liv. You opened a damn portal. Remember? This is nothing compared to that. First, you have to believe in yourself. Then concentrate on the spot you want to hit and picture the energy blasting it off. It's really that simple."

"There's no way!" Olivia shakes her head. "The last time blue bolts came from my hands, Jimmy disappeared."

"Look, I'm trying to teach you how to control all that energy." Patricia takes her hand and aims it toward the stone. "Now, focus on the edge and release the heat."

Holding her breath, she narrows her eyes at the boulder and points to the edge. Her arm begins to tremble, and she can feel her body heat, but nothing happens. Finally, she drops her arm and expels the hot air from her lungs. "I can't!" She waves her hand in front of her face. "All that did was make me hot."

"Because you're fighting it, Liv. You have to release that energy, and for goodness sake, don't hold your breath."

Flopping down on the ground, Olivia closes her eyes and takes a big breath trying to calm herself. "Maybe I can't manipulate energy like you."

"Nonsense. I've seen your glow. Besides, I hate to keep bringing it up, but you opened a damn portal. Based on that fact, I would say you are hiding at least two prominent elements in this body of yours." Animating her movements, she outlines Olivia's frame. "Now get up, and we'll try something I know has worked in the past."

Groaning, Olivia pulls herself to her feet. "Maybe we should wait—" She stops as the sound of rustling trees draws her attention toward the far end of the stream. "Did you hear that?"

Growling, Mr. Green sits, peering into the tree line. "Mmhmm. Looks like kitty cat sees something he doesn't like either." Patricia squints, trying to see through the leaves. "I suppose the good news is that they can't come out till dark." She fans her hand toward the house. "Unless, of course, they're part of your BFF's family."

"Vampires? You think there are vampires in there?"

Patricia gives an uncommitted shrug. "I'm not a hundred percent, but if I had to guess—" She tips her head, still peering out at the dense forest.

"Cash!" Olivia calls out without another thought.

She shrinks back as Patricia flashes her a perturbed glance. "Why would you call him down here? I can handle a damn vampire, Liv."

"That might be true, but you didn't know there is more than one out there, and sunset will be soon enough." Cassian places his hand on Olivia's shoulder. "I'm glad you called me."

Olivia's heart starts to race. "How many are out there?"

"Two, possibly three, but between your aunt and I, we can handle them." he glances up at Patricia and is met with a curt nod.

"Go on up to the house, Liv."

Cassian's head flies around, his eyes flashing red. "No. You stay with us. The sun is already beginning to set." He peers back at a scowling Patricia. "You do not want to make her a moving target. It's as good as ringing a dinner bell."

"Concentrate on the target and release the heat," Patricia reminds Olivia as shadows begin to fall over the stream.

"And whatever you do." Cassian glances back briefly before anchoring his sight on the tree line. "Do not run."

Three paths of swaying treetops converge as they move toward them. Patricia steadies herself, her arms outstretched and her fingers splayed. Blue bolts dance along the lengths of her fingers as she waits for them to emerge, but it's as if time has suddenly stood still. All sounds from the forest have ceased. There are no croaking frogs, chirping crickets, or buzzing tree beetles—just silence. Even the rustling of the trees has stopped.

"What happened? Where did they go," she asks, dropping her hands as she straightens.

"Don't—" Cassian starts, but it's too late. Three hideous vampires with red eyes and fangs bared rush toward them.

Cassian disappears into the forest, taking one with him, while Patricia quickly regathers her stance to remove the second, bearing down on her.

The heat of fear rushes through Olivia's body quicker than the vampire's approach, and she swings her arms forward, repeating the words in her head, 'concentrate on the target and release the heat.' Blue bolts bursts from her hands, knocking her off her feet as she watches the charge flash over the stream.

"Woohoo!" Patricia howls as she grabs Olivia's hand and yanks her to her feet. "You did it, Liv!"

"Did I get him? Are they gone?" Olivia pulls back and looks around. "Where's Cash?"

"Right here." Grinning, Cassian walks out between the trees with his hand raised. "Vampires love the element of surprise."

"Yeah, well, they didn't really surprise us, and I had them."

"You had one at best," Cassian says, smiling over at Olivia. "Thankfully, your niece was here."

Feeling the heat rise to her cheeks, Olivia looks down at her hands. "I'm still not sure how I did that. I heard Aunt Trish's words in my head, and it just happened."

"Hell-o-o. Anyone down there?" They turn to the sound of Clara's voice carrying down the path.

Patricia cranks her head toward the house. "Coming, mom!" Her eyes narrow on Cassian as she pats Olivia's arm. "I always knew she had it in her. Anyway, we should go fill them in."

Cassian smirks at Patricia. "That you did." He reaches out for Olivia's shoulder, but noticing the blood on his hand, he quickly pulls it back and tucks it into his pocket. "I believe I should escape for a shower." As he starts up the path, he glances back. "I'll be in my room if you need me, Olivia."

As they enter the kitchen, Clara stops arranging her herbs and turns toward the door. Her focus quickly moves to Olivia. "Okay. Spit it out. I can tell by the look of you two that something happened. What have we missed?"

Olivia flops down on one of the kitchen chairs while Patricia grabs two mugs. "Vampires," she says.

"What?" Clara and Helen chime in unison.

"Yep. That damn book has been nothing but a curse since it hit your store and even worse since Liv has been reading it. Just like I said." Pouring two cups of tea, she slides one across the table and takes a seat at the end, taking a sip from hers. "On the bright side" — *she smiles at Olivia*— "Liv zapped one of them."

Clara slides into the chair next to her granddaughter and rests her cheek on the back of her hand. "How many? Were you reading the journal when they came?"

Patricia holds up three fingers, wiggling them in the air as she sips her tea. "One for each of us, and no, she wasn't reading the journal."

"One for each of you?" Helen's brows draw together. "Oh, Cash was with you?" Her eyes spring open as her gaze shifts between her niece and sister. "Wait. Did you say Olivia zapped one?"

"Yeah, she did," Patricia says proudly, holding her hand up to high-five her niece.

"I might have zapped one, but I still don't know how." Olivia glances down, toying with her fingers.

Rising from her seat, Clara places her hands on the table. "I think it's due time to involve Elizabeth. I can call her over to see just what elements you're connecting with. The sooner we know, the easier it will be to work with them. The one thing I'm certain of is that you're still rejecting your Goddess given abilities."

"I swear I'm not, Gran."

Patricia reaches across the table and pats her hand. "I hate being the bad guy here, Liv, but I have to agree. I watched you trembling out there today until your body was about to burst into flames."

Olivia's shoulders sag with a heavy sigh. "I'm not sure I know how to release it. It really just happens spontaneously."

Helen places her hand on her shoulder and takes the seat Clara had been occupying next to her. "Aw, honey. You obviously tucked it away and fastened a little knot around it. I have seen Elizabeth and mom unbind someone before. So don't worry. We got this," she winks.

"Good news," Clara says, walking back into the kitchen. "Elizabeth is on her way." Her eyes scan those staring back at her around the table as she takes a deep breath. "She said she's been waiting for my call. So I imagine she won't be long at all."

"Does she know about the journal?"

Clara brushes back the stray hairs on the sides of her head, tucking them back into her bun and forces a smile. "No, I haven't told her yet. Nor have I mentioned that we have a vampire staying under our roof. Though it's not something that will escape her once she enters the archway. Besides, we'll have time to discuss those details when she gets here."

Olivia twists her lips, peering sideways at her aunt Patricia as she shrugs. The sound of the Westminster Chime echoes through the old house, and she points toward the front entrance. "Ah, I assume that's the old battleaxe now? Wanna remind me why you can't do this yourself, mom?"

Helen chuckles, slapping her sister's hand. "Hold your tongue."

"Yes. Hold your tongue," Clara scowls. "I may be able to speculate elements, but Elizabeth can clearly see them. Plus, she is one of my dearest friends, and let's not forget she has been appointed the high priestess of the coven since I stepped down. So, do not embarrass me, Patricia."

"But Gran—" Olivia begins to protest when Clara raises her hand.

"Nah-uh. You just stay put. Everything will be fine."

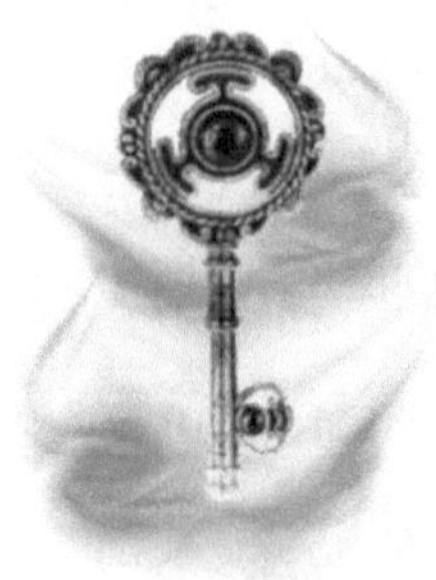

CHAPTER 27 ~ BOUND?

Gabriel perches himself on the bathroom vanity. With his arm draped across his knee, he twists Cassian's toothbrush between his fingers while he waits for him to emerge from the shower. It's only moments until the water shuts off, and Cassian steps out, grabbing a towel from the rack. "Did you really think your presence would surprise me, little brother?"

He chuckles, placing the toothbrush back in the holder as he steps down. "Nah. I knew you'd sense me. I was hoping to hurry you along."

Wrapping the towel around his waist, Cassian grabs another and scrubs his dark hair. "And to what do I owe this honour?"

"Clarentina drank this morning. Drained half our stock," he smiles as his brother stills and stares at him. "It's true. She's not a hundred percent, but she's mobile and speaking." He flips his hand out. "She's been asking for you. Keeps questioning when you will return with father."

Walking out to his room, Gabriel follows, and their heads turn toward the door—to the voices just outside.

Like everyone else, Olivia listens closely to the exchange as her grandmother greets their guest. "Good evening, Elizabeth. Thanks so much for coming by so quickly. Please, come in."

"Don't be silly, Clara dear. As I said, I've been waiting for this call. I have already prepared the sacred knot and incantation."

There's a moment of silence where Olivia can almost picture this old woman's head spinning around with her nose in the air. Then comes the expected gasp. She exchanges a glance with her aunts and lowers her head.

"Sweet Goddess, help us! Do I sense—"

"Elizabeth, try to stay calm. We're aware of his presence. He's actually our houseguest. At least for the time being."

"Guest?!"

"Yes. Guest. I don't care to go into the entire story just now, but Olivia's journey seems to require him here."

"Oh, Clara. A vampire? You poor dear."

Hearing Elizabeth's gasp, Olivia rolls her eyes, places her hand on her chest and drops her jaw. Stifling her laugh, Patricia swats her hand down while Helen shakes her head, 'shushing' them.

"It's not as awful as you'd suspect. Cassian is unlike any vampire *we've* ever encountered. He's a scion. His father was the vampire king, Julien Laurent."

"Julien Laurent? As in the first original?"

"Mmhmm."

"I see. Well, I can tell his stay here holds great importance to you. So I won't question your reasoning. At least not yet."

"You shouldn't. Though I will tell you that his father was important enough to have one of our own create a timekeeper journal for him," Clara says.

"A timekeeper journal? Oh my! You never mentioned that. Only a powerful ancient would have been able to create a timekeeper journal."

"Yes, I'm aware. That ancient happens to be one of my ancestors. That's why I am trusting you not to share this information with anyone. You know the attention it will attract if word gets out."

"Don't be silly. Of course, you have my word," Elizabeth smiles. "Now, where is our little Olivia?"

"Right this way." Clara waves her hand toward the french doors. "They're all waiting in the kitchen."

As they enter the room, Olivia drops her gaze to Mr. Green in her lap while Helen graciously tips her head. "Good evening, Ms. Fletcher." With a flip of her hand, she mutters, 'gingiberi ti citrea,' producing a steaming cup of ginger lemon tea at the end of the table.

"Good evening, Helen." She cranks her head toward Patricia and forces a smile. "Well, hello, Patricia dear. Why is it we never see you at the meetings anymore?"

Clearly unamused by her presence, Patricia rests her chin on her palm and scrunches her nose. "Well, Elizabeth dear, that would be because I have a standing date with the altar here on Thursdays. As I see it, the Goddess isn't particular about where we give thanks. We're free to worship wherever and however we see fit."

"Hmm. Yes, fair enough, I suppose." Olivia raises her head, and Elizabeth's stare floats to meet hers. "Ah, Olivia. You've grown so much since I've last seen you. Not that you'd recall, I'm sure. I first met you when you were a mere youngster." She extends her finger and slowly glides it to the side, moving the teacup Helen had positioned at the end of the table to the seat next to Olivia. Pulling out the chair, she smiles down at her. "Mind if I sit next to you?"

Peering up at her grandmother, Clara lazily blinks as she gives a slight nod before taking her seat at the end of the table. "Of course. It's nice to meet you, Elizabeth," Olivia says, fanning her hand toward the chair.

"Oh, I tend to doubt that. Not that I'm hurt by it, mind you. I am fully aware that my presence is making you nervous. I'm not new to this situation, dear. Only new to you. I also know you've been hiding from magic for far too long. However, I understand you're ready to fix all that, and I" —*she places her hand to her chest with a smile*— "am more than happy to help." Grabbing her teacup, she leans back in her chair and takes a sip. Her eyes widen as she smacks her lips together and peers over at Helen. "Oh my. This is absolutely delicious. You must share your recipe at the next meeting."

Tapping the table, Clara clears her throat while peering at Elizabeth from under her brows. "Right," Elizabeth says with an apologetic smile. "It's not often that I get to be social these days." She holds her hand out to Olivia, unfurling her fingers toward her. "Shall we get on with it then?"

She places her hand into Elizabeth's outstretched palm and immediately feels her insides begin to heat. Every muscle tightens, flexing under her skin. Finally, she tugs her hand free with a grunt, sending Mr. Green leaping from her lap with a squeal. "What the hell was that?"

Elizabeth opens her eyes, her jaw tensing as she takes a deep breath. "That was you fighting me, dear. You have your magic tied in such a tight knot that I can't break past your barrier."

Gabriel steps back from the door and turns his attention to his brother. "A knot? Like her powers are bound?"

Cassian nods. "It seems so."

"But how can that be when she can clearly read the journal and was able to summon you and Elias here?"

"It's a long story, but her powers seem to be selective. Or maybe it's a partial binding. I'm not sure how these things work exactly. Though she has recently hit a wall with the journal—she can't see anything since reading the last entry."

"Shit. Well, who bound her?"

Cassian pulls on his pants. "She did," he says, fastening the button.

"She bound herself?"

"Yes."

"Why the hell would she do that?"

Shrugging on his shirt, he begins doing up the buttons. "Her reasons are just as valid as mother trying to starve herself." He tugs at his cuffs, narrowing his eyes on his brother. "You know it's impolite to eavesdrop."

Gabriel raises his hands. "Hey, it's not eavesdropping if they're talking loud enough to hear."

"Right. How silly of me." Cassian releases an exhaustive groan, running his hands down the front of his shirt. "Come away from there, and I'll get you a drink. I'd like to hear more about what's been happening with mom anyway."

Back in the kitchen, Olivia chews on her bottom lip as she peers around the table at the long faces. For the first time in her life, she not only needs to access her magic—she wants to. "Can we fix it?"

"Hell yeah, we can," Patricia blurts, slapping her hand off the table. "Right, Lizzie? Tell her we can fix this."

Helen gasps while Clara drops her forehead to her hand, but the high priestess remains unscathed by Patricia's ignorance. Instead, she shifts her focus from Patricia to Olivia. "My preference is Elizabeth, if you don't mind, but to answer your question – yes. I believe this can be rectified. As long as you truly want it, that is. This isn't something someone has done to you. This is self-inflicted. You must want to undo it. That's the only way this will work."

Olivia straightens, meeting her gaze. "I want to. I'm ready to do this."

"I was hoping you'd say that. That's why I came prepared." Elizabeth grabs her large tapestry bag and sets it on her lap. The well-worn wooden handles drop open, and she pulls out a white cotton rope tied into several knots with what appears to be red hair. Setting it on the table in front of Olivia, she peers up at Helen. "Could you put two of your largest jars of purified water into a cast pot, Helen dear?"

"Of course."

"Thank you. We'll be needing it out at the altar."

Olivia stares at the rope, her brows drawing together as she runs her hand over her head. "Is that my hair?"

"It most certainly is. Your grandmother was so kind to scavenge it from your brush for me." Stuffing her hand back into her bag, Elizabeth continues pulling out items and placing them on the table. A few bottles of liquid followed by some bags of herbs. Next, she draws out a small satchel containing white powder, a large pair of silver scissors and a white pillar candle. Taking inventory of the items, she sets the bag down next to her, picks up the baggies and small glass jars then hands them to Clara. "We'll need to work together." Holding her arms open, she sweeps them forward toward the backdoor. "Come now, everyone. This will take all our energy to create."

As Olivia stands, Elizabeth places her hand on her shoulder. "Grab your rope and take a seat around the altar. I'll tell you when we're ready."

"Should I call on Cassian?"

Elizabeth's back straightens. "The vampire?" she asks incredulously. "Heavens no. A vampire should not be in the vicinity of a sacred circle. Besides, this is not for show, Olivia. We're trying to help you untie the binds you've placed on yourself—to allow you to work with your elements. Right now, it's forcing through whenever it can. That, my dear, is unpredictable and extremely dangerous. Thankfully, it hasn't backfired yet. And believe me when I say it can only be by the good grace of the Goddess that it hasn't." She turns toward the backdoor, glancing over her shoulder with her finger raised. "So do not insult her by inviting a vampire to the altar."

In an attempt to conceal his grin, Gabriel lifts his fist to his lips. "Eww, it doesn't sound like your presence here is overly welcomed."

Holding out one of the golden chalices Soloman had delivered with the stock of blood, Cassian shrugs. "Olivia wants me here. That's all that matters as far as I'm concerned."

Gabriel snickers. "Yes, I can tell." He takes a generous drink and sets his glass on the end table. "I've only been here but a few minutes, and I can already see what Elias was talking about."

"And what might that be," Cassian asks, running his fingers over the etchings on the stem of his goblet.

"Meh, it's nothing."

"Spit it out, little brother."

Scratching his temple with a smirk, Gabriel lowers his head. "Just something about you being sweet on the little sorceress."

"Is that so?" Cassian's gaze shoots up to meet his sired brother's smirk with narrowed eyes. "Well, Elias should mind his mouth, and so should you. It seems the pair of you have forgotten I am the standing sovereign as long as father is not here." Placing his glass down, he walks over to look out the window, keeping his back to Gabriel. "Tell mother I'll be home as soon as possible and remind her to stay strong. I'm confident we'll have father back before long."

"I'm sorry, Cash. You're right. I didn't mean any disrespect. I'll do my best to appease Clarentina for a little while longer," Gabriel says, bowing as he disappears, leaving the door swinging behind him.

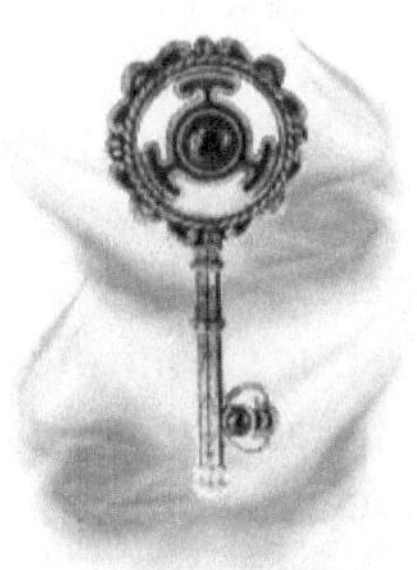

CHAPTER 28 ~ THE UNBINDING

The ladies gather around the common altar as Olivia has a seat on the stone bench. She sits cradling the knotted rope in her hands, attempting to ignore the nervous churning of her stomach when Mr. Green wraps around her ankle. He lets out a louder than usual 'Meow' and leaps onto the bench beside her, nudging her elbow with the top of his head. Shushing him, she runs her hand down his back as she watches the four older ladies prepare the altar.

Patricia lights three incense on the mantle while Clara stacks the wood on the hearth. Elizabeth stands back for a moment, muttering under her breath and checks the area before waving Patricia forward. "That should do it. I believe we're about ready to begin. If you could like the fire, please, dear."

"You got it, Lizzie." Ignoring Elizabeth's dirty look, she winks at Olivia and flips her hand toward the neatly stacked wood. "Flamma!" As the wood ignites, Helen hangs the cast pot over the flames and steps back, grabbing two of the ingredients from Clara's hands. "Shall I give the water a bit of a kick?" Patricia wiggles her fingers toward the pot. "You know, add a little heat to that baby," she grins.

Olivia can't help but chuckle, watching Elizabeth tense as she closes her eyes and shakes her head with a feigned smile. Patricia is undoubtedly doing everything in her power to irritate the high priestess, and Elizabeth is doing everything within her power to ignore the attempts. "No, dear. That won't be necessary. The water is already beginning to simmer."

"Alrighty then. I'll just sit with Olivia and let the rest of you do your thing."

But before Patricia can walk away, Clara holds out two small jars of liquid. "Not so fast. It's your job to deliver the dragon's blood and clove oil. Once Helen has delivered her offerings, you'll add three drops of each to the pot, calling out your element, and you'll take your position when required. Understood?"

The corner of Patricia's mouth tightens as she nods. "Yeah, I got it."

"Look, I know you don't like these ceremonies, but I need—" Clara stops herself. "No, Olivia needs all of our strengths right now."

"I said I got it." She lowers her gaze and quietly joins her sister, watching as Elizabeth draws the invoking pentagram in the air above the altar. She then takes one of the glass bottles marked verbena and counts to nine, dripping it into the simmering pot above the fire. "Goddess, we ask you to help us loosen these binds that hold Olivia from the gifts you've granted her." She waves her hand through the steam in a circular motion, then pushes it skyward. "I come to you with the power of air."

As the air element, etched on the bricks below, begins to glow a brilliant yellow, Clara steps forward. She drizzles tiny pieces of vetivert root into the pot and opens a small satchel of soil. Pouring the pouch into her palm, she rubs her hands together, letting the granules fall into the simmering water as she speaks. "I offer my strength from earth and air." Then, just as Elizabeth had done, she waves her hand through the steam in a circular motion and pushes it skyward before stepping aside.

The earth symbol shimmers a vivid green, and Helen steps forward to join Clara, emptying the lemon juice and rose water into the mix. "I come with the strength of water," she says, moving her hand over the pot in a stirring motion.

Blue illuminates the water symbol around the pentacle, and Helen shifts to the side as Patricia moves toward the altar. Then, just as Clara instructed, she adds three drops from the first jar and three from the next. Finally, she holds out her hands and looks skyward. "I bring the power of storm and fire." Thunder rolls above as the fire sign glows red.

Clara takes the large wooden spoon from the side of the altar and begins to stir the pot. Three times to the left, then three times to the right before carefully resting the spoon across the top of the bubbling brew. She then pulls a small anointing flask from her pocket and dips it into the mixture. "Come kneel here in the center and place your binds in front of you," she says, gesturing to the ground just in front of the altar.

Olivia takes the knotted rope in hand and points to the center of the etched pentacle. Her eyes flit to her grandmother's. "You want me to stand inside there?"

Clara lights the tall white pillar candle and places it on the mantle before turning to face her. "Yes. You are the focus."

As she moves to kneel in the center of the pentacle, the small circle etching at the top point glistens, and the outer circle begins to glow. Olivia gasps, turning to watch as a vibrant violet slowly surrounds her. "I feel like I'm being locked in."

"We've called to the Goddess, and her attention is now focused on you." Elizabeth hands her a thick piece of paper. Not like something you'd purchase from a store. It screams ancient, similar to the pages of the journal. "This is what you'll read aloud. It's a standard unbinding incantation."

Olivia can hear the high priestess speaking, but movement has caught her eye. Her gaze bounces to the ladies shifting their positions around the pentacle to stand on their elements. Her mind suddenly vacates the conversation, making a note of their places. *Aunt Helen is on the top right—water. Aunt Trish below me on the bottom right—*

fire. Gran's on the bottom left—earth. Is this something I'll need to know?

Elizabeth snaps her fingers. "Olivia, you need to pay attention. You mustn't be distracted by what's happening around you."

"Right. I'm sorry. I'm so nervous," she says, trying to control her shaking hands.

Mr. Green lets out a *meow*, flopping next to the altar as Clara reassuringly squeezes her hand. "It's normal to feel anxious. Take a breath and try to relax. Just read the words and envision the knots in the rope unravelling." She holds up the anointing flask. "We'll begin when you're ready."

Watching Elizabeth take her place at the top left of the pentacle, Olivia asks, "If you're all on your elements, does that mean I'm spirit?"

"Yes, dear," Elizabeth responds, her tone sharp with annoyance. "Just tell us when you're ready."

Olivia takes a deep breath. "Okay. Then, I guess I'm as ready as I'll ever be."

Elizabeth's lips tense into a slight smile as she nods. "You must place the rope on the ground in front of you and stay focused. The turmoil you feel in your stomach are the knots that bind you. Visualize them loosening as you think about why you tied them in the first place and why you want to be set free. You'll continue to repeat the verse I gave you until all nine knots have been undone."

"Wait. How am I supposed to undo the knots if I'm not holding the rope?"

Patricia leans forward. "They'll undo as you accept who you are. That includes your inner strengths, your fears and your desires."

The four women begin to hum, moving slowly to the right around the etched pentacle's edge. Their low tone rising as they spread their arms, twirling past each element. A splash of liquid hits Olivia's cheek, and she's met with her grandmother's glare. Chucking her chin toward the paper, Clara lowers the anointing flask, turning across the water sign as she hums.

Come on, Olivia. They're doing this for you. Now, think about why you locked magic away and read.

She closes her eyes, and the flaming ceiling falls on her parents, sending a shiver down her spine. Taking a deep breath, she looks down at the paper, her hands trembling as she begins to read. "Goddess, I kneel before you strong but bound." Thunder rolls overhead, and she pauses to look up as the clouds close in. Another splash hits her cheek, and she continues.

"By Earth, Air, Water and Fire,
I ask you to undo these knots I've tied
—Hecate, this is my desire."

The fire roars, and Olivia looks up as flames lick the sides of the pot. She can see the knots in the rope loosen. No, her eyes aren't supposed to leave the paper, but the temptation is simply too great. A few more drops from the anointing flask, and she quickly drops her gaze.

"By the power of three and nine,
my elements shall realign.
By sky and sea,
magic shall be one with me."

The first knot unravels.
As she peers up with a smile, another splash hits her forehead.

"By moon and sun,
my will shall be done.
For this power is mine!"

Around her, there's an echo of *'So mote it be'* as the women continue to dance methodically.

"Keep going, Liv," Patricia calls out, earning a nasty scowl from Elizabeth.

Taking a deep breath, she begins again. No knot unties on her second try nor her third, not even on her fourth. Frustrated, she finally tosses the paper down and gains her feet, calling out to the sky.

"Mother Goddess, I stand before you stripped of my dignity to ask for your help."

Elizabeth stops. "What is she doing?"

"She's finding her own way," Clara says, nudging her to continue around the circle.

There's a low roll of thunder above as a gust of warm wind wraps its arms around Olivia, whipping her hair across her face. Unwavering, she pulls the hair from her eye, wipes the tear before it hits her cheek and glances down as a knot unties. "I know I have unwisely ignored the gifts you've given me. I'm asking for your forgiveness. I was afraid of them. Scared that eventually, I might misuse them like my parents did—that I would hurt someone I love."

The wind picks up, whipping her hair around her face as rain begins to fall. She clenches her hands and stares into the storm, licking the droplets from her lips as the next knot untwists. "Please, Goddess. I can't help Cassian and his family if I'm bound. The words in the timekeeper journal are no longer visible to me," she cries.

The four women stop dancing, their hum silenced as their eyes anchor on Olivia. The ground rumbles below them—another knot comes undone as Cassian appears at the backdoor. He stands watching in awe as she continues to pour out her heart. "I swear to accept the gifts you've given me. Goddess, please. I'm offering you my mind, body and spirit."

Lightning strikes the top point of the pentacle, and she drops to her knees with gut-wrenching pain. Moaning, she folds over as the rain stops, taking the ache and the wind with it. A calm silence surrounds her as she flops to her back and stares up at the starry sky. Feeling defeated, she closes her eyes, her body limp and her mind numb.

In the distance, she can hear the women gasp. Their voices echo as if they were miles away. She can barely make out what they're saying but can't seem to decipher the difference between their voices.

"For the love of the Goddess, will you look at her!"

"I've never seen anything like it."

"She's glowing!"

"Stay back."

Then a strange tone drapes over her like a vibration, blanketing all external sounds. It's delicate, like an angelic melody mixed with an authoritative hum. "It's been centuries since someone has dared to bare themselves to me after such blatant denial, child. Yet, you do it not for your own desires. Instead, you ask this so you can assist a vampire—a dark creation that has been your enemy since the beginning of their existence?"

"Yes, Goddess." She tries to open her eyes or turn her head to seek out the presence, but she can't move. "He's not like the others. Cassian and his family are good."

"What makes you think this vampire is good? They are a direct product of the Divine's fallen. Built to gorge on human blood."

"The Laurent family are different," Olivia responds, recalling her and Cassian's conversation. "They don't seek out prey. Instead, they've learned to tame their hunger, surviving only off what is given by free will. And Cash is—"

"Yes, child? Please, continue."

"He's kind, caring, honest, strong and more human than most people I have met."

"I see. This vampire sounds to have qualities much like yourself. Why would anyone want to cage someone of this nature?"

"Cage?"

"You summoned this vampire then refused to release him, keeping him bound just as you have done with the gifts I've given you. Like traping a butterfly."

"I - I tried to release him."

"Yes, but did you truly want to? I'm not convinced you wanted him to go." The hum gets louder for a brief moment before she asks, "Who wrote this chant for you, my child? I know these are not your words."

"I'm not sure. I think it was the high priestess from the Eternal Flame coven— Elizabeth."

"I see. Do you even know what the power of three and nine means?"

Olivia thinks about that for a minute. "No. I suppose not. Though I have heard of the rule of three from my grandmother. She has explained that our deeds, whether good or bad, will come back to us threefold."

"Ah, yes, that is true. Though the power of three holds much greater meaning than that, my child. Most, if not all, phases come in threes. Think of the moon. There may be many changes between each stage, but there are truly only three phases—waxing, full and waning. Though it may run a repetitive cycle, it has a beginning, middle and end. When we think of nature, we think of land, the sea, and the sky. Likewise, there are three phases of humanity— birth, lifespan and death. As well, each individual can be further defined by yet another set of three—body, mind and spirit. And then there is me, known to many as the triple goddess, representing the maiden, the mother and the crone."

"I guess I never looked that deeply before."

"No, I don't suspect you have. Many haven't."

"And nine? What's the significance of nine?"

"Nine has its own magical meaning for you and this journal you speak of. It's the reason you were chosen. Though not knowing of any such reasoning, the high priestess would have tied nine knots following the typical rule of a binding."

"But what does nine mean to me and the journal?"

Hearing a faint sigh, Olivia feels a soft touch on her cheek. "My child, all will be clear when the time is right. For now, the only thing you need to know is that only you have the power to undo the final knot that is keeping you from obtaining your goals."

"But how?"

"Accept who you are. Embrace your gifts— get a feel for each element without restricting yourself to one. You have much to learn, but I have faith in you and your decisions."

The weight of the blanket begins to lift, and Olivia starts to hear low ramblings around her. "You are much wiser and braver than you believe and have many strengths. Be sure to use them wisely, my child."

"Wait, but how will I know," Olivia calls aloud as the night sky comes back into focus.

"You'll know," the voice echoes faintly as her heavy eyelids flutter closed. She can hear footsteps shuffling closer and Cash's voice in the distance, asking if it's over.

"Well, the circle has dimmed," Helen says, her voice laced with a bit of uncertainty.

"Then why isn't she moving? Liv?" Patricia calls out, but Olivia barely stirs as she drifts back into darkness.

"Poor thing is likely exhausted. Maybe we should—"

But Clara doesn't allow Elizabeth to finish before turning to Cassian. Instead, she waves him over and points to Olivia. "Can you take her up to her room, please? I'll be right behind you."

"Of course," Cassian nods, stepping into the circle.

The high priestess steps back, placing her hand on her chest with a slack jaw. "You called the vampire into a sacred circle? Clara, I'm shocked. I half expected your granddaughter or even Patricia to attempt something like this, but you?"

Clara watches as Cassian gently lifts her into his arms. Her cheek resting against his shoulder as a barely audible *'Cash?'* leaves her lips. He smiles down at her. "Yes, I've got you."

"I'm sorry I couldn't release you," she mutters.

Slowly turning her head, the muscles in Clara's jaw tense as she narrows her eyes. "Elizabeth, I appreciate you and your position as the high priestess at the Eternal Flame Coven, but I think that'll be quite enough. I'll have you know that Olivia has battled many fears in the past few weeks, all to ensure the obligation set out by one of our ancient elders is met. So if befriending a vampire is part of her journey, I stand behind her. In fact, he's proven to be very honourable and caring. As for Patricia, not that it's your business, but she is entitled to pay her respect to the Goddess as she sees fit. It was your strength that was required here, not your judgment. So if you can't accept the decisions made in my home, then I think you should leave."

Elizabeth gasps as Cassian disappears with Olivia in his arms. "I didn't mean to sound judgy, Clara dear."

"Oh, bullshit," Clara snaps. "You just never expected to get called on it." She turns to walk away and pauses, glancing back over her shoulder. "Helen will gladly see you out. Now, if you'll excuse me. I have a granddaughter to check on."

Patricia breaks into laughter, earning a whack from Helen. "Stop it," she whispers, walking toward the backdoor as she plasters on a smile that only Helen could. She holds the screen open and fans her arm out. "As always, it's been a pleasure, Elizabeth."

"Right. Yes, I suppose I should be going," Elizabeth says, taking hold of the old worn tapestry bag she had brought with her. "Do tell your mother not to be a stranger."

Upstairs, Cassian sits on the edge of Olivia's bed and pulls the covers over her as Clara walks through the door. "Has she said anything?"

Standing, he shakes his head. "No, not a word."

She places her hand on Olivia's forehead, scanning her face. "It's not surprising. What she did tonight took a lot of guts—calling out to the Goddess." She runs the back of her fingers lightly down her cheek. "You know, she never had that kind of will or strength until you got here. She merely breezed through her days trying to avoid magic at every turn."

Cassian lowers his head as he takes Olivia's hand. "I sensed her reluctance that first night she read the journal. I'm sure having such a supportive family has helped her become more accepting." Leaning down, he lightly kisses her fingers. "I'll be in my room if you need me. Sleep well, Olivia." But as he tries to walk away, she tightens her grip.

Clara gazes down at their hands. "Well, I was going to settle in and watch over her for the night, but it looks as if she would rather your company for now." A slight smile settles on her lips, and she kisses Olivia's forehead. "Get some rest, child. We'll talk in the morning."

As the door closes, Olivia tightens her grip on Cassian's hand. "Cash?"

"I'm here."

"I don't want to hold you here against your will. I release you."

Smiling, he runs his hand over her hair. "Get some rest, Olivia."

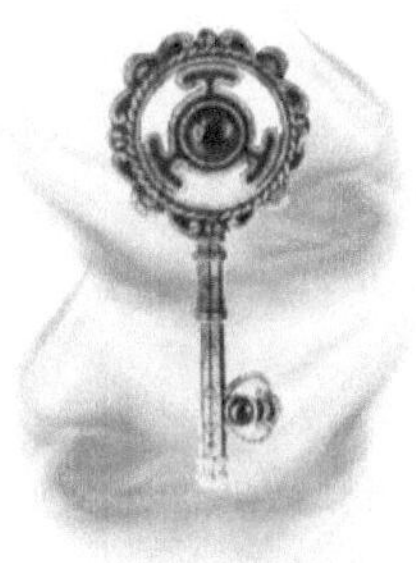

CHAPTER 29 ~ THE GODDESS!

Olivia licks her lips, rolling away from the light sneaking through her bedroom curtain with a groan. "I wondered when the sun might hit you," Patricia says in her usual playful tone. "I was about to sling the drapes back and give you a full dose of the morning sun if you didn't stir soon."

"Ugh, what time is it," Olivia asks, pushing a persistent Mr. Green from her face.

"Almost noon." Patricia walks over to her dresser and tosses a t-shirt and shorts on the bed. "Get dressed. We're all dying to hear what happened when you" —*she grins, making air quotes with her fingers*— "Goddessed out last night."

"Goddessed out?"

"Yeah!" She nods exaggeratedly. "You totally did." Smacking the bed, she heads toward the door. "Now come on, get dressed. I'll see you downstairs."

Pulling on her shorts, Olivia rolls her head across her shoulders, recalling the bolt of lightning and her conversation with the

Goddess. She smiles down at Mr. Green and pets his head. "Can you believe I spoke to a real Goddess last night?"

He presses the top of his head against her hand with a high-pitched 'meow,' eliciting a chuckle. "I know, right? I never thought I'd say this, but I finally feel like I *want* magic in my life." Grabbing the journal, she slips it under her arm and glances back. "Well, what are you waiting for? We've got a book to read."

Three heads turn as soon as she steps into the kitchen, and she stops dead in her tracks. "Geez, way to make a person feel self-conscious." Dropping the journal on the table, she takes her seat.

"You must be hungry. Isbeanan agus uighean," Helen says as a plateful of sausage and eggs materializes in her hand. "Care for a cup of tea with your breakfast?"

"Yes, please." Olivia takes her fork, eyeing the plate as Helen sets it down in front of her. "Thank you. I'm starving." She stuffs a forkful of eggs in her mouth and looks around. "Where's Cash? I could have sworn he was in my room last night."

"He was. He watched over you all night while you slept, then Patricia took over this morning."

"Oh." She takes another bite of her eggs, part of her dying to know if he left, thankful that she finally released him. "Did he leave?"

"No, but he decided it was best to wait in his room until after we had a chance to talk." Clara watches her jam a few more forkfuls of egg into her mouth. "Do you recall the ceremony last night? Your conversation with the Goddess?"

Putting her fork down, Olivia takes a sip of her tea and nods. "How could I possibly forget? The flash" —*she pauses*— "and the pain. Then the most beautiful melody surrounded me, blocking out everything until I heard her voice." She leans back in her chair, taking another sip of her tea. "At first, she sounded angry that I had called on her. Even asked why I would call on her after denying her gifts. She didn't seem happy that I was asking only to help a vampire." A smile brightens her face. "But once I gave my reasons, she seemed to understand." Shrugging, she runs her finger along the rim of her cup, peering around the table. "She told me that only I had the power to undo the final knot. That I had to embrace my gifts." Placing a hand on her chest, Olivia raises the other. "Which I do." She looks around the room. "Where's the rope? I did undo the knot, right?"

"Hell yeah!" Slapping the table, Patricia walks over to the counter, shoving Helen aside. "It's more than undone." Holding up three singed strands, she grins. "You blew that dang thing clean apart!"

Clearing her throat, Helen shrugs. "Well, the knot was blown off by the energy bolt, and I don't think that's what she meant."

"No, I don't believe so either." Clara takes a breath, setting down her cup. "It's not about physical binds. It's about you limiting yourself."

Helen narrows her eyes, focusing on Olivia. "Wait. So that's it? That's all the Goddess said? Did you at least get to see her?"

Olivia shakes her head. "No. I couldn't see anything. I guess it sounds strange, but I didn't have to. I could feel her all around me like a blanket." She twists her lips, recalling the conversation. "But yeah, I guess that's pretty much it. Although she did mention that nine had a significant meaning for me and the journal—that it was the reason I was chosen. Not that it had anything to do with a physical binding. Oh, and that I still have a lot to learn, but she believes in me and my decisions." She peers over at her grandmother. "Any idea what's so important about me and the number nine?"

Clara shakes her head. "I can't say off the top of my head." She slides her fingers through the sides of her hair, tucking the loose strands of hair into her bun before finally resting her cheek against her hand. She studies her granddaughter's face for a moment. "Have you checked the journal yet to see if you can read it?"

Olivia shakes her head. "Not yet, but I can't see why I wouldn't be able to read it now. I mean, the final knot is undone. I've accepted who I am—that magic is in my life."

Resting back in her chair, Clara tips her head, eyeing her skeptically. "She also said you still have a lot to learn. Isn't that what you just said?"

"Well, there's only one way to find out," Helen says, shoving the book in front of her.

Pursing her lips, Patricia folds her arms. "Yeah, I guess you may as well give it a go."

She takes a drink of her tea, washes down the remainder of a sausage and stands. "All right. I'll go get Cash."

"Maybe you should make sure you can read it first." Clara points down to the journal. "If you can, one of us will make sure he joins us."

Sitting back down, Olivia huffs, pulling the book in front of her. "Fine." She peels back the cover, flipping the pages to the last bit she had read—Julien and Harold's argument. She can feel the expectant stares as she thumbs past the remaining pages, but there's nothing there. The pages are still bare.

Slowly closing the cover, she shakes her head. "I don't understand why I still can't read it."

"I believe the Goddess may have meant you'll have to *prove* you've embraced your gifts by working with them— learning about them," Clara says, pursing her lips. "Which makes me think, one way or another, you'll need them to complete your obligation to the journal."

Throwing her head back, Patricia groans. "Christ. We're never gonna get rid of this damn bloodsucker, are we?"

"Aunt Trish!" Olivia shoots her a dirty look. "Cash is not our enemy." She focuses back on her grandmother. "Fine. When do we start?"

"Well, there's no time like the present. However, I have to get down to the store. I should have been there two hours ago, but Elizabeth was kind enough to open for me," Clara says, pushing out from the table.

"Pfft. You mean the bloody old battleaxe is trying to earn your friendship back."

Olivia raises a brow, staring at her aunt. "Why would she need to do that?"

Patricia's mouth forms the shape of an '*O*' as she spins to face her. "Oh, right! You had Goddessed out and missed mom telling her off."

"Ahem." Clearing her throat, Clara shoots her a look.

"I mean, defending us. You for your terrible choice in company" —she fans her hand toward Cassian's room— "and me for not attending meetings."

Clara puts her hand up. "It's not worthy of discussion. When you reach our age, you learn to move past these minor altercations without holding grudges. Instead, we note what not to do next time because worthy friends are not disposable. You should all jot that down for future reference." Getting up from the table, she leisurely pulls a piece of tissue from the box on the counter and lays it in front of Olivia. Then grabs a tiny seedling from the window sill and fills a bowl with water from Helen's collection. She pushes a candle forward from the center and points as she sets them down. "Practice," she says, turning for the stairs. "I'll be back for dinner."

Olivia looks down at the objects. Her shoulders slump as she peers up at her aunts with a long face. "What does she expect me to do with these?"

"Well," Helen says, wiping her hands down her apron as she steps up to the table. "These" *—she points to the objects and feigns a smile—* "can all be manipulated by each element."

Twisting her lips, Olivia looks up at her. "I kind of guessed that. But *how*?"

"Aw, come on, Liv. Don't look so defeated. You know you can light the candle." Patricia stands and starts toward her. "Let's give it a try."

But Helen puts her hand out to stop her. "No," she says, shaking her head. "Mom left her no instructions for a reason." Her gaze softens as it falls on Olivia. "Liv, there is a reason mom gave you these objects and some space. We can help you until the heavens open up, but you are the only one that can make that initial link with each element. We can't do that for you, nor can any of us tell you how. We all relate to each element differently." She takes a deep breath, offering her an encouraging smile. "On the bright side, you had a relationship with them when you were young. It's just a matter of remembering how."

Olivia glances at the items, then back up at her aunts. "All right. I guess I'll give it my best shot."

"Thata girl." Shoving Patricia toward the doorway, Helen taps her thigh for Mr. Green to follow, but instead, he curls into a ball on the chair next to Olivia. "Oh, fine. I suppose he can stay, but don't let him become a distraction."

"He won't." Turning her attention back to the objects, Olivia taps her fingertips on the table, trying to decide which to attempt first. She looks at the candle and quickly shakes off the image of her grandmother's sleeve in flames. "I'm not ready for you yet," she says, shifting her mind to the other three items.

Her focus lands on the tissue, and she holds her hand above it, imagining it lifting to meet her palm. When the kleenex doesn't budge, she sticks out two fingers and flicks her hand, but still nothing. Finally, throwing her arms forward with a scowl, she tries yelling at it, "Fly, damn it! Move. Do something."

Mr. Green meows, offering his typical unamused look as she peers down and sags into her chair. "Oh, hush. It's not as easy as they make it look."

On the other side of the house, Cassian is sitting by the window reading when he feels the presence of another vampire approaching. He drops his feet from the ottoman. The book in hand is all but forgotten as he charges the unfamiliar body as it enters his doorway. His jaw drops, and he steps back to examine the shimmering dark locks and glistening cornflower blue eyes. "Has it really been that long, son?" Clarentina reaches out, placing her hand on his cheek. "Tell me you have not forgotten your mother."

"Of course not. I'm sorry, mother. Please. Forgive me." He throws his arms around her. "It's been so long since I've felt your presence. I was caught off guard for the briefest of a moment." He steps back, holding her at arm's length as he scans her from head to toe. "You look absolutely radiant. How on earth did you get here?"

"You're so much like your father. Always so complimentary." She runs her hand down his arm. "How could I ever stay upset with you." Her blue eyes sparkle, just as they did when he was a child. No longer sunk in and lifeless. "Soloman had the family helicopter carry me to the field just beyond the stream," she says, her tone jovial as she makes her way around his room. "So tell me, darling. Where is this witch that can bring your father back, and what seems to be the holdup? I asked your brothers, but neither one had an answer for me." She glances over her shoulder with the crimson smile he hasn't seen in so many years. "So I thought I would come and find out for myself."

Cassian tucks his hands into the front pockets of his trousers, watching her run her hand over the books on the shelf. "Well, she's very young and really has little skills to speak of yet."

Clarentina stills, her hand poised over Daniel Defoe's edition of Roxana: The Fortunate Mistress. "Obviously, she's not too young to read Daniel's book or enjoy the company of my son." Her hand slowly continues feathering the spines along the shelf. "The smell of a young sorceress doesn't just linger in this room, Cassian. I smell her on you."

He chuckles nervously, pulling his hands from his pockets. "I assure you, mother, it's nothing like you might be imagining." Folding his arms across his chest, he watches her continue to make her way around his room. "Olivia suffered some trauma in her childhood and has blocked out magic. At least as much as possible while living in a house filled with it. What little she has allowed through has given her the ability to read only a couple of journal entries so far, but she is determined to learn—to help us."

She turns to look at him as she shifts her weight to one hip. "You seem awful sure of yourself and this young witch's capabilities." Pausing for a moment, she stares at him as if waiting for a response. "Is it safe to assume you've been in her head?"

"I have. She has seen nothing that can help us locate Roger or the key yet."

"I see. Well, I'd like to meet this young sorceress you claim is willing to overcome her lifetime of fears for a vampire. In fact, I'd like to meet the family of witches that have been keeping my son comfortably hostage." She spins toward the door. "Where are they?"

Shifting to stand in front of her, Cassian shakes his head. "No."

"No?" Her brow darts into her hairline. "What do you mean no?"

Gently turning her around, he walks her back toward the two chairs by the window. "What I mean is I don't think it would be a great idea to introduce you like this."

"Like what?" Her tone rises as her eyes narrow.

"I just mean unannounced. This is their home, and they've been very accommodating up to this point. But we mustn't forget that they could still change their minds."

Pursing her lips, Clarentina places her hand on his cheek. "Oh, very well. I suppose you do have a point." She runs her hand along the lapel of his suit jacket and pats his chest. "Do promise me that you'll make arrangements then. I would very much like to meet the witches that have been" —*she pauses for a moment to study his face, then forces a smile*— "*accommodating* my son."

"You have my word." Taking her hands, he leans in to kiss her cheek. "I'm so pleased to see you up and about. You look wonderful."

"Thank you, darling. I'll check back with you in a couple of days. That should give you enough time to make arrangements with your little friends," she says, sliding out the door just as quickly as she had come in.

CHAPTER 30 ~ WATER BLANKET

As Cassian turns to look out the window, he sees Olivia striving toward the table in the backyard. She's carrying a fair-sized bowl, has a plant tucked under one arm and a candle under the other. He tilts his head, watching her maneuver around the chairs and smiles. "No one can say you are not determined, Miss Parker."

Olivia sets the bowl on the table, then pulls the seedling and candle out from under her arms. After lining them up in front of her, she looks over at the common altar and shrugs. "I have a feeling I know what the Goddess meant by getting personal with the elements, Mr. Green." She scratches the top of his head and kicks off her shoes. "Feel like going for a walk to the basin? It will be a good opportunity to grab a pebble for the altar anyway."

While Mr. Green tromps off through the vast ferns and foxgloves that populate the forest floor, Olivia makes her way through the tangle of trees. She rarely goes to the basin, but she knows her aunt visits it daily to charge. So she carefully follows the trail that Helen has created over the years to do the same.

The tranquillity of the subtle trickle from the stream and the occasional chirps of the unseen birds above bring a soothing calm. Finally, she spots the enormous weeping willow. Its roots are partially washed out, and it hangs so far over the water's edge that one would expect it to plunge into the basin at any time. Though it's been there ever since Olivia can remember.

Wiggling out of her shorts, she hauls her shirt over her head and hangs them from a protruding branch on the old tree, then walks in across the smooth pebbled mouth of the basin. The water being much deeper than she thought, she lies back, letting herself float. It's not long till she's lost in the serenity of her surroundings.

A muffled voice calls out her name, and she springs forward, her feet hitting the muddy bottom at the far edge. "Ew! Oh my god!"

She jumps up, meeting Cassian's stare. *'Oh shit! I need a blanket!'* She throws her arms around her chest, and the water forms a blanket around her. Cassian stands, a smile forming on his face as he points.

"That's incredible. I've never seen anything like that before."

Her heart racing, she peers down at the water swirling around her. "I did it!" she shrieks, flinging her arms out to the side. The water blanket plunges back down around her, and she quickly throws her arm back across her chest, ducking below the surface. "Okay, that may not have been perfect, but it's the most progress I've made all day!" She points to her clothes hanging on the tree. "Can you toss me those and turn your back, please?"

Tossing her shorts and t-shirt, he turns. "How did you do that?"

"I thought about needing a blanket, and when I wrapped my arms around myself, the water rose to cover me." She buttons up her shorts. "Okay. You can turn around now."

"Liv?" A panicked Helen's voice echoes through the forest. "Liv, are you down here?"

"Right." The corner of Cassian's mouth tightens as he throws his thumb over his shoulder, gesturing toward the path. "I meant to tell you your aunts are looking for you."

She peers up as they break through the trees. "For all the times I've asked you to come with me, you choose now to scare the bejesus out of us," Helen says, slamming her hand on her hip. "You do understand that vampires are seeking you out, don't you?"

"It's still daylight, Aunt Helen. Only Cash and his family can walk around in the sun. Besides, I made a water blanket," she grins.

Unamused, Patricia scrunches her face. "Water? But you never had a problem with the fire element, Liv."

Helen swats her arm. "A water blanket?"

"Mmhmm. I wanted a blanket. So I threw my arms around myself and poof. The water surrounded me. Ask Cash!"

"Yes, it was quite incredible," he smiles.

Patricia's eyes narrow on the vampire. "You were supposed to find her, not peep on her!"

"I was not peeping," he says, quickly throwing his hands up defensively.

"Why else would she need to cover up?"

Kissing her teeth, Helen grabs her arm. "Stop." Her gaze falls back to Olivia. "Have you tried doing anything else?"

"Like what?"

"Well, everyone thinks water is just some universal solvent that is only good for cleaning, cooking, and potions, but it can also be manipulated. In fact, it's a powerful element, one that most overlook." Helen waves her over to the edge of the water. "Come, let me show you something." She points her finger down toward the basin and moves her hand in a circular motion. When the water begins to ripple and swirl, keeping time with the movement of her hand, she gradually raises it. A spout forms, continually growing with each turn of her finger. She glances back at Olivia with a smile. "Now, I could send that off, but it wouldn't last long over land." She drops her hand, squashing the funnel with a splash. "I'll admit I may not be able to create fireballs, but I can douse them if I need to."

Patricia rolls her eyes. "Yeah, yeah."

Laughing, Olivia steps up beside her. "How do I do that? Do I simply think about wanting to make a spout?"

"Not exactly. Here, pay attention. I imagine the water is one with my hands." Helen puts her thumbs together, lays her hands out straight in front of her, and steadily lifts them as the water rises. Then, flipping her fingertips skyward, she pushes her hands to the sides.

Olivia gasps as a wall of water forms in front of them, but it doesn't remain erected long. Helen lowers her hands, brings them back together, then forcefully pushes them out, slicing the basin to reveal a muddy bottom. Awestruck, they watch as she moves her hands back together, filling the gap until the swimming hole returns to normal.

"That was amazing."

"Pfft. Yeah, I suppose it was all right," Patricia shrugs.

"I imagine if you can create a water blanket, you too can likely influence it in many ways." Giving her a nudge, Helen gestures to the basin. "Go on, Liv. Can't hurt to give it a try."

Taking a deep breath, Olivia glances over her shoulder at Cassian. Offering her a smile, he pushes off the birch he's been leaning against while quietly observing and folds his arms across his chest. "I agree with Helen. There's no harm in trying. After all, how are you to know anything about your abilities if you don't attempt to use them."

"All right. Here goes nothing." Olivia shakes out her arms and concentrates on the movement of the water. Then just as Helen had done, she slowly lifts her hands, inviting the water to rise. At first, it doesn't seem to respond, but she tries again. Finally, the water begins to ripple, and tiny beads dance along the surface as if a speaker were blasting underneath. She lifts her hands higher, fighting the pull against her muscles. When the strain becomes too much, she lets go. "Ugh! I can't. You make it look so simple."

"I told you," Patricia declares. "Fire is her true element. It comes naturally for her."

Helen shoots her sister a sideways glance before focusing on Olivia. "Go easy on yourself, Liv. You can't fight the flow. You have to be one with it. Only then can you boss it around," she smiles. "Don't forget I have been doing this for a while. It's one thing to create elixirs and potions, but not everyone can influence the flow of water." She nudges her arm, pointing to the pebbled shoreline. "What do you say we grab a pebble for the altar and head up to the house? Mom should be home soon anyway."

Feeling defeated, Olivia stuffs a pebble in her pocket and starts up the path with the rest of them. But with each step she takes, the sound of the stream seems to call her back. Finally, she turns around, runs toward the shore and steadies herself.

She holds her hand out and takes a deep breath, letting the vibration of the water settle into her palm. Swallowing down a nervous flutter, she glances at her shaking hand. *'Calm down, Olivia. You can do this. Now concentrate.'*

Slowly raising her hand, the section below begins to rise. She flips her hand on its side, smiling as a wall of water erects next to her. "Eeee! I did it!" she shrieks, peering back over her shoulder as it crashes against the shore. "Did you see that?"

Patricia tries to hide her smile while Helen throws her hands up. "I sure did! I knew you could do it."

"Where did Cash go?"

"I'm not sure." Helen looks around. "He was here just a moment ago, but don't worry. We'll tell him and mom all about it," she beams, placing her arm around her.

"Yeah, yeah," Patricia bawks, rolling her eyes as she follows along behind them.

As they break the opening of the path, Clara stands on the back patio, staring at the table of items she had set out for Olivia. "These all look very much just as I had given them to you. Except now they're outside."

"I know, Gran. I tried. It felt stifling in there. So I thought this might help." She fans her arms out. "You know, bring me closer to the elements."

"Oh, will you just tell her you moved water, for pity's sake," Patricia snaps.

Helen shoots her sister a nasty look as Olivia's face brightens. Clara's gaze bounces between the three of them. "Moved water?"

"Created a water wall and blanket on demand," Helen corrects enthusiastically.

A slight smile tugs at Clara's lips as she places her arm around her granddaughter's shoulder. "Now, that is wonderful news to come home to. Though seeing that smile back on your face is what makes this one of the most precious moments."

"Thanks, Gran." Olivia stops. "Oh." She reaches into her pocket to pull out the small pebble she collected from the basin's edge. It may not look special, but this one came directly from the water that helped her believe in herself again. "I almost forgot." She walks to the common altar and nestles the stone among the rest.

"Oh, imagine the beauty of the fountain with two people adding stones and shells," Helen beams, "the variety of selections—beautiful."

"Yeah, yeah," Patricia spits as she holds open the backdoor for everyone to enter. "Let's not forget she already knows how to zap a vamp."

"Not like she can test that theory by trying to catch a lightning bolt to charge," Helen snarls.
"You don't even know what you're talking about. The bloodsucker and I saw her fry a vampire," Patricia snaps.

"In case you two have forgotten the fundamentals," Clara's voice rises, halting the banter. "This is not a competition. Each element holds many perplexing pieces. Some even the best may never be able to attain." She pulls two dusty bottles of wine from the rack, sets them on the table, and slaps a corkscrew between them. "We all have personal journeys in this mystery we call life and should not be making comparisons. Instead, focus on the objective. Live and enjoy life with the abilities given."

"Meh, I suppose so. Though I tend to believe the competition keeps life interesting around here." Patricia grabs a bottle of wine, pulls the cork and holds it up to Olivia with a wink. "I really am proud of you, kiddo." She rests her cheek against the bottle and lowers her voice. "Besides, your accomplishment today got us booze," she grins, filling her a glass.

Olivia takes a sip of her wine and smiles. "I'll be right back."

"Aw, come on, Liv. Where are you going?"

She holds up two fingers and continues out of the kitchen. "She's going to see Cash," Helen offers.

"What?" Patricia slumps in her chair, still gripping the bottle of wine firmly in her hand as she shakes her head. "No. Why would she do that? We're having a family night."

"I see no harm in Cash joining us." Clara shrugs, putting her hand up. "Fine, I confess. Perhaps the vampire is growing on me too."

Olivia taps on Cassian's door and barely drops her hand to her side when it opens. Her breath catches as she places her hand on her chest and peers up to meet his gaze. "Wow, that was quick."

His nod is as slight as the smile tugging at the corner of his mouth. "I didn't mean to startle you." Stepping aside, he fans his arm out. "You're welcome to come in if you'd like."

As she walks past, she glances over her shoulder. "I was afraid you might have left."

"Left?" he asks, raising a brow. "What on earth would make you believe I had left? In case you have forgotten, I am bound to the master of the journal—to you, Olivia."

She shakes her head. "Not that I wouldn't rather you be here with me, but I'm certain I released you." She throws her arms out with a smile. "Go on. See if I'm right."

A small smile plays on Cassian's lips. "Very well." As quick as she can blink, he disappears from sight.

"Ouch," she frowns as her heart sinks. As much as she wants him close, she's happy she is no longer responsible for keeping 'a butterfly' in a cage. Her shoulders lift as she draws a deep breath. "Don't stay away too long, Cash," she whispers as she turns for the door.

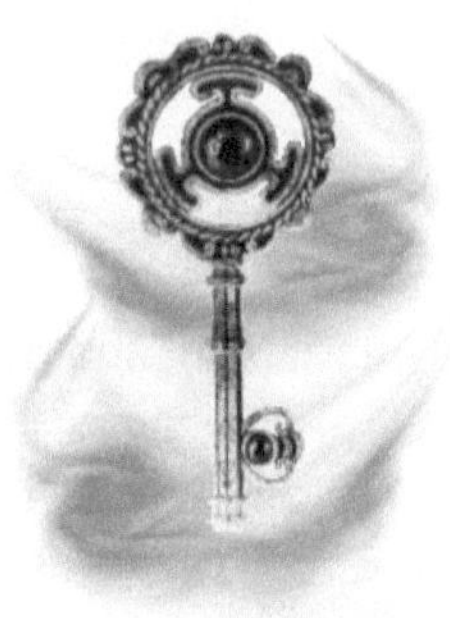

CHAPTER 31 ~ ENCHANTED WINE

Laughter from the kitchen makes her smile when a *'Psst'* from above the fireplace halts her. As she turns toward the picture, Aunt Millie cranks her head. "Don't worry, little Olivia. He'll be back."

"Oh. Yes. I'm sure you're right," she shrugs, shaking her head as she walks toward the fireplace. "After all, I still haven't completed the journal."

"That too, but I'll bet dollars to your pennies that it wasn't the magic holding him here."

"What do you mean?"

"I think you know," Aunt Millie smiles. "Anyway, you had better go get some of that wine before those old hens drink it all."

Chuckling, Olivia kisses her fingertips and touches them to Aunt Millie's cheek. "I wish you could join us."

"I'm here. Thanks to our darling Clara, I still get to witness every one of these joyous moments." She winks, chucking her chin toward the kitchen. "Now, you go spread your wings."

The volume of the women around the table rises as Olivia walks into the kitchen. "There she is." Patricia pulls the chair out next to her and pats the seat. "Come sit." She pushes a glass of wine in front of her. "I have no idea where yours went," *—she holds up her wine glass with a grin—* "for all I know, this could be it."

Olivia drinks back half, then stares at the goblet, twisting it in her hand as she exhales. "I have to admit. This is perhaps the most delicious wine I've ever tasted." She studies the shimmering contents, the tiny glistening specks as they swirl about the glass. "Is my mind playing tricks on me, or is this twinkling?"

Clara holds her glass up to the light. "Mmhmm. I do believe it is," she smiles. "This, my dearest granddaughter, is a special grade of wine. I can assure you, you've never had anything quite like this before."

Her body begins to tingle as laughter erupts around the table. "What do you mean?" Her stomach flutters, and she glances at the ladies, flipping her hands over to examine them. "Did you drug me?"

"Oh, don't be so silly," Clara exclaims, patting her hand as she takes another sip of her wine.

"It's enchanted wine, Liv." Helen extends her glass. "Cheers, Mr. Cobb."

"What?" Olivia eyes her aunt suspiciously. "Who is Mr. Cobb?"

Patricia giggles. "Mr. Cobb was a coven member. Bit of a sourpuss, as I recall." She waves her hand, shooing off the Mr. Cobb topic. "Anyway, haven't you noticed alcohol really doesn't affect you?" Spinning the wine bottle, she turns the label toward her niece.

Handwritten in red paint on plain old cream paper, Olivia reads it aloud. "Enchanted Wind Brew—Dillon Cobb?" She tips her head toward her grandmother and rolls her eyes. "Really, Gran?"

Laughter erupts around the table as Patricia refills Olivia's glass. "Yes, really." Clara brushes a strand of hair back with a smile. "This is a special blend. I haven't made them since I stepped down from the coven, but they last forever. When the moon was full, and we were at our strongest, I would extract the tiniest sliver of essence from a select few to add to Elizabeth's homemade wine." She stands, waving her arm, causing the glass jars of water on the shelves around the room to rattle. Her hand flies to cover her smile. "Oops. Apparently, I've allowed our wind element, Mr. Cobb, to get a little restless." She points to Olivia. "Give it a try."

"I'm not sure what to do."

Clara looks around, then gestures to the box of kleenex on the counter next to Mr. Green. "Concentrate on gently pulling out the tissue. The key is to determine a final destination for it."

Olivia pulls her bottom lip between her teeth and peers around the room, her eyes landing on the trash bin in the corner. She lifts her hand, pinching her fingertips together as if plucking the tissue from the box, then flicks it toward the corner of the room. Mr. Green lets out a wail as he leaps from the counter, kicking the box behind him. "Oh no," she snorts, trying to conceal her laughter. "I'm sorry, buddy."

"Well, we might need to work on that," Clara says, patting back the sides of her hair as she clears her throat. "Once you've connected with the elements, this will work much smoother. Keeping that in mind, I have hidden bottles with the essence of some of our most powerful coven members. I believe it could come in quite handy when it comes down to having to fight off some vampire enemies."

Olivia cocks her head, staring at her curiously. "I thought you could only do that with photos and life-like statues."

"One shouldn't give away all their talents, child," she chuckles.

Helen's head swings around before her gaze settles on Olivia. "Speaking of vampires, where's Cassian? I thought you were going to get him."

"Oh—" she begins when he casually strolls into the kitchen. "Right here."

Patricia frowns, slumping in her chair while Olivia's stomach flutters. A smile grows on her face as she meets his gaze. "But I thought when I—"

"...left my room I wasn't following?" he finishes with a smile. "I just had a few things to check on first. I wouldn't miss your celebration for anything." He gestures to the chair next to Clara. "Mind if I sit next to you, young lady?"

Blushing, Clara shifts her chair. "Flattery is not necessary, but always welcome," she winks, patting the cushion. "Have a seat. We're thrilled you've decided to join us." She pushes a glass in front of him and pours him a drink. "In fact, I think this would be an excellent opportunity to see if this has the same effect on you."

Cash's eyes dart around the table. "Should I ask?"

"This is Gran's Enchanted Wind Wine," Olivia offers. "We get the power of the wind element from it."

"Well, only for a very brief period," Clara explains. "About ten minutes at best."

"I've never heard of such a thing." Cash's eyes broaden as he twirls the contents of his glass. "And you're offering *me* to try it?"

"Yes. We may not require it, but something tells me these vampires have been feeling us out. Testing our strengths and abilities. So I thought now is as good a time as any to pull these out." She motions to his glass. "Well, go on. Give it a try. It won't hurt you."

Cassian tips back the glass of wine, and his deep brown irises swirl with gold. "Well, it certainly is tasty."

"Yes, and unlike our blood, it's not addictive to your kind. Nonetheless, it's not available in large quantities. So this will be the only time we'll be using this unless we absolutely require it," Clara affirms, waving him toward the backdoor. "Now, I think we should test you outside, given your strength."

As they gather on the back porch, Clara points to the stone at the corner of the yard. "Without touching it, I want you to move it. Even rolling it will be sufficient."

Cassian stares at the rock for a minute, then shakes his head. "I'm not sure it works for vampires. I don't believe we connect with the elements like you do."

"Think of it like compulsion but use your hand to guide the desired motion. Place all your power behind the movement in your hand and aim it at the stone," Clara directs.

He lifts his hand, and the rock raises. Then with a flick of his wrist, it takes off, sailing through the air as if he had tossed a pebble. Branches snap as it breaks through the forest, followed by a loud thud as it lands. Cassian stands speechless, staring down the path while Olivia covers her mouth, trying to conceal her grin.

"My word!" Helen exclaims, turning to her mother as she stares down the path in silence.

"Yeah, yeah," Patricia huffs. "He's a bloodsucker that just received a boost from a wind witch. What did you all expect?"

Cassian turns to face Clara. "I apologize for the trees, Ms. Redfearn."

Clara finally turns to meet his gaze and bursts into laughter. "Well, my goodness. I certainly wasn't expecting that." She pats his arm. "Not to worry. You can help me plant a couple of saplings tomorrow. The Goddess will understand," she winks, motioning everyone back into the house. "I do believe this may work in our favour." Taking her seat, she peers around the table. "Of course, we know from Jimmy's bracelet that these vampires have a witch working with them. So I believe we'll need to use everything we have available to gain the advantage."

"Agreed." Helen takes a look around the table and gestures to the glasses. "Are we done with the wine for now?"

Emptying her glass, Olivia sets it down with a grin. "I am."

"Oh yes. I'd say it's time for tea." Clara chucks her chin toward the counter and turns her gaze to Olivia. "Maybe you should give the journal another try. See if you can read any further now."

She takes a deep breath and peers around the table. "And what if I still can't?"

"Then you can't," Patricia pipes up. "It's no big deal, Liv."

"Of course, you'll never know if you don't try. Why don't you let me get it?" Clara places her hand on the table and begins to stand when Olivia stops her.

"Wait." She stands, raising her hands toward the journal. Taking a deep breath, she closes her eyes and slowly releases it. "Thigibh thugam," she repeatedly mumbles as she draws her fingertips toward her. Finally, she opens her eyes, and the journal is hovering between her hands. She grasps it with a squeal. "I did it!"

A slight smile forms on Cassian's lips as he leans back in his chair and folds his arms across his chest. "Remarkable. You've come so far in only a few days, Olivia. How did you know what to say?"

"I'm not exactly sure. The words echoed in my mind."

Turning her head toward Cassian, Clara's gaze remains on her granddaughter. "The infused wine may have been the tiny boost she required to unlock the door she bolted fifteen years ago," she whispers, her thumb and forefinger barely pinching together. "Of course, this is Olivia." Clara shrugs. "She has always been our greatest mystery. In all my years, I have never seen a child so young who could manipulate the elements like her, nor one that could shut them down so quickly and completely."

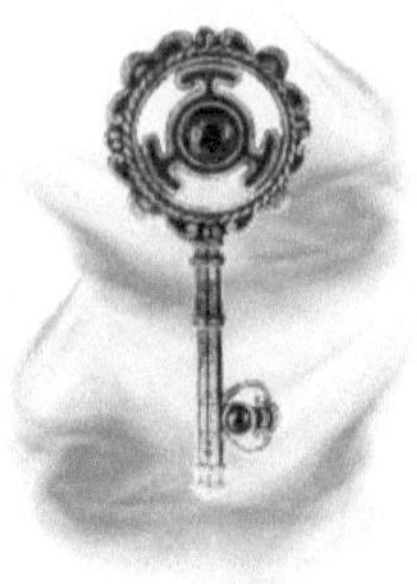

CHAPTER 32 ~ THE KING'S MEN

Olivia runs her hand over the smooth leather, watching the letters shimmer. She smiles, her eyes darting to Cassian's as she excitedly flips open the cover. The pages begin to turn, stopping at the next waiting entry.

She glances around the table as Mr. green circles her ankle with his usual offering of reassurance. Finally, her hand drops to the page, and she begins to trace the beautifully scribed heading with her finger as she reads it aloud, "May 15th, 1796 – London, England."

Olivia's hand covers her face, her stomach churning as a pungent stench of rotten fish and feces fills her nostrils. "For the love of the Goddess! This has got to be the most disgusting place I've ever smelled!"

Laughing, Clara pats Cassian's arm. "Well, wherever she is, she doesn't sound pleased about it."

"Eighteenth-century London didn't smell very pleasant, as I recall. Shall I take a look at exactly where she is?" As Clara nods, he leans forward, resting his elbows on the table. He stares at Olivia, concentrating on her mind's eye as it opens.

The hustle and bustle of the surrounding streets are different from the previous periods the journal has shown her. She examines the nearby buildings packed tightly together. The area feels familiar in an oddly unfamiliar way. As she looks for a point of reference, her eyes land on two women floating about out front of the well-lit window of a noisy tavern. While their heavy silk gowns drag along the dusty ground, their bosoms nearly bust from their corsets. *'This must be one of the most baffling periods in time. How did they justify women's ankles must be covered, but their breasts can protrude till their nipples nearly burst free,'* she grumbles, turning to look down the opposite side of the street.

When her sight lands on the three-story Palladian-style building in front of her, she smiles. *'The Brooks Club! Finally, a place I know.'* Though given its pristine condition, beaming with those brilliant yellow bricks and iconic creamy white Portland stone, it's clear the elements have yet to damage its surface.

As she steps back for a better look, the clomp of heavy hooves and exhaustive snorts startle her. Righting herself, she turns just in time to see an assemblage of soldiers on horseback emerge from the night fog. Most late-night patrons pay them no mind as they trot through the street in a three-wide by four-long formation. On the other hand, Olivia can't help but stop to admire the pristine condition of their long red coats, shiny black boots and tricorn hats.

While they disappear back into the night fog, the door to the Brooks Club swings open, and two dark shadows make their way toward the road. Olivia gasps as the light from the oil-burning streetlamps illuminate their faces. Walking side by side, the resemblance is extraordinary. She's never seen father and son next to each other before.

Julien and Cassian casually stroll in front of her, heading down the hill of St. James Street toward Pall Mall, their every step tugging her forward. Cassian lifts the lapel on his coat and glances at his father as she falls in behind. "I was thinking that since Elias and I will be remaining here in the Stepney Castle when you return to France next week, maybe Gabe could come stay with us. He's technically an adult now, and Elias and I can show him around London."

"I'm not convinced your mother will be pleased with that idea. You know how she tends to baby the boy, and to be perfectly honest, I find it difficult to fault her for that. Being a young human, he's much more delicate than you and Elias ever were." Smiling, Julien slaps his son on the back. "Why don't you leave it with me? I'll have a talk with her. I'm sure I can at least get her to agree to let him visit for a few weeks." He winks, adjusting his hat as he peers over at his son. "Although, I'm not sure he's quite ready for the Brooks Club just yet."

Laughing, Cassian stops to drop a coin into a vagrant beggar's tin. "We'll do our best to keep him away from the gentlemen's clubs."

Olivia barely hears the rush of rapid footsteps approaching from behind when Julien glances over his shoulder. He reaches for Cassian's arm and speaks lowly through gritted teeth. "Son, head back to the Castle. I'll be there soon."

"No. I'm not leaving you," Cassian says, peering behind them as the cluster of men gains momentum.

"Stop in the name of the King!" they hear a familiar voice call out behind them.

Julien tenses, his shoulders rising into his neck as they stop and turn to face the group of men. His eyes narrow on his former comrade, and his lip curls into a sneer. "Harold Windsor. My apologies. I should have recognized your stench."

"Odd, I smelled *you* the moment you stepped foot back into London, old friend." He takes a step closer, his gaze jumping from a shifting Cassian back to Julien. "You look surprised to see me. Surely you haven't forgotten about our last conversation." He drops his hand into the fold of his elbow, then wraps the other around his beard. Stroking it as if petting an animal, he chucks his chin toward the chain around Julien's neck. "You seem to have forgotten that key rightfully belongs to me."

Scanning the group of men standing guard with their hands ready on the grip of their swords, Julien quickly recognizes the golden 'V.H.' sown on their regal cloaks. Their glazed-over appearance is obvious even to Olivia's untrained eyes. That can only mean one thing—Harold has compelled the entire lot of them.

When Cassian turns toward his father, Olivia takes a step back. His irises swim with crimson while a perfect outline of his fangs sits visibly under his top lip. Julien raises his authoritative hand. "Easy, son. This is a public street."

"Yes. You should listen to your father." An arrogant grin forms on Harold's face as he extends his hand, pointing in their direction and yells. "What are you imbeciles waiting for? These are the vampires responsible for all the bloody murders in London! Get them!"

Shshinng

As the shrill ring of a dozen men unsheathing their swords echoes around them, Julien and Cassian take off down Pall Mall. Once they've gained enough distance from the King's men, they cut left down a dark alley off Fleet Street. Keeping his voice a low whisper, Julien grasps his son's sleeve. "Let's take a minute to collect our thoughts. I'm sure they're not more than a few minutes behind."

Cassian's eyes widen. "Father, they may be under compulsion, but those men are nothing more than mere mortals. We can easily remove them from this equation and go after him." He glances at the opening of the alley, then narrows his gaze back on Julien. "It's not as if we're some disobedient plebs—you're the bloody Sovereign. Why are we running from Windsor instead of removing his head?"

Julien reaches into his shirt and pulls out the key. "This key was given to me because someone believed in my ability to do good— believed I had a soul worth saving. It will bring me back if anything ever happens to me."

"But how?"

"Magic, my son. Magic." He steps closer. His eyes soften as he meets Cassian's gaze. "But you need to understand that very same magic that powers this key will disappear if I am no longer worthy. That means if I were to slay a dozen men who have been stripped of their free will, well, then I am no better than Windsor." He shakes his head. "That is why there will be no fighting *here tonight*, son. I need to focus on getting your mother and you boys out of London before that immoral immortal heads to the castle, and I'm sure he will. You see, it's not merely the key he wants—he's after my throne. I'm afraid the very woman who created this had warned me of this moment." He tucks the key back into his shirt and pats his chest.

"Oh, you've got that right, old friend." Their attention is immediately drawn toward heavy boots hitting the ground near the opposite end of the alley. Striding toward them is Harold sporting a sinister grin. He stops and leans forward, narrowing his eyes on Julien. "And as I recall, the last time we spoke, I told you this face" —*he raises his hand, circling his smug expression*— "will be the last face you'll ever see."

"Ah, yes. That conversation does ring a bell. It was one led by a coward. However, we both know that you alone cannot defeat me, at least not muscle for muscle. You seem to have forgotten something. I am your sovereign."

The corner of Harold's mouth pulls into an arrogant smile. "Yes, well, as I see it. That is about to change." Curling his forefinger to meet his thumb, Harold sticks them between his lips and whistles. "Come this way! I found the vampires! They're over here!"

Olivia's heart races as the thundering clatter of footfalls close in on them. She turns with Cassian to face the mob of cloak-wearing men. *'Damn it,'* she mutters, *'wind be with me.'* Her hair blows forward with the breeze as she flicks her hand toward the men, but nothing more happens. At least not in 1796. Present-day, however, Helen has been flipped on her back in her chair.

'Ugh! I felt it. Why can't I make it move anything else,' Olivia huffs as the men get closer. She moves back, watching Cassian's eyes swirl with red as they inch nearer.

One brave soul slashes his sword toward him as his back meets his father's. "I can take them," Cassian growls.

"No. Harold has turned these men into puppets. They have all but one goal – to remove our heads. We need to get back to the castle. I must get your mother and you boys to safety. I can handle Harold, but it must be done without innocent men involved."

"Come on, Laurent," Harold spits as he grabs a sword from one of the men and swings it toward Cassian, narrowly missing his cheek. "What has happened to you?" He swipes the blade toward him, and Julien knocks it from his hand. "Ah, there might be a bit of fight left in the big bad sovereign after all."

"Not toward compelled civilians, Windsor. They are merely a clumsy distraction. If it's my throne you're trying to gain, you'll need to do better than this." He peers at Cassian and tips his head toward the tunnel's opening. "Now!" Julien yells as they dash past Harold and the King's men.

Back at the Stepney castle, Elias is in the den, putting the final touches on a cameo carving for his mother, when his father and brother bust through the main entrance. Julien starts for the stairs. "I can't believe that son-of-a-bitch had the nerve to compel the King's men! I'm afraid your plans to stay here are now out of the question, boys. We'll need to stay clear of London for a while. I'm going to get your mother." He throws his arm out toward the den. "You and your brother prepare to return to France. Time is of the essence."

Cassian meets Elias's questioning gaze. He places his hand in the air and shakes his head. "Don't ask. You heard father. We need to grab a few things and prepare to leave. There'll be plenty of time to explain later."

Julien yells for his wife as he makes his way up the south tower toward their rooms. "Clarentina! My love, you must prepare a bag."

Standing at the top of the staircase, Clarentina nervously wipes her hands down the front of her gown. "Julien? Are you all right? What's happened?"

His hands cup her elbows as he steps closer. "I'm fine, but I'm afraid we need to leave London. Windsor has corrupted the King's men – the V.H. unit."

"What?" Her eyes grow wide as she follows him into their bedchamber. "The Vampire Hunters? How did he ever—"

"He compelled them, Clarentina. The entire lot of them. Look, never mind that now. I'll explain everything once we're all safe in France. We have a small army heading our way at this very moment, and they aren't coming to talk. So, only prepare what is absolutely necessary. Anything else can be replaced, or I'll have one of the plebs come for it later." Lifting the large painting of their sons out of the way, he reveals the safe. Twisting the dial several turns to the right, then to the left, and again to the right, he grasps the handle and pulls it open. Taking out a leather satchel containing a few precious stones and some gold coins, he grabs the scroll and places it inside. Sliding the bag into his suit coat, he secures the string to an inside button and turns back to his wife. "Do you have everything you need for now?"

"Yes. I'll let Soloman know that we'll be leaving for France." Twisting her hands nervously, she peers up at him. "What will become of the others?"

Julien offers her a crooked smile. "They will be fine, my love. I believe they have proven they are no longer a threat to the city. They're welcome to remain here on Laurent's Hill. In fact, we can send Francis and Francine back to watch over the castle. They're fresh faces and can let us know if anything goes awry while we're away. Soloman is just as well known here as we are. He'll need to come with us."

"Of course, darling," she agrees as she turns to leave.

As Julien joins his sons in the den while they wait for Clarentina, he places his hand on Elias's shoulder. "I assume your brother has explained why we must leave."

"Yes." Elias turns to face his father, his jaw tight as he nods. "Though I must ask why we're leaving for France when we should be heading to the Windsor house. Our focus should be to rid ourselves of them once and for all."

"All in good time, my son." With a proud grin, he pulls him against his side. The boy might not be next in line, but he was bred to be sovereign. "First, I must ensure my family is safely out of London. Only then will I settle my score with Mr. Windsor."

Soloman enters the room with two female donors. "Julianna and Catherine have been waiting for you two to get back. At the very least, you should take some nourishment before you leave," he says, gesturing to the two young women.

Saying nothing, Julianna sits next to Cassian and offers her arm with a demure smile. He closes his mouth around her wrist, and Olivia feels her face heat. She quickly looks away. *'I am not jealous!'*

While Julien discusses the final details with Soloman, Elias joins his mother as she nervously paces by the window. Digging his hand into his pocket, he pulls out the cameo he had been putting the final touches on when his father and brother came home. He holds it out in the palm of his hand. "I know this may not be the most favourable time, but with the sudden feud between the Windsors and us—" Forcing a smile, he lowers his gaze to his outstretched palm. "Well, anyway. I carved this from the cowry shell the traveller gave me last month. I thought you could add it to one of your lace chokers."

She presses her hand to her chest, staring down at the beautifully carved image of herself and her husband. "You carved this?"

"Yes, I only completed it this evening. My intent was to save it for your birthday, but, well, I'd feel better knowing you're wearing it." He shrugs. "You know, for luck."

Carefully taking the cameo from his palm, she closes her hand around it. "Oh, Elias. It's absolutely beautiful. I love it. Thank you, my darling." Just then, movement catches her eye outside and her gaze darts to the window. Her face darkens as she rushes to close the curtains. "Julien! Come quickly! Harold is making his way up the laneway!"

Arriving at her side, Julien peers out the window. "You must leave now. Take the boys and go to France, my love. I'll meet you there."

"No, father." Cassian appears next to Julien, his fists clenched at his sides. "I'm not going anywhere. I'm staying right here with you."

"Absolutely not. This isn't a request. You'll go with your mother." Cassian shakes his head, and Julien narrows his eyes. "Cash, you will obey me not only as your father but as your sovereign. Now, go."

Straightening his shoulders, Cassian expands his chest. "No. I'm staying to fight. Not only next to my father but alongside my sovereign."

The muscle in Julien's cheek tightens as he gives his son a curt nod. "All right, son."

"Please, Julien. I saw at least a handful of cloaked men behind him."

"Well, of course. That coward wouldn't have come alone," Julien spits.

"Then the two of you are greatly outnumbered. Mortals or not, they'll be yielding swords. Elias and I will remain. We can fight them as a family," she cries.

"Not a chance, my love." Julien's eyes soften as he pulls her into his arms. "Cassian and I will be fine. We'll lead them into the old dungeon. Without the aid of nocturnal vision, the men will be blind. They'll be easy to overtake, and Harold will be ours. Besides, Soloman will stay behind for now." He slips his hand into the breast of his jacket and retrieves the scroll. Taking her hand, he sets it into her palm and closes her fingers around it. "Take this with you and hide it in a safe place. Somewhere no one will ever think to look. Now, go. Soloman is waiting with your bags at the south tower. Go straight to Dover. There will be a boat waiting for you. You can rest while you cross to Calais."

Tucking the scroll into her skirts, she swipes a tear from her cheek. "No more tears. We'll be there before you know it." Leaning in to kiss her, he turns her toward the den. "Now, take our son and go." His voice deepens with authority as he points to Elias. "Take care of your mother."

Harold bangs on the heavy wooden door as Julien watches his wife and son disappear toward the south tower. "Surrender, Laurent! We know you're in there. The commander and his men witnessed your predatory rage, and the King demands your head. Now come out, or we're coming in!"

"That's ridiculous! Those offences you speak of are yours, and it is *you* that will pay for your crimes. We both know this is nothing more than a ruse concocted to gain a key and throne you're not entitled to," Julien shouts back. He glances toward the lounge as Cassian shoves the sofa off the old dungeon entrance. "Mark my words, Windsor. If you enter my home, you'll leave me no choice but to remove your head."

"We'll see about that, Laurent. Ready the ram!" Harold barks as he orders the soldiers to advance.

"Father," Cassian shouts, gesturing toward the dungeon's opening.

Julien drops the large plank into the bracket, reinforcing the door before darting for the lounge. He glances back as the heavy wooden entrance shakes with yet another tremendous bang, and the hinges finally give way. As he enters the room, Cassian yanks the heavy draft curtain, and together they drop into the tunnel.

Olivia can barely make out her hand in front of her face without the benefit of nocturnal eyes, and the black void of the dank musky tunnels gives a new meaning to darkness. She suddenly understands what Julien meant by the soldiers will be blind. Thankfully, their invisible tether remains intact as she floats along behind him.

When they reach the bottom of the narrow winding staircase, Cassian waits next to his father. Olivia can hear the clanking of the blades and the cries of those tripping their way through the darkness. It's not hard to tell from the groans and gargles that some have met their fates before even getting close.

In the blackness of the room, three soldiers stand before them, their swords drawn as they blindly advance. Another five descend from the staircase behind them, but there is still no sign of Harold. "I can't see a damn thing," one of the soldiers calls out.

Finally, Julien tosses a stone into the center of the room, and the soldiers turn their swords on each other. Olivia lets out a squeal as she covers her mouth. The thrash of blades searing through flesh, accompanied by the cries of dying men, tells her all she needs to know about the soldiers. Sight isn't required to understand the sounds of death.

Julien leans toward Cassian. "I'll let the last of these pitiful fighters finish each other, then find that pathetic excuse for a friend, Windsor. You head to the south tower. Go meet your mother and brother in France. This is now between Harold and me." He pats him on the shoulder, chucking his chin toward the south tunnel. "Go. I'll be there soon."

"But father—"

"Son, the only fight left is mine. These sad sacks are killing themselves down here." He points toward the opening of the dimly lit tunnel. "Now get out of here."

Pursing his lips, Cassian turns, reluctantly taking off through the tunnel toward the south tower.

CHAPTER 33 ~ LOYAL PRIMEVAL

Commana, France

Olivia steps forward. At first, she's unsure if she will follow Cassian or remain with Julien. But when dank darkness turns to well-lit warmth and Clarentina speaks next to her, she realizes she hasn't followed either. "Walking into the castle without Cash and your father feels strange."

Elias forces a smile. "I'm sure they'll be here soon."

Just then, an extremely tall man appears in front of them, and Olivia is quick to notice that even though his voice sounds light and friendly, his face is void of expression. He bows slightly to Clarentina. "Good evening, Madame." Taking their bags, he tips his head toward her son. "Sir Elias. We weren't expecting you back so soon. You two must be exhausted. Shall I have Florentine request a donor for you both?"

She peers into the distance and nods, her face tense with concern. "Thank you, Francis. That would be greatly appreciated."

"Forgive me, Madame, but I noticed Mr. Laurent and Sir Cassian hadn't accompanied yourself and Sir Elias," he says, peering past her at the laneway through the window. "Will they be joining us this evening, or will they be remaining at the castle in Stepney?"

Clarentina straightens her shoulders, meeting his questioning gaze. "I should be expecting them shortly. They had some business to tend to first."

Francis bends at the waist as he steps back. "Not to worry, Madame. I'll notify the other donors so they can prepare for their arrival."

"Thank you. I suspect they will be completely exhausted by the time they arrive."

Elias takes her by the elbow and leads her into the sitting area. "Mother, try not to worry. They will be fine. Father is much wiser than Mr. Windsor, and you can't get any quicker than Cash."

"Oh, I know, darling," she says, patting his hand reassuringly. I have complete faith in your father. Now, why don't you go find Gabriel? I'm sure he'll be ecstatic to know you're back. I'll inform you the moment they arrive."

Clarentina glides up the steps to her room and closes the door behind her. When she's confident she's alone, only then does she carefully retrieve the scroll from the pocket of her skirt. She unrolls the thick parchment paper just enough to reveal the glistening words *Resurrection Key* before quickly rolling it back up. "May you never require this, my darling," she whispers.

Tapping it off her chin, she draws the corner of her bottom lip between her teeth and peers around the room. Finally, her gaze lands on the large portrait above the bed. "No. This needs to be *my* secret," she declares, heading for her dressing room.

As Olivia steps through the door, she's just in time to witness Clarentina swiftly pushing a block back into the wall, then shoving the bureau in front to cover it.

Tap tap

"Mrs. Laurent?" a sweet voice calls out as a petite brunette peeks around the door.

"Oh, Jinny. You startled me." Clarentina spins, settling her back against the dresser as she dabs her face with a handkerchief and paints on a smile. "Please, come in."

Jinny tips her head slightly as she dips into a curtsy. "My apologies, Mistress. I just wanted to welcome you home. It won't take me but a minute to turn down your room."

"Oh, there's no rush, dear. I'm going downstairs to wait for Cassian and Mr. Laurent to arrive anyway." She stops by the doorway and peers back at her chambermaid. "Could you be sure to prepare the boys' chambers as well, please?"

"Yes, Mistress," she dips slightly. "Of course."

After leaving Gabriel's empty room, Elias catches up with their house steward heading down the long corridor. "Hey, Francis. Where's Gabe?" He jumps in front of him, bearing a wide smile as he holds up his hands. "No. Don't tell me. Let me guess. He's out courting a new lady," he grins, falling back in next to him as he grips his shoulder playfully. "That sly fox."

An unusual sombre expression falls across Francis's face. "I'm afraid not, Sir Elias. He's come down with smallpox. He's been locked up in the west tower to keep him away from the other humans." Tightening his lips, he shakes his head. "Such a delicate race, these humans."

Elias puts his head down, keeping stride next to him. "But he's going to be okay, right?"

Francis stops to look at him. "I'm honestly not sure. Sadly, young Gabriel's condition has become increasingly grim over these last couple of days." Lowering his gaze, he shakes his head. "The poor boy. It reminds me of his parents' failure to recover from the disease not so long ago." He continues down the hall toward Florentine's courters, then turns back. "Sir Elias, just one more thing. After seeing him, be sure to wash your hands thoroughly when leaving his chambers. As vampires, we may be immune to disease, but our human donors are not." Nodding, Elias turns and heads back down the hall in the direction of the west tower.

Downstairs Clarentina is staring out the window when she spots Cassian walking up the laneway. She springs to her feet and flings the door open. "Oh, thank god you're all right." She searches behind him, her face dropping as she meets his gaze. "Where is your father?"

"Still in Stepney. He ordered me to leave once the soldiers met their demise, insisting on finishing Mr. Windsor himself." Cassian hangs his head. "Forgive me, mother. I know that disappoints you. I feel as though this is the one time I should have defied him."

"No." She places her hands on either side of his face, lifting his head to look into his eyes. "Your father is aware of his capabilities." She forces a smile. "Besides, he is sovereign, and you were right to obey him. Now, come on inside. We'll wait together."

Hours pass as she sits by the window with Cassian pacing behind her. Finally, he stops for the third time and stands before her with his arms folded across his chest, his brows knit tightly together as the muscle in his cheek tenses. "Mother, please. My intent is not to upset you, but father should have been here by now. I believe I should go back to London. He may need my help. What if Mr. Windsor not only brought the King's men but his own army of plebs?"

Standing, she meets his dilated pupils and takes his hands. "I know you're concerned. I am too, but we must have faith in your father's abilities. If he thought he needed you there, he would have had you stay. Besides, Soloman is still there." Forcing a smile, she kisses his cheek. "Elias is up in the west tower with Gabriel. The poor boy is gravely ill, and I fear he may be facing the same fate his mother and father suffered. He's contracted smallpox. I know he's always looked up to you boys. You're the older brothers he never had. Why don't you go check on him for me?" Cassian starts to open his mouth in protest when she raises her hand and shakes her head. "If your father hasn't arrived by the time you come back down, we'll discuss you going back. But, first, go check on Gabriel and your brother."

Elias sits in the wooden chair at Gabriel's bedside when Cassian enters the room. His elbows resting on his thighs, he stares down at his folded hands in front of him. "He can't even open his eyes, Cash."

"His suffering must be unbearable." He places his hand on Elias's shoulder. "I hate to sound cruel, but maybe it's best if he passes. He'll finally find refuge from this horrendous disease. Besides, what does he have to wake up to? He has no family."

"How can you say that?" Elias springs from his chair, shoving Cassian against the wall. "He was born here. Right here in this tower, in fact. Hell, we've practically raised him ourselves for a good part of his twenty-two years. Remember when we helped him build the tree fort outback?" Cassian slides his hands into the front pockets of his trousers and rocks back on his heels. "Right," he points down at Gabriel. "That's him, Cash. And don't forget all the fishing excursions we took him on because his father was too busy working here for our family. It was father who taught him to use a sword, and I taught him to carve. Shit, the first time he got drunk was with us. How can you be so callous to say he'd be better off gone? *We* are his family! He has us to wake up to!"

Before he can leave the room, Cassian grabs his arm. "Elias, I know he's our friend, but he is human. They are not like you and me. They are a vulnerable species—born to die."

Pulling his arm free, Elias glares back at him. "Not Gabe! Gabe is our brother, and he doesn't have to die! I swear, if father doesn't turn him, then I will!"

"Elias, stop!" Elias pauses with his hand on the door. "You know you can't. Only the head of the family has that option." He slams the door behind him, leaving Cassian staring at the door as chips of plaster fall to the floor. His voice drops to a near whisper. "Father would never forgive you."

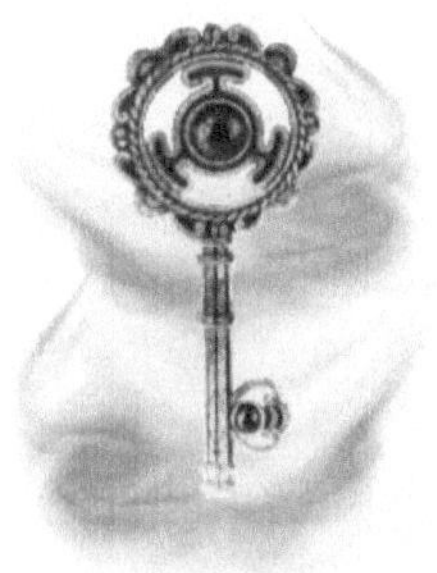

CHAPTER 34 ~ FRIENDSHIP SEVERED

Stepney Castle, London

The clang of a sword hitting the floor, followed by a grunt, leads Julien back to the lounge. As he leaps through the dungeon door, the sight before them causes Olivia to gasp. Soloman is pinned against the wall by the tip of Harold's sword. "Forgive me, Sir. The new army outside distracted me."

Harold's sinister laugh echoes off the castle walls as he pushes the point into Soloman's sternum. "Such a loyal primeval you have here, Julien. It will be a shame to lose him. Don't you think?"

"Let him go, Windsor. This isn't his fight."

"Oh, but it is, Laurent." He swipes his blade across Soloman's stomach, letting him drop to the floor and turns to face Julien. "You see, a loyal primeval is an obstacle for me, old friend." kicking the weapon away from his body, Harold's lip curls into a sneer. "I have but two purposes here today. First, I'll take your head, then I'll be leaving with that key to remove the other two obstacles. I had hoped I could finish this all right here in London, but I see you have sent your sons to hide under your wife's skirts in France," he says, blood splattering off his blade as he throws his arms in the air.

Julien's eyes narrow, a snarl settling on his face as he steps closer. "I guarantee you will not get within miles of my sons. This will end here."

"You're awful sure of yourself for a lone man facing a small army." Harold kicks Soloman's sword toward him. "At least pick up the blade. I'd hate for this to be an unfair battle."

Julien glances down at the knife. His eyes rise to meet Harold's as he kicks it against the wall next to Soloman. "I need no weapon to defeat you and your newborn hellions, Windsor."

"Very well. The choice was given." He raises his sword. "I've let your ridiculous rules threaten our lifestyle for far too long."

"My laws have not impinged on *your* lifestyle one bit. In fact, *you* have paid them no mind at all. Instead, *your* reckless plebs are drawing as much attention to the vampire community as possible. Carelessly leaving dead bodies all over town with no regard for humanity will only bring trouble," Julien spits. "They're treating our city as a damn buffet!"

The calm Julien has thus far been able to maintain washes away with the steady flow of Soloman's blood. Before Harold anticipates his move, Julien knocks his sword to the floor and snaps his forearm.

He drops to one knee, holding his arm as a heavy hiss fills the room and several of his men circle them. Julien turns. "Easy little plebs," he growls, raising his arms as he eyes each ready vampire. "Let me remind you" —*he shifts slightly, gesturing to Harold*— "this imbecile may be your sire, but I am your sovereign. Should you attempt to go against me, your death will be swift."

Slowly recovering, Harold narrows his eyes, groaning as he rises. "Get him!"

Olivia squeals, but as the first vampire charges forward, Julien runs his hand straight through the pleb's chest. He yanks it back with the sound of wet *slosh* reminiscent of pulling a stuck boot from mud.

The newborn drops like a brick as Julien holds his heart in his hand. "You think these misfits can defeat me," he screams, tossing the unusually dark heart at Harold's feet. He turns, staring at the unsure crowd and yells. "Choose your fate!"

Instantly, the room clears, leaving only four. Harold's quick to issue a command, and they move in, fast as light from all directions. Julien spins. His foot connects to a pleb's throat with a thundering crack, but three others pounce before his foot touches the ground, sending him back. The sound of bones cracking as his shoulder smashes into the brick floor causes Olivia to cringe.

"Seems my misfits aren't as useless as you may have thought." Harold reaches for his sword. "Get him on his knees," he orders, flopping the mess of hair from his face.

Olivia watches Julien grimace as the plebs wrench on his arms, pulling him to his knees. She can't begin to fathom his pain as they stand on his ankles and yank his head back. Her heart racing, she closes her eyes, wondering if this is the dreaded moment—the moment he meets his end.

The jarring screech of scratching metal across stone causes her to cringe, and she looks up to see Harold dragging his sword along the floor. He stops in front of Julien, slowly running it along his neck, then flips the gold chain with the tip of his blade. "Ah! The anticipation of this moment makes this that much sweeter." His mouth forms an evil grin as he grasps the key and snaps it free of Julien's neck. With a sinister laugh, he holds it up, turning it to admire its glow. "True immortality!"

Julien flexes his shoulders while the plebs holding him absorb themselves in their conversation. "That's why you wanted the key? You thought it would be of use to you?"

"Of course! Why else would I want it?" His eyes fall from the key to glare at Julien. "You told me the key brought Soloman back—mended his severed neck as if it never happened."

Olivia looks at the bloodstain on the floor where Soloman had been lying and smiles to herself. "Yes," Julien affirms, "**A** key did. But the key you're holding was created specifically for me. It's furnished with a piece of my soul to ensure it would be deemed useless to anyone who wrongfully tried to claim it."

"You're lying!"

"You know, as sovereign, I cannot."

Harold's eyes darken as he turns back to look at where Soloman had been, and a roar resonates from deep in his chest. "Well, don't just stand there," he barks, directing the two plebs standing at his side. "Find him!"

"This isn't Soloman's fight," Julien growls. He tosses the distracted plebs from his arms and charges at Harold.

Dust bursts from the bricks at the opposite end of the room as they hit the wall, and Olivia's body tenses. She watches the young vampires swiftly regain their feet, sending her heart pounding against her chest as they dart past her for Julien. Her eyes squeeze shut, reopening to the sound of Soloman's booming voice. "You will bow to your sovereign, you ingrates!" he bellows as he spins, his sword slicing through the midsection of the advancing plebs.

"Surrender, Windsor," she hears Julien shout, followed by a guttural groan at the opposite end of the room. Turning, she finds his hand lodged in Harold's stomach, suspending him against the wall. "Agree to live by my laws, and I'll let you live. Otherwise, Ancina's prediction will become a reality."

Harold attempts to laugh, spitting blood across Julien's face. "Never. *You* have grown weak, Laurent." He raises his boot between them and kicks Julien back. "You are no sovereign of mine," he yells, steadying himself against the wall.

"You will concede, Windsor," Julien growls, drawing back his hand as he extends his claws. "Or you leave me no choice."

Pushing off the wall, Harold lunges forward, his fierce roar triggering Julien's swift swing. Their movements are so rapid that Olivia doesn't have time to cover her eyes before Harold's head sails across the room. His body drops to the floor with a thud, and the victorious sovereign reaches down to pry the key from his hand. "I do believe this belongs to me."

Olivia gasps. Her eyes spring open, and the journal falls to the floor, her hand flying to her mouth. "What is it? What did you see," Patricia asks, bounding forward in her seat.

"He cut off his head," she mutters. Her gaze locks with Cassian's as a tear trickles down her cheek.

"Who?" Helen's eyes bounce between the two of them. "What happened in there?"

Clara raises her hand, glaring at her daughters. "Let her take a breath before pouncing on her, for goodness sake." Her eyes flit to Helen as she gestures toward the steaming pot on the stove. "Why don't you get her a cup of tea and something to eat? She's been in there an awfully long time."

Olivia's eyes focus on Cassian. "Why is this key so important? After all, you're immortals, right?"

"Yes, but as you just witnessed, death is not entirely out of our reach. Not to mention, that key was infused by a very powerful witch. So it offers much strength to the wearer of its own—something my father did foolishly mention several times."

"But all that means nothing if the key only works for Julien, and Ancina made that point clear when she gave it to him."

"Actually, Ancina said it was garnished with a piece of his soul and could only resurrect an original. There are only three *true* originals, my father, my mother and Harold. That's something only discovered recently through the journal. I assure you, if that information wasn't shared with us—his family. It wasn't shared with anyone." Cassian drags his hand down his face. "In fact, as you read, I'm discovering many things my father kept to himself."

"Then Julien lied when he told Harold it wouldn't work for him. I thought originals couldn't lie."

Cassian walks over to the window, peering out at the darkness. "As long as my father wore the key, he was unable to lie. That's true. However, if you'll recall, Harold had torn it from his neck at that point." He turns back, offering a slight smile as he peers at each woman. "But you should know the other originals can be untruthful without consequence. It is only the key-bearing sovereign who is unable to speak dishonestly. Ancina clarified that when she gave him the key, but I believe it may have been overlooked. Mr. Windsor could spin a tale perfectly fine, and my mother has been known to stretch the truth on occasion as well."

"But you—" Olivia's voice fades as she watches him shake his head.

"No, Olivia. I promise it's all a myth. I can lie if I choose to. I simply haven't because I want you to know that you can trust me. Besides, I'm only a scion, not a true original. So that fable wouldn't apply to me anyway."

Patricia eyes him suspiciously. "Wait, then how do we know you haven't been lying all along?"

"*You* don't. But quite frankly, Patricia, **your** opinion means nothing to me. I wanted to ensure Olivia knew the truth." Cassian bows slightly. "I'll be in my room if you require me."

Watching him leave the room, Olivia stands. "I'm quite exhausted myself." She nudges Mr. Green from the top of the journal and hugs it to her chest. "Come on, Mr. Green. Time for bed," she says, clicking her tongue for him to follow.

"What?" Helen's jaw drops. "Just like that? You're not even going to tell us what you saw in there? You can't come out with Julien cut off Harold's head and not tell us why, Liv."

"Actually, I believe that's a good idea." Taking a deep breath, Clara stands. "Cassian's mother is visiting tomorrow evening." Patricia's hand slams against the table, and her mother shakes her head. "Nah-uh, hear me out before you raise to protest. She would like to meet the family of witches willing to help reunite them with their sovereign," *—Clara points around the table, squinting at her daughters—* that means all of us, and we will welcome her."

Patricia bounds to her feet, igniting the candles around the room as she throws her hands up. "This is utter bullshit!"

Raising her finger, Clara gives it a quick swirl, blowing the flames out and narrows her sight on her daughter. "You will watch your tongue in this house."

"Oh, I'm sorry. It's difficult to tell what's acceptable around here anymore. It appears the house rules have drastically changed these past few weeks." She turns her gaze toward Olivia. "Liv, I love you, but I no longer want anything to do with that damn demon diary." She scowls at her mother and sister. "Nor do I care to entertain any more royal pain in the ass vampires. You're all on your own!"

"Patricia, wait," Clara calls out, but any attempt to reason with her falls on deaf ears as she storms out the backdoor.

"Well, that's just bloody wonderful," Helen huffs, flopping back in her chair. "Thank goodness for your enchanted wine."

"Accepting change has never come easily for Patricia." She places a reassuring hand on her granddaughter's shoulder. "Your aunt will be fine once she's had some time on her own to think. You go on up to bed. Everything will be fine tomorrow."

"I hope you're right." Olivia lowers the journal, allowing Mr. Green to hop on top and makes her way to the stairs. "I guess we'll see you two in the morning."

CHAPTER 35 ~ FRENEMIES

As Olivia approaches the door to her room, the bust at the end of the hall tips his head. "Sleep well, Olivia."

"Goodnight, Uncle Chester." She sets the journal down on her nightstand and draws back her duvet. She can't seem to shake the image of Julien's eyes filling with rage. The very thread still holding his humanity intact, severed within moments by his need to protect his family and throne. "This wasn't your fault, Julien. Your reaction was out of necessity." She runs her hand over the journal as if to comfort him or possibly her, then slides into bed. "I need to find that key."

Tap tap tap

"Olivia?"

Cassian's deep voice glides through the crack of the door like a quiet melody, bringing a smile to her face. "Come in, Cash."

"Your thoughts—" He lowers his head as he steps in and tucks his hands into the front pockets of his pants. "They're loud." His gaze lifts to meet hers. "You wouldn't have actually attempted to read the journal without letting anyone know. Would you?"

She can't help but laugh. "You make it sound like a Ouija board or something."

He pulls his hands from his pockets with a shrug and gestures to the bed. "Mind if I sit?"

"Of course not." She nudges Mr. Green aside, then shifts and pats the edge of the bed. "I don't honestly understand the concern. I mean, you've all been pushing me to read it, and I believe I finally understand why." She pulls the journal to her lap and smoothes her hand over the cover. "I have to read it if I'm going to find the key and figure out how to bring your father back."

Cassian takes the book from her hands and places it on the nightstand. "I wouldn't necessarily say pushing, but as someone who has been waiting over a century to hear about the entries" —*he tips his head side to side*— "you could say I am anxious. I wouldn't argue with that. However, we must keep in mind this is a timekeeper journal. An ancient tome created by a remarkably powerful source. And as your grandmother has explained to us, this isn't just something you're reading, Olivia. You travel into another dimension of sorts. So is it plausible to think that you could enter it at some point, and we may have to fight to bring you out?" The muscles in his jaw tense. "Or maybe the question I should ask is will we be able to?"

"Cash, you're scaring me."

He swings his knee on the bed and takes her hands. "I'm not trying to frighten you. I am merely suggesting that you practice caution when using anything that yields this much power." He runs his thumbs over the back of her hands. "There's no harm in letting someone watch over you while you're inside."

A small smile tugs at her lips. "Fair enough." Pulling her hands from his, she adjusts the blankets around her hips. "So, your mother is coming to meet us tomorrow?"

His gaze falls to his pant leg as he busies himself with straightening the seam. "Yes. We spoke of her intentions to come by," his eyes meet hers, "don't you recall?"

"I remember. I just didn't think it was going to be right away. I haven't finished reading the journal yet."

"It will be fine, Olivia. I've given it some thought, and if you summon her here, then you can also release her whenever you're ready." Winking, he pats her hand and stands. "Now, you should try to get some rest."

"Cash?"

"Hmm?"

"I saw where your mother hid the scroll. I'm sure you did too." He confirms with a nod. "Where is your father's body?"

Shutting her bedroom door, Cassian turns back to face her. "Olivia, your grandmother made it very clear that I am not to interfere with the process of the journal. Both our families could suffer consequences if I do. Besides, we still don't have the key."

She lowers her head, twiddling with her fingers. "I understand that, but I would like to prepare myself." Her eyes meet his. "You know, mentally. You can at least tell me if you have his body. Can't you?"

Cassian's mouth opens, his eyes shifting from hers to the window. "Yes. We have his body." His nostrils flare as he inhales, his deep blue eyes swirling with crimson. "Forgive me, Olivia, but I must go. Get some rest."

Leaving her door slightly open, he disappears before she can say anything more. "I hope I didn't offend you by asking," she murmurs, staring at the door as if he'll walk back through any moment. But when he doesn't, she flicks her hand toward it. "Prope ostium." Watching it close, she pulls the string on her bedside lamp and snuggles down in her bed. "Goodnight, Cash."

Outside, Patricia stands in front of the common altar. She's staring into the blazing fire when the backdrop of croaking bullfrogs and chirping crickets turn to silence. Her ears perk to the sound of cracking branches in the distance, and she spins. Her eyes strain toward the path, but she can see nothing through the darkness. Shaking her head, she curses, turning back toward the fire. "Damn coyotes."

"I'm afraid you're losing your touch, Miss Redfearn." Her shoulders stiffen as she peers up to see two darkened figures on either side of the altar.

Patricia starts to raise her hand when they're quickly tugged behind her. "No, no. There will be none of that. We only want the young witch and the journal, then we'll gladly be on our way." He finally steps forward, and his eyes lock with hers. "Now, why don't you be a good host and invite us in?"

Futilely tugging her arms forward, she glares at the fair-haired figure and spits. "Over my dead body, you disgusting leech."

He widens his stance and chucks his chin toward the vampire restraining her. "I'm sure that can be arranged if you're not going to play nice."

Clouds move to cover the starry sky as the vampire's grip tightens. His teeth graze the side of her neck, and thunder rolls above. Patricia rubs her fingers together, and a blue charge brightens between them. "Ow!" the vampire shrieks, trying to maintain his grip on her arms as he bounds backward. "I swear it, she-devil, I'll drain you if you try that again!"

"You'll hold her until I tell you otherwise," the second vampire demands as he steps forward. He grabs Patricia by the hair and yanks her head back, stopping her struggle, if only for the moment. "You are a feisty one, aren't you." He lifts his hand, slowly smoothing his claw-like fingernail along her cheek. "If you're not going to invite us in, why don't you call young Olivia out here?"

"Olivia can't help you. She has no powers," Patricia spits.

His gaze shifts to the vampire holding her as he steps back. "You're lying." He takes a step forward and inhales. "Did you know fear warms the blood?" Patricia glares at him but remains silent. "Oh, yes. Not only can I hear your heart racing, but the scent of your blood heating is utterly alluring."

"I'm not afraid of you, you filthy leech!"

"No?" His swift response opens a gash on the side of her face. "How about now?"

Blood trickles from her cheek, spurring an agitated growl from behind her. "Oh, get control of yourself," he snarls, his eyes narrowing on the vampire baring his teeth. "You see, Nathaniel here—" he starts when suddenly his mouth falls open, and his knees buckle, leaving Cassian standing in his place with a dripping heart in his hand.

Patricia's arms are released, and she falls forward with a gasp, landing on the bloody corpse of the heartless vampire. As she scrambles to her feet, she frantically brushes her hands down the front of her bloody shirt as if it will clean the blood-soaked mess and peers over at Cassian. "Where the hell did you come from?"

"You're welcome." He tosses the heart into the fire and turns the corpse over.

"Is this the infamous Roger?" She toes the vampire's arm, wincing as her hand covers the open gash on her cheek.

"No, I'm afraid not. This is one of Roger's plebs—Holden. I recall him from the night my father was killed."

"Well, that's great." She points to the hole in his chest. "I think it's safe to assume you regret ripping his heart out of his chest now, huh? You can't question a dead guy."

Cassian smirks. "You really must work on your people skills."

"I have people skills. It's my vampire skills that are in *I don't give a shit mode.*" Forcing a smile, she points down at the body. "You need a hand disposing of this mess?"

"Sure. A nice hot flame should do the trick." He gestures to the gash on her face. "Then you ought to clean that wound before it gets infected."

"Yeah," she cringes, "those nails looked like they hadn't been cleaned in centuries." Rubbing her hands together, she extends them above Holden. "Flamma!"

"Well, look at you two getting along," Helen chirps, holding the backdoor open with a grin. She flips on the outside light and steps down. "Before what gets infected?" Taking a few steps forward, she stops, throwing her hand over her mouth as she watches her sister set the body ablaze. "Is that?" She waves her finger, her face set in horror. "Is that—"

"Relax, Helen. It's a dead vamp." Patrica grabs her arm, turning her toward the house. "Come, I need your help to bandage this up."

"Oh my goodness," she shrieks, her attention immediately shifting to the blood dripping from Patricia's chin. "I can see your tongue through your cheek! Not even with the love of the Goddess can I fix that. That is going to need stitches and likely mom's healing."

"A few drops of my blood will seal that wound quicker than any stitch." Making a small cut with his thumbnail, Cassian holds out his wrist. "Unlike stitching, it won't leave a scar. Here, just dab a bit on."

"No way, Bloodsucker!" Patricia throws her hand up. "You are not recruiting *me*. I would much rather deal with mom's wrath."

Breaking into laughter, Cassian pinches the cut on his wrist together and licks the blood from his thumb. "As you wish. Though, to be clear, I wasn't offering enough to change you. Only a few drops to heal your wound. I'm not careless. Not everyone can withstand the change, and although we might be frenemies, you're still Olivia's aunt."

"Frenemies," Helen laughs. "I have to admit. That is perfectly termed."

CHAPTER 36 ~ NEVER READ ALONE

Olivia is about to doze off when Julien flashes before her. He's standing in his blood-soaked shirt with the key in his hand when his gaze locks with hers. She bounds up in her bed. "Solas air!" she shouts, turning the bedside light on without giving it a second thought.

With her hand pressed to her chest, she looks around the room. "I could've sworn I just saw Julien in front of me." She reaches down, running her hand over her cat's head. "I know this sounds silly, but I think he needs me back in the journal. And yes, I am aware of my promise to Cash, but technically, I'm not alone if you're here. Right?"

The lazy feline stretches with his signature *'meow,' and Olivia smiles.*

"I knew you'd agree." She reaches for the journal and pulls it to her lap. "Maybe I missed something important in the last entry." As she opens the cover, the pages begin to flip, stopping on the last page she read. The final line glows, marking the spot where she left off.

Julien reaches down and pries the key from his hand. "I do believe this belongs to me."

She places her finger on the next line and continues reading. Before she knows it, she's standing next to the blood-soaked Julien she just saw.

One final swipe of Soloman's sword and the last of Harold's plebs fall to the floor. He appears at Julien's side, his clothes bloodied and torn. "That's the last of the remaining intruders, Sir."

"Well done, Soloman. I'm grateful for your loyalty." He smiles down at the key. "This key holds much more value to our kind than even you may know. With it, I am sovereign and responsible for holding every vampire accountable for their pleb creation and transition. Unfortunately, Harold's careless neglect of his pleb propagation has resulted in blood rage and indulgent feeding frenzies." His gaze drops as he toes Harold's body. "As a fellow original and friend, I allowed him far too much room, hoping he would stop and gain control of his clan. Instead, he chose to continue with his irresponsible ways drawing attention to our kind more than once. Finally, today, when he involved the King's men, he left me no other choice but to put an end to it."

Bowing slightly, Soloman looks around. "Having witnessed the danger and chaos firsthand, I completely understand, Sir."

Julien pats him on the back with a smile. "I knew you would, Soloman. You're a wise man."

He wraps the hair on Harold's head around his hand and lifts it into the air to stare into his face. "You fool, Windsor. I hate that our friendship had to end this way." Tucking the head under his arm, he peers back at Soloman. "I have a message to deliver to the rest of his clan. I trust you can find your way to France?"

"Of course, Sir." Soloman smiles as he fans his arm around the room. "I'll head out after the pig roast."

"Thanks again. I'm not sure what I would do without you, Soloman." Leaving the door to the castle swinging closed behind him, Julien takes off toward the Windsor residence.

Appearing on Harold's front step, Julien grabs the heavy iron knocker and slams it against the door. "Harriet! Come on out here. I have something for you."

The heavy wooden door opens, and Harriet steps out with her arms crossed. "Julien? You're covered in blood. Is everything all right?"

His bloodied face tightens, and tears start to trickle down Harriet's cheeks as she shakes her head. "No." He steps closer as her hand flies to her mouth, and she takes a step back. "That's Harold's blood." Her eyes drop as he reaches down to grab the hair on Harold's head.

"I don't have to tell you your husband was a traitor. He compelled the King's men to come after my son and me—to kill us. When they failed, he released his crude plebs into my home. I want you, your half-breed son and your clan of illegal plebs out of London. And if anyone thinks of coming after my family or me again, they stand to suffer this same fate. "

He tosses Harold's head at her feet and turns, her scream echoing in the night as he disappears through the fog.

Olivia covers her mouth as darkness settles around her. Finally, warmth fills the air, and she blinks to bring her view into focus.

Clarentina is sitting by the window in their castle in Commana, France, as Julien crests the hill of the gates. "Oh, thank goodness!" She rushes out to greet him, her strides stuttering to a halt as she scans his bloody figure.

"Come here, my love. It's okay. It's over," he smiles, reaching out to hold her.

Her arms fly around him. "Julien?" She steps back, placing her hand over her nose and stares into his eyes. "Oh my goodness. Is that Harold's—"

"I'm afraid so, my love." He cups her face in his hands as his solemn gaze lifts to his sons standing behind her. "I had no choice but to kill him. From this point on, the Windsor clan has been declared rogue. I'm afraid the castle in London is inhabitable, and I believe it would be best if we made our presence there scarce for a while."

Clarentina loops her arm through his, turning him toward the Castle. "We have everything we need right here, my darling. Come, let's get you cleaned up. You must be starving."

Stepping into the main entrance, Julien looks back at his sons. "Where is Gabriel? Did the boy go out?"

Elias's face drops as he takes a step forward. "Oh, father, he—"

"Yes, we must discuss young Gabriel once you've taken some nourishment," Clarentina says, cutting him off with a glare.

Julien stops, his eyes bouncing between his wife and son. "What are you two hiding? Is the boy all right? Oh, for goodness sake. Tell me he hasn't gotten some young lass into trouble."

Unexpectedly, Cassian speaks up against his mother's wishes. "Unfortunately, it's nothing that simple, father. Gabriel has come down with smallpox. When I arrived home, Francis informed me of his illness, and he's been declining by the hour."

Elias steps up next to Cassian. "Father, he's in and out of consciousness. He may not make it through the night. I know you swore not to change any more humans, but this is Gabe. He's our brother."

Julien's shoulders slump as he places his hand on Elias's shoulder. "Son, I know you believe that we have the ability to change anyone into our kind, but that is simply not so. The change is never guaranteed, and even if they accept our blood, seeing someone through the transition can be difficult. Fortunately, you boys have never known that type of hunger, but I can tell you from personal experience it is excruciating while trying to tame it."

"Could you at least try?" Cassian pleads.

Closing his eyes, Julien offers him a sympathetic smile. "I'm sorry, son. Now, your mother's right. I need to go get cleaned up."

The front door slams before Julien and Clarentina hit the second step. She pats her husband's hand and smiles up at him. "We'll all have to adjust to his loss if you decide not to, but you should at least go and say your goodbyes to the boy while he's still breathing."

"Clarentina, I know what you're trying to do, and we've discussed this before. The creation of new vampires should be wisely considered, if not completely eliminated. At least until we have these rogues under control. We aren't humans. We're immortal, and thanks to Windsor's reckless disregard for the laws I set out to protect humanity, a community such as ours is overpopulated."

Opening their bedroom door, she steps aside to let him pass before following him in. "I know we have discussed this, but this would not be a reckless creation. Gabriel may as well be one of our own children and has our entire family committed to assisting with his transition." Brushing her hand over his shoulder, she kisses his cheek. "At least consider it. Please, darling. For me."

Julien nods. "I'll go see the lad once I get cleaned up."

"Of course. I'll have Francis request a donor for you."

The strain on Julien's face as he struggles to decide right from wrong weighs heavy on Olivia's chest as the room darkens. She rubs her arms as the chilly night air settles on her skin, but the feeling of being pulled in all directions sets her heart racing, and she tries desperately to steady herself, to focus on her surroundings. Cassian lifts his head from his book and inhales deeply. "Damn it, Olivia!" His book hits the floor, and within moments, he's shoving her bedroom door open.

"You silly, silly girl," he runs his hand over her back. "Olivia, can you hear me? You need to come toward my voice."

Clara bursts through the door as her granddaughter begins to tremble. "Dùin na dorsan uile nad inntinn!" she yells with arms extended toward her.

Olivia's head falls back against her headboard, and as Clara lifts her hand from the page, Cassian knocks the journal to the floor. Sitting next to her, he cups her face in his hands. "Olivia? Olivia!" he yells. Her eyes spring open with her mouth as she gasps for air. "Damn it, Olivia!" He pulls her into his arms for a brief moment, then leans back to look at her face. "What were you thinking? I thought we had just discussed this."

Stepping back, Clara raises a brow as Cassian scolds her granddaughter. "I take it you had no idea she was reading then."

"No, Gran," Olivia speaks up. "I'm afraid this is on me. Cash warned me not to read the journal without someone present."

Scrunching her face up, she holds her hand out toward Mr. Green. "Though technically, I wasn't alone."

Clara's face tightens as her voice rises. "This is not something to joke about, young lady. That book opens doors to both good and evil. Thankfully Cassian was here to—" She stops herself, peering at Cassian. "How exactly *did* you know she was in trouble?"

"I smelled her fear." Instinctively he licks his lips as Patricia steps into the room.

"Right. You mean you *tasted* it," Patricia snarls. "That's what you really meant. Isn't it, Bloodsucker?" Shoving him aside, she sits next to Olivia and throws her arm around her.

Clara takes a second glance as her sight sets on Patricia's cheek. "What the hell happened to your face?"

"I told her we should get you," Helen blurts as she steps through the doorway. Clara's questioning gaze shifts, and Helen quickly points to Cassian and Patricia. "Don't look at me like that. Take it up with those two. Like you, I only saw the aftermath."

Gasping, Clara's gaze shifts between them. "Cassian did not—" she starts when Helen lifts her hand and shakes her head.

"Goodness, no. Cash saved her."

"I'm not sure *saved* is the word," Patricia says, rolling her eyes. "A couple of vamps showed up and caught me off guard."

"Yeah, and Cash ripped his heart out to *save* you," Helen retorts.

Rubbing her temples, Clara drags her hands down the sides of her face and looks around the room. "That's the last time I take my own sleeping remedy. Is there anything else I should know before we start addressing these current matters?" Watching heads shake, she takes a deep breath. "Well, thank the Goddess for that." Her sight lands on Helen, and she tips her head toward the door. "Why don't you make us some tea? It seems I have a wound to tend to, and we have a journal to discuss."

"Gran, I'm sorry. I don't know what came over me. I just had to know what happened with Julien."

"Olivia," Clara pauses for a minute, choosing the right words. "Imagine the Timekeeper Journal as a medium—a Ouija board of sorts." Cassian glances at Olivia with a smirk. "It will draw you in every chance it gets. It's spelled to entice you, call to your curiosity, and make you want to continue reading it at any cost. That journal has a task set out for you, and I've told you that it will not leave you rest until you have completed it. These stories are getting more and more intense. That tells me you're nearing the end. It will soon guide you through how to complete your mission, but you must not, and I can't stress this enough, you must not read it alone. Do I make myself clear?"

"Yes, Gran."

Clara looks over at the alarm clock on Olivia's nightstand. "Well, it looks like this is going to be an early day. You may as well get dressed. Once I've mended your aunt's face, we can all have some breakfast." She peers up at Cassian with a smile. "I'd like to know a little more about our guests before they arrive tonight."

Meeting her stare, Cassian draws his brows together. "Guests? I thought it was only my mother you were having over."

"Yes, well, I figure as Julien's wife and children, the anticipation must be overwhelming. If it were me, I would like a full update on Olivia's journey through the journal thus far. I assume you'll remind them that we're not the enemy."

"Absolutely, Ms. Redfearn. That's very thoughtful. I assure you, you have nothing to worry about."

"I didn't assume so." Shooing everyone toward the door, she grabs the journal. "Now, let's go. Olivia will meet us downstairs." She stops in the doorway and holds up the book. "I'll take this with me just to ensure you aren't tempted to dive back in. You can finish the entry after you've eaten something."

Watching her bedroom door close, Olivia runs her hand over Mr. Green's back. "A house full of witches and vampires. What do you make of that, Mr. Green?" He stands, nudging her hand with his head as he lets out a 'meow' and flops on his side. Chuckling, she hops off her bed and chooses her clothes for the day. "I suppose you're right. What's to worry about? I mean, outside of them being blood-drinking immortals and our apparent natural enemies." She pulls her hair back into a ponytail and waves him forward. "You coming?"

CHAPTER 37 ~ SMALLPOX

Olivia stops dead on the bottom step as Cassian slices into his wrist and drips a small amount of the darkest blood she's ever seen into a dish. He pinches the cut together and hands the bowl to Clara. "I'm sure that's plenty."

Patricia cringes. "I'm telling ya, if I grow fangs and start craving blood, I'm coming for you first, Mom."

Clara soaks a cotton ball with his blood and meets Patricia's scornful gaze with a smirk. "Oh, hush and stay still. That's not how this works, and you know it." She dabs the blood-soaked puff along the gash on Patricia's cheek, cursing as she flinches. "Damn it, child! I said stay still."

"Ptui," Patricia spits, her tongue hanging from her lips in disgust. "You got it in my mouth!"

"Well, the cut goes straight through. What did you expect?" Clara steps back cocking her head to the side to have a better look, as Olivia steps up next to her. "It's quite amazing, wouldn't you say, Liv?"

Bending to have a closer look, Olivia steps back, shaking her head. "I've never seen anything like that."

"Pfft." Patricia rolls her eyes. "Oh, please. Mom has mended many wounds. This would have healed just fine without that petrified gunk."

Twisting her lips into a half-smile, Clara shakes her head. "Not this quickly and certainly not without a few stitches and a hideous scar. You ought to be thanking Cassian for parting with some of his life source to save your flesh."

"Seriously, Aunt Trish. I just watched the fibres of your skin knit back together." Olivia's eyes flit to Cassian. "I knew you healed almost instantly, but I didn't realize your blood works like a miracle bandaid."

"It does heal human tissue remarkably well." His gaze moves to Patricia as she turns her head to gag. "However, without *human* blood to aid me, I wouldn't be able to regenerate myself."

Helen sets a platter of bacon and eggs on the table. "Okay, not to be a prude, but can we stop all this chatter about blood now? Breakfast is ready, and I'd like to enjoy mine, please."

A broad smile lights up Cassian's face as he holds up the travel mug that Clara was so kind to supply him with. "I was just about to go get a refill anyway. Of coffee, that is."

"Ha!" Patricia laughs sarcastically. "Yeah, right!"

Grabbing a plate, Clara shoots her a dirty look. "Well, be sure to come back once you've replenished." She forces a smile as her gaze shifts to Cassian. "As you know, Olivia is antsy to get back into the journal, but we can't have her back in there alone."

"I'll be back before she can finish loading her plate with bacon," he winks.

Clara picks up her fork and stops to peer at Olivia. "Now, why don't you tell us what had you so determined to jump back into the journal on your own. Especially after you were warned not to."

Olivia holds up her finger, taking a sip of her tea to wash down her mouthful of bacon. "It was as though Julien needed to show me what happened next." She picks up a piece of bacon and takes a bite. "Or maybe his reasoning behind his actions. I'm not sure, but he appeared in front of me in his blood-soaked clothes just as I had last seen him."

The three women exchange glances. "Appeared to you?" Helen asks, setting her fork down.

"Mmhmm."

"I'm still hung up on him cutting Harold's head off. I would have expected him to rip his heart out of his chest like Cash did to the bloodsucker last night," Patricia smirks as she eyes Cassian. "Isn't that how your kind takes care of business?"

Meeting her stare, Cassian takes a drink from his mug. His tongue sweeps across his lips, gleaming with remnants of the bright red contents. "Not necessarily. We try to ensure the penalty fits."

Patricia shudders as she raises her hand. "Okay, that is so disgusting." Turning toward Clara, she scowls. "Why are you allowing him to drink people here?"

Rolling her eyes, Clara rubs her hand over her cheek. "I think we may have lost focus." She peers around the table. "From this point on, we need to stick together. No more travelling outside the house alone." Her gaze anchors on Olivia. "And you, my child, may not read that journal by yourself. I don't care if Julien appears to you. I have told you before, Timekeeper Journals are spelled to draw you in."

"There's certainly no denying that." Helen rests her chin on her hand and smiles, her gaze fixed on her niece. "You went from completely avoiding magic to using it without even realizing you are."

"I'm not sure how I know what to say. Words just pop into my head."

"You've been around it your entire life." Clara smiles. "You may have thought you weren't paying attention, but you were." Her gaze shifts to Cassian. "This may sound silly, but do you eat at all?" She lifts her finger. Her cheeks redden as she shakes her head. "I only ask so that Helen might prepare something for when your family arrives."

Cassian runs his hand across his chin, scanning Olivia's face before meeting Clara's gaze with a nod. "We do. Occasionally, we enjoy some basashi or carpaccio, even some ossenworst."

"So raw meat dishes then." A smile brightens Helen's face. "I can easily accommodate that."

"There's really no need to go out of your way—"

"Yeah. I'm sure we can assume they're just like this one" — *Patricia gestures to Cassian*— "and come packing their own blood supply anyway."

Clara shoots her a dirty look. "You will be on your best behaviour." Her scowl turns to a smile as she looks up at Cassian. "It's settled then. We'll let Olivia finish her journal entry, and then she can summon them here for dinner."

Helen snaps her fingers, clearing the table, and Olivia pushes her chair back. She runs her hand over the black furball curled up in her lap, then gives him a gentle nudge. "You should probably get down, Mr. Green. My reactions while reading the journal have been pretty unpredictable so far."

She watches him hop down with a disgruntled *'meow'* and pulls the journal in front of her. Her fingertips tap the cover lightly as she looks around the table. "Ready?"

Tipping her head toward the old leather tome, Clara turns her hand out. "Whenever you are."

Olivia slowly opens the cover, letting the pages flip to where she had finished reading only a few hours prior. "Okay." Her gaze flits to Cassian before her finger drops to the page—to the next glistening line of script.

The cool night air wraps around her as Cassian and Elias come into view. They're staring up at the rickety timber of an old tree fort in the field behind the castle when Cassian shoves his hands in his pockets. Exhausting a breath through his nose, his brother nudges his elbow. "Remember when Gabe fell from the top of there and broke his leg?"

"Yeah, I remember. You gave him some of your blood to heal him so nobody would know." Swiping his thumb across his nose, Elias chuckles. "Father would have had your head for that."

"I know. I should never have done that. I recall father telling me a few years after that our blood is actually toxic to some humans. That not all humans can be turned. Some die a painful death instead of changing."

Elias's face lights up. "Wait." He paces in front of Cassian, pinching his bottom lip, then stops. "So then, if Gabe has already had some of your blood and it didn't kill him, it will likely work. He'll accept the change. Right?"

Cassian rubs his hand across his forehead. "It's not the same, Elias. I gave him such a minimal amount. Only a drop at best to heal him."

"Come on, Cash. We have to try. If we don't, he doesn't stand a chance. You can smell death seeping in."

"Absolutely not! Father is the head of this family. If any human is to be turned into a Laurent, it will be by him."

Putting his head down, Elias kicks at the stones along the path. "It seems so wrong to do nothing when I know we can save him."

Swiping a tear from her cheek, Olivia barely blinks before she finds herself back in Julien's bed chamber. A clean pair of trousers and shirt are slung over the end of the bed, where Clarentina waits patiently for him to emerge from his bath.

There's a light knock on the door when Clarentina calls out, "Come in, Francis."

A young lady, possibly in her mid-twenties, walks through the door and curtsies. "Miss Lillian has offered to come for Mr. Laurent, Madame."

"Wonderful. Thank you, Francis." Clarentina smiles at the young lady. "It's nice to see you again, Lillian. Mr. Laurent will be out in a few moments." She gestures to the seat on the other side of the room. "Please, make yourself comfortable."

With a slight curtsy, Lillian takes the offered seat and twists the long tie on her smock around her fingers while she waits. When

Julien emerges from the bathroom with a towel wrapped around his waist, his gaze falls to his wife. "You know," he starts when she slowly closes her eyes and lifts her hand slightly from her lap to point in Lillian's direction.

"Why don't we discuss it once you've taken some nourishment, darling."

"I can wait until we've talked."

Shaking her head, Clarentina gestures to the young lady. "Don't be silly. This can wait a few more minutes. We don't want to keep Miss Lillian any longer than necessary."

"Oh. Right. Of course." Julien walks to the opposite side of the room and sits next to Lillian. She automatically draws her hair back from her neck and tips her head to the side. He shifts uncomfortably, glancing at Clarentina. "If you don't mind," he says, taking Lillian's hand and gesturing to her forearm. "I'd prefer to take from here." Pushing up her sleeve to acknowledge his request, he graciously bows his head and sinks his teeth into her arm.

Once his hunger has been satisfied, he releases her arm and runs his tongue over the puncture wounds to heal them. "Thank you, Miss Lillian." Standing, he eases her to her feet.

She offers him the slightest smile, her face noticeably paler than when she entered. "You're most welcome, Mr. Laurent."

Carefully escorting her to the door, Julien places her hand in Francis's. "Please see that she eats something before you show her back to her room."

"You know I will, Sir."

"Oh, and Francis?"

"Yes, Sir?"

"How is young Gabriel doing?"

His smile fades. "I'm afraid his situation is quite grim. We've made him as comfortable as we can for now. He's in the west tower if you'd like to see him."

"Yes. Thank you." Julien's gaze lowers as he closes the door. Turning back to face Clarentina, he forces a smile. "What is it you wished to speak to me about, my love?"

Returning his smile, she steps up and takes his hands. "It was nothing, darling." She reaches up, brushing her thumb across his tense brow. "I'm just pleased to have you home safe. We all are." Her palm rests against his cheek as she stares into his eyes. "Should I come with you to see Gabriel, or would you prefer to see him on your own?"

The corners of his mouth droop into a frown, and he lowers his gaze. "No, my love. Saying goodbye to the boy will be difficult enough. I wouldn't be able to shoulder your tears as well."

"Fair enough, darling. Take your time. I'll go speak with the boys."

Kissing her hand, he lets it slide from his and reaches for the door.

CHAPTER 38 ~ GABRIEL

Olivia follows him to the west tower, her heart heavy as Julien pauses outside Gabriel's door. She watches him place his hand over his mouth. Then taking a breath, she realizes the stench of imminent death seeping from the room is almost too much to bear.

"Are you all right, Sir?" Francis lays his hand on Julien's shoulder and gestures to the door. "I can accompany you in if you'd like."

Julien shakes his head. "You know, if it were anyone else on the other side of that wall, it would be just another goodbye, but this is young Gabriel. A young child we have all watched grow into a man."

"Yes. I can assure you his condition saddens us all, Sir."

Dropping his head, Julien slowly opens the door, taking a moment to collect himself before entering. The young man that was so full of life the last time he saw him now lies completely still. Naked, all but the small towel across his groin, his frail form is ninety percent covered in pus-filled blisters. Julien starts to turn around when he hears a groan.

Gabriel lifts his index finger, pointing at Julien, and he steps inside, closing the door. As he nears the bed, he hears a slurred attempt at his name, "Misser Larran."

"I'm here, son."

Rushing to his side, Julien takes his hand, a tear escaping from the corner of his eye. "Son, what I'm about to say goes against my own rule, but I believe if anyone ever deserved eternity—you do." He swallows, studying the horrific blisters covering the joyous face they've all come to know so well. "Do you know what we are?" Gabriel nods. "It's not a glamourous lifestyle, but the boys and I will help you adjust if this is what you choose." Slowly closing his eyes, he tightens his hold on Julien's hand. "You must understand that not all humans can tolerate our venom. There is a chance you may not survive. Are you sure you want me to attempt this?"

Gabriel closes his eyes, his response a wet slur. "Yesss."

Forcing a smile, Julien gently pats his hand. "As you wish, my boy." He slides his hand behind the young man's neck and draws him forward. As his head rolls to the side, Julien sinks his fangs into his artery.

Olivia cringes, covering her face with her hands. *"For the love of the goddess, I can't watch!"*

She hears the bed creak and peers up to see him unbutton the cuff of his shirt, rolling his sleeve halfway up his forearm. His thumbnail elongates into a knifelike claw, and he runs it across his wrist. As the dark blood rises to the surface, Julien places it to Gabriel's mouth. "Go ahead and drink."

While he swallows the offered blood, Julien runs his extended nail across the young man's neck, draining what's left of his human life. When Gabriel finally weakens enough that he can no longer drink from him, he pulls his arm from his lips and sits in the chair next to the bed. "That's it, son. You're doing great."

Watching the pulsing flow of blood slow, Julien once again slices his wrist and places it back to Gabriel's lips. With very little response, he tips the young man's head back to let the blood seep down his throat. "Gabriel, if you can hear me. Swallow." Julien eyes his adam's apple trail slowly up and down. "That's very good. You should be just fine, my boy."

The pulse in his neck ceases, and Julien knows the only thing left to do now is wait. He removes his wrist from Gabriel's lips, wets his fingers with his saliva and seals his wound. He knows it could be hours, even days before Gabriel wakes up - if the lad wakes at all. So he wets the washcloth next to the washbasin, and wipes the blood from the young man's lips, then calls for Francis.

Within moments, Francis is standing in the doorway, his eyes shifting between the pool of blood on the floor to Gabriel's lifeless body. "Well, don't just stand there. Come in and shut the door. I'm going to need your help," Julien snaps.

"Uh—of course, Sir." He grabs the bloody washbasin and cloth. "I'll retrieve some fresh water and linen."

"Thank you, and could you get the boy some clothes? There's certainly no fear of fever now."

"Right away." Francis hurries from the room. When he returns a few minutes later with fresh water and linen, he perches one of the human donors in front of Julien. "You should feed, Sir. I have another waiting for when the boy wakes."

"You seem sure the boy will make it."

Francis smiles as he wrings out the cloth and wipes Gabriel's face and neck. "Oh, I'm certain of it. He has the purest of blood running through his veins. His body just needs time to adjust and heal."

Brushing aside the donor's hair, Julien glances up at him. "I do hope you're right, Francis. If it weren't for seeing one of my own sons every time I look at this boy, I never would have attempted this."

"I understand, Mr. Laurent. I can imagine it would be a difficult decision."

Staring over at Gabriel's lifeless body, Julien rubs his hand across his chin and thanks the donor. Under normal circumstances, he wouldn't have needed to feed. Instead, he would have drained

Gabriel's blood to replenish his own, but with the boy's body covered in blisters, he couldn't stomach it.

Francis's voice cuts through his thoughts. "Sir, it's been hours. If you'd like to go get some air, I'll stay here and watch over him."

"No. I appreciate that, but I need to be here when he wakes." Julien's voice trails off. "*If* he wakes." Julien pushes himself up in his chair and straightens his vest. "Maybe we should change those sheets."

Julien starts to stand, and Francis puts his hand up. "I've got it." He gently turns Gabriel, rolling the bloodied pus-laden sheet from under him and slides a clean one in its place. As he tucks the corners under the mattress, he places the young man's fallen arm back at his side. "Sir." He glances over his shoulder. "I believe the boy's blisters are beginning to heal."

He scans the body, his sight landing on Francis's uncommon smile. Before another second can pass, Julien and Olivia stand at Gabriel's side. Their sight anchoring on a sizeable pus-filled blister as it gradually shrinks and returns to smooth flesh. "Well, I'll be damned. I believe you're right, Francis. I think he's healing." As Julien places his hand on the young man's arm, Olivia lays her hand on his. He stills. His head turns toward her as he whispers, "Is that you, Ancina?"

"Did you say something, Sir?" Francis asks as Olivia pulls her hand away and steps back.

"No." Julien shakes his head. "Just mumbling to myself. He grabs the clothing Francis had brought up for Gabriel and tugs the trousers over his feet. "Help me pull these up for the lad, will you? We don't want him waking up bare as the day he was born."

Francis grabs the other side of the waistband and gives it a tug. "Of course, one might argue this *is* his second birth."

He pauses to look over at him before fastening Gabriel's button. "Yes. I suppose you're right."

"I know I am," Francis smiles. "Should I retrieve the other donor now, Sir?"

Rubbing his forehead, Julien walks to the head of the bed. "It's been so long since I've turned a human. I haven't the foggiest idea how much longer it will be." Using his thumb, he gently retracts Gabriel's eyelid. The once familiar brown eyes are now swirling to life with streams of red and gold. "But if his eyes are any indication, I'd say it shouldn't be much longer now."

"Very well," Francis bows. "Then I shall be right back." He steps toward the door, stopping abruptly. "Shall I let Mrs. Laurent know that young Gabriel is doing well?"

"No. In fact, let's not say anything to anyone just yet. I want to be sure the lad is awake and fed first."

"As you wish."

Julien paces back and forth beside the bed, and suddenly every hair on the back of Olivia's neck stands at attention. The pressure in the room changes, and the vampire sovereign stops as his new pleb's eyes spring open. "Gabriel?" Julien takes his hand. "Son, can you hear me?"

Gabriel's hands fly to his throat. With his mouth wide, he begins gasping as though he's desperately trying to take in oxygen that he no longer requires. Julien stands in front of him and grabs his hands. "It's okay, son."

Francis rushes through the door with a sword in hand as Gabriel jumps off the bed, sending Julien across the room. Quickly gaining his feet, Julien stands with his hands out in front of him. "Francis, drop the sword. He's fine. Gabriel, I know you're scared, and you feel like you need to breathe, but oxygen isn't a requirement for you any longer. It will just take you a few minutes to adjust."

Gabriel's eyes frantically dart to Francis, still holding the sword at his side, and for a moment, his eyes swirl from black to red. Julien glances over at his house steward. "Bloody hell. Put the sword down. He's still coming around. You're frightening him."

"He looks pissed, Sir. Not frightened."

Julien knocks the sword to the floor. "Gabriel, do you recall our conversation before you closed your eyes? About changing you?"

Gabriel's demeanour shifts. His shoulders relax as he nods. "I was dying. You asked me if I wanted you to try and change me—make me one of you." He holds his hands out in front of him, turning them over. His gaze springs to Julien, his light brown eyes swirling with occasional streams of red as he smiles. "You cured me! Does this mean I'm a vampire now?"

"Yes. Well, no. Not exactly. We must complete the change, son." Julien holds his wrist out to him. "Take only a small amount. It will seal your bloodline, and I need to ensure you don't tear the flesh. Francis has brought a donor up for you. Then we must have a quick talk before letting the family know you're okay."

Gabriel looks down at Julien's offered wrist and licks his lips. His canines lengthen, and he sinks them into Julien's flesh. "All right, son. Very good. That's enough."

Releasing Julien's arm, Gabriel wipes the back of his hand across his mouth, his red eyes locking on the female donor next to Francis. "Calm yourself," Francis warns. "Come and sit on the chair, and above all, be gentle. We must only take enough to sustain ourselves. I assure you. You will not starve."

As instructed, he sits in the chair and gently grips the back of the woman's neck when Julien halts him. "No. Until we're sure you can control yourself, you'll drink only from the wrist." He stands beside him, patiently waiting as he feeds. "Okay, son. That's enough for now." He chucks his chin toward Francis. "Could you take her back to her room and ensure she gets something to eat? I need some time with our new pleb."

Bright blue eyes with red streams dart toward him. "Pleb? What does that mean?"

Chuckling, Julien takes a seat on the edge of the bed in front of him. "It's what we call a sired vampire. You're no longer a fledgling. You've now fed from your first human. Soloman, our house steward in London, he is my primeval — my first sired." A bright smile forms on Julien's face. "And, of course, Cassian and Elias are scions." He lays his hand on his chest. "They were naturally born to a sovereign."

"Can I still have children?"

Lowering his eyes, Julien shakes his head. "No, I'm afraid not. Only original vampires and their scions can reproduce. Sired vampires do not have that ability."

"But we can create others just like you changed me."

Julien's forehead furrows as his expression hardens. "Yes and no. You have the ability to, but you must have your sovereign's approval before attempting to change a human by our laws. There are no exceptions, Gabriel. Our population must be kept in check. Our blood can be used to heal a human in small quantities, but it has also been known to be toxic to some, denying the change. Instead, their deaths are excruciatingly painful. These vampires attempting to turn humans hoping to build armies will meet their fate." Standing, Julien begins to pace in front of him. "You mustn't be careless. My blood now runs through your veins. If you step out of line, as your sovereign, I'll be forced to end the life I've given you."

Gabriel's eyes open wide, obviously realizing the weight behind Julien's words. "I understand. No turning humans."

A smile forms on Julien's lips as he pats Gabriel on the back. "Good. That's very good, son. Now, as for feeding, we have sixteen human donors who live here in the castle. You'll only feed here at the castle." Making eye contact with Gabriel, he stops pacing for a minute, the corner of his mouth tugging slightly into a crooked smile. "Our saliva offers a euphoric sensation to humans, and a few young females here crave the bite. However, if you decide to partake in the pleasure offered, you must be careful not to get carried away. You only take enough to quench your thirst. We don't drain our hosts."

"How will I know when to stop? I know you say I've taken my fill, but I still feel hungry."

"Give it a few days. This is still new."

Gabriel looks at him in disbelief. "That's all there is to this?"

Julien laughs. "It sounds easier than it is, but you are going to do just fine, my boy. Oh, I'm sure small things will come up occasionally. Just be sure to talk to me as they do. You can always ask or tell me anything." He holds his hand out with a wide smile. "Welcome to the family, son."

Gabriel grins as he takes his hand. "Thanks—" he stammers. "I'm not sure what I am supposed to call you." Twisting his lips, he squints. "Father? I've heard Francis and Soloman call you Sire."

"Let's not make a thing of it, Gabriel," he smiles. "Now, shall we go let everyone know your new status? I'm sure they're still worried sick."

Taking off toward the door, Gabriel grabs the handle ripping the doorknob off in his hand. Staring down at it, he turns back to face Julien. "I—I didn't..."

Bringing his hand to his face, Julien smoothes it over his beard in an attempt to conceal his smile. "It's fine. You'll get used to the additional strength. For now, try to think of everything you touch as a delicate young lady."

"Right," Gabriel nods, setting the doorknob on the dresser.

When they enter the parlour, Clarentina gasps, leaping to her feet with a squeal. Her arms wrap around Gabriel's neck as she plants a kiss on his cheek. "Oh, I just knew you'd be okay." Her smile softens as she moves to stand next to her husband.

Elias slaps him on the back with a huge grin. "Welcome back, brother! You have no idea how great it is to see you standing here!"

"Thanks. I feel like a new man."

Cassian sticks his hand out with a smile. "That's because you are a new kind of man." As Gabriel takes his hand, Cassian pulls him in for a hug. "Not that you weren't always part of it, but welcome to the family, brother."

CHAPTER 39 ~ YOU SHOULD BE FRIGHTENED

The warmth of their welcome seeps into Olivia's bones, causing an audible *'aww'* to leave her lips as the journal closes. Her eyes slowly open, and Patricia falls back in her chair with a huff. "Great. Now that damn demonized book is pulling on your emotions."

"Knock it off." Helen slaps her arm. "Pay her no mind, Liv. Tell us what you saw."

"Well, at first, I wasn't quite sure why it was showing me Gabriel's creation. I knew Julien sired him, but now I think I understand," she says, a smile settling on her face as she peers at Cassian. "I believe the purpose was to show me the Laurent family's love and respect for one another—for humanity. Julien wouldn't consider turning a human without welcoming them into his family as one of his own." Her smile broadens. "Gabriel truly is your brother."

Cassian smiles. "Yes. He very much is."

Clara rests her chin on her thumb, narrowing her eyes on Cassian as she runs her index finger across her pursed lips. "What happened to all the vampires he created before he gained a conscience and decided population control must be considered?" She drops her hand, turning her palm up toward her granddaughter. "Olivia never mentioned how he dealt with them."

"He rounded them up." Cassian leans back and runs his hand over his chin. "Any that were willing to accept his help, that is. He brought them back to the castle and helped them through their hunger cravings. He taught them how to respect our donors. Then when they were no longer a threat to society, he offered them housing on Laurent's Hill."

"And what of those that weren't willing?" Patricia asks.

Without hesitation, Cassian meets her stare. "He beheaded and burned them. They were his creation and his responsibility."

"They had lives and families before he thoughtlessly turned them!" Patricia blurts, slamming her hand on the table.

Olivia grabs her arm. "Aunt Trish."

"What? That's just a fact, Liv."

"Yes." Unaffected by her outrage, Cassian nods. "That's true. Once. Though, there was no possible way they could ever return to those lives. As much as he would have loved to, he couldn't undo what was already done. And since most rogues were killing humans onsight, my father did what he felt was best for the safety of humanity."

Placing her elbow on the table, Helen rests her cheek in her palm. "I would think that must have been difficult for him."

"It was. He struggled with having to end those who refused to conform. His guilt was unmistakable to all of us, even Mr. Windsor, who fought him daily about the law. He felt vampires should be free to sire and feed as they saw fit." Cassian shrugs. "Of course, he also felt that he should have been made sovereign the night they were created."

Clara sets her cup down and smiles at him. "I obviously can't say I know the three originals as you do, but the journal entries do give us some insight. With that, I think I speak for us all when I say I'm thankful Harold Windsor was not given that kind of power." She peers down at her watch and places her hands on the table, pushing herself to her feet. "I'm going to take Patricia and check in with Elizabeth at the store before Olivia summons Cassian's family. We won't be long." She scans Helen, Olivia and Cassian. "Do be sure that you look presentable by the time we get back."

Patricia releases a huff. "Why me?"

"Quite simply because I can't trust you not to try and kill Cassian." She turns toward the stairs and glances back over her shoulder. "Well, come on. Let's not doddle. We have company coming."

The words *'You Suck'* appear crossed Patricia's chest as she sticks her tongue out. "Fine. I'll see you guys soon." Scrunching her face, she raises two fingers, points to her eyes, then directs them back at Cassian as she mouths *I'm watching you.*

Cassian shakes his head. "I'm not sure what I did to get on her bad side."

"Well, that's easy. You're a vampire," Helen chuckles. "Speaking of vampires, what shall I prepare for your family's visit?" she asks. "They must have a favourite dish."

"That's tremendously kind, Helen, but that's not necessary. In fact, I'm sure Soloman will come prepared."

"Oh." She turns to face him, her hand falling to her chest as her jaw drops. "Ohhh. Gotcha," she says, slowly nodding with a wink. "Well then, how about a drink for now while we wait?"

"That would be lovely. Thank you."

Olivia throws her hands out. "Wait! I can do this." Cassian leans back, and she circles her hand. "Rubrum sangue," she says, producing a goblet of red liquid on the table in front of him.

Helen spins around, her face tight with concern. "What did you just ask for?"

Cassian stares down into the glass, his eyes swirling with red as he lifts it to his nose. Then, quickly setting it back down, his hand flies over his mouth as he squeezes his eyes shut.

"What's wrong? It's red wine. Right?"

Grabbing the crystal goblet, Helen Holds it up to her nose, then marches to the sink. "That was not wine, Olivia."

"I don't understand." She watches Helen dump the contents, then peers at Cassian. "What did I do wrong?"

"That was blood, Olivia," Cassian says, his voice low, his eyes unable to meet hers. "*Your* blood." His shoulders heave as he disappears from the table, leaving the backdoor swinging.

"I'm not sure how I could have gotten that wrong. I'm sure I've heard you say that before."

Helen shakes her head. "Close, but not quite. Where did you get those words from?"

"I'm not sure." She shrugs. "Lately, the words just pop into my mind. Isn't that how it works for you?"

"No. I'm always fully aware of what I'm asking for. What were you thinking when you conjured that drink?"

Olivia's face drops. "I was thinking of what Cassian's desired drink would be."

"Oh." Helen takes a deep breath. "Well, I believe we should keep this to ourselves." Feeling her cheeks burn, Olivia nods. "But no more offering Cash anything to drink. If Patricia were here, you could have gotten him killed."

"Right." Sighing, Olivia looks at the doorway. "I should probably apologize to Cash."

"Don't be too long. Mom and Patricia should be back anytime, and they'll be expecting you to summon his family."

"I know," she calls back, striding through the living room when an old woman's voice stops her. "Aww, what's wrong, young Livy? You look like you have the weight of the world resting on your shoulders."

She stops and stares at the picture above the mantel. "Oh, Aunt Millie, I've done something terrible."

"What on earth could you have possibly done?"

Olivia stands in front of the portrait and lowers her eyes. "I said the wrong words and served Cash my blood. Now he's upset with me."

"And did he drink it?"

"Goodness, no!"

Millie smiles. "I don't believe he's upset with you, child. I think he was tempted, and the thought of that frightened him."

"Frightened him? That's ridiculous. He drinks blood all the time. Did you forget that he's a vampire?"

Millie shakes her head. "He drinks human blood, not blood singing with magic. A little over a century ago, the vampire sovereign made it punishable by beheading to drink from a witch."

"But he drank Gran's infused wine."

"Yes, enchanted wine. Essence and blood are not the same. Essence can only be retrieved if willingly given, whereas blood can be taken. And our blood is like a power rush for vampires—highly addictive." Smiling, Millie chucks her head toward Cassian's door. "Now, go on and don't make a deal of it. That vampire is kind of growing on me."

"Wish me luck." Olivia crosses her fingers and turns toward Cassian's door. Tapping lightly, she calls out, "Cash?"

Opening the door, he immediately lowers his gaze, and they begin to speak simultaneously. "I was—"

"I just—" Pushing past him, she steps into his room. "I just wanted you to know that it wasn't intentional. I'm still new to this magic thing." She looks down at her fidgeting fingers before meeting his gaze again. "Half the time, I'm not really sure what I'm doing." His eyes finally meet hers.

"It's me that should apologize. My thoughts—" he stammers, reaching for her hand. "This was the first time I have felt your mind connect with mine. You read my thoughts. That glass was a product of my desires. I can't apologize enough, Olivia."

Heat rushes to her cheeks. She's not honestly sure how she should feel about that. Her heart begins to race, and she looks up, her eyes meeting his. "I'm not sure if I should be—" she starts, but he cuts her off.

"Scared, Olivia. It should terrify you that I long to taste your blood. That I can hear your heart racing at this very moment and smell the scent of your fear—*your* desires." He lets go of her hand and holds his door open. "Never forget that I'm a vampire, Miss Parker."

Taking a deep breath, Olivia bites her bottom lip. "Fine. I'll leave, but you better pull yourself together before your family comes." Walking toward the door, she stops and raises her finger. "Oh, and in case you missed it. I'm not afraid of you, Cassian Laurent."

"Olivia," he starts, but before he can finish, she raises her hand and walks past him. "Olivia," he says once again as she steps into the hallway.

She stops, closes her eyes, and takes a breath. "Push or pull, Cash. Which will it be?" Releasing her breath, she spins to face him, flicks her hand to the side, and slams the door in his face.

She can hear a chuckle from over the mantle, but she's too upset to stop. Instead, she gathers Mr. Green from the sofa and continues toward the stairs. Still grumbling as she reaches the top of the steps, she hears a deep voice from the opposite end of the hall.

"Easy with your words now, young lady. What is it that has your britches in such a knot?"

Setting Mr. Green on his feet, she turns toward the plaster bust. "I'm sorry, uncle Chester. I didn't mean to disturb you."

"I'm not disturbed, but *you* seem to be. Why don't you tell me about it?"

Leaning over the bannister, Olivia releases a huff. "It's nothing, really. Vampires, I guess." Peering up, she feigns a smile.

The plaster bust lets out a hearty laugh. "Ah, yes. I never thought I would see the day one would be staying within these walls."

She twists her lips. "Yeah, well, I think he blames *me* for having to be here."

"Nonsense. Don't forget he chose to come back, and I wouldn't let that whole blood incident bother me too much, either. It's not you that he's upset with. He's mad at himself."

Straightening, Olivia stares at the bust. "How do you know about that? There's no way you could have seen that from up here."

"See it? Heck no. Regrettably, I wasn't that fortunate. But these walls have ears, my dear."

Olivia rolls her eyes. "Right. Well, I hope you all enjoyed the show." Turning, she stomps off to her room and slams the door.

CHAPTER 40 ~ ACCIDENTAL SUMMONING

She's about to bury her face among the pillows when Olivia spots it. There in the middle of her bed, sits the old leather tome. She places her hand on her hip, scolding the book as if it were a disobedient child. "What are you doing up here? I left you in the kitchen!"

Mr. Green hops onto the bed and flops down next to the journal. His jaw separates with his enormous yawn as he stretches his paw across the cover and peers up at her with a squeaky *'meow.'*

She shakes her head. "No. I promised Gran I wouldn't read it alone anymore, and you know *you* don't count as a worthy companion in this case," she says, shoving him aside. But as she reaches to retrieve the book, it opens to the list of names. A golden glow illuminates Clarentina's as if she had already laid her finger on it.

"That's odd." Sitting on her bed, she pulls the journal onto her lap and stares at the page. "Why only Clarentina Laurent?"

Mr. Green hisses, and Olivia drops the journal, jumping to her feet as a gray cloud forms in the corner of her room. "Damnit! I didn't mean to—"

"To summon me?" Clarentina steps forward, running her hands over the length of her black velvet gown. She straightens her shoulders, giving them a roll, and as her sight finally lands on Olivia, she extends her hand. "Well then, you must be the little sorceress my son is smitten with. Olivia, is it?"

Olivia stands staring at her, unsure what to say when Clarentina takes her hand. "Oh, come now. You're the one that summoned me here." Her deep red lips pull into a smile, showing just the tip of a fang. "Relax, darling. I'm not going to bite. Any friend of my son is a friend of mine." She strolls around the room, taking in her surroundings before turning back with a questioning gaze. "Where is my son anyway? I don't feel his presence in the house."

"I'm not sure. If he's not in his room, he may be down by the creek."

"Well, I'm sure he'll sense my presence and turn up soon enough. Besides, this gives us some time to get acquainted." Clarentina gestures to the bed. "Mind if I sit?"

Olivia shakes her head, bending to pick up the journal when long thin fingers grasp the corner. The smell of charred skin fills the room as Clarentina jolts back with a squeal. She holds her hand out, examining each blackened digit as they slowly rejuvenate. "What is this voodoo spell you've placed on my husband's book?"

"None!" Olivia exclaims, slowly stepping back. "Timekeeper journals are created with a magic of their own."

"Hm." Clarrentina's eyes narrow as she sits on the bed and crosses her legs. "I have heard that you don't just read the journal. Instead, you view the scene from within." Olivia confirms with a nod. "That sounds impressive. I've never heard of any such magic before." Her cornflower eyes search Olivia's face. "Could you read some for me?"

"I'm not supposed to read it alone. Cassian usually watches over me while I'm in the journal."

Smiling, Clarentina throws her arms out. "But, you're not alone, darling. I'm here."

Mr. Green nudges Olivia's arm with a meow. "It's okay, buddy," she says, running her hand down his back. "This is Cassian's mom, Mrs. Laurent." But his persistent meow only gets louder as he hops off the bed and struts for the door.

"He probably senses my dislike for cats," Clarentina offers, getting comfortable as she watches him scratch the door. "So tell me, darling. What was the last thing you saw? Are you nearly finished? With the journal, that is."

Letting Mr. Green out, Olivia sits back down on the bed. "Um." Tensing her shoulders, she bites her lip and takes a deep breath. "Julien had just turned Gabriel."

Clarentina smiles. "That's probably one of my fondest memories. Gabriel was always meant to be one of ours." She points to the journal. "Can you show me where you left off?"

Olivia glances at her door, then back to the journal. *There shouldn't be any harm in just showing her where I left off. Right?*

She grabs the old leather-bound tome. The all too familiar tingle travels up her arm, now an almost welcoming feeling as she opens the cover. The pages begin to flip, turning to the last page she had read. She hears a gasp as the script begins to glow, and her eyes dart to Clarentina. "You can see this?"

Moving closer, Clarentina peers down at the page. "I could have sworn I saw flaming words burn into the page, but no. I don't see anything." She sits back down, staring at Olivia. "Are you telling me that you can see writing there?"

"Yes. It's beautiful script. I wish others could see it."

Clarentina leans forward with wide eyes as she stares down at the page. "What does it say?"

Olivia turns her attention back to the book, and before she realizes she has begun to read, she finds herself standing in the grand entrance of Julien's castle in France.

"I so wish I could come with you, darling," Clarentina says, adjusting the lapel on Julien's jacket before leaning in to kiss his cheek. "Do be sure to give the boys a kiss for me and tell them I love them."

"You know I will, my love. Once the boys and I have cleared up the mess of unruly plebs young Windsor has created, you'll be able to visit London freely. Until then, I think it's best you stay here where I know you're safe."

Sighing, Clarentina nods. "I know." She Pats his chest. "Do you have everything, darling?"

"Everything I need is either here or at the castle in London." Julien smiles. "You made sure to send the telegram to the boys, letting them know I would be arriving late this evening, didn't you?"

"Yes. I asked them to meet you at Blackfriars pub. Just as you requested."

"Excellent. Then I suppose I shouldn't keep Granger waiting. I sent him to get the boat ready." He leans in, kissing her cheek, then disappears out the front door.

Olivia will never get used to how quickly vampires travel by foot. Her head spins as colours flick by her too quickly to determine what they're actually passing. She closes her eyes, and before she knows it, they've already reached the dock. A short, stocky man in a long black coat extends his hand to Julien. "Sire. It's so great to see you."

Shaking his hand, Julien pats him on the back. "You're looking well, Granger. How's the wife?"

"Stunning as the day I met her, Sir," Granger grins, leading him onto the boat.

"Ah, that's what I like to hear, my boy. That's what I like to hear."

Though Olivia is certain the trip across the English Channel takes longer than it does to blink, she opens her eyes to the port of Dover. Julien exits the boat with a wave and darts across the fields, only slowing when he crests the edge of London. Once his pace slows, he strolls casually through town, tipping his hat to the odd patron as he makes his way to the Blackfriars pub.

He opens the door to the pub and scans the room. With no signs of his sons, he heads for a table near the back. Taking no more than a few steps, he hears a grating voice, "Well, look who we have here, boys. It's the almighty murdering sovereign."

Julien spins towards the annoying tone, coming face to face with none other than Roger Windsor. "I see the apple hasn't fallen far from the tree." Only recognizing two from his last trip to London, Leonard and Holden, he fans his hand out, pointing toward the plebs standing on either side of the young halfbreed. "We have laws against pleb creation for a reason, young Windsor."

"You say that like I should care, old man."

"It seems you may have forgotten who I am. It might do you well to watch your tone with me."

Roger's jaw tenses as he steps closer, his words leaving his pressed lips in a growl. "You killed my father and left my mother a mess. So as I see it, it's *you that* should watch *your* tone when speaking to me." His plebs hiss, and he puts his arms out to hold them back. "Now, hand over the key. Its power is not lost on me, old man, nor is the fact that it rightfully belonged to my father."

Julien looks back to the pub's main entrance, noticing two of Roger's plebs have moved to stand guard by the door. "Oh, you are a treat, young Windsor. Like your father, you're falsely granting yourself undeserved entitlements."

Roger smirks, his eyes landing on the key as it swishes around his rival's neck. He steps forward, pausing as the door to the pub swings open.

"Windsor plebs to your sides!" Julien yells to his sons as he darts for the stairs.

Swinging his attention to the door, Roger flings his arm toward the stairwell. "Well, what are you waiting for, Leonard?! Go after him!"

Men seem to come from all directions, and the three brothers are left to fight their way through the pub as Leonard follows Julien upstairs. When Olivia's invisible tether tugs, she finds herself standing on the second floor's landing. She follows the voices to a door halfway down the hall on the right and finds the standoff. Julien is standing mere feet from Leonard when he reminds him, "Easy, young pleb. Let's not forget who I am."

"I care none for your sovereign title, ancient one," Leonard spits. "My loyalty stands solely with my sire." Reaching over his shoulder, he draws his sword and gives it a swift swing, the tip barely missing Julien's midsection as he bends around it.

Just then, Roger's shadow darkens the doorway, with Holden quick at his heels. Julien straightens, his fang digging into the corner of his bottom lip as he growls, "Then it seems you just sealed your fate, young pleb." He extends his claw and swipes in a motion so quick that his rival is left frozen. Nearly slicing clear through Leonard's neck, he yells over his shoulder as he disappears, "Be sure you clean up your trash, Windsor!"

Blood splatters from the gaping wound as his head drops to the side. He teeters toward his sire, and Roger grabs his dangling head. "You useless Sac!" he screeches, ripping it from his shoulders. Tossing it to the floor, he gestures to the steps. "Bring him to me!" he commands.

Holden darts upstairs, stopping on the fourth floor when a door swings shut at the end of the hall. With a sly grin, he slowly makes his way down the corridor. "Come out, Laurent. If you turn over the key, my sire may just let you live." He spins to footsteps running up the stairs behind him but quickly focuses back on the room.

Olivia stands on the fourth-floor landing as Julien sprints past her toward the roof. *'Hurry, Julien! Go!'* He stops for a brief moment and peers back over his shoulder, causing Olivia's heart to race. Her brows pull together as she squints through the darkness. *'You can hear me?'* But his pause is too brief for a response, and when a woosh of cool air blasts past her, she understands why. *'Holden,'* she mutters as their tether yanks her forward.

When she reaches the roof, Julien kicks the sword from Holden's hand and grabs him by the throat, lifting him into the air. "Your sire has this all wrong, little pleb," he starts when the heavy metal door flies past them, and Roger steps out.

CHAPTER 41 ~ THEY HEARD ME!

"O—liv—ia!" Clara calls out as she walks through the living room. Her sight sets on Helen as she enters the kitchen. "Where's Olivia?"

"I'm not sure," Helen shrugs. "I think she might have gone to lie down."

"Well, that's just great! You were supposed to keep your eye on her," Patricia huffs.

"Oh, settle down," Clara says, heading for the stairs. "I'm sure she hasn't gone anywhere."

The corner of Patricia's mouth tightens as she glances over her shoulder toward the end of the hall. "Fine! I'll go check with the bloodsucker."

"Why? What's going on?" Helen asks, scurrying along behind her mother.

"We had a vampire show up at the store."

"What?!"

"We're fine, but your sister recognized him as the vampire that was here with Holden the night she was attacked. They tend to only pop out when Olivia's reading." Clara knocks on the bedroom door. "Olivia?" Not waiting for a response, she reaches for the handle as Cassian appears at her side and pushes his way past.

He pauses, his eyes narrowing on the woman at the foot of the bed. "Mother," he growls.

"Watch out, Julien! He's coming!" Olivia yells as Cassian rushes to her side. He reaches for the book.

"Wait!" Clara puts her arms out, her attention shifting to Clarentina. "How long has she been in there?"

She shakes her head with a shrug. "I'm not sure. An hour. Maybe."

"How did you get in here," Cassian demands, the muscles in his face stiff with anger

"I was summoned here."

"Mother, don't lie! You've been dying to get Olivia on her own!"

"True, but the fact remains that she summoned me. How else could I be standing in her room?"

"Cash." Clara reaches out and touches his hand. "I believe her. These journals can be quite persistent. We've all witnessed that. My guess is that she must be nearing the end." She points to the open book in her granddaughter's lap. "There doesn't look to be much left. Why don't you try to connect with her? See where she is."

Nodding, Cassian closes his eyes and reaches out to Olivia's mind. Within moments he joins her on the roof of the Blackfriars Pub.

Roger steps toward them. "Let Holden go, Laurent. He's merely a grunt."

"You mean your primeval," Julien spits back, tightening his grip on Holden's throat as his eyes stream with red. "The stench of halfbreed rests thick in his blood." His nails dig into the side of Holden's neck as he heaves him at Roger. "Just take your misfits and get out of London!" he roars.

Shoving his primeval aside, Roger springs to his feet. "I'm afraid I can't do that." His eyes drop to the sword in front of Julien's boots as he takes a step forward. "Not until I have avenged my father's death."

Before Olivia sees him move, Julien snatches up the sword and charges toward his young rival, but Roger is just as quick. He grabs the heavy door and holds it in front of him, but the force behind Julien's strike cannot be stopped. The blade sears through the metal with a high-pitched squeal, piercing the young halfbreed's abdomen and pinning him to the wall.

Confident he has secured Roger long enough to tend to the commotion below, Julien walks to the edge of the triangular-shaped roof and peers down. The crowd of plebs has moved from the pub to the street with his sons in the center. He stands tall, holding the key from his chest as he addresses the group in a commanding growl. "Windsor clan, heed your sovereign!"

Behind him, Roger stirs, and Olivia yells, *'Julien! He's moving!'*

'I wish he could hear you, Olivia,' Cassian mutters as he stands next to her, looking on helplessly.

'Julien! Behind you!' she cries out, but it's too late. Roger has already shoved the door off and rid the blade from his body. He grabs the hilt of the sword, looks up at Julien as he continues to address the crowd below, and storms toward him.

"Your sire has agreed to conform to my laws, and so shall—" His final words lost as his hand drops to the blood-drenched steel protruding from his chest.

"**Windsor**!" Olivia hears Cassian roar from below as a hush falls over the crowd. She looks over the edge as he turns to his brothers and points to the pub. "Take care of these plebs. I'm going after Roger!" he shouts. Leaving Gabriel and Elias to fight the plebs in the street, he pushes his way back into the pub.

There's a burst of sinister laughter behind her, and Olivia turns to see Roger land a kick to the back of Julien's calf that drops him to his knees. Her hand flies to her mouth as he grabs the hilt of the sword, then places his foot against his back and yanks the steel free. "Any last words, Laurent?" he asks, drawing the sword over his shoulder.

"Only in your mind will you ever be king, young Windsor," Julien wearily replies as he struggles to rejuvenate.

"I'll be happy with that as long as you're not!" With that, Roger swings his sword, beheading the sovereign.

'No!' Olivia's scream is so loud it shatters her bedroom window in present day.

"For the love of the Goddess! Pull her out!" Patricia wails, moving for the journal. But before she can reach it, Clara grabs her hand.

"No. I'm afraid this is not an entry we can pull her from." Her expression is sullen as she shakes her head. "Just look at how difficult this is for him." She points to the tears trickling down Cassian's face. "This is not a memory he wanted to relive. The only reason I can see him remaining in there is for Olivia's sake. This must be the piece to this puzzle we've been waiting for."

Confused, Clarentina looks at the women. "Why would he remain for Olivia's sake?"

"You mean, why is Olivia in that cursed book for **your** sake?" Patricia turns, throwing a brilliant blue fireball at Clarentina as she jumps out of the way. "Because she's trying to fix *your* eternity, you selfish antique."

"All right!" Clara shouts. "That's enough."

Back on top of the Blackfriar's pub, Cassian leaps through the doorway to the roof. Olivia runs toward him, but he lunges straight through her. "Windsor!" His scream booms through the air as he jumps across the rooftops after Roger and his primeval, but it's of no use. They're already long gone, disappearing into the night with Julien's head and the key.

Cassian returns, slumping next to Julien's body. His fingers curl around the material of his shirt, fisting it in his hands as he pulls him closer. Olivia wishes she could console him, but it's not possible. Not in this world. All she can do is watch as tears spill from his deep red eyes as he lifts his head, releasing a horrendous wail. "You're dead, Windsor!"

Elias storms out onto the roof, digging his hands through his hair. "How the hell could you have let this happen, Cash?! Where the hell is Roger?"

"They took off, and what do you mean me?! Where were you, Elias?"

"Gabe and I were fighting off his clan of plebs! Just like you asked us to.

"The plebs were a distraction so Roger and his primeval could get to father!"

"Everyone either ran," Gabriel puffs as he emerges through the doorway, "or has taken a knee—" his words slowly trailing off as Cassian lifts their father's body over his shoulder.

Elias turns, scanning the rooftop. "Where the hell is his head?"

"I don't know! Pick one, Elias!" Cassian bites, continuing toward the door. "Windsor or one of his goddamned heathens took it!"

"Cash, wait." Gabe grabs his arm. "Where are you taking him? You can't bring a headless corpse to Clarentina.

"Well, we sure the hell aren't going to leave him here!"

Pressing his fingertips to his temple, Elias stares at the body. "Mom will never forgive us, Cash." He drops his hands, meeting his brother's glowering stare. "We need to track down Windsor and get that key back.

"And what?! Do you know how to use it? 'Cause I sure the hell don't, and we have no witch on standby."

Elias scrubs his hand over his face. "No, I don't know how it works, but I do know we can't use it if it's not in our possession. That means that halfbreed needs to be found."

"Great! And what do you suggest we do with father's body in the meantime? Leave it here to rot?"

"Of course not!" Elias runs his hand through his hair. "Okay, look. Why don't I run the body up to Ben Nevis Mountain while you and Gabe search for Windsor? There's a snow cave there that will keep it from decomposing until we locate the halfbreed and the key. Hopefully, by then, we can figure out how it works and bring father back before mother is any the wiser."

Running his hand over his mouth, Gabriel lowers his eyes. "I hate myself for saying this, Cash, but I have to agree with Elias. I'm not ready to break mother's heart. I'd rather her think he simply extended his stay. At least until we can find Windsor and the key."

Cassian sets Julien's body down and shakes his head. "Ben Nevis is in Scottland. Even at top speed, it's at least 2 hours away. There's no way you'll get there unseen."

"The most anyone will see is a blur as I pass. I'm quicker than you. Three hours tops to get there, stash the body and get back. I should be here before sun up."

"This is our father you're talking about *stashing*," Cassian barks. "How can you be so callous?"

Elias points to Julien's body. "That is not our father. That is nothing more than a headless corpse. Now, stop wasting time and hand it over so I can leave. You and Gabe need to go look for Windsor."

Gabriel steps between the two brothers breaking Cassian's glare. "Honestly, Cash. I think Elias is right. This is our best chance to preserve Julien while we locate the key."

Cassian drops his head. "Go. Take him and hurry back. Gabe and I will search the city."

'Cash, I'm so sorry you had to see—' Olivia starts, but before she can finish, his image begins to fade and streams of light flash around her. Her stomach churns as she's tugged in all directions. When she finally steadies, she's standing in front of Julien's castle in France, watching a blood-soaked Roger slam his fist against the massive wooden door. "Mrs. Laurent! I have a message from Julien."

Olivia throws her hand over her mouth as the door swings open, and Roger raises Julien's head, holding it out to Clarentina. Her pale complexion turns gray as she lets out a bloodcurdling scream. Shaking her head in disbelief, she steps back, burying her face into Soloman's chest. "The sovereign sends his love, Mrs. Laurent."

Tossing Julien's head through the doorway, Roger tips his nonexistent hat. "Do tell your sons I'll be seeing them."

Clara points at Cassian's tense jaw and clenched fists. "Helen, I'd back away from him if I were you. I'm not picking up an amiable vibe at this moment, and we certainly can't fault him if he lashes out while in this trance."

Patricia bounds to her feet. "That's it! I've had just about enough entertaining magical diaries and vampires!" she huffs, pointing to Clara. "Let it be known that if he attempts to lash out, I will torch the toothy bastard right where he sits!"

Clarentina springs to her feet, standing face to face with Patricia. "You will not touch one hair on my son!"

Clara shoves her way between them. "Knock it off! The pair of you will sit down!" She motions to Olivia as her hand stills on the page. "I believe she's done.

Cassian slowly opens his eyes as the journal closes and reaches for Olivia's hand. "Never apologize to me for what I have to see while you're in there. It's me that is sorry. You shouldn't have to witness these events," he whispers, pulling her against his chest.

She leans back, blinking him into focus. "Could you hear me in there?" He nods. "I'm almost certain Julien heard me too, but he thought I was Ancina."

"Ancina?!" Clarentina huffs, moving to stand in front of them.

"Yes." Olivia stands, peering at the anxious faces. "When I told him to run, he looked straight at me and called me Ancina."

"How can that be?" Helen asks

"Yeah." Patricia glares at her mother. "How come all of a sudden she can communicate with the bloodsucker and his father while she's in there? I thought you said they were on different planes."

Clara runs her fingertips over her pursed lips, shaking her head. "I'm not exactly sure. The only answer I have is that Olivia's powers are getting stronger. I never thought it was possible, but somehow, it seems she may be able to manipulate the planes, partially crossing them while in the entries."

"I tried to reach out to her—lay my hand on her shoulder, but I still couldn't make a physical connection," Cassian says.

"How about you, Olivia? Were you able to touch anything?" Clara asks.

"No. Well, now that I think about it, I don't believe I tried."

Patricia jams her hands on her hips. "Is this finally over now? Do you know where to find the key so these bloodsuckers can leave us alone?"

"Patricia!" Helen scolds.

Olivia shakes her head. "No. All I know is that Roger has the key, but I still have no idea where he is." She raises her hand, pointing at Clarentina. "But Cassian's mom hid the scroll, and Cash and his brothers know where his body is. So—" She looks around the room, her eyes finally landing on her grandmother. "I assume we should be able to get the key if I were to summon Roger here. Right?"

Clara chucks her chin at the journal. "Something tells me that was not the last entry."

"Well, it's not as if any of us are in any shape for a fight right now," Helen says, gesturing toward the door. "Let's talk about this during dinner."

"That sounds good to me. Reparatione fenestra," Clara says, waving her hand toward the shattered window.

As the shards of glass magically return to an unmarred window pane, Clarentina stands staring in awe. Squeezing her eyes shut, she points to the window and looks at her son. "Okay. That truly is amazing."

"Yes," he smiles, escorting her from Olivia's room. "They are all incredibly gifted."

Clara gestures to the old book at the foot of Olivia's bed. "Don't forget the journal. You'll need it to call on the rest of Cassian's family."

CHAPTER 42 ~ LAURENT FAMILY DINNER

Olivia pats the cover of the journal as everyone takes their seats around the kitchen table. "Who am I summoning exactly?"

Clarentina wrings her hands together, her smile lighting up the room. "Oh, imagine having the whole clan here at once!"

"Whoa!" Patricia raises her hands. "Hold it, fangy barbie!" she scowls. "No one said anything about having your entire clan here!"

"Patricia!" Helen shoots her a nasty look. "Forgive my sister. We're having her tested for Tourette syndrome."

"Tourettes, huh? Well then, that opens a big old door of indiscretions I won't need to apologize for this evening," Patricia says, forcing a grin.

"You will mind yourself," Clara commands as she folds her arms and sinks into her chair. "Forgive my daughters. We don't often have an opportunity to entertain guests." Her gaze flits to Olivia. "Just the immediate members we had discussed with Cash earlier, dear."

Nodding, Olivia opens the cover of the journal to the list of names and drops her finger on their first guest. "Elias Laurent." All eyes focus on the grey mist in the corner of the kitchen. As it slowly dissipates, Elias steps forward with a smile.

Cassian quickly stands with his hand out. "Good evening, brother."

Shaking Cassian's hand, Elias walks over and stands next to their mother, offering Clara a slight bow. "Ms. Redfearn. It's great to see you again. Thank you for the invite."

"Welcome, Elias." Clara turns her attention back to Olivia. "I think we're ready for the next one."

Olivia places her hand on the next name. "Gabriel Laurent."

A handsome young man with dark curly hair steps out of the mist, and just like Julien's other two sons, Gabriel's complexion is flawless. He throws his arms around Cassian, slapping him on the back. "Great to see you, Cash." He turns to face those around the table, and as his sight sets on Olivia, he bows. "It's such an honour to finally make your acquaintance, Miss Parker."

Heat rises to Olivia's cheeks. "Thank you, Gabriel. I'm pleased to finally meet you too."

Patricia clears her throat, and Olivia places her finger on the last guest to be called. "Soloman Laurent."

Soloman steps forward, his arms filled with unlabeled wine bottles. He bows slightly toward the room. "Thank you for having me, Madame." As the brothers relieve him of his stash, he runs his hands down his chest, then over the length of each arm. "I must say, that certainly is a different way to travel, now isn't it?"

Laughter seeps through the room, and Helen pats the chair next to her. "Come sit, Soloman. Being summoned can be a bit disruptive to your system if you're not used to it," she says with one of the sweetest smiles Olivia has ever seen her wear.

"Careful not to mix those bottles," Soloman says, raising his finger toward Elias. He turns back to Helen. "My apologies, Miss Helen, but that's private stock, if you know what I mean. We wouldn't want that getting confused for actual wine."

"Oh. Right, of course not," she chuckles. "Why don't you put them on the ledge by the bay window then?"

Patricia gags into her hand. "So gross!"

Clara shoots her a look. "Why don't we all sit?" She fans her hands out, gesturing to the chairs around the table. "Helen has prepared some dinner for us all to enjoy."

"Not to seem ungrateful, Ms. Redfearn—" Clarentina starts when Clara interjects.

"Just Clara is fine." She looks around the table with a smile. "I'd like to think we may be somewhat friends."

"Speak for yourself," Patricia huffs.

Paying her no mind, Clarentina returns Clara's smile. "Very well. Clara. I'm sure you must know that we work with a very select menu."

Helen stands and twirls her hands above the table. "Laminam de basashi, laminam de carpaccio et laminam ossenworst," she grins as three large plates of raw horsemeat, raw beef and ground spiced meat (raw, of course) appear in front of their guests. "Cash might have mentioned your preferences."

"So very thoughtful, Miss Redfearn." Soloman sits next to her eyeing the plates. "It all looks divine."

Her smile broadens. "Thank you. I do hope you all enjoy. Now for something I'm a little more familiar with." Leaning back, she mumbles, "coquam bubulae, potatoes et asparagus." Then with a snap of her fingers, four plates of roast beef, potatoes and asparagus appear." She slaps her hands together. "Well, let's dig in!"

Gabriel leans in towards his brother. "Is it like this every night?"

"I don't often eat with them, but yes," he nods. "I've watched Helen conjure up a gourmet meal with only a few words quite a few times."

Clarentina rolls a piece of basashi and takes a bite. "This is quite delicious, Helen. I'd say we'd have you up to the castle one evening for dinner, but I'm afraid you'd still be serving dinner there."

As everyone is finishing their meal, Elias turns toward Olivia and asks, "So do you care to share what you've read in the journal thus far?" Cassian nudges his elbow. "I just mean have you been able to locate Roger or the key yet?"

Olivia swallows a mouthful of food and takes a sip of her wine. "No," she says, shaking her head. "At least not in the present day. Though I tend to believe I might be able to call him out."

"Call him out?" Clarentina asks.

Gabriel wipes his mouth with his napkin and peers over at her. "You mean just like you summoned us here tonight?"

"Exactly."

Clara clasps her hands together, interlacing her fingers and stares at Olivia. "We've already discussed this. You must complete all entries in that journal."

"But Gran—" Olivia begins to protest when an old woman's voice cuts her off.

"Nah-uh, Livy," Aunt Millie chimes in. "Listen to your grandmother. She's right. To not complete the journal could cause undesirable results for both families."

Heads flip around, searching for the voice when Cassian points to the portrait sitting among the jars of spices. "That's Olivia's Aunt Millie speaking. In the photograph."

"What?!" Clarentina walks over to the image for a better look when Aunt Millie purses her lips and tips her head to scan the length of the tall, beautiful vampire.

"My, Olivia wasn't kidding. You really do resemble a china doll."

Olivia's cheeks redden as she lifts her hands. "I meant that as a compliment!" she declares.

"Oh, I'm not offended, dear. In fact, I'm flattered," Clarentina says, never taking her eyes off Aunt Millie's image. She reaches out, then quickly yanks her hand back when Millie squeals.

"No touching!"

Clasping her hands together in front of her chest, Clarentina stares at the portrait. "My apologies. I've never seen a talking image before."

"Well, it's best you get used to it. I'm not the only one around here. I'm just the only one with a tendency to put her two cents in when I feel it's necessary," Millie says, her lips settling back into her posed smile. Her response causes Olivia to giggle while Cassian lowers his head to hide his smirk.

"I'm sure she meant no harm, Aunt Millie. If you can't mind your tongue when speaking to our guests, I'll be forced to put you in the wardrobe for the evening," Clara scolds the woman in the portrait as she escorts Clarentina back to her chair. "You'll find our home is quite eccentric. It's been in our family for centuries—built by our ancestors entirely out of spells." She holds her arms out as she takes her seat, looking around the room. "These walls see and hear everything. Literally. At times you'll even hear them mumbling as they pass the information along to each other."

Clarentina remains facing forward as her eyes scope the room. "Intriguing." Her focus finally shifts to Olivia. "And yet, somehow, among all this, you were able to ignore who you are. I find that absolutely fascinating."

"Fangtastic! Cause our main goal these days is to entertain bloodsuckers," Patricia scowls. "Though I suppose tit for tat, I found it quite amusing that an original such as yourself would try to starve herself to death."

Clara slaps her hand off the table, shooting her a dirty look. "Patricia!"

Grinning, she shrugs. "Whoops. It must be that damn Tourette's kicking in again. Hopefully, it doesn't trigger random fireballs. I'd hate for one to hit our guests."

A shiver runs up Olivia's spine as that all too familiar feeling travels along her arms. Her attention is immediately drawn to the counter where Mr. Green lies next to the journal. She stands, and silence falls over the room as she stretches out her arms. "Thigibh thugam," she says, slowly curling her fingers until the journal hovers in front of her.

Elias leans over, nudging Cassian with his shoulder. "I see she has overcome her fear."

"Mostly," he whispers back.

Closing his eyes, Soloman gently sways his head, a slight smile playing on his lips. "I haven't heard magic sing like that since the night that journal was created."

Patricia scrunches her face. "Really, Liv? You're going to read that dang thing right now?"

"Yeah. I mean, this might sound odd, but it feels right. As if we were all meant to be here." She looks around the table for further objections. "As long as Cash doesn't mind joining me." Her eyes land on Cassian. "It's up to you. I know your family is here."

His gaze travels to Clara before nodding. "Of course."

Smiling, she takes her seat. "All right then." She sets the journal down in front of her, and the pages automatically begin flipping to the last entry she has read. Though for some reason, the script isn't glowing like it usually does, so she places her finger on the first word but still nothing. "Odd," she mumbles.

"What's odd?" Clara asks.

"The text usually glows once I touch it." Shaking it off, she places her finger back down on the script. "I'm sure it'll change once I start to read." With her finger on the page, she peeks up at the eager eyes waiting for her to start, a shadow of uncertainty rattling her nerves. Still, she clears her throat and begins to read.

"After twenty-four hours of turning London's underground upside down, Cassian and Gabriel still haven't been able to locate Roger or the key. In fact, they haven't seen a single member of the Windsor clan, and knowing Julien was only supposed to be in town for two days means Clarentina will soon be expecting him back in France. When he doesn't return, the boys know she will likely make her way to London to be with him."

Olivia looks up, uncertainty shadowing her features. "I have never read this much before without being immersed in the events."

Clara lifts her hand. "Just keep going. You've also never had such a big audience before."

Nodding, Olivia continues. "Cassian slips into the tailors on Queen Victoria Street and purchases two dinner jackets along with a 7-inch top hat. Dark will soon fall again, and he and Gabriel need the proper attire if they're going to attend the Gentlemen's Club tonight. Rumour has it that Roger Windsor and his clan like to frequent the place."

Olivia shakes her head, blinking as the script begins to glisten. She slides her finger forward, welcoming the tiny waves of energy that travel up her arm. "As he leaves the tailors and strolls toward the club, Gabriel catches up to him, matching his stride—"

Her mouth stops accompanying her finger as it continues across the page, and Clara nods toward Cassian. "I believe she's finally made her way inside. Can you check on her, please?"

"Of course." He closes his eyes and reaches out to Olivia's mind.

She's standing in the middle of the street, taking in her surroundings, when Gabriel approaches. "Hey, Cash. Where you headed?"

Never losing his stride, Cassian slowly glances to his side. "*We* are headed to the Gentlemen's Club," he says, handing him the other dinner jacket. "I'm assuming you had no luck finding the sewer dwellers?"

Gabriel's voice lowers as he slips on the new coat. "No. I even searched the darkest corners of Regent Circus, took a tour through the depths of the market, then backtracked under Regent Street toward the bridge, but nothing." He knocks him with his elbow. "Anyway, I thought you hated the Gentlemen's Club. Did you run into a tart that works there or something?"

Shaking his head, the corner of Cassian's mouth tugs into a smirk. "I am not you, little brother. However, I did run into Dr. Neilson, who mentioned he had seen Windsor there several times this past week." Shrugging, he glances at Gabriel. "I figure it's worth checking."

Olivia purses her lips. *"I bet you do, Cassian Laurent,"* she huffs.

"I have only been as far as the foyer myself," Gabriel says when Cassian stops walking and looks from side to side.

"Did you hear that?"

"Hear what?" He looks around as Cassian seems to be listening for something before shaking his head and continuing. "Anyway, as I was saying, I was waiting for Julien. He promised he would bring me next time he was in town." Pausing for a moment, he lowers his head. "Hey, Cash? How are we ever going to manage without him?"

Stopping in front of the Carlton Club, Cassian opens the door and offers him a slight smile. "He swore that key worked. So all we have to do is find Roger. We both know he has it, then we'll bring him back, little brother."

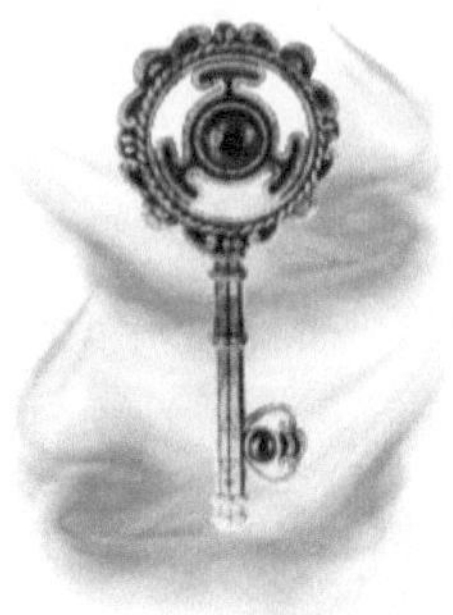

CHAPTER 43 ~ THE BEAST'S TRUE NATURE

As the brothers enter the small foyer of the Gentlemen's Club, a man standing with his white-gloved hands folded in front of him nods toward Cassian, then tips his top hat. "Mr. Laurent. Splendid to see you, Sir. It's been some time since we've last had the pleasure of your company. If there's anything we can get you, please, just ask."

Folding her arms, Olivia purses her lips. *"For a place you don't enjoy, they seem to know you quite well, Mr. Laurent."*

"Thank you, Henry," Cassian nods as Gabriel raises his brow at their friendly exchange and silently watches as he scans the crowd before entering the main room.

"Oh, I'm with you, Gabe," Olivia huffs. *"It is indeed a strange greeting for a man who doesn't come here."*

As they near the middle of the club, he glances over his shoulder at his wide-eyed little brother. "I don't sense any other vampires in the club. At least not yet. Honestly, if I were alone, I'd leave. But since father promised you an evening here, why don't we grab a seat near the window? We can have a drink or two while we watch people pass. If he doesn't come in, one of them may at least walk by. Besides," he pulls out his pocket watch and checks the time. "It's still relatively early. I wouldn't expect to see Roger and his clan out and about for at least another hour."

As they take their seats, a beautiful young brunette saunters up next to Cassian. Olivia folds her arms, eyeing her suspiciously. The square neckline of her bodice is low-cut and squishes her breasts so tightly that a nipple could appear at any moment. Gabriel's sight locks on the young woman's bosom, and Cassian kicks him under the table as he graces her with a smile. It's a proud moment for Olivia. That is until she notices Cassian focusing on her deep-red lips as she speaks. She twists a tendril of her hair and shifts her weight to one leg, returning his smile. "Good evening, gentlemen. My name is Beatrice. I'll be your server tonight. What can I get for you two?"

Gabriel gulps, and Cassian quickly responds before his anxious little brother can make a spectacle of himself. "Good evening, Beatrice. I'm Cassian Laurent, and this is my younger brother Gabriel. Two shots of your finest bourbon, please."

Beatrice rests her hands on the table, squeezing her breasts together with her arms. "It sure is a pleasure to finally meet you, Mr. Laurent," she says in a low sultry voice. "Are you sure there isn't anything else I can get for you tonight?"

Olivia huffs as his eyes drop to her cleavage, but he merely graces her with a tight smile and shakes his head. "Just the bourbon, please, Beatrice."

Pursing her lips, she straightens. "Of course. Mary, your cigar girl, will be by in just a minute." She wipes her hands down the front of her dress and adjusts her breasts. "If you think of anything else while I'm gone, don't hesitate to ask." Turning toward the bar, she glances over her shoulder, licking her top lip with a wink. "I'll be right back with your drinks, gentlemen."

Gabriel flops back, throwing his hands in the air. "What the hell, Cash? That girl may as well have asked you to take her to bed." He shakes his head, his eyes wide as he leans over the table and lowers his voice. "Surely, there's no harm in taking her for a spin while we're here."

"That's not why we're here, little brother." Cassian leans back in his seat and opens the button on his dinner jacket. "Try to stay focused. These ladies are a distraction we don't need. We're looking for Windsor and his men. Remember?"

"Sorry, Cash. You're right." He inhales back into his seat. "These ladies certainly are a distraction."

Just then, the sweet slithering voice of a female chimes next to them, and their heads snap to attention. "Cigar, cigarette or tobacco?" a blonde calls out as she struts toward their table. Her pale complexion nearly blending with her even paler hair. She's wearing the crimson smile of a sinner as she rolls a wooden cart laden with an array of cigars, layers of cigarettes and multiple dishes of loose tobacco.

Gabriel leans forward. "Damn. Now, that girl is bloody gorgeous." His eyes scan the length of her body, and he slowly sits back as his nostrils flare. "But ew, is that halfbreed blood I smell?"

"I do believe you're right, little brother." Cassian raises his hand and motions for her. "I'd like to have a look at those cigars, Miss." As she approaches the table, his eyes narrow. "You must be Mary."

Fear flashes across her face as her eyes meet his, and she quickly drops her chin to her chest, dipping into a curtsy. "Yes, Sir. I hope everything is to your liking, Mr. Laurent."

Cassian takes a cigar from one of the boxes and clips off the end. His eyes trail back to hers. "Everything has been wonderful. Thank you. Why don't you join us for a moment, Mary? That would please me very much."

Noticeably nervous, she passes him a rather fancy leather-wrapped lighter. "Oh, uh, I'm afraid I cannot, Sir. My only duty here is to deliver tobacco, but your server, Beatrice." —*she gestures toward the scantily dressed young lady leaning against the bar*— "she would be happy to accommodate any such requests, Mr. Laurent."

Wrapping his hand around hers, his eyes narrow. "Well, Mary. Maybe I wasn't making myself clear. It wasn't a request." He shifts and pulls her onto his lap. "Let's talk about your sire. Shall we?" Mary's eyes bounce between Gabe and Cassian as Beatrice drops their drinks on the table. "Thank you, Beatrice. That will be all for now," Cassian says, his eyes never straying from Mary.

Lowering her voice, Mary avoids his gaze. "I'm not sure what you're talking about, Mr. Laurent."

Tightening his grip on her hand, Cassian speaks into her ear. "What do you say we cut the shit, Mary? Your sire, Roger Windsor. Where is he?"

Gabe appears almost as stunned as Mary as he silently watches the interaction unfold, and when he shifts uncomfortably in his seat, Olivia can tell he has never seen this side of Cassian before. The anger in Cassian's eyes when they dart to his is enough for him to remain silent. Taking a drink of his bourbon, he leans back in his chair.

"I—I'm not sure where Roger went, Mr. Laurent. I haven't seen him since he and a few others left last night."

"Where did he go?"

Mary's pleading eyes glance up at Gabriel. "I truly don't know, Mr. Laurent."

Leaning forward, he finally interjects. "Come on, Cash, you're drawing attention."

But when Cassian glares at him, he quickly throws his hands up and sits back, offering the patrons watching their exchange a smile. "It's not that you don't know, Mary. It's that you won't say." Adding pressure to Mary's hand, he watches her face tense. "You may heal just fine, but I assure you it will hurt like hell if I crush every bone in this dainty little hand of yours. Now, let me ask again. Where did your sire and his men go?"

"Mr. Laurent, please. I'll lose my head if I tell you."

The corner of Cassian's mouth lifts into a devious smile. "Well then, it seems you're damned if you do and damned if you don't. Although you should know that I'll make it much more painful."

"You can't do anything to me," she stammers, nervously looking around the room. "Everyone here has seen you – they've all witnessed our exchange."

Cassian throws his head back with a sinister laugh. "You seem to have underestimated me, my dear. These mortals can easily be compelled to forget we were ever here. In fact, by the time Gabe and I finish here tonight, I can ensure none will even recall that a pretty little blond named Mary ever worked here." He brushes a strand of hair behind her ear with a sweet smile. "Now, for the last time. Where was Roger going?"

Mary moistens her lips, her gaze bouncing between the two brothers as she winces. "I may have heard him mention something about France."

"France?" His hand tightens around hers. "Where in France?"

"I don't know." Tears well in her eyes as she shakes her head. "All I know is that he told Bando that he had the key and was going to France to get his father."

"Who is Bando?" Cassian demands, squeezing her hand hard enough that Olivia hears bones crack.

Mary's face contorts. "Ow, ow, ow!"

As she cries out, Olivia swats at the glasses sending droplets of bourbon across the table and shocking not just the two brothers but herself. Gabriel quickly puts his hands up and shakes his head. "Don't look at me."

"Why do I need to see this?" Olivia screams, squeezing her eyes closed.

A familiar hum fills the air, and she opens her eyes to a starry sky. "You needed to see that your vampire isn't always as sweet and gentle as he appears to you, my child."

"Goddess?"

Cassian's eyes spring open as he sits forward, his gaze locking on Olivia, still deep in a trance. "Is she stuck in there? She yelled out, then everything went black."

"What did she yell," Clara asks.

"She asked why she had to see this." Cassian closes his eyes. "It wasn't one of my finer moments, I'll admit, but I needed to get information from one of Roger's plebs. A female."

"Mary," Gabriel confirms with a nod. "Even I had trouble watching that side of you."

Helen points to Olivia's hand. "If she was still reading, her finger would still be moving. Right?"

Clarentina looks around at the three older witches. "So, what now?"

"Now we pull her the hell out of there, or I'll zap that damn book from her hands!" Patricia screeches.

"No!" Clara stands with her hands out. "I felt the pull last time she got lost in there. That's not what's happening. Does she feel confused?" she asks, glancing back at Cassian.

He shakes his head. "No, she feels—"

"Oh, for pity's sake!" Patricia lifts her hands, and brilliant blue bolts dance along her fingers. "I don't care how she feels. She needs out!" Aiming toward the book, she fires, but the energy bolt barely ripples the pages. "Ugh! I hate that damned thing!"

"Patricia, knock it off!" Clara scowls, her face softening as she turns to Cassian. "Can you keep trying to reconnect with her, please?"

"Of course."

But Olivia is still out of reach, surrounded by the Goddess's tranquil hum and a sky full of stars. "Yes, my child. It is I who felt you needed to see this. You spoke of Cassian Laurent as sweet and kind, and with you, he very well may be, but you need to see the beast's true nature. See that the vampire is capable of cruel and unthinkable behaviour before he steals your heart."

"This doesn't change my opinion of Cash. Even when he's done something bad, he's done it for a good reason, like ripping the heart out of another vampire to save my aunt Patricia. The very one who has done nothing but try to kill him since he's been in our house. I trust Cassian with my life," she yells, her voice echoing through to present day.

"Liv?" Patricia squints across the table at her. "Are you back? Who are you yelling at?"

Clara places her finger to her lips. "Shhh. No, she's not back, but that's a good question." She peers over at Cassian. "Still no luck?"

He shakes his head. "I'm getting nothing but complete darkness."

"Very well, my child," the Goddess's voice booms around her. "Then I hope the vampire is as you expect when you require him to do the same for you."

The stars fade and the sounds of the Gentlemen's Club overtake the soothing hum, and Cassian finally finds himself back in Olivia's mind.

She blinks the room back into focus, watching Mary squirm as Cassian twists her hand further. "Maybe you didn't hear me. Who is Bando?" he asks again, articulating each word.

"The witch Roger's been feeding off," she sobs. "I don't know anything else. I swear."

Cassian purses his lips as he scans her face, then grabs her cheeks and stares into her eyes, his pupils dilating. "If anyone asks, we had a pleasant conversation about the tobacco you had available this evening. I purchased a cigar and told you that you were a beautiful young lady." He wipes the tears from her cheeks with his thumbs. "Now smile." Wiping her eyes, she graces him with a demure smile. "Your smile is quite beautiful, Mary."

"Thank you."

He lifts her hand, guiding her to a standing position and takes a cigar from the cart. "Might I have a light, please?"

"Of course, Sir."

"Thank you, Mary. You've been very pleasant." He tosses a shilling on her cart. "Buy yourself something pretty."

Her eyes wander between Gabriel and Cassian as she curtsies. "Thank you very much, Mr. Laurent. Enjoy your evening, Sir." Grabbing her cart, she glances back as she slowly walks away.

Cassian swallows half of his drink, then drops his cigar into the glass. "Let's go. You heard the young pleb. Roger left for France to retrieve his father."

Jumping to his feet, Gabriel buttons his jacket as he strides toward the door behind Cassian. "Wait. As in dig up his bones from the grounds of the Laurent Castle?"

"Yes." Picking up his pace, Cassian glances over at him. "At least his torso. Father delivered Harold's head to his wife the same night he turned you." He stops, his face tense with concern as he looks at Gabriel.

"You don't think he's—"

"Don't finish that statement! Let's grab Elias and get to mother."

Elias is sitting on the sofa with his feet propped up on the coffee table and a glass of red wine in his hand when they storm through the castle doors. He quickly turns to face them. "Making that kind of an entrance, I thought you would've had the halfbreed with you."

Cassian slaps his feet as he attempts to set them back on the table. "Unfortunately not. However, we did locate one of his plebs, who goes by the name of Mary, at the Gentlemen's Club. She informed us that Roger has left for France with a bloodied sack."

"Oh shit!" Elias sets his glass down and stands. "You don't think he's taking father's head to—"

"Indeed. I believe that is his plan. So let's go. We need to get to mother. Now."

CHAPTER 44 ~ CLARENTINA'S MISERY

Back in the kitchen of the Redfearn home, Gabriel impatiently taps his fingers on the table. "Is she usually in there this long?"

"It all depends on the entry," Clara says, adjusting herself on her chair.

Elias throws his arms up. "Well, I don't understand why we're just sitting around while she's lost in this journal." He looks around the table. "Can someone enlighten me, please?"

Patricia shoots him a dirty look. "Because when she reads that cursed thing, bloodsucking demons much like yourself tend to show up, you ungrateful twat."

"Patricia!" Helen scolds.

"What? They need to be reminded why she's in that bloody thing. It's not for her sake," she shouts as she gains her feet. "She didn't even like magic before that damn thing came along!" Slamming her hands on the table, she leans over, coming face to face with Elias. "She's in there for you!" Her ignited finger scans across the shocked faces. "For all of you. So if anything happens to her, it's on the Laurent clan! Remember that."

Clara closes her eyes and takes a deep breath. "Patricia," she says calmly. "Sit down."

Pursing his lips, Elias puts his hands up. "My apologies."

Taking her seat next to him, Patricia folds her arms. "Just be quiet and prepare for your enemies."

"Right."

Back in 1896, the three brothers arrive at the castle in France to find the grounds completely dug up. "Mother," Cassian yells, taking off toward the castle doors with his brothers quick at his heels.

As they enter the grand entrance, their nostrils flare. A trail of blood leads from the massive double doors to the bottom of the staircase. Olivia's heart drops. Then all heads turn toward the large archway on the right—to the sound of hysterical sobbing.

"Mother?!" Elias calls out as they disappear into the next room.

Following them, Olivia quickly throws her hand over her mouth as her own tears begin to freely flow. Clarentina sits sobbing uncontrollably on the sofa, her teal gown dripping with blood as she rocks back and forth, cradling her husband's head in her arms. Elias slowly moves to sit next to her, and the air leaves the room. "Mother, give Soloman father's head so we can get you cleaned up," he says softly.

"No!" she wails, hugging Julien's head tight to her bosom.

"Mother, please," Cassian pleads, offering her his hand, but Clarentina doesn't reach for him. Instead, she glares up at him, her eyes cold enough to throw France back into the ice age.

"No! This is your fault! All of you!" she screams.

Olivia's heart sinks, knowing the guilt Cash has carried all these years and the weight of Clarentina's grief. She has to try something. "Goddess, please let this work," she whispers as she throws her hands out toward the sobbing widow, willing her to rest her heartbroken mind. "Caudal a-nis," she commands.

Clarentina's head drops to the side as the three brothers stand in awe. "What just happened?" Gabriel asks.

Elias bends down to have a closer look at her. "Did she pass out?"

"Did you hear that?" Cassian looks around the room.

"Yeah," Gabriel drops his head. "She didn't mean it, Cash. She's just lost the love of her life."

"I didn't mean mother." His gaze jumps from Elias to Gabriel's bewildered stare. "Never mind. It doesn't matter. She's resting peacefully, at least for the moment." He waves Soloman over to retrieve Julien's head from her arms. "Gently, we don't want to disturb her."

Cassian turns his gaze to Soloman, his face hardening as he points to her dress. "Where did all this blood come from? Is she hurt? Did Roger attack her too?!" he demands, his glare cutting into their trusted house steward.

"No, Sir Cassian. She slashed her own throat several times before I was able to stop her. Thankfully she was well nourished and healed too quickly to cause serious harm." He gestures to Julien's severed head. "Giving her the sovereign's head was the only way I could calm her enough to prevent her from doing more damage."

Cassian folds his hand into the crevice of his arm, pressing his fingertips to his lips. "Thank you, Soloman. You did what you could. Can you send Jinny to her chamber to clean her up?"

"Of course." He sets Julien's head on the table. "I'll leave Mr. Laurent with you until you have decided what to do with him."

As Cassian lifts his mother into his arms and starts for the stairs, he glances back over his shoulder at Elias. "Reunite father's head with his body on Ben Nevis until we can get that key."

"You got it."

"Rest easy, Clarentina," Olivia says aloud as she opens her eyes in the kitchen of her family home back in present day.

"I used my powers in the entry!" Olivia blurts before anyone can say anything. Cassian opens his eyes, and she points at him. "And Cash heard me!"

He nods slowly as all heads turn to look at him. "She's right. I did. Though back then, I brushed it off and quite honestly, I had forgotten about it until now. But I did hear her."

"That must have been the final entry. Right?" she asks him.

He shrugs, and Clara taps the table. "Okay. The pair of you need to slow down and fill us in."

Olivia holds her hands out. "Here. Take my hands," she says. "If we all hold hands, I might be able to project it to you. Like a dream." Her gaze falls to her grandmother. "They should all be able to see it, too. Right?"

Clara nods. "They should if we all share our energy." She points to Patricia. "Switch places with Elias, so you're between him and Gabriel, and I'll shift in next to Soloman."

Rolling her eyes, Patricia stands to switch seats. "For the love of the Goddess! The things I agree to for your sake, Liv," she shakes her head.

Once everyone is situated in their new positions, Olivia looks around the table, taking note of the newly formed circle—the *nine* vampires and witches. Starting at her left is Cassian, Helen, Gabriel, Patricia, Elias, Clara, Solomon, then finally Clarentina on her right. *The significance of nine—bringing these nine enemies together for one greater purpose.*

Smiling, she holds her hands out for Clarentina and Cassian, then watches as everyone offers theirs to those next to them. Clearing her throat, Clara narrows her eyes at Patricia.

"Fine!" she huffs, finally extending her hands to Gabriel and Elias. "Let's get through this quickly, Liv."

"Before I start," she turns to look at Clarentina, "I need you to know that this was probably one of the darkest times for you. We'll all understand if you wish to sit out."

Forcing a smile, Clarentina meets Olivia's gaze. "I appreciate your concern, sweetness. But knowing I'll finally have him back soon, I think I'm ready to see what happened to my Julien."

Mr. Green circles Olivia's ankle, and she squeezes Clarentina's hand. "All right." She peers around the table. "Just close your eyes, and I'll start from the beginning."

Cassian releases her hand and stands. "Actually, I think I'd prefer to sit this one out if you don't mind. I think someone should be walking around on this side should any rivals decide to appear."

Clara smiles. "Of course not. Soloman, can you take Cassian's seat, please?" While Soloman moves across to take his new position, Clara addresses everyone at the table. "If for any reason any of you feel you need to leave the circle, simply guide the two hands you're holding together to ensure the circle remains unbroken." Once everyone acknowledges, she turns her attention back to Olivia. "We're ready when you are, dear."

Cassian puts his hand on Olivia's shoulder, giving it a light squeeze. "I'll be right here watching over everyone with Mr. Green," he smiles down at the black furball curling around her leg.

Mouthing *'Thank you,'* Olivia closes her eyes, taking them all back to Julien boarding the ship for Dover.

While they're walking through the dreadful events of Julien's last day, Cassian pours himself a glass of blood and sits on the bumped-out window seat, looking out into the backyard. "I'll never get used to how fast vampires travel," Olivia says aloud, causing him to turn. But the circle is still intact, and she is just as he left her, eyes closed, holding hands with his mother and Soloman.

"It's strange, isn't it?" an old woman asks.

"What's strange?" Cassian asks, looking around.

"Up here," she says. "The spice shelf."

"Ah, Aunt Millie," he smiles. "My apologies. You've been so quiet."

"Yes. Well, I thought I should mind myself. I'd hate for Clara to stuff me in a closet to shut me up," she grins, making him laugh. "The occasional outbursts young Livy has. They're peculiar."

"Oh." He looks back at Olivia and shrugs. "I suppose."

"I believe that's her mind trying to keep her grounded to her body—to her time." Cassian stares at Millie. "Why do you look shocked by that? You've been in her mind while she's been in those entries. You have seen what she is capable of. The ability to have people, centuries before her lifespan, not just hear her but recall it today as if her voice had been there during their time is baffling enough, but now she can use her magic to interact not just with objects but cast spells." Millie tips her head, looking at him from under her brow. "Not just anyone could do something like that."

"Clara mentioned the timekeeper journal had a magic of its own. Do you think it could be fueling Olivia's abilities?"

The corner of Millie's lips tighten as she nods. "It's possible. She does seem to come out of each reading stronger than when she went in."

"Roger Windsor," Olivia says aloud, and Cassian spins to face the grey mist in the corner of the kitchen.

Millie's eyes widen. "Goddess, help us," she utters.

CHAPTER 45 ~ ROGER WINDSOR

The hair on Mr. Green's back stands on end as he hisses at the figure standing in the corner of the kitchen. "Easy there, Kitty," Roger says with his hands out as he tries to calm the furious feline.

Refusing him an opportunity to adjust to his surroundings, Cassian leaps over the crowded table and pins him to the wall by his throat. "I've been waiting centuries for this moment, Windsor," he spits.

Roger looks past his rival at the group sitting around the table. As his eyes land on the journal next to Olivia, he laughs. "As have I, Laurent. As have I."

Cassian glances over his shoulder, and Roger doesn't waste the opportunity. He swings his arms underneath, breaking Cassian's hold, and sends him flying against the far wall of the kitchen. Jars of Helen's waters crash around him as he tries to regain his feet.

"Come to daddy," Roger says, reaching for the journal, but as his fingers meet the cover, he's jolted back against the counter. "Damn it!" he growls, cradling his hand to his chest as the stench of burning flesh fills the kitchen.

"You shouldn't touch things that aren't yours," Cassian snarls. Lunging forward, he grabs him by the waist and tosses him over his back into the broken glass, but it doesn't take long for Roger to recover.

Pulling a large shard of glass from his bicep, Roger tosses it onto the portrait of Aunt Millie. "Ah, but it *is* mine, Laurent," he taunts, grasping the once golden key around his neck. "It belongs with this little jewel."

"I beg to differ," Cassian replies as Mr. Green lets out a long angry yowl, swiping his paw toward Roger with a hiss. "Even the cat knows you're a liar. Neither that key nor that journal were ever meant for a Windsor. I'll bet that key tarnished the moment you put it around your neck."

Olivia screams, *"Julien, watch out!"*

Cocking his head with a smirk, Roger slowly walks around the table, examining the anguish on each of their faces. Finally, he peers over at Cassian and points to Clarentina. "Aw, look at the horror on your mother's face. If I were to guess, I'd bet they've just witnessed the beheading of your loving sovereign."

He reaches out to wipe a tear from Clarentina's cheek, and Cassian rushes him, driving his shoulder into his midsection. Wood and glass shatter around them as the force of his blow carries them through the large bay window and onto the back patio. As blood splatters across the sacred circle, Cassian slowly rises to his feet with a groan and places his hand over the hole by his collarbone. He looks down at the spear of wood protruding from Roger's stomach and grabs him by the scruff of the shirt, lifting him to stare into his eyes. "It's a pity they won't witness *your* beheading," he snarls, extending his claws.

"Nor will you, Laurent," Roger chokes, blood spraying across Cassian's face as he twists the ring on his forefinger with his thumb and shouts, "Bando!" disappearing into thin air.

"No!" Cassian yells, angrily punching the bloodied circle where Roger had laid, smashing the cement slabs into tiny bits. Furious, he rests back on his haunches and stares at the empty space. That's when he sees it, nestled between the pieces of stone. The tarnished key.

Digging it from the rubble, he holds it up to examine it as Mr. Green jumps through the window with a friendly *meow*. "At least all is not lost," he groans, dangling it from his fingers. The furry feline offers another *meow* as he rubs against Cassian's side. "Don't worry, little kitty. I'm not finished with Roger Windsor yet." Cringing, he leans back against the house and looks down at his wound. "That is if I can get this thing to heal."

There's not a dry face around the table when Olivia opens her eyes. Clara swipes the pad of her hand across her cheek. "I'll get some tissue," she says, stopping as she takes in the state of the kitchen.

Helen's mouth falls open. "Oh, my waters!" she cries.

"Don't forget your Aunt," Millie mumbles among the broken glass. "And Olivia's vampire needs some help."

The vampires rise, their nostrils flaring as their eyes swirl with red. "Cash!" Olivia yells, taking off out the backdoor.

"Yeah, where the hell is that bloodsucker?" Patricia snarls, knocking her chair back as she stands.

Elias leaps in front of her. "I don't know what you're suggesting, but I know my brother! If anything—"

Gabriel wraps his arms around him. "Easy, Elias."

"Boys, stop! I smell halfbreed blood," Clarentina says, darting for the broken window with Soloman and her sons following close behind.

Outside, Olivia rounds the corner and freezes at the sight of Cassian's limp body leaning against the common altar with Mr. Green's head on his lap. "Cash!" she screams, running barefoot through the blood and glass, not noticing the splinters driving into her feet. As she reaches his side, Elias and Gabriel leap through the window but quickly step back when Mr. Green swipes out with a hiss. Sobbing, Olivia lifts his head, placing her hand over the gaping wound by his collarbone. "Oh, Cash. Who did this to you?"

"Windsor," Elias growls, taking a step closer to his brother. "I can smell that halfbreed blood all over him." His eyes narrow on Olivia. "You have the power to summon him here. Do it now, and let's finish this!"

A bright blue bolt strikes his foot, and Elias jumps back. "Stay away from my niece, Bloodsucker, or I will fry you where you stand!" Patricia warns, rounding the corner.

Clarentina gasps and Soloman turns her into his chest. "Enough of that, Patricia! Everyone needs to calm down and back up so I can have a look at the boy," Clara orders trotting over with her medicine bag. She gently moves Mr. Green aside, then lifts Olivia's hand. "Honey, I need to look at the damage. There must be a reason he's not regenerating." She points to her feet and knees. "You stay put, and I'll tend to those when I'm done here."

"He needs blood," Elias shouts.

Helen gestures to the broken glass and blood sprayed across the patio. "I'm afraid everything Soloman brought is gone."

Clarentina moves next to Cassian and takes hold of his clenched fist as Clara pulls a finger size piece of wood from his wound. "I believe this may have been the culprit that was stopping him from healing. I'm afraid most of the house was constructed of ash wood so it could be used against our enemies."

"Well, that's just great." Elias swipes a frustrated hand across his forehead, pacing back and forth at Cassian's feet. "We need to get him some blood. Just look at his clenched fists," he exclaims, gesturing to his hands. "He's starving. There's no way he'll be able to fight that kind of poison."

Soloman nods. "I'll take care of it, Sir Elias. You boys and your mother stay here while I return to the castle and get a few more bottles," he offers. "It shouldn't take more than an hour if the young miss could release me and I bring the helicopter back."

But before anyone can move, Olivia runs a shard of glass across her wrist and shoves it into Cassian's mouth. "Drink," she commands.

The commotion stops. Everyone is left speechless for the first time this evening as they stare at her, cradling Cassian with her wrist between his lips. Sobbing, she tips his head back to help her blood run down his throat. "Cash, please. Take my blood. You need it to heal, and *I* need you with me if I'm going to see this through."

Patricia lunges. "Olivia, No!" But her plea falls on deaf ears as Olivia utters something barely heard and a golden shield surrounds them.

Clara's face drops. She looks at Mr. Green lying across Olivia's ankle and grabs her daughter's arm. "Patricia, stop. The Goddess will protect her."

"You can't be serious! We have to break through the barrier!"

Pursing her lips, Clara shakes her head. "We'll never penetrate that barrier. Olivia requested it from the Goddess. There must be a lesson in this." She gestures to Mr. Green, then to her granddaughter, cradling Cassian as she feeds him. "Maybe for all of us."

"That's bullshit! If anything, this is a lesson we can all do without! And there is no way I'm sticking around to witness Olivia's demise!" she spits, storming down the path. "That goddamn cat doesn't know anything!"

Gabriel stares over at Clarentina. "But Julien's law—"

"Hush. Your father will understand."

Cassian swallows, and Olivia smiles. "That's it," she says, stroking his hair. "Stay with me, Cash."

"I'm sorry," Helen sniffs, turning toward the backdoor. "But I can't watch anymore of this."

Clarentina's gaze never wavers from her son as she taps Soloman's hand. "I need you to fetch as many bottles of O negative from our stockroom as possible." He dips his head and begins to turn when she raises her finger. "Be as quick as you can and bring the helicopter back."

"I release you, Soloman," Olivia whispers with a quick intake of breath as Cassian sinks his teeth into her flesh. Slowly relaxing into his bite, she kisses the top of his head. "Thank you, Goddess. I can't complete my obligation to the journal without him."

The key falls from Cassian's hand as he grabs her arm, repositioning himself to sink his teeth deeper. And though the key goes unnoticed by all around them, Mr. Green plucks it from Olivia's lap and darts for the house.

A familiar hum surrounds them as the melodic voice fills Olivia's mind. *"I warned you this was the nature of the beast, my child. That he would do anything to sate his thirst. Even feed on you—the* *forbidden. You should ask yourself, how can the journal's obligation be met without **you**?"*

"Am I going to die? Goddess?" Olivia calls out as the soothing hum begins to fade.

"That depends on your vampire's will, my child," she hears in the distance as her eyes begin to close.

"Cassian! That's enough," Clarentina orders, but he's too lost to his hunger to hear her.

As Olivia's shoulders slump, the golden shield that protected them dissolves, and Gabriel rushes to her side. "Cash," he snarls. "You have to stop yourself. Release her arm. You're taking too much."

Thunder rolls in the distance as a bright blue bolt zaps the ground at Cassian's knees, jolting him away from Olivia. "I warned you too many times, Bloodsucker. Now, back away from my niece!" Patricia rushes toward them with her hands pointed at Cassian as they dance with energy.

"For the love of the Goddess. Let her be okay." Hurrying to her side, Clara stands back as Clarentina scoops her into her arms. "Let's get her upstairs. Soloman shouldn't be long."

"Wait!" Elias steps between Patricia and his brother with his hands out defensively. "It was bloodlust caused by hunger." He glances over his shoulder at Cassian. "He's no longer a threat."

"Yeah, well, now I am!" The firepit ignites behind Patricia, and Helen runs out of the house, tossing a bubble of water over her sister, then stands in front of them.

"No. You're not. You're upset. We all are, but you forget that Cash saved *your* life only days ago."

"I didn't ask for his help!" she barks.

"And he didn't ask for Olivia's," Helen quickly reminds her.

Groaning, Patricia drops her hands. "This is not over, Bloodsucker!" she yells, stomping off into the house.

Cassian sits back on his haunches and blinks, the deep blue returning to his eyes. He holds his hands out in front of him, his fingers splayed. "The key! Where is it?"

"What key?" Gabriel and Elias chime in unison.

Frantically sweeping the ground with his hands, Cassian glares up at his brothers. "Father's key! I tore it from Windsor's neck before he disappeared!"

Gabriel and Elias exchange glances. "We didn't see any key, Cash."

"You lost so much blood. You were probably delusional," Gabriel adds.

Leaping to his feet, Cassian grabs him by the throat. "I wasn't delusional! I had the key in my hand!"

"Cash!" Elias yells, grabbing his wrist.

"Yeah?" Gabriel strains. "Were you thinking clearly when you almost drained Olivia?"

His eyes dart to Olivia's window. "Damn it! Olivia." He drops his gaze. "I can't hear her thoughts." He releases Gabriel and grips Elias's shirt, his eyes desperately seeking the answer. "Is she—"

Elias shakes his head. "Thankfully, no."

"Thanks to blondie. She had to nearly blow you to pieces to get you away from her," Gabriel huffs.

"She should have." Cassian runs his hand through his hair. "I had the key. It's here." Staring at the ground, he gestures to the broken stones where he had been lying. "Somewhere. Make sure you find it. I can't be here," he says, taking off through the trees.

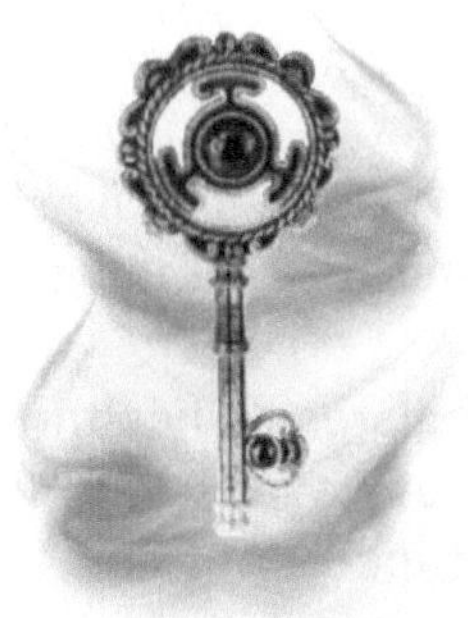

CHAPTER 46 ~ SHE NEEDS BLOOD

"Is young Livy going to be okay, Clara," a deep voice asks as they reach the top of the stairs. "We've all been worried sick since Millie told us of that ruthless vampire appearing in the kitchen. Thank the Goddess for that lad Cassian being here. Who knows what he would have done to all of you if not for him."

"Yes, we are very fortunate for Cassian's presence, Uncle Chester," Clara says, glancing back at the plaster bust. "And Olivia should be fine once we get her some blood."

"Blood?! Oh, no! Did that bastard get her? Has she been turned?!"

"No, Uncle Chester. She's lost a lot of blood." Clara pushes Clarentina toward Olivia's door. "Her feet are full of glass."

"Such a strange house, Clara."

"Hm?"

"Talking plaster and pictures."

"Oh, right. Well, after a while, you don't even notice these things."

Clara shoos Mr. Green from the foot of the bed as Clarentina lies Olivia down. "I've sent Soloman to retrieve our O-negative supply. He shouldn't be long."

"Now, we just have to figure out a way to administer it," Clara says, brushing the hair from her granddaughter's face.

"I don't understand what you mean." Clarentina flares her hands out to the side and looks down at her incredulously. "Can't you just wave a magic wand or something? Isn't that what you witches do?"

Sighing, Clara glares at her through the corner of her eye. "First, *us witches* don't use wands. Secondly, this is completely beyond anything our magic is capable of fixing."

"Tell me what you need," Gabriel says, standing in the archway of her room. "I can slip into the hospital and get it. They won't even know I've been there."

Watching Clarentina shrug, Clara nods. "Okay. Then I'll need an IV line and an IV needle or PICC line. At least if I have those, I can figure out how to rig up a drip system."

"Done," he says, disappearing from the room.

"Tell me then. If this little hiccup" —*she points to Olivia, lying on the bed*— "can't be fixed by magic. How am I to believe that she can bring my Julian back?"

"Well, to put it simply," Clara says, adjusting the pillow under Olivia's head. "That resurrection key was created by an ancient form of magic. By one of the very first in our line of descendants. That kind of power simply doesn't exist today."

Clarentina stares down at Olivia. "And yet this little one has enough power to be able to use it?"

"She must have," Clara shrugs, "or the journal wouldn't have chosen her."

The clanking of china outside the door alerts them to Helen's presence. "I brought tea and your medicine bag," she says, setting the tray on top of Olivia's dresser before handing Clara the bag. "How's she doing?" She walks to the end of her bed to look at the condition of her feet when she spots it. "What's this," she asks, picking up the key from the foot of the bed. Running her thumb over the stone, she holds it closer and examines the markings along the shaft. "Is this—"

Clarentina lunges forward with her hand outstretched. "My Julien's key!" she cries, tearing it from Helen's grip.

"Easy!" Helen steps back, her eyes wide as she watches Clarentina kiss the key. "You almost removed my hand."

"Don't you know what this is?" She holds it out, her grin clearly showing her fangs. "This is the resurrection key. The one Roger stole from my Julien." She hugs it to her chest. "Cassian must have gotten it back during their scuffle, but how would it have gotten up here?"

The three women look at the cat lying on the window sill. "Mr. Green must have picked it up," Clara smiles. "He can be quite intuitive."

"Hm. Well, thankfully, he didn't run off with it." Clarentina gives the key another kiss and slips it into the breast of her gown. "Where are my sons anyway?"

"Oh, um, Cash took off into the forest, and Elias went after him," Helen says.

"And Patricia," Clara asks, removing a fragment of glass from Olivia's foot.

Helen shakes her head. "I'm not sure."

"She'll turn up." She pulls another shard and dabs the blood.

"I hate to alarm you, but her pulse is becoming weaker," Clarentina steps forward and grabs one of the small dishes Clara has next to her. Slicing her wrist, she lets the blood drip until the cut reseals. "Here. Dab this on her wounds. It'll close those gashes. The last thing the child needs is to lose any more blood before Soloman gets here."

Clearing the last piece of glass from Olivia's foot, she dabs a cloth into the blood and wipes it across the cuts. As they watch the wounds close, Clarentina smiles. "See that? Seems we're both capable of a little magic."

"Yeah, except *we're* good, and *you're* pure evil," Patricia barks, entering the room.

Rolling her eyes to meet Patricia's glare, Clarentina elegantly glides toward her. "I'll have you know that we're *both* capable of good and bad."

Patricia raises her hand, letting sparks dance along her fingers. "Yeah? Well, if you get any closer, I'm gonna show you how bad I can be."

Mr. Green jumps up on the bed to lie next to Olivia as Clara bounds to her feet. "Will the pair of you can it already!" She takes a bottle from her bag, expels a dropper full of liquid and empties it into Olivia's mouth. "Come on, Child. Swallow."

Bending her head around Helen, Clarentina tries to get a better look at the bottle before it disappears into Clara's bag. "What was that you just gave her?"

"Just something to help build her red blood cells. Not that it's gonna do much good without some blood."

"I could give her a few drops of mine," Clarentina offers. "It might help."

Patricia shakes her head. "Oh no, you don't! You're not turning my niece."

"I said a few drops." Clarentina purses her lips. "It would take a heck of a lot more than that to change her. Besides, I don't believe you witches can be changed." She makes a tiny cut on the pad of her hand, letting the blood pool into her palm and looks to Clara for approval. "It's up to you. At the very least, it could keep her going until Soloman returns."

"All right, but only a few drops."

"Ugh!" Patricia groans. "I can't believe you guys!" she shouts, about to leave the room when she runs into Cassian.

"Mother, Stop!" he yells past Patricia.

"No! No no no! You are the last" —*she looks him up and down*— "bloodsucker that should be anywhere near her."

"Patricia! Let him in," Clara demands.

Cassian's gaze anchors on Olivia. "If it's going to be any vampire's blood, it will be mine." He slowly makes his way across the room and kneels next to her bed. "This is my fault."

"I'm going to try and clean up some of that mess in the kitchen." Helen starts for the door. "I'm not sure I have the stomach for this."

Unlike his mother, Cassian cuts the tip of his finger and pushes a small bubble of blood to the surface. Then pressing down on her chin, he runs his finger under her tongue. "We should hear her pulse pick up in a minute or two, but she still needs blood."

Just then, Gabriel walks through the door, pulling packages of clear tubing, needles, gauze and tape from his shirt, and dumps them on the chair. "I think I got everything you asked for and some," he smiles.

Footsteps come padding up the stairs. "I hear the helicopter! I think it's landing in our backyard!" Helen yells, her voice tapering off to a pant as she grabs the doorframe and doubles over. "Elias has gone to help him."

"He couldn't have arrived at a better time." Clara begins sifting through the sterile packets. Grabbing the IV line and a needle, she pats Gabriel on the back. "You are a God send, young man," she smiles.

"Pfft! Unlikely," Patricia snarls, eyeing him disgustedly. "That's just another making of the devil."

Pursing her lips, Clara shoots her a dirty look. "Patricia! I think it's best if you wait downstairs."

"No problem. There are way too many beasts in here for my liking anyway."

Elias pushes her aside as he walks through the door with four bottles in his arms. "This is all the O-negative Soloman could get for now. He insisted on getting it fresh from the four O-negative donors in our village instead of what was in our storage. That's what took him so long."

"Soloman is a very smart man, and it's plenty," Clara declares, taking one of the bottles from his arms. "And the cork is perfect." She pushes the spike at the end of the IV line through the cork, and the blood starts to fill the line. "Fantastic!" Crimping the line, she hands the bottle to Gabriel. "Could you hold this a moment, please? Helen! Bring up one of your macrame plant holders!" she yells over her shoulder.

Clarentina's brows draw together. "A plant holder?"

"To hang the bottle."

"Oh, of course."

Clara takes Olivia's hand from Cassian. "Now, the Trick is going to be finding her vein."

Cassian gains his feet and holds his hands out to Clara. "I can do this. If you'll allow me, that is."

She hands over the IV needle. "I'm sure you'll do a better job than I."

With a faint smile, he takes Olivia's hand and gently pushes the needle into her vein, then attaches the line. As Clara uncrimps the hose, the blood begins to flow. "Now we wait," she says.

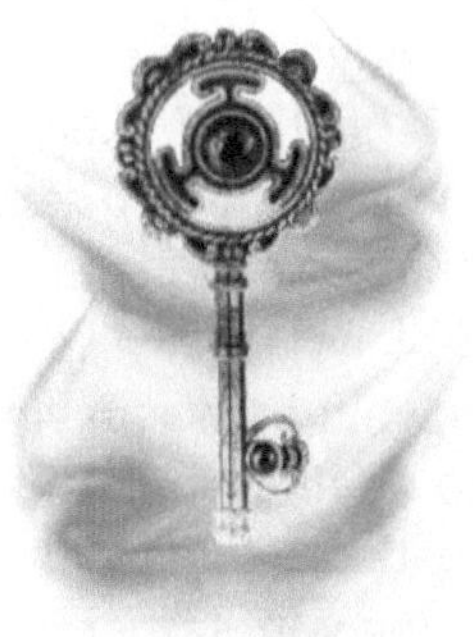

CHAPTER 47 ~ THE KEY IS TARNISHED

They change out the first bottle and secure a fresh batch of blood to the drip. "Will she need all four of those," Helen asks.

"No," Clarentina responds. "I would say two at best. Her pulse is already getting stronger."

"She's going to be all right then," she probes impatiently.

Clarentina nods, confidence ringing in her tone. "Yes, darling."

Sitting on the floor with his back against Olivia's bed, Cassian lowers his head. "No thanks to me," he mumbles.

Helen's face drops as she places her hand on her heart. "Oh, Cash."

He drags his hands down the sides of his face. "I don't know how she'll ever forgive me. Offered or not, I know better than to drink from your kind." He shakes his head. "And I didn't even have the willpower to stop myself. I went against one of father's main laws."

Clara places her hand on his shoulder. "No use in beating yourself up about this. We were all aware of your weakened condition, including Olivia. She made a choice. There is no room for blame here."

"Your father would have understood," Clarentina says, her face lighting up as she reaches between her breasts. "Oh, my goodness, with everything going on, I nearly forgot." She extracts the key and holds it out. "Your father's key!"

Cassian's eyes widen as he stands and jabs his hands through his hair. "You had it all this time? I searched the rubble, and when I couldn't find it, well, I didn't want to disappoint you again. So I thought it best not to say anything. I had planned to have another look for it once I knew Olivia was okay," he says, his words leaving his lips so fast one could barely catch what he was saying.

"She's going to be fine, son. And once she's stronger, we can take her back to the castle so she can wave her hands or whatever it is she needs to do to bring your father back."

"It's a little more complicated than waving her hands, and I'm afraid my granddaughter will not be accompanying you to your castle alone." Clara fans her hand out toward Olivia. "Must I need to remind you of what can happen? Besides, I believe the outcome would yield much greater results if she were to perform the ritual where she feels most comfortable, and that would be here."

Frowning, Clarentina places her hands on her hips. "But my Julien is at our castle."

Helen tips her head with a questioning gaze. "I thought he was in a cave on Ben Nevis mountain."

"Only until we had electricity in the castle, then more recently we had a walk-in freezer installed," Elias smiles.

'Meow.' Mr. Green jumps onto Olivia's bed and flops down against her leg. "Hi, Buddy. I missed you too." Olivia's voice rasps as she reaches down to pet him. "Cash?"

"I'm here, Olivia." He flips around to his knees and takes her hand. "Thank goodness you're okay," he says, lowering his gaze from hers. "I can't apologize enough."

She scans his clean white shirt. "You're healed?"

"Thanks to you," he nods, kissing the top of her hand.

"You drank from me," she breathes, a smile dancing on her lips. "Was I all you had imagined?"

Helen gasps as Cassian's face drops. He leans back to look at her, but as her smile grows, he pulls her into his arms. "So much better than imagined," he laughs.

"Watch her IV," Clara calls out.

"My IV?" Olivia looks around. "How in the world did you get all this stuff?"

Gabriel smiles, raising his hand. "I might have visited the ER and borrowed a few things," he winks.

"Did I hear someone say we have the key?" She lifts her head, but the weight of it demands the comfort of her pillow.

Clara puts her hand out. "Just lie there. Your body needs some time to recover. Try rotating your feet and hands to get your circulation moving before you try sitting up."

"We do have the key," Cassian smiles. "But your grandmother's right. You're in no condition to try any spells just yet. You need to rest before we even think about the resurrection."

"And you must eat," Helen grins, lifting her finger as she spins toward the door. "I'll be right back with some scrambled eggs and tea."

Struggling, Olivia props herself against the headboard. "Can I at least see it?"

Focus shifts to Clarentina, and she folds her arms across her chest with a huff. "Oh. Alright. But just for a moment." She reaches into her gown, pulling it free from her bosom once again, but as she holds it out, Olivia's face drops. "What? What is it?"

"Well, it's just that I'm not sure if that will work."

"Why not?! This is my Julien's key. I'd know it anywhere."

"That may be so, but it's tarnished."

Clarentina yanks it back. "Well, of course, it is. It's centuries old and likely never been cleaned by that ingrate that had it."

Olivia shakes her head. "No. I mean, Ancina told Julien when she gave it to him that if it ever tarnished, it wouldn't work. But I would have seen it if Julien had done something to make it turn." She holds her hand out. "May I see it, please?"

Reluctantly, Clarentina hands her the key, and the moment it touches Olivia's hand, the stone begins to glow. Gold sweeps across the dark dinge, leaving a shimmering beauty in its wake. "It must have been the bearer that changed its appearance," Clara says, walking over to have a closer look.

"This key is just the beginning. I still need Julien's body and the scroll for the spell." Her eyes meet Clarentina's. "Is the scroll still hidden in the wall in your dressing room?"

Placing her hand to her chest, she gasps. "How did you know that?! Not a soul saw me hide it there. I'm certain of it."

"Until the journal revealed it to Olivia, that is," Cassian smiles.

"Oh." Closing her eyes, Clarentina gives a slight nod. "Yes. I have it."

Olivia looks around her room. "And the journal? Who has the journal?"

Clara shrugs as she places her hand on her shoulder. "I don't know. I'll ask Aunt Millie if she saw what happened to it. Right now, you need to concern yourself with rest."

"I agree. Right after you eat," Helen smiles, entering with a tray of food and Patricia on her heels.

"Hey kiddo!" Patricia shoves Cassian aside and leans down to hug her. "How are you feeling?"

She takes a mouthful of eggs and nods. "I've felt worse," she shrugs. "Have you seen the journal?"

"Really?!" Patricia straightens, slamming her hand on her hip. "Haven't we had enough of that damned thing yet?"

"I have to be sure I read the final entry and that I don't need it for the resurrection, Aunt Trish."

"Who cares?! The only thing that damn book has brought is misery."

Helen waves Patricia off. "Ignore her. She's a bit moody, Liv. I know I didn't see it when I cleared the mess in the kitchen."

"What about Windsor," Elias asks. "Is there a chance he might have taken it?"

Cassian shakes his head. "No way. I wouldn't be surprised if the kitchen still smells of burnt flesh from when he grabbed it."

"Ouch," Clarentina cringes as she puts her hand up. "Been there."

"Then it must be here," Olivia says, pushing her tray aside and attempting to swing her legs out of bed when Clara stops her.

"Absolutely not, Child. You still look pale. Once you've rested, you can set out on a wild goose chase for that journal. Besides, we all know that if there is more to read, it will find you."

Helen claps her hands, drawing everyone's attention. "Sorry to interrupt, but Soloman, that wonderful, handsome man, is setting the table. I made tea and something that should appease everyone's pallet. So why don't we detour to the kitchen and let Olivia get some rest?"

Twisting his hands together, Gabriel licks his lips. "That sounds good to me." Heading for the door, he stops, glancing back at Olivia. "I'm glad you're feeling better. You had us all worried."

"Thanks for getting the loan from the hospital." She cocks her head toward her hand as Clara prepares to remove her IV.

"I don't think Olivia should be up and—" Clara starts when Cassian jumps in.

"Don't worry. I'll stay with her."

She stares at him for a moment. "All right. I suppose that would be okay." She leans down to kiss Olivia's forehead. "Just make sure she stays put and gets some rest."

"You got it," he nods.

"I can't believe you would agree to leave him alone with her," Patricia scowls. "Especially after he almost drained her dry!"

Placing her hand on her back, Clara aims her for the door. "Her blood was not his choice, and he feels guilty enough. Now, let's go."

Looking over her shoulder, Patricia raises two fingers aiming them at her eyes, then jabs them toward Cassian. "I'll be watching you, Bloodsucker." As she reaches the door, she waves four brilliantly blue charged fingers in his direction. "I'll be back sooner than you think."

He looks down, shaking his head. "Honestly, I couldn't even be upset if she zapped me."

"She's not going to zap you." But then, as they watch her leave, Olivia scrunches her nose. "Meh, scratch that. On second thought. She might."

Smiling, he nods in agreement. Then as soon as her bedroom door closes, Olivia pulls her blanket back and swings her legs off the bed. A sharp 'meow' comes from under the covers as Mr. Green pokes his head out and stares at her. "Oh, stop. We need to find that journal. I'm not sure if I need it for the resurrection."

Cassian quickly grabs her feet and places them back onto her bed. "I don't think so, Olivia. Clara would have my head if she knew I let you out of this bed."

"Fine," she huffs. "Then I suppose I'll just have to try and make it come to me." She wiggles her bottom back toward her headboard and crosses her legs. Then resting her forearms on her knees, she opens her hands with her palms facing skyward and closes her eyes, picturing the book's cover. "Acta, veni ad me," she commands.

"You shouldn't be doing this, Olivia. You need to rest."

"Shhh!" She glances at him through the corner of her eye. "I need to concentrate."

He sits in the chair beside her bed and exaggeratedly crosses his ankle over his knee. "You're spending energy you don't have. You're not strong enough to work spells yet."

Her shoulders drop as she exhales. She then focuses on the large cushion at the end of her room and flips her finger towards Cassian, sending it sailing toward his head with a chuckle. "See? Perfectly fine. Now please, be quiet for a few minutes."

Smiling, he shakes his head and clasps his hands behind his head. "Very well. Continue."

"Thank you." She closes her eyes and once again imagines the journal. The weight of the soft leather cover. The script glistening as it appeared to her, and the smell as she turned its pages. But when nothing happens, she opens her eyes and bellows to the unseen entity of the book. "If you're not going to come to me, then I suppose I'm ready to move forward with the resurrection!"

Cassian springs forward in his chair as she flings the blanket off. "Olivia, what you need to do is lie down."

"Do you know what tonight is?" He shakes his head. "No, I didn't assume so. Tonight is the full moon. We won't see another for thirty days. If I recall correctly, Ancina used the full moon's glow to activate the key when she brought Soloman back."

Remaining quiet, he bites the inside of his cheek. "Cash, you and your family have been waiting over a century for this. Not to mention I have overcome my fears and followed every rule thrown at me to get to this very moment. I don't want to put it off another month when we can do this tonight."

"Olivia, I appreciate what you're saying, but the likelihood of you being strong enough is slim to none."

"I promise, I'm fine." She throws her hands in the air and starts to twirl, nearly losing her footing when he catches her by the waist and sets her on the bed. "Stop." She pushes him back. "I'm fine," she says, brushing her hair from her face. "Just clumsy."

"Right. Even if that were the case, you don't have everything you need, specifically the body and the spell."

Her eyes narrow. "Why are you trying to stop me? This is my obligation as the journal's master —*she raises her hands, making air quotes with her fingers*— Remember? Isn't that what you told me?" She stands with her finger in the air. "No, wait. Isn't that what everyone has told me?"

Pursing his lips, Cassian closes his eyes. "You're right, and the last thing I want to do is to interfere, but I've already put your life in danger once tonight."

"Technically, I summoned Roger, which led to this entire mess." Shoving past him, she heads for the door. "Well, don't just stand there. I either need Soloman to take us to the castle, or he needs to bring Julien and the scroll to me." Cassian stands staring at her blankly. "It is Solomon that flies the helicopter isn't it?" He nods, and a smile grows on Olivia's face as she rounds back to take his hand. "Great! Then what are you waiting for? It's already dark, and we need all the moonlight hours we can get!"

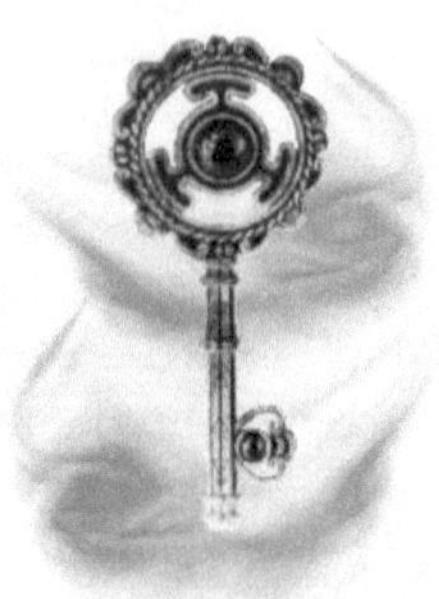

CHAPTER 48 ~ RISE, SOVEREIGN!

Wide eyes turn toward the doorway as Olivia bursts into the kitchen. "I need Julien's body and the scroll. If there is anything I am sure of, the key must be used during a full moon, and that's tonight," she says, pointing to the window.

Standing behind her with his hands raised, Cassian meets Clara's stare. "I'm sorry. I tried to talk some sense into her, but she is determined."

Clara feigns a smile, her shoulder tensing as she leans back in her chair. "That she is." Her attention shifts to her granddaughter. "Olivia, you need some rest."

"No, Gran, I'm not waiting for the next full moon. We need to do this tonight. I can feel it. The Goddess told me nine had a specific purpose for me, and I believe this is it." She points around the table, stopping on each of them. "Nine of us. Vampires and witches coming together to make this happen. I can't do this without you," she says, fanning her hands out to include everyone around the table.

"I'm with you, sweetie," Aunt Millie chimes from the spice shelf. "There's no time like the present."

Patricia purses her lips and stands. "Well, if that's what it's gonna take to get rid of these bloodsuckers. Count me in, Liv."

Clarentina pats Soloman's hand. "Can you fit us all in the helicopter?"

"Nuh uh," Clara says, waving her finger. "I already told you. This would have to be done here, where Olivia is most comfortable."

"Right. Of course," she agrees, eagerly turning to face Soloman. "Then you must get the scroll. You'll find a loose brick in my dressing room behind my wardrobe. The scroll is behind it." As he stands with a nod, she quickly directs her attention to Elias and Gabriel. "You boys go with him and be extra careful with our sovereign."

"Then I guess Patricia and I will prepare the altar," Helen says, rising from the table.

"Why me?"

Grabbing her arm, Helen drags her toward the backdoor. "Because you volunteered, sister dear."

Clara gestures to the two chairs across from her and Clarentina. "You and Cassian, come sit. Tell us everything you remember about the night Ancina resurrected Soloman."

Cassian sits across from Clara and his mother, clasping his hands under his chin while Olivia paces behind him, looking skyward as though the answers may be written there. "Okay. Well, there was definitely a full moon, and I remember Ancina used Julien's blood to draw the elements on Soloman's body."

"And what about the key," Clara asks. "What did she do with the key?"

Olivia glances at Clarentina. "She lodged it between his neck and head." Just then, Mr. Green meows, jumping from the counter to reveal the journal he had been using as his bed. "There you are!" she exclaims, darting for it. She slams it down on the table and begins flipping the pages. "I tried calling it earlier, but it didn't appear."

Clarentina cranks her head around Clara to look at the counter. "That's odd. I don't recall seeing it there when we came down earlier."

Resting her arms on the table, Clara leans forward to look at the journal. "Yes, well, it has always had a mind of its own. What is it you're looking for in there? I thought you had completed the last entry."

"I did, but I wanted to see if there are any hidden notes. You know, something that tells me if I have to have it during the resurrection or anything really." She slams the cover closed with a huff. "But there's nothing. It just ends abruptly."

Clara studies her face. "I don't understand why you're upset, dear. If you don't feel you're ready, then we'll wait till you are."

"No!" Olivia's face softens. "I'm sorry. I didn't mean to snap. I just feel like something is missing." She taps her fingers on the cover of the journal, then locks eyes with Clarentina. "Can I see the key, please?"

Her gaze bounces from Clara back to Olivia. "Now?"

"Yes. I don't recall feeling anything the last time I held it. I know it responded to me, but when I hold the journal, it feels alive—it's pure energy."

Pursing her lips, she slowly retrieves it from her bosom, and just as before, the moment it touches Olivia's hand, the stone begins to shimmer. "I see it glowing, but there's still nothing, no energy." She dangles it above the cover, and golden fingers reach up towards it. Gasping, she quickly pulls it back. "Did you see that?"

Cassian sits forward. "Maybe Roger knows more than we think."

"What do you mean?" Clara asks, her attention shifting from her granddaughter.

"When he was here, he mentioned that the key and the journal belonged together." He gestures between the two. "He was quite desperate to get his hands on that book even after it seared his fingers."

Closing her eyes, Olivia lays the key on top of the journal and covers it with her hand. They watch in awe as her back straightens and eyes fly open, rapidly shifting from side to side. Clarentina throws her hand over her mouth. "What the hell has she done?"

"Damn it." Clara's gaze springs to Cassian. "Can you get inside her mind? See what she's seeing?"

"I'll do my best."

Helen and Patricia enter the room as golden script feeds from the journal along the length of Olivia's arms. "What the hell are you letting it do to her?" Patricia shrieks aiming her charged hands toward the offending book, and releases a brilliant blue bolt.

"Patricia, stop!" her mother orders. "That does nothing."

"What's happening," Helen asks, pushing Patricia aside as they watch the golden letters radiate across Olivia's face.

"She put my Julien's key on top of the book," Clarentina points to Olivia's hands, "and—" Tears trickle down her cheeks as she starts to cry. "Now the key is lost, and I'll never get my Julien back."

Clara shakes her head. "I've never seen anything like this, and I can't be certain, but it very well may be part of the process."

Cassian opens his eyes. "She's watching the entire book on fast forward."

"Did she request this?" Patricia asks.

"No." Clara glances at Clarentina. "At least not out loud."

The script along her arms begins to fade until finally, no words are left visible on her flesh. She sits staring straight forward, and with a quick intake of breath, the journal disappears. Olivia blinks, her eyes falling to her hands as she turns them over to reveal the key. She clenches it in her fist with a smile. "I feel it. The energy. Stronger than the journal ever was."

"For the love of the Goddess," Helen mutters. "She absorbed the journal."

Clara takes a deep breath. "Yes, I dare say."

"My Julien's key!" Clarentina reaches for it when bright arcs sear the tips of her fingers. "What have you done?!" she cries, holding her hand to her chest.

Cassian puts his arms around her. "That key now only has one purpose, mother." He looks skyward. "The helicopter has returned."

He follows Olivia through the backdoor, and Clara stands. "Then I suppose we should get ready." She grabs five bottles of her enchanted wine and heads outside. The altar is lit with candles, and the smell of jasmine sits heavy in the air. Mr. Green is lying next to the large stone bench when he lifts his head to watch the helicopter land. She hands the bottles to Cassian. "For you and your family."

Taking the bottles, he stands next to Olivia, watching as Clarentina rushes toward Soloman to retrieve the rolled parchment in his hand. Her eyes meet theirs, and she kisses the scroll with a heavy sigh. "I believe you'll be needing this, darling."

As the side door of the helicopter slides open, Elias jumps down with a cooler in his hand. "We sent word to Granger to spread the word through the Laurent clan of father's rising. Most had already left before we finished loading his body, so I suspect it won't be long till they arrive." He glances back as Gabriel and Soloman lift the stiff figure from the floor of the chopper. "Where should they put father?"

Clara's sight lands on the stone bench. "If two of you can bring that closer to the altar, I believe that would be ideal."

"Of course." Cassian waves him over. "Set the cooler down and give me a hand, little brother."

Elias hands the cooler to Helen. "Careful with this. It's my father's head."

"Oh." Helen cringes as she cautiously takes the cooler and sets it down gently next to the altar.

Once the bench is in place, Soloman and Gabriel lie Julien's body across the large slab of stone. His shirt is still bloodied and torn, exactly as Olivia remembers from the night in 1896 on the roof of the Blackfriar's pub. She gestures to the cooler. "We need to put his head in place."

"Wait." Cassian grabs four of the five bottles of wine Clara had given him and hands one to each, his mother, Soloman, Elias and Gabriel. "It's enchanted wine." He opens his own bottle and takes a drink. "It will enhance our strength. In case we have any unwanted visitors."

Olivia rerolls the scroll, then grabs a knife and clay dish from the altar. Making a small cut to the soft pad of her hand, she lets a tiny pool of blood form in the bowl. Her eyes meet Cassian's. "I'll need a few drops of yours and Soloman's as well."

She opens the front of Julien's shirt and dips her finger in the bowl. Using the mix of blood, she draws four elements across his chest—earth, air, fire and water. Then finally marks his forehead with the symbol representing spirit. Her heart begins to race, and she pulls the key from her pocket as the cool touch of Cassian's hand comes to rest on her shoulder. "I have faith in you, Olivia. Just relax and concentrate. Nothing can stop you now."

"Except maybe me," an unwelcomed voice growls as Roger shoves a grotesque-looking woman out from behind the helicopter and stands at her side. "Bando! Get me the key and that witch!" he yells.

Clara reaches for Patricia and Helen. "Take my hands. Now! We need to form a protective barrier around Olivia and Julien."

"But Cash!" Olivia cries.

"You need to worry about completing the ceremony," Clara says sternly. "We can't hold this barrier in place for long, and Roger's witch is stronger than I thought."

Shaking, Olivia drips the blood onto the key's stone and lodges it between Julien's head and body. She turns it, allowing the moon's glow to shine directly through the bloody gem, then raising her hands above Julien, she closes her eyes. Her voice rises and lowers with each change of direction as she recites Ancina's incantation. The glow from the key gets brighter with each pass of her hands, and Julien's body begins to respond. His legs bend, then straighten—his abdomen expands and deflates like a balloon.

Vampires appear from all directions bringing growls, screams and the sound of cracking bones. Still, Olivia continues to chant.

"I don't think I can hold it any longer," Helen cries out, her face straining as she struggles to remain upward.

"Just a few more minutes," Clara says, looking over her shoulder at the carnage as the Laurent clan battles against their rivals.

But Helen's hand slips from theirs, and she falls back, breaking through the barrier and into the clutches of two of Roger's plebs.

"Helen! No!" Patricia yells, attempting to release Clara's hand, when a strange old woman rises between them and clutches both of their hands.

"We must hold strong now. Olivia and the sovereign need us."

"Screw the sovereign!" Patricia is about to let go when Helen steps back through the barrier, holding hands with Bando. "I was going to let the walls crash to save you, and you recruit Roger's demon witch?!"

"She's on our side," Helen says as Olivia's chanting gets louder.

With a nod, the old woman takes Bando's hand. "We need all the strength we can get to keep this protective veil in place. Now, concentrate, Patricia!"

A resounding buzz surrounds them as electricity sends their hair skyward, and a thick fog drapes across Julien's neck. Booms of thunder crack above, and a magnificent beam of light disperses the haze as the key's stone connects with the moon. Mere moments pass when brilliant golden spikes begin to stitch along the severed flesh, sealing the wound as if it never existed. When the final arc fades, the key drops to the ground, leaving Olivia to slump over Julien's body. Patricia attempts to break free from Clara and the old woman's grasp. "Liv!"

"She will be fine. We must hold the barrier until the sovereign rises," Bando orders. "Mr. Windsor would love nothing more than to catch him while he's still weakened."

"I don't give a damn about the sovereign! We've given enough for these bloody demons!" Thunder claps above as Patricia sends bright blue bolts rushing through their hands and tossing them back against the shield. She pulls Olivia onto her lap and cradles her in her arms. "Open your eyes, Liv," she sobs.

Swiftly gaining her feet, the old woman's image flashes, her face changing before their eyes from a black furry feline to wrinkly flesh. She reaches out, grasping Clara and Helen's hands. "I know you're all exhausted, but we must hold this barrier steady. Both Olivia and the sovereign need time to regain their strength."

Bando begins to chant, and the old woman quickly accompanies her, "Eirich a righ! Eirich a righ!"

Just then, Julien sits up, and Olivia opens her eyes. "Thank the Goddess." Patricia kisses her forehead. "I swear, I'll never press you to use magic again." But Olivia barely acknowledges her as her eyes shift to meet Julien's, and she pushes herself to her feet. "Liv? What are you doing?"

"Sealing my journey by completing Julien's rebirth." Reopening the cut she had made on her hand earlier, she lets the blood pool in the palm of her hand and holds it out to him.

Bowing his head, he gently takes her wrist, accepting the offered blood. "I can't thank you enough, young sorceress." Olivia lowers her head, gesturing toward the old woman. "Ancina?"

"I'm afraid there is no time for pleasantries, Julien." Releasing Bando and Clara's hands, she drops the protective veil, revealing the bloodbath around them. "You have a score to settle, and your family needs their sovereign."

His eyes widen as he spots a pleb gaining ground on Clarentina. With a roar, he takes off in his direction, his fist slamming through the unsuspecting pleb's chest. Barely stopping to toss the corpse aside, he turns to seek out the one who caused his demise—Roger Windsor.

He sweeps through the crowd of half-breed plebs, tearing through their necks like a hot knife cutting butter. To everyone else, he may have been gone over a century, but for Julien, that fateful night in 1896 on top of Blackfriar's pub was only moments ago.

Removing the head of an advancing rival, he spots Roger from across the yard. "Windsor!" he bellows, bringing the commotion to a halt. His eyes land on the young man he has dangling by his throat. "I command you, as your sovereign, to let go of my pleb. Now! This is between you and me."

The fighting comes to a halt as everyone turns toward the boom of his voice.

"Not a chance, Laurent," Roger grunts, stepping over a bloody corpse as he extends his claws with a snarl. "You should have stayed dead, old man. We don't require a Sovereign. He draws back his fist and drives it through Gabriel's chest. Holding up his blood-drenched hand, he laughs. "Meh, the lad never had much heart."

Clarentina screams, and Julien's nostrils flare as his eyes swirl with crimson. "You're dead, Windsor."

"Easy now, old man." He tosses Gabriel's limp body to the side and steps forward. "If I were you, I'd send my little family home. It would be a shame making your sons watch me take that head of yours a second time," he grins, his gaze settling on Clarentina. "Oh, and your poor wife. The state she was in the last time I saw her," he says, feigning a frown as he shakes his head.

Julien lunges, wrapping his hand around Roger's throat. Glaring into his eyes, his other hand rests over his young rival's heart. "I've heard just about enough. Now, pledge your allegiance and agree to conform to my laws, or I'll be forced to remove your heart."

"Do it, Julien! Tear out his heart," Clarentina cries out. "Rid us of the mutant and his wretched lifestyle once and for all."

"Never!" Roger growls, snapping Julien's hand from his chest and tossing him across the yard. The echo of cracking bones as his body smashes against the stone bench makes Olivia cringe, and she raises her hands as plebs from both factions move to surround him.

"Olivia, no," Ancina orders, taking hold of her hand. "We must have faith in the resurrected sovereign."

Sluggishly slinging his arm over the bench, he lifts his head to look at his wife as she cradles Gabriel's limp body, his sons at her side. His shoulders sag, and Roger stretches his arms out, his maniacal laughter filling the air. "Would you look at this pathetic bloke you all call a sovereign? He's clearly unworthy of the title." Dropping his arms, his stance shifts as he glares at his rival. "There's no key to bring you back this time, Laurent."

Roger rushes toward him as Julien unexpectedly rises with a roar, his clawed hand ramming straight through his young rival's chest. A loud gasp fills the air as he extracts his fist and drops the bloody heart in front of him. His shoulders broaden as he scans the crowd of plebs. "Anyone else feel I am unworthy to stand as your sovereign?" he asks, watching as they drop to take a knee in front of him. "Good. Then get rid of this garbage!"

Several plebs move toward the heartless corpse of their sire when Patricia zaps the ground at their feet, sending them back. "Unless you want to join your maker, don't touch it!"

"I hope you don't mind," Bando says, stepping up next to her with her fingers ignited. "This bastard took a century from me."

"Give it your hottest flame," Cassian shouts, accepting Olivia's outstretched hand.

"You heard the man." Patricia kicks the bloody heart next to the body and throws her hand out. "Set it ablaze."

Bando extends her hands. "Ignis diaboli!" she commands, sending brilliant blue flames into the night sky.

Standing next to Ancina at the altar, Clara gestures to the expanse of bodies scattered across her yard. "What am I to do with this massacre site?"

"I will see that it is cleared when I leave." She places her hand on Clara's back and smiles. "Hell has been waiting a long time for this package, and I promised to deliver it." She flips her hand out, producing an old worn book with pages sticking out between the bindings, and Clara steps back.

"Another one?" Clara asks.

"No, dear. My grimoire. It's yours now," Ancina says, her sight focusing on Helen and Olivia standing with the family of vampires huddled around the fallen boy. "I learned centuries ago that our bloodlines were fated to forever be entwined. I had hoped Annabel would have passed this down through the lineage, but she didn't find the package I had left, and I—well, I was busy trying to save our own kind during those times."

"And what of Gabriel?"

"I'm afraid nothing can be done, Clara dear. Gabriel was a sweet boy, and I'll see to it that he is finally reunited with his parents."

"Ancina!" Olivia calls out, darting toward them. "I never thought I'd get to meet you." She twists her lips. "I mean, not in person." Squinting, she cocks her head. "Were you really inside Mr. Green all this time?"

Smiling, she nods. "Yes, child. Though, I'm afraid Mr. Green's time here is done, as is mine." She holds out her arms, and Olivia steps in, giving her a hug. "I'm so very proud of you, Olivia." Her sight lands on Cassian across the yard. "Your fondest desire is here to watch over you now. Go be with him."

Then, as quickly as she appeared, she was gone again, taking the mess of bodies with her as promised.

EPILOGUE

"Hurry up," Helen hollers. "I hear the helicopter landing."

"I don't see why they're staying in France with his family when they could be staying here," Patricia huffs, entering the kitchen in a pair of worn blue jeans and a bright pink t-shirt.

Cocking her brow, Helen jams her hand on her hip. "Well, maybe Cash got tired of dodging fireballs. Did you ever think of that?"

"But this is where Olivia belongs. With her family."

"Yes, and soon enough, they will be her family too. Besides, once the castle in Stepney is restored, they'll be living right around the corner."

"I still don't like it," Patricia grumbles.

"Oh, stop it," Clara says, putting the backing on her earring. Her arms drop, and she trails the length of her youngest daughter. "Is that really what you've chosen to wear today?"

Looking down at herself, Patricia scrubs her hands down the front of her jeans. "What's wrong with it? It's not like it's their wedding day."

"It is their rehearsal. Surely you could have chosen something nicer than jeans and a t-shirt."

"Eeee," Helen squeals, running toward the back door. "It's too late to change now anyway. Soloman's here!"

Clara places her hand on Patricia's shoulder, turning her toward the back door. "I expect you to be on your best behaviour while we're there," she whispers. "Do not ruin this for Olivia and Cash."

Rolling her eyes, Patricia shrugs from under her mother's hand. "Like I would," she smiles.

S.J. Turner

About the Author

Author of the steamy erotic romance series Contracted to Mr. Collins, SJ Turner took a big step out of her comfort zone with the paranormal fantasy Immortal Treasures. Primarily written in fragments, many original pieces never made it into the final storyline. And those that did required artful blending to create the ultimate tale that hopefully finds its way into many hearts and homes.

SJ's love for books began the moment she learned to read. By her early teens, she was sneaking her mother's romance novels into her room and tucking them under her pillow for late-night reading.

While a steamy romance is still her personal favourite, SJ can't deny a fondness for the many other genres she often enjoys. After all, how could she not indulge in magical fantasies, exhilarating adventures, heart-stopping horrors and relentless drama?

Among her favourite authors are Deborah Harkness and Sylvia Day.

Visit SJ's website https://www.sjturnerstories.com

Publishers website https://cozyreadspublishing.com

Follow SJ on Twitter -
https://twitter.com/SJTurner_Author

www.ingramcontent.com/pod-product-compliance
Lightning Source LLC
Chambersburg PA
CBHW032041050726
47590CB00001B/89